A SHADOW PASSING

Shirley Carnegie

ISBN 978-1-4466-0460-1

A SHADOW PASSING

Shirley Carnegie

For my husband Andrew

Independence came

But Freedom was not there.

An old woman saw Freedom's shadow passing,

Walking through the crowd. Freedom to the gate.

All the same, they celebrated for Independence.

'A Mysterious Marriage'

poem by

Freedom Nyamubaya

1

The African squatted on his haunches and watched the two young boys playing in the distance. Out in the bush, a lonely jackal's cry pierced the twilight, but the African did not move. He would not betray his presence. He sat, silent and brooding, hidden by the thorn bushes that bordered the land the white men had called Scarfell Farm.

The sun was slipping towards the horizon and soon the land would be cloaked in the jet black mantle of night. Then, the two boys would gather up their things and go their separate ways. And the African would disappear into the gloom.

But for now, while the sun still bathed Scarfell Farm in its soft, warm glow, the two boys remained blissfully unaware of the malevolence that had cast a shadow over their childish game. One day, that shadow would plunge their world into darkness and tear apart the bonds of friendship that had sustained them in their early years. For their destinies were inextricably bound to that of their beloved Rhodesia – to Africa. To the place they called home.

Miles Cameron did not know he was being watched. He was too busy concentrating on the solemn ritual before him. He sat on the ground with his legs crossed and his hands clasped in his lap. In the distance, the dying embers of the African sun cast amber lights on the tips of his hair and flecked his dark brown eyes with gold. Opposite Miles, also cross-legged, sat Joseph Hungwe, the Cameron's gardener and Miles' hero.

'It is ready.' Joseph lifted the tin pot from the flames and swirled the butter in its base.

'It is ready.' Miles echoed, imitating Joseph's inflexion with all the gravity his four tender years could muster. He turned to his playmate, six year old Julius Khumalo, who was leaning against the trunk of an ancient

African fig tree holding another container. Julius acknowledged the command and lifted the bowl to his lips. Gently he blew across the bodies of the flying ants until the air was filled with tiny gossamer wings.

Joseph Hungwe nodded his approval.

Julius handed the bowl to Joseph then moved closer to the fire for the final part of the ritual. Joseph tipped the ants into the butter and stirred them with his finger. His hands, the texture of blackened boot-leather, were clearly more suited to manual labour than this delicate task, but he performed it well and the boys were impressed. Within minutes, the bright yellow flames had cooked the contents of the pot and the procedure was complete.

'Are they ready, Joseph?' Miles was eager to reap the rewards of their evening's work.

'They are ready, Nkosizana, little lord. Here see for yourself.'

Miles dipped two fingers into the pot and plucked out the fat, juicy body of a buttery ant. Tilting his head back he popped it into his mouth and closed his eyes. A trickle of butter ran down his chin, which he wiped away with the back of his hand. 'Yummy!' he enthused.

Julius leaned forward to claim his share. He grabbed a handful and stuffed them into his mouth before helping himself to a second portion and shuffling back against the tree.

The fig tree grew alongside the kopje in the Cameron's garden and was as much a part of Scarfell Farm as the Camerons themselves. It was one of the boys' favourite haunts and they had spent many hours tracing the paths of the roots which wound their way around the kopje in search of water.

Julius sat with his knees drawn up to his chest munching his way through the inch-long body of a flying ant. He scrutinised the remains of his dwindling share lying in the pink palm of his hand. His eyes were black, fringed with long, thick lashes, and his skin was the colour of caramel. This would darken as he grew to manhood under that fierce African sun and his skinny frame would fill out into the muscular physique common to his race. Julius was a handsome child. He took after his father, Moses Khumalo, who worked on the Camerons' farm.

Miles was a Rhodesian-born white boy, the great grandson of one of the early pioneers who had come to this land and claimed it as their own. He was a Cameron and, generations down the line, Camerons still farmed the rich, red earth of Rhodesia. It was their heritage and they loved this wonderful country. It was their home. They knew no other way of life.

'Looks like a storm brewing,' Rachel Cameron, Miles' mother, stood up on the verandah and looked beyond the Blue Hills to the distant horizon. 'Let's hope we get some rain here.'

Her husband, Ralph, frowned and squinted into the distance. 'Guti,' he declared. 'Nothing more. We'll not see any decent rains until next year. It's been a dry season.'

Guti - that irritating drizzle which made it too damp for effective gardening and too dry to be of any value to Rachel's ailing flowers. 'Next year I'm going to pull up all these wretched flowers and plant some good old Rhodie shrubs.' she declared flatly. 'At least they'll stand the drought and won't just give up and die on me.'

Ralph grinned. 'You say that every year, my darling, and every year you tend those pathetic little English flowers with more loving care than I could ever hope for!'

'You were born here,' Rachel responded, flicking his arm with her spare knitting needle. 'You weren't transplanted from the lush soils of Shropshire and carted off to this miserable place. They need me more than you do.'

'You'll be telling me next that you want to uproot Scarfell and move us all to the north of the country. There's more rain up there. Your garden could be the envy of Mashonaland.'

'Hmm!' Rachel snorted at her husband's tease. 'Uproot you from your beloved Matabeleland? Never! I'm quite sure you would wither and die among the Shona. Matabele and Shona? Chalk and cheese! Heaven knows why Cecil Rhodes couldn't find a way to bring the two warring tribes of Rhodesia together when he conquered this country.'

'The Matabele and the Shona have been at each other's throats for generations' Ralph pointed out. 'Not even Cecil Rhodes could change that. Anyway, I like Matabeleland. I'm a Matabele!' he added proudly. 'Born and bred here.'

'A Matabele of Scottish descent,' Rachel teased. But gently. She knew how much her husband treasured his third-generation African birthright.

Out in the garden, the boys' ritual was cut short by the entrance of Bliss, the Cameron's nanny and Julius' mother. Swiftly, Julius jumped to his feet and scampered away to avoid his mother's wrath. Joseph on the other hand chose to ignore the fuss. He simply shrugged and distanced himself from the domestic upheaval by rolling a cigarette and edging back into the shadows.

Bliss ignored them both, concentrating instead on her young charge. Her expression softened as she bent down and scooped Miles up into her arms like a pet puppy. 'Come my baby,' she cooed in his ear. Miles fought feebly, but knew better than to expect victory. His nanny may be a soft touch at times, but when it was time for supper and the dreaded 'bed' there was no arguing.

Bliss approached the verandah, or stoep as it was called, eyes down as a mark of respect to her employers.

'See that he's washed before we eat, will you Bliss,' said Rachel with a frown. 'His face is greasy.'

'Yes Madam,' Bliss bobbed a curtsey. Inwardly she cursed Joseph Hungwe for feeding her babies at this time of night. It was not right. But then Joseph never was one for sticking to the rules. No doubt he would be making his way to some seedy village bar right now, arriving back drunk in the early hours. It was a common occurrence. Sometimes he would be escorted by Moses, her husband, and the two men would stagger home, arm-in-arm, in a spirit of drunken camaraderie, before parting with a great show of emotion and making their way to their respective quarters.

Bliss shook her head and sighed. Then her gaze fell upon the small boy who was waiting for the sign that his ablutions were about to begin. She bent down, ruffling his silky locks, and her heart melted with love. 'Come, Master Miles,' she said sternly in an effort to rid herself of the urge to gush with affection. 'Let Bliss get you nice and clean and ready for some proper food. And then we shall wake up your little sister.'

At around 12,000 acres, Scarfell was a thriving dairy farm with over 100 head of cattle. But not just any cattle - Ralph's father had gone for good quality Friesland-Holsteins, and Jerseys with a high milk yield which were serviced in the main by their own bull. Travelling from town Scarfell Farm was approached by a long drive flanked by soft-wood marulas. The house had been built by Ralph's grandfather in a choice position on top of the hill, well away from the milking parlour and grazing land. It was surrounded by lush jacarandas that were turning yellow with the onset of autumn. The farm by Rhodesian standards was small, but it had been home to four generations of Camerons and they had no reason to doubt that it would serve future generations just as well.

Bliss followed Ralph and Rachel into the house. As she turned to close the door behind her, she spotted a rustle of movement in the thorn bushes at the edge of the lawn. Puzzled, she peered into the darkness, when a sudden chill caught her and she shivered as though touched by one of the evil spirits that purportedly roamed the African bush at night.

Hurriedly, she closed the door and ushered Miles towards the bathroom where a tub of hot water was waiting.

'Should I serve supper now Madam?' Sixpence Dube, the Camerons' house-boy entered the sitting room and spoke to Rachel.

'First check how long Bliss will be will you Sixpence? Miles was so grubby when he came in.' Sixpence nodded, bowed and turned to leave. 'Oh, and don't use the new napkins I brought back from Jo'burg. I'm saving them for Beth's birthday party.'

'Yes Madam.'

'I'll have a cup of coffee while I'm waiting Sixpence.' Ralph settled into the easy chair and picked up the newspaper.

'Yes Nkosi.' Sixpence used the Zulu term of respect then bowed before returning to his kitchen.

Rachel smiled and watched him go. Over the years the comforting sight of the little black man pottering around the house pushing the ancient Hoover, or with hands thrust deep into a sink full of washing up, had become a source of stability to her. He had kept the house running while she was laid up with her two difficult pregnancies, and he had watched over young Miles in his early childhood. Sixpence, so it seemed, would always be there for Rachel and her family and she would always treasure him.

Ralph picked up a copy of the Bulawayo Chronicle and sat down to read, but his attention was soon diverted by the arrival of his youngest child, Beth. Clinging to her nanny's fingers, Beth plodded with a curious sideways walk to her mother. Chubby arms outstretched, fingers spread wide and with a big grin on her face, she completed her journey across the sitting room in record time.

'How's my beautiful little girl?' Rachel leaned forward in her chair. 'Oh, is this for me?'

'She wished to give it to you Madam.' Bliss answered on behalf of the child.

'But this is your special-favourite rag-dolly,' Rachel enthused. 'And you carried it all by yourself, just for me? Why thank you, darling.'

Beth chuckled and delivered her gift with fat little hands still bright pink from her bath. Having divested herself of the rag-dolly, which she had protected from the attentions of her troublesome older brother, she turned to her nanny. 'GoiGoi Blish?' she asked.

'Here you are Miss Beth. Here is your GoiGoi, all nicely washed and pressed.'

'You actually managed to wrest the GoiGoi away from her?' Rachel marvelled at this rare achievement.

'While she was asleep Madam. It needed to be washed.'

'Well done Bliss,' Even Ralph knew how hard it was to remove Beth's precious tea-towel from those fiercely protective arms. It was her 'comfort blanket' and she would not settle without it. It had been called the GoiGoi after the suckling noises she made as a baby when she dropped off to sleep with the corner of the towel in her mouth. It was, without doubt, one of the family's most treasured possessions.

Later, Rachel left her husband snoozing quietly in his chair and went to say goodnight to her children. She peeped round the door of Miles' room. 'Sleepy now pet?'

Miles nodded. He was in bed, having lost the battle to stay up late.

Rachel perched on the side of the bed and brushed a wisp of tawny-brown hair from her son's eyes. She pulled the sheet up round his chin and settled Pandaloo in his arms. Pandaloo had been sent out from England three years ago. The toy panda had been a Christmas present from his English grandmother. Now threadbare, and crammed with old stockings when the original stuffing fell out, the one-eyed panda was an essential night-time companion.

'Mummy?' His voice was barely a whisper.

'Yes, my heart.'

'Is Chuff here?'

Rachel glanced around the room until her eyes fell upon a bright orange ball. 'Yes sweetheart. Chuff's nice and cosy in his box.'

Miles sighed and snuffled deeper into the warmth of his bed. Mummy was sitting beside him, Pandaloo was in his arms and Chuff was safely tucked up in his box. His worldly requirements were complete.

'Sandman coming eh?' Ralph entered the room and stood behind his wife at the side of the bed. 'Looks like he's already arrived if I'm not mistaken.' Ralph laid a hand on his wife's shoulder and gazed at his son.

Rachel nodded and signalled to her husband to leave. Once outside she closed the door quietly and followed Ralph into the sitting room. She sat on the sofa and automatically picked up her knitting. 'He's really quite obsessed with that rubber ball,' she mused, her fingers clicking expertly as the wool transformed itself into the cuff of a sleeve for Beth's jacket. 'I hope it's not unhealthy. It's as though he really believes it has a life of its own.'

Ralph re-lit the half-finished cigarette and turned on the radio. 'I wouldn't worry too much,' he fiddled with the dials in a bid to find the BBC World Service. 'I was just the same when I was a kid. Only my little friend was a stone that my father used to sharpen his knives. At least Chuff can move!'

He chuckled at his own recollection, then returned his attention to the task in hand. Suddenly the radio crackled into life and the sounds of the Glen Miller Band burst into the room. Ralph drew heavily on his cigarette, eased himself into the chair and opened the creased copy of the Bulawayo Chronicle.

Ralph and Rachel enjoyed these quiet evenings together. They were precious times, for Ralph was a farmer, and Scarfell a thriving dairy farm, and they would both be starting another hard day's work before sun-up. It was their life. They had chosen it and, so far, it had served them well.

Miles had important things to do today. He was on his way to find Julius. Halfway down the path that led to the Khumalo kia, Miles stopped, turned and sped back to his room to collect Chuff. The rubber ball had been imbued with a life of its own and was it Miles' favourite toy. He grabbed it and ran through the house, his leather sandals slapping noisily on the wooden floors.

The path to the servants' quarters led him past the tennis court by the bee-hives where Joseph was slashing at the tall grasses now that the rainy season had come to an end. Miles waved and went on his way, whistling a breathy tune in unconscious imitation of his father.

The route took him down a steep slope. Here the ground became uneven and littered with stones and the path less well-defined. A few rough-hewn steps led further down the hill. There were two whitewashed buildings at the bottom. The larger kia was home to Moses and Bliss and young Julius. It had a room at either end and a central space that served as living room and kitchen. The smaller kia was occupied by Joseph Hungwe and Sixpence Dube.

Julius was sitting on a log outside his kia. 'I see you Julius,' Miles made the traditional African greeting in fluent Sindebele.

'I see you too, Miles.'

'What are you doing?' Miles stood looking down at his friend with Chuff tucked neatly under his arm.

'Chongololo.' Julius said simply.

Miles watched while Julius worried the little millipede with a stick. He was fascinated by the way some chongololo curled up into a ball while others rolled over and writhed. It provided the two boys with an endless source of entertainment, particularly in the rainy season when there were dozens in the garden. Miles, riding over them on his bicycle, had been amazed to discover that the end with the head attached kept wriggling even when the rest of the body was crushed under his wheels! It was a miracle of nature demonstrated with such simple clarity to two young boys.

'Don't pick it up or it'll pong like crazy and make your fingers go yellow,' Miles said knowingly.

'I know that.' Julius countered.

Miles watched the stick darting about in the sand for a while. Then, bored by this particular miracle of nature, he turned his attention to Chuff. Bending down close to the ball he whispered: 'Off you go and play, naughty Chuff. Me and Julius are busy.'

With that, he dropped the ball and gave it an encouraging tap with his toe to help it on its way. Julius allowed himself to be distracted from his own game while he watched the ball bounce down the path towards Joseph's kia.

'Chuff!' Miles cried, feigning a note of anger. 'Don't you go near Joseph's kia you naughty ball.'

The ball, of course, continued on its way down the slope, bouncing slightly off course when it hit a particularly large stone. It was this independence of movement that had allowed Miles to attribute life to Chuff. 'It's magic.' He turned to Julius with a menacing look.

'What kind of magic?' Julius was happy to be convinced.

'Tokalosh magic!'

Julius affected a shiver at this mention of the feared African goblin. At night in the dark he would be genuinely frightened but now, with the sun high in the sky and the Heugelins robins singing their hearts out in the paw-paws, he was only pretending to be scared. Miles understood this, but he was content to play along.

'Chuff only does what I say,' he declared importantly. 'Anyone else gets the chop!'

With that, he stood up and strode purposefully towards the ball that had come to rest at the corner of the kia. He picked it up, showing off a little now that he was sure of Julius' attention, and whispered bits of nonsense against the hot smelly rubber. He walked back towards his friend, paused for a moment, and then lobbed the ball at him. Julius yelled and ducked, whether from fear of the tokalosh or being clobbered by the ball was not clear, but he soon recovered and was up on his feet and lunging for Miles with all the strength he possessed in his skinny young arms.

Miles took him head on and the two lads fell sprawling on the path. As always the wrestling match would continue without purpose until either an angry grown-up, a scratched knee or something more interesting diverted their attention. They were young and they were friends, and the odd scrap didn't really count. And how they would long for such innocent pleasures in the years to come.

It was 24th July 1964 and it was a very important day in the Rhodesian calendar. It was the second birthday of Miss Elizabeth Cameron, and a special birthday party was being held to honour the occasion.

Out in the garden, Sixpence was preparing the braai. The wood had crackled into life and flames danced over it. Although it was winter, the temperature was a pleasant 26 degrees at mid-day and Rachel's gamble had paid off. Everyone loved a barbecue and it was an ideal way to celebrate Beth's birthday.

'Leave that now, Sixpence. I'll take over,' Ralph called as he strode across the lawn. 'Go get some beer out. You can store it under the table.'

'Yes baas.'

'And keep the flies off the salad.' Rachel added.

'Yes Madam.'

With the onset of winter the rains had stopped and the lawn, thirsting for water, had lost some of its green lustre. In the far corner the jacarandas were starting to shed and parts of the garden were covered in a layer of yellow leaves. Out in the bush, the familiar rusts and browns of Africa were transformed into various shades of creamy-grey with only occasional flashes of orange to brighten the landscape.

'Mummy!' Beth, shaking herself free of Bliss, came hurtling, sideways-fashion, across the lawn to the welcoming arms of her mother.

'Hello my birthday girl!' Rachel swept her daughter up and plonked a wet kiss on her cheek. 'And don't you look a princess!' She planted the child firmly on the floor and turned to thank Bliss who kept a respectful distance and stood with her hands clasped in front of her. 'Is Grandma Cameron ready to join us?'

'She certainly is!' The question was directed at Bliss, but it was more than adequately answered by the individual who marched resolutely to greet them.

'Mother,' Rachel smiled warmly. 'Did you enjoy your nap?'

'Very much so, thank you dear. Does Grandma Cameron get a kiss child, or do I have to try to bring this creaky old body down to your level?' Rachel laughed and lifted her daughter up to her mother-in-law's level.

Rose Cameron was not one for excessive displays of affection. She was made of sterner stuff. Short and stout with hair gone prematurely grey, she was a fighter. All alone she had kept Scarfell Farm afloat after the untimely death of her husband - and she had single-handedly raised two healthy sons to boot! Rose came from tough, pioneering stock and she was proud of her pedigree. She belonged to the generation that had struggled and toiled to win this hostile land and who had suffered untold heartache in the process. But they had not abandoned their quest. They believed in themselves and they believed in God. God had given them this land in order to save the natives from themselves. As civilised whites, they had a duty to be worthy of that gift.

'When is your brother expected to grace us with his presence?' she enquired in her usual abrupt manner.

'Looks like he's on his way now,' Ralph pointed to the battered station wagon thundering up the drive. They all turned to watch the cloud of dust that heralded the approach of Charlie Cameron and his Afrikaner wife, Clara.

'Is it oom Charlie?' Miles approached the group followed by Prince, his father's favourite Rhodesian ridgeback. Both children had been taught to use the Afrikaner terms for aunt and uncle. It was at the request of Clara, a descendant of a Boer hero who had fought at Spion Kop, and who prized her own pedigree way above that of the 'newcomers'.

The station wagon spun round at the top of the drive and screeched to a halt causing the nearby chickens to squawk among themselves. Prince, Ralph's dog, barked loudly, working himself up into a frenzy of territorial supremacy, while the entire Cameron family crossed to the lawn to greet their guests. Charlie had arrived! Rachel breathed deeply, straightened her shoulders and prepared herself for the chaos that was to come.

The car door swung open with a harsh scraping of metal on metal and Charlie clambered out. Prince continued to bark, but warily now having recognised the invaders.

'Voedsak, you mangy mutt! Bugger off dog!' Charlie flicked the dog's nose. Prince withdrew, but only so far - Rhodesian ridgebacks were not prized for their timidity!

'Howzit boet!' Charlie slapped his brother on the back. 'Mother! A new frock!' Charlie kissed his mother on the cheek before lifting young Miles high off the ground and swinging him full circle above his head. Miles squealed in delight. Oom Charlie was his most favourite person in the whole wide world - save for Mummy and Pa, of course. Beth, who was overwhelmed by her uncle's immense physical presence, clung wide-eyed and anxious to the hem of her mother's polka-dot dress.

'Beth - come and give oom Charlie a hug!' Charlie leaned forward and extended both arms to embrace his niece. This was all too much for Beth, who promptly burst into tears and disappeared into the folds of her mother's skirt.

'Now see what you've done.' Charlie's wife tutted her disapproval. 'Fool! Hello Ralph... Rachel. I hope I find you well, Mother?'

'Quite well thank you, Clara.' Clara proffered Rose a cursory air-kiss.

Eager to dispel the cool that had arrived with Clara, Rachel gently disengaged the clinging child from her skirt and gave her sister-in-law a hug. 'I shouldn't worry, Clara. Beth's been a bit tearful all morning. I think the excitement is all too much for her.'

'It's not helped by Charles and his tomfoolery.' Clara rarely gave in. Peace must be on her terms or not at all. Rachel recognised this, but she was willing to surrender for the sake of the party. Threading an arm through Clara's she said: 'Come along Clara. We've got some of your favourite boerewors on the braai. Do you know, I've been dying to see you. I wanted to ask your advice about my latest painting. I just can't decide on a frame...'

Ralph and Charlie made their way over to the braai. There were only two years between the brothers but they had little in common. Although both had inherited their father's good looks, and both shared a love of sports, the resemblance stopped there. While Ralph was the studious one, the son to whom Rose had entrusted Scarfell when she moved out to the eastern highlands, Charlie was the carefree one, a likeable loafer who could be relied on to be the life-and-soul of any party.

Not for Charlie Cameron the responsibility of 12,000 acres, cattle and kids. His life revolved around snooker, tennis and the Bulawayo Club. He and Ralph had come to an agreement over the farm and he had already spent most of his share when he met his wife-to-be, Clara Van Vuuren, at an Afrikaner festival in Cape Town.

'Get me a drink, boy! Shumba will do.' Charlie thundered at Sixpence who scurried off to find the beer. 'I'm as dry as a bushman's backside!'

'Bushman's backside?' Ralph laughed. 'That's a new one.'

'Bloody munts!' Charlie snatched a sausage from the flames and crammed half of it into his mouth. 'All they do is sit on their bloody arses out in the bush complaining about the whites.'

'Ja. I see the connection, but I'm not sure it's completely accurate.'

Charlie wiped the grease from his chin. 'Knew you wouldn't. You've always had a soft spot for the poor old Af. Take it from me, little brother, you've got to keep at them the whole bloody time or they'll end up either doing sod-all or causing trouble for everyone. Sixpence! Get your useless backside over here, boy. I'm dying of thirst!' Charlie folded a piece of ham into his mouth and chewed vigorously while continuing his analysis of the African's propensity for work.

Clara watched him with icy cool. Charlie had exaggerated his own financial prospects, Scarfell Farm being one of his many assets, in order to satisfy the elder Van Vuurens and capture the heart of their daughter, Clara. It was not long after her arrival in Bulawayo that Clara had realised the truth.

Her new husband had frittered away his share of the farm and now made a living as an electrician in the Matopos. Instead of a beautiful farmhouse set in the Blue Hills, home was a small bungalow in a Bulawayo suburb. Clara's dreams of a rich life beyond the Limpopo River crumbled into ashes. As time passed, even her dreams of providing grandchildren for the Van Vuuren family were crushed, although this final ignominy she was forced to attribute to her own barren body.

Clara was a woman embittered by her life. She had few friends, no children and she despised her husband. She loathed her mother-in-law, who stubbornly refused to acknowledge her daughter-in-law's impeccable credentials, and she envied Ralph and Rachel so completely that sometimes it quite overwhelmed her. She was a deeply unhappy woman.

'Miles, don't you dare use that catapult here!' Rachel pointed a stern finger at her son. 'Beth darling, stop clinging to my skirt. You'll tear it. Sixpence, more wood, please...' Rachel swept across the lawn and snatched the catapult from Miles. 'I told you ...Now where did you get this?'

'Joseph made it.' Miles thrust his hands into the pockets of his shorts and sulked. 'I wasn't going to use it. I just aimed... that's all. It's not fair!'

Rachel stuffed the weapon into her own pocket. 'You know full well what you were planning to do, my lad. Now stop fibbing or I shall be cross. Go and sit with tante Clara, there's a darling. Beth, don't go near the fire! Ralph - watch her will you!'

Thoroughly fed up now, Miles trudged over to his aunt with his hands in his pockets. He walked slowly, eyes fixed on the floor in protest, and kicked at a stone in front of him. Tante Clara made him feel uncomfortable. He didn't like the way she fixed him with her eyes when she talked. It was scary. He had tried to explain it to Julius, savagely imitating his aunt's expression to convey the point. Julius had nodded. It looked scary enough. He would trust Miles' judgement.

Fortunately, just as Miles was about to fulfil his duty, he was spotted by oom Charlie and a welcome detour ensued. Delighted to be lifted onto his uncle's back for a giddy piggy-back ride, he felt quite justified in being diverted from his earlier mission. Even the sight of tante Clara sitting alone in the midst of the revelry could not detract from the thrill of being swung from side to side and tipped upside down by good old oom Charlie, and he screamed with mock terror and laughter. Beth's birthday, he decided, was turning out to be a really special day.

Moses Khumalo sat on the step in the doorway of his kia and chewed on the end of a strip of biltong. Joseph sat on the ground opposite fashioning a more sophisticated catapult for baas Miles. His hands worked carefully, stripping the wood with his knife into a perfect curve. Later he would polish it with rags until it gleamed. It would be a fine weapon, Joseph thought with pride.

Moses watched with eyes that were dark and brooding. He bit another chunk of the dried meat and chewed it thoughtfully. On the step beside him was a carton of Chibuku - the millet beer produced by a black brewery in Salisbury. He picked it up and gulped the contents greedily, belching loudly as he flung the empty carton into the bushes. Joseph paused in his labour, nodded his approval, then continued with the task in hand.

'Why do you do that?' Moses stared moodily at his companion.

'The Nkosizana, he is an expert shot.' Joseph could not contain a note of pride. He had taught the young baas himself.

'But why do you make weapons for the whites? Why do you wish to arm the enemies of your own people?'

Joseph shrugged. 'Baas Miles is only a child.'

'A child who will grow into a man. Are you a fool Joseph Hungwe? Can you not see what is all around you? Already our people have been thrown off their land to make way for the white man's farms. Now we struggle to make a living out of dust while the white man grows fat with our labour. The weapons that you make should be weapons of war. Weapons that your black brothers will use in their fight for freedom.'

'But baas Miles…. he is only a child.' Joseph repeated his argument, certain now that it was too feeble to win any war of words with Moses Khumalo.

'Yes. But when he comes into manhood he will follow the tradition of his ancestors and he will steal yet more of our land for himself. There will be nothing left for the children of Mzilikazi - for our sons. The white man is hungry for Africa and he will destroy us all with his greed. He will destroy your sons, Joseph Hungwe, with weapons you have taught him to use.'

Joseph stared miserably at the catapult in his hands. He laid it to one side and reached into his pockets, searching for tobacco to help conceal his guilt. Try as he might he could not match the revolutionary fervour of Moses Khumalo. Later, when he was halfway through his nightly quota of beer, he would have plenty to say. He would tell himself that his life was good. He had food in his belly, a bed to sleep in and money in his pocket. If the whites wanted the responsibility of ownership he would not stand in their way. He was content with his lot

'Already our great leader lies rotting in the white man's prison,' Moses continued. 'Joshua Nkomo, the leader of the Zimbabwe African People's Union, is suffering for you Joseph Hungwe. And for what? Because he dared to speak out against white privileges and white oppression. He dared to give the black man a voice in Africa. For that crime, they took away his freedom. Bah!' Moses spat in disgust.

'But what can I do about that?' Joseph wailed, drawing heavily on his cigarette. He longed for a drink, but dared not let Moses see that mere physical pleasures were uppermost in his mind.

'You can fight, that is what you can do. ZAPU needs you. And you need ZAPU. You will never know real freedom if you do not join the struggle against white tyranny, my brother.'

'But…' Joseph hastily abandoned his half-formed response in the face of Moses' displeasure. He ground the remains of the roll-up into the dirt and kept his eyes fixed firmly on the crumpled cigarette paper.

'Do not be ashamed my brother.' Moses softened his tone. 'The Camerons have made you as you are now - weak as a woman. They have fooled you with their kind words and with ... with this!' Moses waved a hand at the comfortable servants' quarters. 'But you are still a slave Joseph. Even though you have money to spend and the Camerons' food in your belly you are not a free man. I speak the truth and one day you will come to know this. When that day comes, and it will come soon enough, you will be ready to fight alongside your black brothers in the chimurenga.'

Joseph sagged with relief. He did not want to relinquish his place alongside his black brothers completely, for that might incur the fearsome wrath of Moses Khumalo, but he was content to await the coming of the chimurenga in the comfort of the local shebeen.

Moses leaned back against the doorframe and shielded his eyes against the glare of the mid-day sun. The light illuminated his smooth skin until it shone like polished ebony. His nose was long and straight with nostrils that flared evenly, and his eyes were as black as the Kimberley mines, dark and fathomless. It was a beautiful face.

He was thinking about Joseph, whom he knew to be a fool. There were many of his brothers who, like Joseph, had been emasculated by the white man. It would be difficult to rekindle the fire that had once made them men but he, Moses Khumalo, would do it. It was a promise he had made to his ancestors, and it was one which he would keep.

The whites were building their homes, their roads and their farms on the blood of black Africans , but Moses knew that one day his people would rise again and reclaim this divided land they called Rhodesia. He would bide his time quietly in the shadows. He would pretend to be the inferior being they believed him to be. But when the time came, he would stand alongside his African brothers while the white man's blood mingled with the dirt of the land he had stolen. And it would be a great day for Africa.

Moses Khumalo sighed deeply and let his gaze swoop like the wings of a predatory eagle across the hills and fields of Scarfell Farm. But he did not see the awesome majesty of the landscape, nor the beautiful azure skies and shimmering sunlight, for his gaze was blinded by hate.

2

Rachel was planting a herb trough ready for her parents' Christmas visit. With winter now past the temperature was soaring, thirty-five degrees by noon, and she wore a floppy hat to keep the sun out of her eyes. Nearby, Joseph was sweeping up the leaves from the frangipani that blossomed in front of the dining room windows. It was in full bloom and Rachel could smell the heady fragrance from its sunshine-coloured flowers that drifted on the breeze.

She glanced at her watch. It was time for lunch. Beside her, kneeling on a blanket, Beth was force-feeding Spot with a jelly-bean. The push-dog remained rigid on its wheeled platform while Beth jammed the jelly-bean against its mouth. Eventually, satisfied that her motherly duties were complete, Beth pushed Spot away and ate the jelly-bean herself. The dog tipped over coming to rest on its side, its expression unchanged while its upturned wheels spun slightly.

'All finished,' Rachel wiped her hands on the corner of a towel and surveyed her efforts with satisfaction.

Beth helped herself to another jelly-bean.

'Don't you eat too many of those you naughty monkey, or you'll make yourself sick.' Rachel returned Spot to his former dignity then looked up as Miles came tearing across the lawn.

'Wow! Jelly-beans!' Miles swooped upon the bag with glee. Beth screamed and clutched at the corner of the bag. She had assumed proprietary rights of the jelly-beans and was not about to relinquish the title without a fight.

'Hey! Let go! Mu-um! Tell her!'

'Come along you two.' Rachel snatched the bag from the warring siblings, took one sweet out and handed it to Miles. The rest she tucked into her pocket as Beth began to cry.

'Boo hoo, cry-baby!' Miles mimicked though sticky teeth.

Rachel took Beth's arm and pulled her to her feet. 'Now just stop it! Both of you. It's much too hot to fight. Wipe your eyes, Beth darling. It's really not that bad. Come on, let's see what Sixpence has made for lunch shall we?'

'Bet we've got Koeksisters.' Miles yelled, bolting across to the house like a young colt. Sure enough, as he skidded to a halt in the dining room, he spotted the sweet plaited pastry on the table. 'See, I told you,' Miles said, climbing on to a chair in order to reach the tasty treats. 'He promised.'

And Miles knew full well that Sixpence Dube never, ever broke a promise.

Miles ate his lunch in a hurry. He had an important assignation. He was due to meet Julius in the bush behind the kopje where the Boer War would be starting shortly, and he had little time for the courtesies which his mother set such store by. Even so, he knew rebellion would be futile so he wiped his hands on the napkin and addressed her with his very best smile.

'May I get down from the table please?'

'Yes dear, but don't go too far. We're going into Bulawayo this afternoon, remember? So try not to get too dirty.'

'Okay,' Miles skipped out of the house before his mother could change her mind. The Boer War could wait for lunch, but it could not wait forever.

The kopje was on the far side of the garden past the jacarandas where the cultivated land gave way to the African bush. Miles ran, oblivious to the scorching heat and the raucous squabbles of the fire finches and mannikins fighting for crumbs on the bird table. The Boer War was about to break out on Scarfell Farm. There was no time to waste.

'I see you Miles,' Julius was waiting on top of one of the huge granite boulders.

'I see you too Julius.'

'The weather is good.' Julius was practising his traditional Matabele address, devoting several minutes to general courtesies, such as the weather, or the health of the cattle, before engaging in proper conversation. Usually Miles was happy to share in these age-old rituals which made him feel very grown-up, but today he was keen to get started.

'Who do you want to be?' he asked, forsaking etiquette in favour of the game.

'Mzilikazi,' Julius declared, equally content to abandon Matabele traditions in pursuit of good fun.

'You were him last time,' Miles whined in protest. 'My dad says Mzilikazi wasn't even in the Boer War.'

Julius shrugged. He was not about to be diverted by historical pedantry. 'I want to be Mzilikazi … or I'm not playing!'

It was a solid argument and Miles conceded defeat. The first battle of the Boer War had been fought. And Julius was undoubtedly the victor.

The two boys loped along the dusty track in companionable silence for a while. Both were barefoot, the soles of their feet impervious to loose stones and cracks in the ground. Miles wore no shirt, only a hat and a pair of red and white shorts in honour of his favourite football team, Manchester United. His grandmother had sent them over from England and he was wearing them for the first time.

Julius was also wearing a pair of Manchester United shorts. He was often the recipient of Miles' hand-me-downs. Miles was thrilled to see his friend in similar colours. They stood chin up, side-by-side to compare how they looked. Practically the same height, determined by a flat palm from the top of one head to the top of the other, the same colour shorts, similar sized feet. Why they even had a similar graze on their knee. They could easily pass as brothers Miles had said, much preferring a veteran of the Boer War to a soppy sister. Julius nodded eagerly. They could indeed be brothers.

Within minutes the two boys came out of the dense bush into a clearing of tall, golden grasses. They squatted down and began to plan their campaign. The grass was dry and it crackled underneath them when they shifted position. In the distance a solitary tree reached up with blackened branches to a sunlit sky. Beyond that, capping the horizon, the Blue Hills loomed large, enclosing them in a world which seemed so safe and secure and full of wonder.

'Why do you always have to be Mzilikazi?' Miles asked, poking the scab on his knee with a blade of grass.

'Baba says that the Khumalo family is directly descended from the founder of the great Matabele nation,' Julius replied, echoing his father's exact words. 'He said that Mzilikazi refused to bow down to Chaka, the Zulu King, and took his people north to find their own land.'

'Did he fight lots of battles?'

'Baba says that our people had to fight and die to reach Matabeleland. He said that the war is not over, and our black brothers will have to fight and die again to keep it.'

'Why?' Miles was intrigued. He enjoyed stories about fighting and dying. 'Why have they got to fight and die to keep it?'

This was beyond Julius. He had learned his father's story parrot-fashion and his knowledge did not permit any deeper analysis. He watched Miles' efforts to lift the corner of the scab with the sharp end of the reed. It made him feel a bit squeamish. 'It will bleed,' he declared stolidly. 'We are far from home. You could bleed to death.'

Miles shrugged. Bleeding to death seemed a most interesting prospect. 'What else did baba tell you? Miles used the Sindebele term for father, or elder.

Julius took a deep breath and prepared to recite the words which his father had taught him. He explained how Mzilikazi had been sent to train under his maternal grandfather, Zwide. He spoke of the bloody battle between Zwide and the rival chief, Dingiswayo. Much to Miles' delight, he explained how Zwide had beheaded Dingiswayo.

Mzilikazi's own tribe, the Khumalo, were governed by his father, Mashobane. Zwide, believing the Khumalo had aided Dingiswayo, had Mashobane killed. He then installed Mzilikazi as chief of the Khumalo.

'Mzilikazi is my great-great grandfather,' Julius declared with pride. 'Baba says he taught the Matabele how to fight.'

'What did he teach them,' Miles lobbed the blade of grass into the bush leaving the scab on his knee curling up at the edges. This was much more interesting.

'He learned from the great Chaka Zulu. He learned how to teach the warriors to form the horns of the bull and encircle the enemy ... like this,' Julius imitated the bull with his thumbs pressed against his temples. He had Miles' undivided attention now. 'And he learned how to use the assegai,'

He picked up his own spear which Joseph had made for him. It was a perfect replica of the short stabbing spear of the Zulus, but rendered harmless by being made out of cardboard. Joseph and his father had told him about the weapon, how Chaka had broken the traditional Zulu long spear in half and created this fearful tool in its place. And it was this weapon, the assegai, which had become the symbol of the strength of the Zulu and which had killed thousands of black and white warriors in the long and bloody fight for Africa.

Julius watched as a tok toki beetle made its way across the undulating folds of his faded Manchester United shorts. He pulled the crease apart slightly so that the creature fell into the crevice. Miles leaned over and peered at the spectacle of the beetle on its back, its legs dancing wildly in an effort to right itself. It was a common enough sight, but death in the insect world, although fascinating, could not hope to compete with tales of human devastation and gore.

'Okay!' Miles jumped to his feet. 'You can be Mzilikazi. I'm going to be General Louis Botha. First one to that tree gets to play with the assegai!'

Julius scrabbled to his feet and rushed after his friend in the race to fight the Boer War armed with a beautifully-crafted cardboard assegai. He kept an even pace. He knew he could outrun Miles and the tree was some way off. He would keep his assegai.

The two boys left behind a circle of flattened grass where they had sat and swapped stories. In the middle of the circle, under the relentless African sun, the beetle had fallen in an upright position and was now recouping its strength before burying itself in the dark, cool earth.

It was Christmas Eve and the children were tucked up in bed. Ralph and his father-in-law took advantage of the peace and quiet to enjoy the brandy and cigars that George Bentley had brought out from England. They sat on the stoep watching the smoke curl in the glow from the paper lanterns that Rachel had hung out earlier. Fluttering around them, emperor moths spun crazily in the pools of light while others flung themselves against the illuminated windows of the house.

George was watching his son-in-law. The lad was troubled. George could sense it. He did not want to interfere in matters which were not his concern, but he felt bound to offer his help if it was needed. 'Penny for them?' he whispered.

Ralph turned and smiled. 'Sorry Dad. I'm a bit of a dull companion, I'm afraid.'

'On the contrary, my boy. It's just that I couldn't help noticing you've been a little ... pre-occupied shall we say?'

Ralph laughed. 'Ever the diplomat,' but then a frown creased his brow. 'I was just wondering how many more Christmas Eves we'll enjoy like this. Things are changing and it worries me. The blacks are angry, but the whites aren't listening, especially now we've got Ian Smith at the helm.'

George drew heavily on his cigar and the tip glittered bright red. 'He's a powerful politician, Ian Smith. Popular too.'

'Ja. The Rhodesia Front are determined to fight anyone opposed to their rigid segregation and supremacist policies. The voters couldn't fail to be hooked. They'll do anything to hang on to white privileges.'

'And you?'

'Me? I'm more concerned about the effects of UDI to dwell on party politics, but I can't help feeling that Rhodesia's stance will isolate us from the rest of the world. I know Smithy says we're self-sufficient, but we'll find it hard to cope if the rest of the world introduces economic sanctions against us.' Ralph batted away a moth and took a swig of brandy.

George leaned forward in his chair with his elbows resting on his knees and his chin propped up on his fist. 'Will Scarfell be hit hard, do you think?'

'Not initially. We're protected by the internal market. Our customers will still need milk, so we won't have to rely on exports. My problem will be development. It may become impossible to get stock-feeds, parts for my machinery, fertilisers - you name it. Ian Smith sure opened the door to problems when he decided to go it alone.'

'And you've got increasing pressure from the black population to deal with. My understanding is that this whole UDI thing is based on the land issue. The blacks believe that the whites have stolen the best land for themselves, and they'll not give up their claims to a fairer distribution of land that easily.'

Ralph was silent for a moment collecting his thoughts. In the far distance, under the cover of darkness, a wild animal's cry rang clear in the night. It was an eerie sound. 'I think we're heading for war,' Ralph said simply.

George stubbed out his cigar and picked up his brandy, swirling the contents in the glass. 'God forbid it should come to that! I'm sure the politicians can reach an agreement with the blacks without resorting to violence. But if you're right, how will it affect you here? Rachel ... will she be safe ...and the children?'

'Oh, they'll be safe, don't you worry yourself on that account,' Ralph sensed the alarm in the older man's voice. 'It'll be tough, no doubt about that, and we'll need to be extra vigilant, but they won't come to any harm out here. It'll take more than a handful of African thugs or tsotsis to beat the Camerons of Scarfell Farm. We're a hardy bunch.'

'True, but you must remain alert to any signs of danger. Even so, right now I couldn't wish for a better home for my daughter. Do you know Ralph, Doris and I were worried sick when she took off for Africa. We were even more alarmed when she said she was going to marry a farmer and stay here for good! But we couldn't have wished for a better life for our girl. You've given her so much Ralph, and we're grateful to you.'

George shuffled uneasily on his chair. It was a rare moment of emotion in this normally reticent English gentleman and he was grateful for the night shadows which helped conceal his face.

Ralph knew his father-in-law too well to imagine that he was comfortable with this demonstration of affection, so he stood up, stretched his back and said: 'If I'm not mistaken Christmas is almost upon us. We'd better go in. I've got a couple of Christmas stockings to fill before I turn in for the night. Heaven help me if Santa fails to do his duty. Then we really will have a war on our hands!'

The two men went into the house closing the doors against the world outside. Christmas was coming and they would enjoy it together. Christmas 1965 was tangible and real and, for now, it was all that mattered. They would not let the clouds looming on the horizon jeopardise what they had today, for each was hoping that those clouds would disappear before long. Perhaps they would be carried away on the winds of change that were purportedly blowing over Africa. Anything was possible.

Joshua Nkomo was experiencing a very different kind of Christmas Eve at the Gonakudzingwa protected area near Gwelo where he had been imprisoned since April 1964. He was not fenced in with wire at Gonakudzingwa, nor his freedom curtailed by locks and chains. There was no need. Escapees were at the mercy of lions and other dangerous animals that roamed the Gonarezhou game reserve, whose survival instinct was oblivious to race, colour or creed. The wild beasts of Africa were his warders, and their locks could never be broken.

But Nkomo was not wasting his time at Gonakudzingwa. As the prison population swelled it was fast becoming a centre for the political education of new and existing members of ZAPU, the Zimbabwe African People's Union. The prisoners did not waste their time. They used their incarceration as an excellent training opportunity for the day when they would finally reclaim the land that was theirs by right.

On Christmas Day, after breakfast, Ralph and Rachel prepared to give out the servants' gifts. A dozen or so had gathered in the hall with their wives and children who would also receive small parcels of sweets and biscuits. This year the men would be given new shirts and ties, together with the traditional Boys' Christmas Hampers containing foods such as rice, sugar and bread.

'Shall I tell them to come in now Daddy?' Miles was eager to start the lengthy Christmas Day tradition. His enthusiasm was not so much Yuletide generosity, but more the urge to hurry things along so that he could open his own presents. Having received permission to summon the queue of Africans standing awkwardly in the hall, he skipped over to the door and addressed them in Sindebele as one. 'Okay you can come in now. Your stuff is over there ... by the tree.'

The workers and their families trooped self-consciously into the sitting room. One or two were sporting shabby brown suits with trousers that were so short they bordered on the comical. Miles was under strict instructions not to giggle and he was happy to obey. He knew what was expected of him, and he did not want to delay the proceedings unnecessarily. A couple of men were barefoot while another had failed to find a shirt to wear and now sported a suit jacket over a bare chest. One man was gripping his prized trilby hat against his stomach so tightly that the rim cracked under the strain. All had gone to great lengths to cobble together a suitable outfit for this most solemn ceremony.

When presented with their gift each man bowed with great formality to the Camerons and their guests before shuffling out of the house clutching their Christmas parcels. Their children, although over-awed by the big house, were thrilled to be given presents, and Julius and a couple of other lads turned to grin at Miles.

At the far end of the line, one man stood tall and proud above his fellows. This man wore his suit with ease and it fitted him well. Moses Khumalo approached the Christmas tree with a dignity that both Doris and George were quick to spot. Moses looked directly at Ralph who nodded in fond recognition. But when Rachel handed Moses his Christmas Hamper, the light in the African's eyes dimmed and a frown creased his brow. Rachel did not notice. After all, it was Christmas and it was a time for rejoicing. Moses accepted the gift and inclined his head towards Rachel.

'Happy Christmas Moses.' She said with a cheerful smile.

'Thank you Madam.' Moses smiled back.

He took the parcel and turned to leave. When he stepped outside the house, the sun warmed his face in an instant. He looked at the European shirt and tie and then at the hamper made by all the white people for all the cook-boys, garden-boys and house-boys who served the white people in Africa.

And he was no longer smiling.

After Christmas, the family planned to spend New Year's Eve at the Victoria Falls Hotel and they were all looking forward to the trip.

'You'll get to see loads of baobab trees,' Miles told his grandparents the night before they were due to leave. 'Julius reckons that African spirits live in them and some of them are a thousand years old.'

'They're known locally as the "upside-down trees" because of their peculiar shape,' Ralph added. 'Their branches look like roots - hence the name.'

'And the seeds taste all minty when you suck them.' Miles was bobbing about from one foot to the other, anxious to impart the full extent of his knowledge about the baobab tree. 'And the flower is a big, white thing that really pongs.'

'It's true,' Rachel laid aside her knitting to join in the conversation. 'The flower actually does smell like rotting meat. It's most peculiar.'

Ralph was standing in front of the hearth. 'And, of course, we'll see Vic' Falls., so it should be quite a trip.'

It was quite a trip. The journey by car took more than five hours, over and above the break for lunch at a family inn near Gwaai. By the time they finally reached their destination, the temperature had soared to forty degrees and even Miles was feeling the heat.

Eventually they arrived at the hotel and were greeted by an army of black porters in smart, grey uniforms, and a pleasant, fresh-faced young man at the reception. The decor was a skilful combination of vibrant African colour with cool marble floors, huge mirrors and exquisite African tapestries hanging from the walls. The bedrooms were luxurious, too, with balconies that had spectacular views of the Falls Bridge in the distance.

The next morning, refreshed from a good night's sleep, they set off early to follow the paved pathway that wound its way through the tropical rain-forests on the cliff-top opposite the Falls. George was awe-struck by the sheer size of Victoria Falls and the awesome power of the Zambesi as it thundered into the deep gorge below.

'That's a heck of a lot of water,' It was all he could think of to say.

'The Kololo tribe called it Mosi-oa-Tunya, the Smoke that Thunders,' said Ralph. 'Do you remember the painting in the Bulawayo Club?'

'I do indeed,' Doris had been impressed by the work of the artist Thomas Baines. He was one of the early explorers who had accompanied David Livingstone's party on the Zambesi expedition in 1858.

'This is where your family came into Rhodesia, isn't it?' asked George.

'This side of the Zambesi,' Ralph replied. 'My great-grandfather was a missionary, as you know.'

'So what brought him to Africa? We never did get the full story.'

They had reached a clearing in the forest where they could sit and enjoy this wonder of the world. Miles and Beth hurried off to try to entice the little vervet monkeys down from the trees with imaginary food. The monkeys were not easily fooled and they continued their merry capers across the branches to everyone's delight.

'It's quite a tale,' Ralph warned, reaching into his pocket for a cigarette.

'So I gather. Well go on, my boy. We've got all the time in the world.'

Ralph paused to wipe the spray from his brow. He offered George a cigarette then shielded the match from the spray with his cupped hand. He drew deeply, enjoying the Rhodesian home-grown tobacco as it filled his lungs.

'It all started with the explorer, David Livingstone, who stayed on the other side of the river with the Kololo tribe.'

'Ah, yes! The people who called this the Smoke that Thunders.' Doris rarely appeared to be listening to the conversation, but would chip in from time to time with evidence that she had actually heard and absorbed every single word.

'Well Livingstone wanted to bring the Kololo over to this side of the Zambesi away from the unhealthy flood plains where they were plagued by tsetse fly.'

'But old Mzilikazi wouldn't let them would he Daddy?' Miles was determined to contribute to the lesson. 'He would have killed them all … cut their throats … like this!' He drew a dramatic forefinger across his windpipe.

Ralph laughed and pulled his son on to his knee. 'Perhaps you should tell the tale. It would be far more exciting I'm sure!'

'No you tell it Daddy.' Miles knew the story off by heart but it was no less wonderful for that.

'Well, as this young pup says, Livingstone knew that Mzilikazi would never allow the Kololo to settle on this side of the river. So he asked his father-in-law, Robert Moffat, to persuade Mzilikazi to let him bring missionaries into Matabeleland. Moffat, who had considerable influence with the Matabele king, got his wish.'

'But how did that solve matters?' asked George.

'David Livingstone planned to bring missionaries up to the Kololo tribe too. He believed that the Christians, working together, could help keep the peace between the two tribes when the Kololo crossed the river.'

'But they all died, didn't they Daddy?' Miles interjected.

'Who?' George was confused. 'The Kololo?'

'No Gramps, silly! The missionaries!' Miles interjected. 'They all pegged it before they reached the Kololo.'

'And poor old Livingstone had to abandon the project.' Ralph ground the stub of his cigarette into the earth with his heel.

'So where do the Camerons fit into all this?'

Miles rolled his eyes and promptly received a tap on the head from his father for being cheeky.

'Luckily the other missionaries, the ones sent to work with the Matabele, survived. There were three of them and they were the first white men to set up home in this part of Africa. One member of that stalwart group was none other than Clive Ewan Cameron.'

'That's us Gramps!' Miles grabbed his grandfather's hand. 'That's us lot!'

George Bentley patted his grandson's head. His hair was damp from the spray and lay flat against his skull. It accentuated his little face, all bright-eyed and eager, and George felt a tight knot of emotion swell in his throat. 'It is indeed my boy. And you must never forget that you belong to one of the oldest, finest white families in all Africa. There aren't many who can claim that distinction, you know. You're a lucky boy. A very lucky boy indeed!'

'And may the Good Lord keep it so,' he whispered to himself.

The ballroom was vast, hung with crystal chandeliers and decorated with wreaths of Flame Lilies. African waiters mingled with the guests, carrying silver trays laden with glasses of sparkling champagne. On stage a trio of young musicians delivered a competent rendition of Sam Cooke's 'Twisting the Night Away'.

Rachel was flushed, partly with the excitement of dancing with her handsome husband and, if the truth were known, partly from that last glass of champagne. Wisps of corn-gold curls fell across her cheeks and crinkled damply in the nape of her neck. Ralph pulled her closer and whispered tantalisingly close to her ear: 'You're beautiful tonight sweetheart.'

'And you sir,' she replied, tapping him lightly on the chest and blushing like a schoolgirl, 'are an incorrigible flirt!'

1965 was drawing to a close. For some it would be good riddance, for others it would a time of fond memory. For all, it would be the past. As the night wore on, the tempo slowed and the lights dimmed. Midnight was approaching and the guests made their way into the middle of the dance floor to celebrate the dawning of 1966. Smiling at each other in a spirit of bonhomie, they took hands and formed a series of circles. And then they waited.

George winked at his son-in-law across the top of his daughter's head. Rachel blew her mother a kiss and then hugged her husband's and father's hands to her chest. The room was silent. Even the African waiters lining the walls were awed by the event. And then the countdown to the new year began, culminating in a flurry of bursting balloons, streamers, giggles and hugs and kisses from friends and strangers alike. 1966 had arrived and a voice boomed from the stage: 'Happy New Year everybody!' They all laughed, happy in this shared moment of optimism, then they grabbed hands again and lifted their voices to the future.

And we'll take a cup o' kindness yet

For Auld Lang Syne.

Charlie and Clara lived in a neat bungalow in a Bulawayo suburb. It was approached by a drive of flattened red earth which swept past the pretty manicured garden to reach the front steps of the house. A verandah circled the building on three sides, supported by sturdy pillars of Rhodesian teak. The roof was made from galvanised corrugated iron that expanded in the sun with almighty cracks, causing mayhem among any lizards or birds that might have chanced to rest upon it.

Clara was in the kitchen at the back of the bungalow baking bread. She refused to employ a cook, preferring to prepare all meals herself. Africans were dirty creatures she had declared on more than one occasion They could not be trusted to meet the rigorous standards of hygiene in her kitchen.

She was wearing a green gingham pinafore as she worked and her arms were dusty with flour up to the elbows. Her hair was plaited into two braids, pulled off her face and gathered in a tight knot on top of her head. An old ginger cat lay sleeping in the washing basket in the corner of the kitchen, curled up on top of a pair of Charlie's pyjamas.

It had rained the night before and the air outside was heavy with the scent of damp leaves. The grass was thick and verdant and the branches of the marula trees along the garden's perimeter wall were drooping with the weight of water. The rainy season lasted from November to March and it had been a good season so far. The dams outside Bulawayo were almost full, and the Matshemhlope had overflowed its banks on several occasions, flattening the tall grasses that had grown up on either side. Relief was palpable. There would be no drought this year.

Clara shaped the dough into a ball and began to knead it vigorously. Her mouth formed itself into a thin line and two vertical creases cut into her brow as she concentrated on the task in hand. An earlier batch was already in the oven and the smell of fresh bread had permeated the house. Clara opened the window above the sink and a cobweb attached to the glass separated into tiny silver strands as she did so. She glanced up at the sky, which was dark with clouds of gunmetal grey. There was a storm brewing and that was always a welcome sight.

Slightly less welcome was the sound of tyres crunching over the ground as her husband spun his company Land Rover into the drive and screeched to a halt at the front of the house. She winced as the car door slammed and the sound of heavy boots thundered up the steps of the verandah. She knew that they would not pause for one moment, but would stomp right into the house leaving in their wake a muddy testament to the man who was her husband ... the man everyone knew as good old Charlie.

'Woman!' Clara heard the call but chose to ignore it. 'Clara!' It was more insistent this time and she knew her token defiance was wasted. She untied her apron strings and washed the flour from her hands. Then, smoothing imaginary creases from her skirt, she went into the sitting room to greet her husband. Behind her, rudely disturbed from his afternoon slumber, the ginger cat leapt down from his comfortable corner and fled in search of a safer refuge.

Charlie was employed by the Electricity Supply Commission whose depot was based on the Plumtree Road that led to the Botswana border. His responsibilities included setting up new power supplies to outlying farms and regular maintenance of the sub-stations that served the districts outside Bulawayo. He did not enjoy these responsibilities, nor did he like the job. In fact, as Clara knew all too well, Charlie did not like work in any shape or form.

'Are you deaf, woman?' Charlie was sprawled out on the chair when his wife entered the room. He was holding a table lighter fashioned in the shape of an elephant. The butt of a cigarette was firmly gripped between his teeth and he spoke out of the side of his mouth.

'No dear,' Clara took the lighter from his hands and a tiny flame emanated from the elephant's trunk. She used it to light her husband's cigarette.

Charlie exhaled deeply and expelled a noisy sigh. 'What a day. What a fucking awful day I've had.' He rubbed his temples in an agony of self-pity.

Clara blanched at the expletive but knew better than to protest. She perched on the edge of the chair opposite and folded her hands neatly in her lap. She was expected to listen to her husband's complaints and agree with them without question. It was her duty as a wife. And it was one she performed well.

'I've been struggling half the day with a dead bloody monkey, would you believe? And on my own too.' Charlie moaned.

'Why didn't you take the Af's with you?' Clara knew that Charlie was normally accompanied by black labourers who would be expected to carry out the more menial tasks. Such work was not for white men.

'The storm brought the lines down at Nyamandhlovu. The depot foreman decided to send all the labour over there to sort it out - which left yours truly halfway up a bloody pole trying to scrape a dead monkey off the lines.'

'Where was it?'

'Near the De Wit farm in the Matopos. The monkey had climbed up the transformer and fried itself on the lines. Short-circuited the entire farm. By Christ, what a bloody chore it was trying to prise its miserable carcass off the line. Damn near killed myself in the process.'

Charlie tugged on his cigarette and shuddered at the memory. The ground around the sub-station had been thick with mud, and he had been forced to abandon his Land Rover and lug his cumbersome equipment through the field. 'It's no joke trying to grapple with a twenty-five-foot ladder, I can tell you!' he added indignantly.

'So... did you succeed?' Clara's subtle attempt to escape sailed ineffectively over Charlie's head. He was still rankling at the thought of that charred, immovable carcass and the gross injustice which had required him to sort out the mess on his own.

'Of course I did! I couldn't leave the farm without power, could I?' An inch of ash was hanging from the tip of Charlie's cigarette. Clara watched silently while it fell on to the rug. 'Not without a struggle though, I can tell you.' Charlie continued. 'It was burned to a crisp and one of its legs snapped off in my hand. Jeez - what a mess!'

Clara eyed the offending ash on the rug and made a mental note to clean it up the moment her husband left the room. She had also spotted a trail of mud leading in from the verandah to the pair of filthy boots that had been kicked off in the middle of the floor. They, too, would be removed as soon as possible. Clara turned to the wall beside her chair and pulled on the bell-cord which hung there. Within seconds the house-boy, Ibbo Tembani, appeared. 'Beer for the boss please, Ibbo.' she said.

'And make it snappy!' Charlie added for emphasis.

Ibbo Tembani was a member of the sprawling Shona tribe whose people had occupied this part of Africa for centuries, but who had proved no match for the great Mzilikazi who had swiftly claimed their territories as his own. The scores of petty Shona chiefdoms were no threat to the fearsome Matabele king and many Shona were incorporated into his kingdom as third class subjects. Matabele children grew to manhood imbued with their fathers' contempt for the Shona. They were an inferior race, a vanquished people, and the Matabele summed it up with the cruel epithet, 'Eaters of Dirt'.

Ibbo Tembani shuffled out of the room. He was slow and ungainly and his feet, clad in a pair of well-worn tackies, flapped against the wooden floor. His apron, faded to grey, had ripped pockets and a hem which was torn in parts. He walked with his back bent, the legacy of a car accident that had damaged his spine, and he rarely smiled. In his lonely, impoverished world there was little to smile about and, over the years, his expression had moulded itself into a permanently sullen pout.

'So help me if I don't send that lousy cripple on his way with his bags packed.' Charlie exploded behind the servant's back. 'Give me one good reason why we keep him on.'

Clara ignored the outburst and used the distraction to scoop up the offending cigarette ash. When the servant reappeared clutching a glass of beer, she seized the excuse to remove herself from the sitting room and return to the sanctuary of her kitchen.

'On the table, boy.' Charlie gestured irritably with his forefinger.

Ibbo's instinct for self-preservation had attuned him to his master's many moods. Sensing that a relatively short fuse had been ignited he quickened his pace. Unfortunately he failed to negotiate the pair of boots that lay in the middle of his path and he tripped over one of them, spilling beer as he did so. Some of it splashed on to Charlie's socks, sending his master flying into a rage.

'For fuck's sake, watch out man!' Charlie jumped to his feet, accidentally clipping Ibbo's elbow as he did so. The movement sent the glass spinning out of the servant's hand on to the floor where it shattered on impact. 'You blithering idiot...' Charlie was seething now and he lashed out at the man with the side of his fist, causing Ibbo Tembani to stagger back with a howl of pain.

In the kitchen, Clara heard the commotion, followed swiftly by the sound of her husband's fist against the house-boy's skull, and her heart sank as she pictured the shards of glass and beer on her beautiful South African rug. She stared fixedly out of the kitchen window watching the progress of the spider as it struggled to re-build the web she had destroyed earlier. It helped divert her attention away from Ibbo Tembani who was now stumbling past the window on the path that led to his kia.

She watched him stop and rub his eye where an unsightly lump was already forming. She watched while he paused and sighed so deeply that his shoulders rose and sagged before turning to retrace his steps as she had known he would. He had made a mess on the carpet, and it would have to be cleaned without delay.

Julius was going to school and Bliss was thrilled. He was enrolled at the Faith Springs Mission School at Ntabazinduna where he would learn to read and write and acquire the skills that would guarantee him a good job in later life. More importantly, he would find his way to God, guided to safety by the steady hands of the good men of the church.

Bliss had accompanied the Madam on a visit to the school and she had beamed with pride at the prospect of her son attending such a fine institution. The headmaster had taken them on a tour. He was anxious to encourage white patronage and had answered Rachel's questions with enthusiasm.

Faith Springs was financed by the church, as were most black African schools. It was a collection of brick buildings with corrugated iron roofs and high windows to keep out the heat. There was no glass in the windows, funds did not run to such luxuries, but each was covered with a wire mesh to protect the children from mosquitoes.

Inside the classroom, the older pupils, many of whom were already young men, sat hunched up on long, wooden benches facing a blackboard set into the wall. The younger children sat on the floor. There was no ceiling, only the roof itself, and strips of sunlight could be seen between the corrugated iron sheets. In the rainy season, water flooded in through the gaps and the children had to evacuate that part of the school.

The missionary and his family occupied a large rambling house on top of the hill, overlooking fields full of mealies. The teachers lived in smaller dwellings further down. The cleaners and other domestic staff occupied traditional rondavels at the end of the jacaranda paths that led to the chapel. Teachers and pupils worked together on the farm and ate the food which they themselves had produced. It was more than just a school. It was a community.

Back in their kia, Bliss held Julius at arms' length and surveyed him from head to toe. He was dressed in the brand new khaki uniform which the Madam had purchased, but which was several sizes too big at present. Julius shuffled about in the massive shirt and struggled to free his hands from the sleeves that dangled beyond his fingers.

'Do I have to sleep there, Mama,' he asked gazing up at her with wide eyes.

'Yes child. It is too far to travel at the end of each day. But you will come home many times. And each time you come you will be able to tell your Mama all that you have learned from the good book of the Lord.'

'Why can't I wear my amabhetshu?' Julius wriggled miserably in his uniform. He would much rather wear the little loincloth suspended from his waist with a thong. He really did not need to cover his body with so many clothes.

Bliss smiled and her cheeks glowed. 'The Madam paid for this uniform herself. It is an honour to be given such a gift. Other children at the school will have to accept clothes that are handed out by the missionaries - like charity. You, my son, will have your very own uniform. Just think of that!'

Julius thought hard, but it did not help. He could see little point in being trussed up in hot, heavy garments all day. He knew that the Madam had paid for his uniform - and his first year's tuition fees - and that he should be grateful, but he would be even more grateful if Mama would let him slip out of the scratchy material and back into his amabhetshu. He was not due to start school until his eighth birthday. He had weeks to go until then.

He was about to protest further when the door of the kia opened and a man's shoulders blocked out the light. It was Moses, back from a day's work on the farm. Suddenly, Julius felt very small indeed and he craned his neck to catch a glimpse of his father's expression. It was sour and angry.

'This?' Moses pointed to the little boy standing before him. 'What is this?'

Bliss got to her feet. 'The Madam has made it possible for our son to go to school. You know that my husband.' Her voice contained an uneasy combination of pride and apprehension.

'A school which is run by white missionaries who will train him to serve their white masters.' Moses spat out the words. 'Besides, he is too small. Too young.'

'I can touch my left ear with my right hand when I do this, baba.' Julius demonstrated the measure of a child's readiness to leave the kraal and go to school. Proudly he stood straight and passed his right arm over his head so that he could touch his left ear. It was a powerful argument.

'Boys do not go to school until they are ten years old,' Moses ignored the graphic demonstration of his son's maturity and turned to his wife. 'Older than that in most cases.'

'True, my lord.' Bliss nodded. 'But the Madam says it will be better for him to go now. He will be ahead of the other boys if he starts school while he is still a child.'

Moses glowered at his wife. 'And what will they teach him at this school?'

'English, Arithmetic and the skills he will need to tend the farm when he is older.' Bliss pulled her son closer. Her husband was angry and she wanted to prevent Julius from making things worse. It would take only one word. She knew her husband's moods well enough.

'They are missionaries. They care little about his education. They care only for his soul which they will take from him and give to this God of theirs - He who lives to eat the souls of the children of Africa. My child is a son of Mzilikazi. He does not belong to the white man's God.'

Bliss crossed herself and whispered a hurried prayer. Moses may have sufficient strength to defy the Lord with these blasphemous ravings, but she did not. And she was not prepared to risk eternal damnation for herself and her beloved son on account of her husband's heresy.

She knew that it was early for Julius to start school, even the Madam had said that he would be the youngest in his class by far, but Bliss cared little for that. She was determined that the boy would have a chance to learn. The Madam had said it was possible. Julius was an unusually intelligent child and they must nurture that gift. The Madam had said this. And the Madam knew best.

'I will build you a house which sits in a tree,' said Joseph Hungwe. 'It will be a fine house. Fit for the sons of great warriors.'

'Where will you build it?' Miles needed precise details.

'I will build it in the old tree over there - the one by the kopje.'

'How big will it be?'

'It will be big, Nkosizana. As big as the King's kraal at Great Zimbabwe.'

'How long will it take?' Julius wanted it finished before he went to the mission school.

'It will be finished in …' Joseph shrugged. 'Days!'

The two boys whooped with delight. Days! That meant they would get to play in it before Julius was sent away to board at Faith Springs. Miles lobbed Chuff into the air and held out his arms to catch the ball that promptly sailed straight through his hands and on to the ground. Julius kicked the ball and Miles wailed in protest.

'Don't you kick Chuff!'

'It's only a ball. Anyone would think it was real.'

Julius had outgrown the myth of the magical ball but Miles still clung stubbornly to the fantasy. There were times, however, when he grew weary of Chuff's inability to function without prompting and he longed for something real to play with. He had already begun to lobby his parents for a puppy, but so far had met with resistance.

Joseph, sensing that a boyhood scrap was imminent, sought to reclaim their attention. 'It will be a place where you can hide and see things that other people will not be able to see. It will be a secret place where only the two of you may go.'

The two boys were captivated by the thought of their very own secret hidey-hole and they instantly abandoned their squabble. Fired by their imagination the project took shape, and before long they were happy to endorse Joseph's scheme.

The following days were busy with everyone caught up in the venture. Ralph supplied urns from the dairy to use as chairs, while Rachel rooted out old blankets and pillows. Even Sixpence contributed to the project, offering to bake a ceremonial cake to celebrate its completion.

And then came the day when the tree-house was finally finished. It was almost six-foot square with low walls and an angled roof supported by wooden poles. Miles and Julius were impressed as they stood gazing up at the elaborate structure supported by the fig's thick branches. A rope ladder had been unfurled for easy access and now dangled against the trunk. Miles had contended that it would be better to climb the tree without a ladder, but he had lost the argument.

'Can we sleep there tonight Mummy?' Miles tugged his mother's arm until she weakened, then he raced over to the tree and clambered up the ladder. His feet kept tangling up in the rope, and the ladder twisted and turned with each step, but eventually he reached the top. He peered over the rim of the outer wall and waited for Julius to follow.

'Hang on, I'll get my camera.' Ralph ran into the house and returned within minutes. 'Stay where you are. That's it. Miles - lean forward more. I can't see your face. You'll have to shift in a bit, Julius.' The boys shuffled sideways into the camera frame. 'Now smile. That's it. Big smiles. Perfect!'

Ralph pressed the button and captured the memory of two little boys standing side-by-side in a newly-built tree-house. Ralph did not know it, but the camera had caught the exact moment when they had turned to look at each other and started to laugh. They waved at the camera and their fingers had locked in mid-air. It was only a second in the lives of these two youngsters, but it represented a time of youth and innocence and joy.

One day in the years to come, Miles would look at that photograph and remember that one fleeting moment in his childhood. He would remember a friendship and a happiness that he had thought would last forever.

And he would hold his head in his hands and weep.

The setting sun had already filled the sky with shades of pink and crimson when the two boys began their adventure. It was their first night in the tree-house and they were far too excited to sleep. It had rained earlier and the air was warm and damp. They lay listening to the constant drone of insects and staring at the curious shadows of the gnarled branches in the twilight. It was going to be quite a night.

'Julius…' Miles whispered. 'Do you want to hear my plan?'

Julius lay on his side on top of his sleeping bag, propped up on his elbow, and waited for Miles to continue.

'Do you want to be blood brothers?'

Julius sat up. This sounded like a major plan.

'I know how to do it. Cowboys and Indians do it. They cut their hands here.' Miles pointed to the centre of his palm.

'What with?' Julius was not keen on the prospect of drawing his own blood.

'With a knife, dummy!'

'Where will we get a knife?'

Miles scrabbled around on the floor. 'I spotted it earlier. It's Joseph's. He must have forgotten it.' Miles held the knife up to the light. It was a fine weapon.

'It looks a bit big,' Julius cringed at the thought of that sharp point piercing his hand.

'You're not scared, are you?'

'No,' Julius lied. He was ashamed of his fear. 'Let me see it.'

They huddled closer to examine the blade and in the dying light of the sun their heads were crowned with halos of gold.

'Is it dangerous?' asked Julius.

'I don't think so.'

Miles pressed the point into his flesh. He paused. It was a scary business, no doubt about that, but Cowboys and Indians did it so it must be okay. He pulled the knife across his palm and winced with pain.

'Are you okay?' Julius was mesmerised by the ritual and by Miles' courage.

Miles nodded and sucked in a deep breath. 'Your turn,' he said shakily

Julius took the knife and immediately cut into the palm of his hand. It was better this way. He wanted to get the nasty bit over with as quickly as possible. Even so, he still felt a bit queasy when he spotted the thin trickle of blood seeping from the wound.

'You'll have to squeeze it a bit.' Miles suggested.

Julius ignored this advice. 'What must we do now?'

Miles tried to remember. 'We have to rub them together, like this.' He took his friend's arm and turned it over so that the cut was visible. He then gripped Julius' hand in his own and pressed the open wounds together.

'See - your blood is all mixed up with mine now.'

Julius inspected the smear of blood on his hand. The cut had stung a little at first, but it was subsiding now and he felt less afraid. They had become blood brothers and it had been a fine ritual. He stared at Miles and felt strangely elated. Again he contemplated the wound.

'Blood brothers.' he mused.

'Blood brothers.' Miles echoed.

3

ZAPU's power in Matabeleland was rivalled by that of the Zimbabwe African National Union (ZANU) led by Robert Mugabe in northern Rhodesia. Shona membership of the fledgling political group grew swiftly and, before long, ZANU recruits were being sent to train in guerrilla warfare at camps in neighbouring Zambia and Mozambique.

In April 1966, a handful of inexperienced ZANU insurgents infiltrated Rhodesia from their training base in Zambia. They had planned to destroy the electrical power pylons at Sinoia, but their plan ended in failure. Undeterred they went on to raid a farm near Hartley, just fifty miles from Salisbury. There they murdered the white farmer and his wife.

Within days all the insurgents had been tracked down and killed by the white security forces, and the incident consigned to history. But for black Africans, especially those proud Shona members of ZANU, the 'Battle of Sinoia' as it became known, heralded something far greater than that. White Rhodesians could not possibly have known it at the time, but the Battle of Sinoia would be recorded in black African history as the beginning of the great chimurenga.

'I see you, old man.'

'I see you too, Moses Khumalo.'

Moses squatted on his haunches so that his eyes, the colour of liquid chocolate, could look deep into the yellowing, rheumy orbs of Chief Nkulumane. 'Do you know why I am here, baba?'

The old man chuckled quietly and nodded. 'I know why you are here, Moses Khumalo.'

Chief Nkulumane was an old man with skin as thin and wrinkled as dry parchment. He had once farmed the prosperous lands in the middleveld, but he and his people had been forcibly resettled under some strange new law known as the Land Apportionment Act. This law, so he had been told, prevented black Africans from owning more than eight acres of land and five head of cattle. Clearly, he had broken that law.

He had been a young buck then, full of fire, and he had truly believed that his people would find prosperity in the new Native Reserves set up by the Government. But it was not to be. Chief Nkulumane would never again know the joys of reaping a rich harvest, of seeing his children at play with bright eyes and plump bellies. He and his people had failed to eke out a decent existence from the arid lands of the Native Reserves. Now he was no longer a young man and he no longer had the strength to fight.

He had come to accept that his earthly life would reach its end in this small, red brick hut at the edge of the kraal. It was a shambling construction with crumbling holes in the brickwork for windows. The front door dangled precariously on only one of its three hinges, and the green paint was now patchy and peeling away from the wood. Mopani flies buzzed noisily around the door. One or two landed in the white woolly cap of the old man's hair, but he did not notice. Only when they gathered at the corners of his eyes, seeking moisture, did he stir himself to flick them away.

'You have come to tell me that the chimurenga has begun,' he said simply. He was old, but his mind was still as swift as the flight of a springbok from a bushman's spear.

Moses nodded. 'You have heard.'

'I have heard that a dozen young Shona warriors in the north have slaughtered one unarmed mukiwa and his woman. Is that what you have come to tell me, Moses Khumalo? Is that your war of liberation?'

'It is a start, baba.' Moses leaned forward, the fanatical fire burning fierce and bright in his eyes. 'At last we can prove that the white man is not invincible. The Shona dogs have shown us that he can be beaten. We have seen that it is possible for a black man to kill a white man. Is that not a start, baba?'

Chief Nkulumane laughed, but the sound was dry and bitter. 'And what will you do when you have killed the last of the white men, Moses Khumalo? Who will run their factories then? You? Who will work their machines? Bah! The black man does not have the skills to use the white man's machines. We are like children now. We cannot survive without the white man. You are young, Moses Khumalo. How can you know where this chimurenga will lead?'

'It will lead you away from this, baba.' Moses jutted his chin at the kraal. Scornfully, his gaze took in the pole-and-dagga huts, the children poking about in the dirt with sticks and the stringy chickens that pecked fruitlessly on the ground for scraps.

His eyes came to rest on the full, round buttocks of a young girl who was draping her washing over a rope hung between two mopani trees. With some uncanny female instinct, she sensed his attention and she turned and pouted prettily, pushing her budding breasts in his direction. Moses felt the heat rush to his loins, but it was quickly followed by a surge of bitterness so great that it burned the back of his throat. Why, he asked himself, should this beautiful young girl have to wither and grow old in this evil place? Why could she not continue to stand proud?

Moses shook his head in despair, lowered his gaze and looked again at the old man. 'We will win this war, baba,' he spat through clenched teeth. 'And then we will teach our people how to use the white man's machines. We will teach them how the factories work, and we will teach them how to be proud warriors once more. This I promise you.'

'I believe you, my son.' Chief Nkulumane had watched the younger man grappling with the demons in his head. 'I believe that you will lead my people out of this barren place, Moses Khumalo, but I shall not be here to help you, you know that. I shall not be with you when you celebrate your great victory at the end of this great chimurenga. I shall be in a better place. I shall be with the spirits.'

'I know that you are longing to join your ancestors baba, and I respect your wish to bring this earthly journey to an end. But you have a job to do first. You cannot leave until you have brought the young bucks in your kraal back to life. You must inspire them with your courage, and you must light their fires again. You must tell them that freedom is coming. Freedom! But first they must learn to fight. Tell them, baba. Tell them that ZAPU is armed and ready to rise up against the white man. We know now that we can win. All we have to do is fight the war.'

Chief Nkulumane did not rise when Moses stood up to leave. He was too old, too frail, and there was no need. Instead, he watched as the younger man strode purposefully out of the kraal, and he smiled. It would take men like Moses Khumalo to light the fires of freedom across Africa. He could see him now, eyes dark with suppressed fury, a neck thick with veins that bulged in anger, strong hands and a proud, square jaw. A fine warrior, Chief Nkulumane thought with pride. He had been such a warrior himself, many moons ago.

He lay back against the wall and chewed thoughtfully on a ragged cheroot. In his hands he held a bundle of pamphlets that Moses had left in his care. They had been produced by the ZAPU propagandists and called for all black Africans to rise up against white tyranny in the great chimurenga. Chief Nkulumane did not look at the publicity material. He could not read. But he would pass it on to his young warriors who would devour the written words greedily.

His thoughts took him back to a time when Matabele warriors did not need pieces of paper and printed words to ignite their passion for war. There had been a spirit of kinship and a lust for blood that had kept this great nation as one even during the devastating Mfecane of Mzilikazi. But he knew in his heart that the Matabele fire could never be extinguished completely. It would simply lie dormant until a flame ignited it once more.

But that was something Moses Khumalo had yet to learn about his African brothers.

Ralph stood beside the snooker table and watched as his brother potted the pink ball in the top pocket. It was a fine shot and Ralph had already conceded defeat. Charlie was on fine form tonight.

'Ah, just the man I'm looking for.' Ralph turned as Sandy Fitzgerald tapped his elbow. 'Ralph Cameron, can I introduce you to the Bulawayo Club's latest recruit, David Llewellyn.'

Ralph smiled and took the hand of the man opposite. 'Doctor Llewellyn?' he asked.

David Llewellyn smiled and nodded. 'The very same. Have we met?'

'Not exactly, but you have met my wife and son. They were involved in a car accident last year. You did a fine repair job on my youngster. He carried those stitches in his forehead with pride and was quite a celebrity for a while, I can tell you.'

'Yes, I do remember. Mrs Cameron and young Miles. Smashing lad, and very brave too. Hardly made a sound. How's he doing?'

'Well as ever, all thanks to you. My wife was full of admiration for your bedside manner. Now please, let me get you a drink? What about you, Sandy?'

Sandy Fitzgerald deposited his ample backside on the barstool and wiped his sweaty brow with a damp handkerchief. 'Make mine a beer, Ralph old chap. I'm whacked. It's a tough business bringing in a new member, especially one of your calibre.'

Sandy took the ice-cold beer and gazed at it longingly. 'Now that's what I call a sight for sore eyes.' He gulped the contents greedily.

What stage is your membership application at David?' asked Ralph.

'Oh please, call me Dai, everyone does. Sandy tells me the application form went to committee last week, so it's just got to go to the vote.

'Dai will be able to poll the forty votes without a struggle.' Sandy chipped in. 'The committee should be bending over backwards to bring him in as a member. He's one of the country's finest surgeons by all accounts.'

'I think the beer must have gone to Sandy's head,' Dai laughed to cover his embarrassment. 'I'm just one of a team. Nothing more.'

'Modest! Far, far too modest!' Sandy spluttered. 'The man's a marvel. I have it on the best authority.' He had heard tales of the young Welsh surgeon who had recently taken up the post at the Lady Halliwell, Bulawayo's largest white hospital. And Ralph, it seemed, was not the only member of the club who had cause to be grateful to the surgical skills of Dai Llewellyn.

Anxious to change the subject, Dai turned to Ralph. 'You live out towards the Blue Hills don't you? Scarfell Farm? I've seen the name on your milk wagons.'

'This country's oldest family, the Cameron's.' Sandy interjected, his face alight with enthusiasm at the prospect of highlighting the impressive credentials of yet another club member. 'You're standing in the presence of the descendant of a true pioneer. The Camerons go back as far as Livingstone you know. Am I right, Ralph? Now that's something to be proud of in my book. Yes indeed!' Sandy slapped Ralph on the back, downed the rest of his beer and hurried off to relieve his aching bladder.

'Not one to stint on the praise, old Sandy, eh?' Ralph watched as the bulky little man pushed and squeezed his way out of the bar.

'I just wish I could accept half of what he's been telling people about me,' Dai chuckled. 'I've got one hell of a reputation to live up to if I ever do get into this club.'

'You think that's bad, huh? I'm practically visiting royalty in Sandy's eyes. I wouldn't mind, but the rest of Bulawayo knows I'm nothing more than the local milkman!'

'And I'm just a local quack. Not exactly one of … what did he call me? … "this country's leading surgeons". Phew! Here's to mediocrity.'

Ralph lifted his glass to Dai's and laughed. He had warmed instantly to this tall, gangly Welshman with the lilting accent and sea-green eyes. He liked the way he could laugh at himself, and at others' perceptions of him. Like Ralph, Dai Llewellyn was not overly troubled by other people's

46

opinions - good or bad. He was his own man. And he was a man, Ralph had already realised, whom he would be proud to call a friend.

'Why don't you come out to the farm one day,' he said. 'Rachel would be delighted to meet you again. Miles too, no doubt. '

'I'd love to.' Dai was genuinely pleased. 'Okay if I bring my wife and daughter?'

'The more the merrier. Sunday suit you?'

'Sounds fine. We'll look forward to it.'

Ralph finished his scotch and soda and left the glass on the bar. 'Sunday it is then.'

Sunday came quickly enough. It came with a glorious blue sky and a dazzling sun that scorched the earth below. Rachel's garden was ablaze with colour from the wild gladioli among the shrubs and, just behind the house, the Cape honeysuckle was covered with bright orange flowers. It was a particularly vibrant scene that greeted Ralph as he strode back from the dairy. His short-sleeved shirt was open at the neck, exposing a tangle of dark springy chest hairs against a ruddy suntan. He walked swiftly, smiling at the noisy party of crested barbets who were squabbling over a tin of plum jam on the bird table.

'Daddy!' his daughter came hurtling across the lawn to greet him.

Ralph bent down to catch her in his arms and swing her high above his head, leaving her squealing and breathless with delight. Having completed a heady twirl, he plonked her squarely back on her feet only to be tugged and pestered for a repeat performance. Beth's demands continued without respite until Ralph reached the steps of the stoep, at which point he deposited his lively youngster on the ground with an audible groan.

'Phew!' he smacked the little bottom underneath the folds of a white cotton skirt as it disappeared into the house. 'Either I'm getting old, or that young missy is growing up far too quickly.' He sank into the rocking chair and grinned at his wife who had been waiting, ice-cold lemonade at the ready, for his return.

'A little of both, I'm afraid.' Rachel wiped her husband's brow where a thin line of sweat had trickled through the dirt on his temple. 'Before you know it she'll be bringing home boyfriends!'

'Not if I have any say in it!' Ralph grimaced. He did not relish the thought of his precious girl entering the complex world of womanhood.

And he was certainly not prepared to stand by and let some young rascal steal his darling away from Scarfell Farm without a fight. He pushed his spectacles back on to the bridge of his nose. 'If she's got any sense, she won't be wasting her time with boys. She's got far too good a head on her shoulders for that. You can see that already - clear as daylight - and besides she's only four years old so why, may I ask, are we having this pointless conversation?'

Rachel smiled behind her cup of coffee. Beth was his pride and joy, heaven help the innocent young Rhodie who happened to fall in love with Scarfell's finest daughter. Rachel had already decided that her husband was quite prepared to see off Beth's future admirers with a shotgun if necessary! Goodness! What fun they were going to have when Miss Elizabeth Cameron came of age.

'Daddy?'

Ralph turned to Beth who had reappeared beside his chair. The sight did much to vanquish any unpleasant thoughts and his relief was palpable. 'Yes, my sweetheart?'

'You know these people who are coming tonight...?' Beth's lengthy conversational introductions rivalled those of the Matabele.

'Yes sweetheart,'

'Well... Miles says that they've got a little girl. Just like me.'

'So I gather.'

'Well... do you think she might want to be my best friend?'

Ralph grinned at his wife over the top of the little head. 'I am sure she would consider it an honour, princess. But I thought I was your very best friend.'

Beth rocked from side to side and stuck out her tummy in an attitude of deep concentration. 'I thought it would be fun to have two best friends.' She concluded solemnly.

'I think that's an excellent idea. Anyway, I reckon she can have as many best friends as she jolly well likes - don't you agree, Mummy?'

'Oh - dozens, at the very least!' Rachel leaned across to pull up Beth's white cotton socks that had fallen in folds around her ankle. Beth angled her toe from side to side to inspect her new strappy sandal with its pretty gold buckle. It shone wonderfully in the light and she wondered if her new best-friend-to-be would have such shiny buckles on her shoes.

'What's her name?' she asked, swivelling round on her father's lap.

'Lydia Llewellyn.'

Beth mouthed the surname with difficulty. 'That's a funny name,' she declared at last. 'It's hard to say.'

'It's Welsh,' her mother replied. 'Lydia's parents come from Wales.'

'I'm going to let her play with Spot,' Beth continued. 'She can look at my new dolly, but she can't play with her. She can play with Spot.'

Given that Beth's push-dog, Spot, was now consigned to the lumber room, having been abandoned in favour of the doll with hair you could comb, this gesture was not as generous as it seemed. Nevertheless, Beth had already anticipated that she may need to share the contents of her toy box with her new best friend, and she was quite prepared to make this sacrifice should the need arise.

This tranquil family scene was interrupted by the resounding thud of sturdy young limbs on hard, dry ground. It was Miles, tumbling from the rope ladder that hung from the tree house. Rachel sighed and shook her head. She had told him a dozen times to tackle the ladder slowly, but he would not listen. 'He'll kill himself, if he's not careful,' she complained with a backward glance at her husband, before hurrying over to examine the latest addition to her son's cuts and bruises.

'Let's see what you've done to yourself this time,' she spat lightly on her handkerchief and rubbed away the smear of blood from his knee to assess the extent of the damage. 'It's more dirt than blood by the look of it. Come on, my lad. Let's get you cleaned up. Our guests will be arriving after lunch and I don't want them to see you looking quite so grubby.'

Later, the Camerons stood waiting as Dai Llewellyn's car made its way up the drive. Ralph stood behind Rachel, both hands resting lightly on her shoulders, as the Austin Cambridge approached. In front of them, as fresh and neat as two new pins, Miles and Beth were wide-eyed and excited.

Miles was smartly turned out in a pair of grey cotton shorts, long socks and a clean, white shirt. His hair had been vigorously combed and parted to one side. In honour of the special occasion, he had been allowed to slick it down with some of his father's Vitalis hair oil and it now lay flat and glossy against his head.

His sister was standing rigidly to attention beside him. She was wearing her favourite dress - the one with the flared skirt that swirled like a saucer when she spun round on the spot. Her curls had been scooped up into a pony-tail and wrapped in a red and gold satin bow, and her cheeks were pink with excitement. She was watching the clouds of dust as the car made its way up the hill, and she paused to cast a quick glance at her feet to check that the shiny gold buckles were still quite shiny.

The car drew to a halt at the top of the drive and Ralph hurried round to help Dai's pregnant wife, Myra, out of the car. She was a petite, pretty woman with bright eyes and black hair cut into a flattering bob that framed her face nicely. She took Ralph's arm, grateful for the support as she eased her swollen belly out of the car.

'Thank you, Ralph.' She straightened her back and brushed the creases from her maternity dress, before looking up and smiling over the bonnet at Rachel.

Dai sprung out of the driver's seat, turned to check on his wife's progress, before loping over to Rachel and clasping both her hands in his own. 'Good to meet you again,' he said with a pleasant Welsh accent.

'And in much happier circumstances, thank goodness,' Rachel agreed.

With his unruly shock of auburn hair and lean, almost gaunt features, Dai Llewellyn was not someone easily overlooked in a crowd. He was tall and thin with a large, hooked nose and a widow's peak in the centre of his fringe that caused his hair to part untidily in all the wrong places. But in spite of this curious physical composition, he was a rather handsome fellow with an unconscious charm and an easy manner that instilled a sense of ease in all those with whom he came into contact. Rachel was no exception to that rule, and she found herself warming to him instantly.

Beth, who had been watching the introductions with the intensity of a lioness at prey, now blushed violently as her father opened the rear door to the car to expose a pair of neat little feet clad in black patent-leather shoes. Beth clutched her mother's hand tightly, overcome with shyness, while the owner of the shoes jumped down from her seat and stood nervously on the ground of Scarfell Farm.

The two girls eyed each other warily. Beth noted the pretty dress with its interesting zigzag pattern, and she was intrigued by the two packages gripped by tightly-curled fingers. She could not bring herself to meet those strange, grey-green eyes, but she did notice Lydia's hair and it took her breath away. It was long and silky, a vivid copper-red, that tumbled like a fiery mane down her back. Beth was astonished. She had never seen hair that colour before and she was very impressed. It resembled an African sunset and far outclassed a pair of shiny buckles any day.

'Aren't you going to say hello to Lydia?' Rachel bent down to untangle her daughter's arms from the folds of her skirt.

'Hello, Lydia,' said Beth, blushing crimson.

'Hello.' Lydia replied, staring fixedly at the floor. 'This is for you.' She thrust a small box of toffee treats at Beth.

'Don't forget Miles,' Myra urged her daughter forward.

Lydia's arm shot out to one side. 'Here you are.' She did not look up at Miles as he sprang forward to claim his gift. Her courtesies complete, she then snatched back her arm as though it had been bitten by a deadly cobra.

Miles, of course, was blissfully unaware of Lydia's discomfort. He was far too busy breaking into the box. He had already extracted one of the contents and crammed it halfway into his mouth before his mother spotted his lack of decorum and tapped him smartly on the head.

'What do you say, dear?'

'Thanks.' The muffled response came from the side of a large chunk of toffee.

'Let's go inside,' Rachel took Myra's arm. 'There's a jug of freshly-squeezed orange juice waiting.'

'That sounds perfect,' said Myra. 'It's such a strain being cooped up in a car these days. I have to keep reminding myself that I've only got only two months to go before I'm back to normal again. I feel so ungainly. I was nowhere near as big as this when I was carrying Lydia. I think I'm about to give birth to a baby hippo!'

Rachel giggled. 'I was exactly the same with Miles. I did so miss wearing my normal clothes. I looked like a balloon most of the time....'

The two men went across to the verandah. They were followed by Miles who had dogged their heels like an eager puppy, anxious to begin the dramatic reconstruction of his crowning moment. He plonked himself down on the top step, from which point he could poke poor Prince in the ribs with his toe while he waited for them to finish their conversation. It took rather a long time and he grew bored with their speculation on the outcome of the talks between Ian Smith and Harold Wilson, the British Prime Minister, in Gibraltar. Miles knew better than to make a fuss, and he kept quiet for fear of being banished from the stoep. His turn would come soon enough, he was sure of that. Meanwhile, he had Prince to annoy. And that was a fairly absorbing occupation in itself.

Beth and Lydia had followed their mothers into the house, each casting surreptitious glances at the other from under their lashes. They had not spoken a word, but they were conversing with equal fluency in the complex body language of the very young. Eventually, Lydia, who was emerging as the more confident of the two, broke the silence.

'What's that?' she pointed at Beth's GoiGoi.

'It's my GoiGoi. It makes me go to sleep.'

Lydia stroked the soft material. 'It's a tea-towel.' She said, matter-of-factly.

Beth stared at her GoiGoi as if to confirm Lydia's conclusion. It was a tea-towel, no doubt about that, but it was a very special tea-towel for reasons far beyond Beth's comprehension. She tucked the GoiGoi under her arm, puzzled, but reluctant to enter into a lengthy discussion on its magical properties. Instead she turned to Lydia, brushing away the last traces of shyness, and said: 'You can come and look at my toys if you like. I've got a dolly with hair you can comb.'

Lydia nodded, eager to see the dolly with hair. She took Beth's hand and followed her through the house to where the phenomenon was unceremoniously dumped under a pile of toy cups and saucers. The two girls scrabbled about in the box, heads together, sunshine curls mingling with a mane of red fire, until they had extracted sufficient equipment to enable a complicated game of 'house' to proceed.

The relationship between Miss Elizabeth Cameron and Miss Lydia Llewellyn had begun.

Later, the entire party gathered together for sundowners and the conversation flowed effortlessly. Dai leaned forward in his chair and spoke with passion on a subject which was clearly close to his heart. 'The main problem is that the primary health services are directed to the cities. The meagre services for the blacks out in the bush are supplemented by the church, not the government.'

'That seems so unfair.' Myra interjected. 'The Africans suffer dreadfully without proper health care. Childhood malnutrition is rife, isn't it Dai? And the infant mortality rate is sky high. It's so sad.'

'Even if they do survive, their life expectancy is appallingly low.' Dai added. 'There's a chronic shortage of black doctors, and Africans can't be treated in our hospitals, so what are they supposed to do?'

Dai was clearly a pioneer of reform and Ralph admired his revolutionary fervour, but his view was tempered with caution. 'So what's the alternative? I can't imagine that integration in the hospitals would work.'

'Heavens, no!' Myra exclaimed. 'There's no question of sharing facilities. I'm sure they wouldn't want to come into our hospitals, and I know I would rather die than be treated by an African doctor. Goodness! I can think of nothing worse!'

Rachel sipped her Mampoer. 'I have to agree. I don't approve of racial segregation per se, but I would have to draw the line at being examined by a black doctor. I should feel most uncomfortable.'

Dai reached across and squeezed his wife's hand. 'I just feel that the government should put more money into health provision for the indigenous population. As it is, the church funds nearly sixty per cent of rural services. That can't be right, surely?'

'No,' said Ralph. 'It isn't right. I've always advocated a fairer distribution of government money, especially when you consider that the blacks outnumber us by twenty to one, but I hardly think the RF will listen.'

Dai scooped up a fistful of nuts. 'In the meantime, I'll continue to work at the Lady Halliwell while trying to immunise the natives out in the bush. And that's no easy task, I can tell you. The hardest part is convincing them that it's in their interest to be vaccinated, and that I'm not trying to inject them with white man's poison! Most of them would rather suffer in silence, or rely on their witch-doctor's muti, even when they're at death's door. It's absurd.'

The conversation ambled along with only the occasional pause to tend to a fractious child or Myra's aching back. Eventually they fell silent, enjoying the spectacle as the sun dipped below the Blue Hills and the sky was hung with strands of shimmering violet. It was a common enough sight in Africa, but to the four friends sitting out on the stoep at Scarfell Farm that evening, it was a particularly gorgeous display. They had warmed to each other and had already bonded as friends.

The land was already wrapped in the soft, black mantle of night when the Llewellyn family piled into their car to head for home. Ralph and Rachel stood at the top of the hill watching the red tail-lights of the car flicker as it drove over the cattle grid. Miles and Beth leaned against each other's shoulders for support, each stifling those tell-tale yawns.

'Time for bed,' Rachel uttered the dreaded words. 'And no arguments tonight, please!' she insisted. 'It's been a long day.'

She shepherded her youngsters into the house leaving her husband to enjoy a quiet moment alone. He breathed deeply, sucking in the rich animal smells from the farm which were carried on the breeze. Once in a while, he heard the gentle lowing of the cattle or the cry of a tawny owl, but otherwise the night was still.

Ralph knitted his fingers and stretched out his arms, yawning a little himself as he turned to leave. Then his eye caught the headlamps of a truck on the road and he was surprised to see it slow down as it approached the farm. He watched the twin spots of light turn into Scarfell Farm and make their way towards the house. They grew larger, illuminating the night sky, and Ralph felt a knot of tension tighten in his stomach.

His sense of foreboding worsened when he realised that it was a police Land Rover. He hurried towards it, caught in the glare of the headlamps as the vehicle drew to a halt and three men got out. Ralph squinted against the harsh, white light trying to make out the features of the man who approached him with one hand raised at shoulder height and an identity card held out at the ready.

'Mr Ralph Cameron?' It was an uncultured voice with a thick Rhodesian accent.

'Yes. What can I do for you?'

'Special Branch,' The man puffed out his chest. He delivered the words with relish, enjoying the importance which people invariably attached to them.

'What can I do for you?' Calmly, Ralph repeated the question. It was not the standard response, but Ralph was singularly unimpressed by status and the man was taken aback.

'You have a labourer name of ….' He shuffled among his papers. 'Moses Khumalo?'

'I do.'

'We have a warrant to search his quarters. I would be grateful if you could direct me and my men to those quarters, if you please sir.'

In other circumstances, Ralph might have smiled at the swollen ego of this pompous individual, but a sixth sense warned him that it would be foolish to risk incurring the wrath one of the country's elite Special Branch. Instead he said simply: 'May I ask what he is supposed to have done?'

'No sir. I'm afraid not! We need to search his quarters first. We'll follow you, if you please.'

He turned and gestured to his two colleagues who were waiting to attention at the side of the Land Rover. At his command, they stepped neatly into action with a brisk, military air. One of the men was armed with a FN 7.62mm rifle, which was slung casually over his shoulder. The other was sporting a Browning 9mm pistol in a leather holster on his belt.

Ralph knew then that this was far more serious than he had imagined and he led the trio down the stony path to the servants' kias without further comment.

The path was dark, lit only by the moon and the twin beams of light from the policemen's torches. Ralph stared at those shiny pools as they swung drunkenly from side to side as he pondered the reason for this visit.

'You all right there, sir?' The younger man shone his torch at Ralph's feet. 'Can you see all right? It's pitch black down here.'

'I'm quite fine, thank you. I know this route well.' Ralph could not resist adding a note of sarcasm to his voice. He was annoyed by their refusal to divulge the reason for the operation, which was being carried out on his land and involved one of his workers.

Eventually, they reached the two kias at the bottom of the slope. The elder man, who was obviously in charge, leaned towards Ralph and whispered: 'Which one is his?'

Ralph pointed to the larger of the two buildings. There was no electricity, but candlelight illuminated the windows and gave the kia a homely air. Bliss had made her own curtains, borrowing Sixpence's old sewing machine, and a golden light shone through the fabric. There was a strong smell of cooking and smoke billowed out of the chimney.

'Looks like we're at home, eh?' The chief officer turned to his colleague. 'But not expecting visitors, I'll bet. With your permission, sir, we'll take a look inside.'

Ralph was quite unprepared for the appalling sequence of events that began to unfurl before him. The three men swooped down upon the kia and crashed in through the door without pausing to knock. He saw Moses make a dash for the exit, only to be stopped by a fierce blow to the head that sent him reeling back against the wall. Ralph heard Bliss scream and it spurred him into action. He rushed into the hut and pulled her behind him, protecting her with his own bulk.

'What the hell are you doing?' he yelled at the men who were now ransacking the neat, little home. 'There's a woman here for Christ's sake!'

He pushed Bliss towards the door. 'Get up to the house,' Ralph snapped the command. 'Tell the Madam what's happening! Do you hear me? And stay put! Don't come near this place.'

Bliss hugged her arms to her chest and rocked back and forth on her heels. She was shocked by what was happening in her home - in her world. She could hear the baas, and she wanted to obey, but she simply could not move. She was mesmerised by the scene of devastation before her. Three mukiwas were tipping her drawers upside down, tearing her blankets apart and slicing open the mattress on her son's bunk. It was too awful, too ugly, but still she could not drag herself away.

Her husband, Moses, lay slumped against the wall, a thick slime of blood oozing down the side of his face. One of the men stood over him and shoved the butt of the pistol into his cheek.

'Okay muntu,' he snarled. 'We know it's here. Just tell us where it is.'

Moses struggled to sit upright. His eyes were fixed steadily on those of his aggressor. He refused to acknowledge the cold steel that was rammed against his flesh. He did not answer. Instead he glared at the man with an even colder steel - the cold steel of hatred.

'You miserable kaffir!' the man smashed the side of the gun barrel against Moses' jaw and Bliss screamed again.

'I will not tolerate this on my land!' Blindly, Ralph rushed across the room, ready to defend Moses from further attack. 'Bliss get up to the house! Now!'

Bliss stumbled out of the door in tears. The night air was cool and she shivered, pulling her crocheted shawl around her shoulders. She hurried up the path, cutting her bare feet on the sharp stones as she made her way in the dark. She did not feel the pain. Something had gone horribly wrong in her world and she did not know what it was. She heard an almighty crash from below, and she clutched at the rusty wire walls of the tennis court to steady herself before rushing into the house and into the arms of the Madam.

Back at the kia, the older man was turning out the kitchen cupboards. He opened the tins and glass jars, tipping them upside down until the floor was covered with rice, sugar and coffee. And all the time he was watching Moses, waiting for a tell-tale sign, a flicker of anxiety.

Ralph was crouching on the floor beside Moses who had not acknowledged Ralph's courageous gesture in his defence. There was no room for gratitude in Moses' heart. He sat bolt upright, his chin raised in open defiance. His eyes, black as pitch, bore into those of his guard who had now removed himself to a safer distance where he stood panting quietly. Eventually, the man began to buckle under the weight of that fierce intensity and he averted his eyes, sweating under his stiff collar.

'For fuck's sake, hurry up!' he yelled over his shoulder.

'No need to fret, lad,' his chief replied. 'If he gives you any trouble, just shoot the bastard. It'll be one less Magandanga to worry about.'

Ralph leapt to his feet in a rage. 'What do you mean Magandanga? This man's no murderer. I can vouch for that. He's my chief herdsman, for Christ's sake.'

'Is he indeed, sir.' The man stopped, peered into the large earthenware pot and raised his eyebrows. He then turned to Ralph, his fat face ruddy with the effort of destruction. 'And what, may I ask sir, would your chief herdsman be doing with these?'

He pulled a pile of printed papers from inside the pot and waved them under Ralph's nose. Ralph glanced at them and his heart sank. He knew immediately what they were. He had heard that members of ZAPU had been distributing anti-colonial literature out in the kraals. But they were political extremists - men who were prepared to fight and die for a cause that no ordinary person could possibly believe in. Surely Moses could not be one of those crazed fanatics. It was just too absurd for words.

'We've been tailing him for months, sir. He's quite a busy little kaffir - when he's not working as your chief herdsman that is.' He scrutinised the pile of evidence that lay in his meaty paws. 'Incriminating stuff this, boy. Planning to wipe out the whites, are we?' He leered at Moses from beneath two bushy brows and then turned back to Ralph. 'Take it from me, sir, old Moses here may not be a Magandanga now, but he sure as hell wants to be in the future. And you, boyo, are in big trouble. Big fucking trouble. So get your gear. You're going on a little holiday.'

Ralph followed the party back to the Land Rover where Rachel was waiting with Bliss sobbing beside her. Sixpence was under strict instructions to keep the children inside the house.

'Mrs Cameron.' The man touched his forehead with his forefinger in an old-fashioned gesture of respect. 'Forgive this intrusion. I do hope we haven't inconvenienced you unduly.'

Rachel moved closer to her husband, seeking his protection. 'What's happening? Where are you taking Moses?' she said.

'Can't say for certain, Mrs Cameron,' the man addressed her with a deferential air. 'He'll most likely end up at Sikombela in Que Que.'

'Que Que!' Ralph gasped. 'My God! That's a bloody hell-hole. It's practically a desert.'

'We reserve it for our country's most dangerous enemies.' The man spoke fiercely, glaring over his shoulder at Moses who was being bundled into the back of the Land Rover. 'And, I'm sorry to say sir, we have reason to believe that Moses Khumalo falls into that category.'

'Moses!' Ralph pressed his hands against the window of the vehicle. 'Don't worry. There's obviously been some mistake. Don't worry, man. I'll sort this mess out. God knows what the hell has happened here, but trust me. I'll sort it out.' He turned to the detective who was climbing into the passenger seat. 'Watch what you do with him,' he warned. 'This man is my chief herdsman. I will not have him harmed. Do you understand?'

'Perfectly, sir,' the man replied with sneer.

Moses had been handcuffed to one of the officers and he now sat, proud and impassive, as the engine roared into life and the vehicle set off down the drive. Ralph expected him to look back, to plead for help, but he did not move.

Moses Khumalo did not look back as the police Land Rover took him away from Scarfell Farm. He did not speak, and his lips were pressed together so tightly that the blood drained from them and gave them a deathly pall. He could feel the metal handcuffs biting into his wrists, but he did not lower his gaze. He stared straight ahead, head held high, rarely blinking. It was a steady, ice-cold stare. His own chimurenga had begun at last. His time had come.

4

Moses Khumalo could not see the long, dusty road that led to his new home at Sikombela in the Que Que bushland north of Gwelo. He was chained to the floor of a windowless prison van that was hot and dark, and rank with the stench of sweat from fellow prisoners who lay huddled in the back.

Occasionally, when the van bounced over a large rock or fallen branch on the road, the men were thrown against the metal sides of the vehicle and they cried out in pain from the heat which scorched their flesh. But their cries were ignored by the armed guards who rode in the driver's compartment. The miserable cargo crammed into the rear no longer had any rights. They had committed crimes against white people and they were about to pay the penalty. From now on they would have no voice. Not even one that cried out in anguish.

The sun had reached its zenith when the prison van came to a halt inside the barbed-wire enclosure. A dozen half-blinded, burned and bloodied men were dumped unceremoniously on the ground and left to find their feet in the harsh glare of the noon-day sun.

Moses got to his feet quickly, ignoring the pain where the metal chains had cut into the raw flesh around his ankles. His gaze swept the compound that was to be his home for the next eight years. It was a primitive place. A place designed to break a man's heart and destroy his spirit.

Crude mud huts had been erected on an otherwise featureless plain of scrub and inhospitable bush. There was little sanitation and no electricity. The huts were unbearably hot during the day and bitterly cold at night. Food was a meagre ration of beans and maize-meal, which the prisoners cooked into a traditional sadza. The police brought rations to the centre, usually on a Friday. If they were lucky, the prisoners would be given meat, which they would dry out in the sun so that it would keep without rotting.

It was a harsh existence. One where survival was the sole measure of success.

And survival, Moses swore to himself under his breath, would be his goal. He would walk out of here alive one day. Without chains. And then he would continue the fight to free his African brothers. This he swore upon the spirits of his ancestors.

The detainees at Sikombela had been forced to build their own shelters. They had already completed most of them when Robert Mugabe arrived from Wha Wha prison. To honour their chosen leader, ZANU detainees built him a thatched dagga hut with a door made painstakingly from reeds.

From day one, Mugabe instituted a strict regime of work and education, rising at dawn to complete his yoga. His self-discipline never faltered. It was a discipline based on hope. Hope that the future would be brighter, that it would come soon, and that he would live to see it.

Shortly after the first white farmer was killed in the Sinoia incident, Mugabe and thirty ZANU members were transferred from Sikombela to Salisbury Central Prison in Mashonaland. But his legacy of self-discipline was maintained by the Que Que detainees long after he had gone. It was all they had left. They had little else to believe in.

Moses inherited this legacy, learning to pace each long day and fill it as best he could. But still time passed slowly. Prisoners came and went. Some died, some lost their wits and some walked to freedom. And for some who remained, the endless monotony of confinement robbed them of any sense of reality. They could not imagine the magnitude of the events which were unfolding in the world that lay beyond the barbed-wire. Many inmates had long been forgotten by the world outside. They had ceased to exist.

Once in a while, new detainees would arrive with news. One man explained how the United Nations had imposed sanctions on Rhodesia, and how the whites were trying to find ways to beat the sanctions and maintain their life of privilege and luxury. In 1967, they heard that ZANU in the north and ZAPU in southern Rhodesia had begun armed revolt against white rule. This was greeted by cheers from the crowd of inmates who had gathered to hear the news. Their hopes were soon squashed by a second arrival who claimed that the South African police had been drafted in to quell the black uprisings occurring on their own doorstep. Life at Sikombela was a roller-coaster ride of hope and despair.

Ralph came as often as he could to visit Moses. He came armed with good wishes from Bliss, food from Rachel and gifts from Julius and Miles. Today, he arrived with a small giraffe, hewn from jacaranda wood, and painstakingly decorated with black ink. It was from Julius. He had made it at school where he was developing a taste for arts and crafts alongside his academic abilities.

Moses took the carved animal. He turned it from side to side, examined the craftsmanship closely and grunted with approval. 'It is a fine carving.'

'Your son is very talented' Ralph replied. 'The teachers at Faith Springs are convinced he'll go far. He's easily the brightest boy in his class.'

Moses shrugged and laid his son's gift on the table between them. 'We hear talk,' he whispered, fingering the smooth contours of the carving. 'We hear talk of more trouble between Sithole and Mugabe. Do you know about this?'

Ralph shifted uncomfortably on the metal chair. 'I don't think we should be talking about such things, do you? It could get you into trouble.'

'Please!' Moses hissed. 'A man can go mad in here. I must know everything that is happening outside.'

'It's difficult to say. The news is heavily censored.' Ralph sighed. 'You probably know more than I do. All I know is that Sithole is serving six years for attempting to assassinate Ian Smith, the Prime Minister. Apparently, he then agreed to disband ZANU in return for his freedom and exile to America.'

'Bah! Shona dogs! They have no loyalty. ZAPU would never agree to such a cheap deal. They have too much honour.'

'That may be, Moses, but I think it would be wise to keep your thoughts to yourself while you're in here. It'll do you no good to cause trouble. Just bide your time. It's all you can do. And then you can come home to Scarfell. Bliss misses you very much. She's finding it heavy going without you.'

'Tell me about this new Republic of yours.' Moses ignored the reference to his wife. Ralph's visit was too precious to waste on women or domestic trivia.

Ralph shrugged. He understood the man's priorities, even if he didn't agree with them. 'Well, I can tell you that the government has decided to allow blacks to be represented in Parliament, although the whites will retain overall control. After that, they will separate blacks and whites into local councils, with black representation depending on income tax paid.'

Moses threw back his head and laughed. It was a deep belly-laugh that brightened the honey-whites of his eyes and momentarily smoothed out the deep frown lines that had etched themselves into his gaunt face. It was a laugh that bore all the cynicism of a man who could see life for what it was. The laugh of a man who scorned all versions of the truth other than that which he could see for himself.

'I understand why you're laughing,' Ralph pulled a cigarette from the packet and held it between his teeth while he fumbled in his pocket for a match. He then lit it, exhaling vigorously. 'It looks as though only wealthy blacks can get the vote. And we all know there aren't too many of those!'

He handed the rest of the packet to Moses who seized it greedily. Cigarettes were excellent currency at Sikombela. Moses had seen a man being beaten to within an inch of his life over a cigarette. Values were different in here. Almost immediately, his laughter subsided and his eyes darkened once more. He stood the little giraffe on its legs, where it wobbled uncertainly on the uneven surface.

'It's a start!' Ralph whispered hoarsely. 'Can't you see that, man? Things will not change overnight. See sense for God's sake!'

'So now Rhodesia is a Republic? This much is true?'

'It's true. Smith couldn't agree to the British Prime Minister's demands, so he decided to renounce all ties with the Crown and the Mother Country and go it alone.'

'He must truly believe in his cause. Perhaps he is a true warrior after all.'

Ralph smiled. 'That may well be. I'm sure he'd be delighted with the accolade. But to answer your question, yes, officially, on 2nd March 1970, we became a Republic. Things are changing out there, Moses. Be in no doubt about that.'

Moses said nothing. He gazed at his son's carving, trying to see into an uncertain future. The baas was right. Things were changing rapidly and he longed to be free, to be able to play a part in fashioning the new Africa. He had little respect for ZANU or their new leader. They were Shona. They could not be trusted. No! His place was with the Matabele, with ZAPU.

He needed to be with his African brothers. He needed to play a part in the changes that were taking place in the world outside. He truly believed that if he were free he would move swiftly. He would not be content to wait for the whites to argue among themselves, to squabble with that distant foreign country and its distant white Queen. He cared only for Africa. There was no place in his vision for the white man.

'And, of course, we're all struggling to cope with the new decimal currency.' Ralph sought to steer the conversation into safer territory. 'We now have a new Rhodesian dollar. Look, here's one.' He pulled out a brown five-dollar note, decorated with the Rhodesian coat-of-arms and a giraffe.

Moses looked at it and held it up to the light where he could see the water-mark of Cecil Rhodes' profile. He placed it on the table between them and stared at it. His brow was deeply furrowed, but his jaw was still firm and square. Eventually he lifted his eyes to look at Ralph and his wide nostrils flared angrily.

'It means nothing,' he said, screwing the dollar into a little ball in his fist. 'It is a worthless piece of paper. An African can thread all his money on a coin necklace round his neck. This is white man's money. A black man can only steal it. He will never be allowed to earn it.'

Ralph looked at Moses. For the first time he could clearly see the anger that burned deep within the man's soul. Moses had lost weight, but hard labour and toil had honed his physique into that of a lithe black panther poised to strike. It was an impressive sight, yet one which was vaguely alarming, too.

Sitting there at the little metal table, sweltering under the sun's rays, Ralph could no longer see his chief herdsman, the father of young Julius and husband to Bliss. This was a man whom Ralph did not recognise. This was a man for whom death held no terror. A man with a cause as old as Africa itself. A cause called freedom. It was a cause, Ralph now knew, that Moses was prepared to die for. And, more disturbingly, one he would be prepared to kill for.

Rose Cameron had moved to the Eastern Highlands shortly after entrusting Scarfell Farm to her son, Ralph. Her house, nestling in the foothills of the Inyanga mountains, afforded spectacular views of the wide open spaces of the Inyanga National Park, beyond which lay the border to Mozambique. The cool climate and high rainfall ensured a lush, green landscape of hills and valleys. It was a land of breathtaking loveliness.

Rose had never regretted her decision to leave Matabeleland. She had always said that she would end her days in a place where water was plentiful and the grass was soft and wet and green. Now, her garden was full of flowers and rich with colour. The lawn, sweeping down the hill, was damp with dew and springy underfoot. At the bottom, a massive granite kopje clawed its way up into the clear blue sky. On top of the kopje was Punch Rock.

'Why is it called Punch Rock?" her grandson, Miles, had once queried, peering up at the assortment of boulders.

'Well if you look closely,' Rose had replied, bending down to his level and tracing the outline of the peculiar rock formation with her forefinger, 'you will see that it looks just like Punch lying on his back.'

Miles had pondered this, following his grandmother's finger with a sceptical eye. He had seen pictures of Punch and Judy and he was not entirely convinced that his grandmother's assessment was accurate. Even when his father had come to stand behind him, confirming that Punch Rock was well-named, Miles had not been completely convinced.

Rose could see the outline of Punch Rock now as she drove home from a shopping trip to Juliasdale. The road curled upwards, flanked by huge msasa trees with their early pink leaves. Wattle trees grew in abundance in the distant Penhalonga valley and the thick trunks of the acacias, with their top-heavy foliage, loomed large at the base of the craggy hills.

Rose Cameron's house was small, but beautifully situated. Surrounded by undulating hills and valleys it was a haven of peace and tranquillity. Her neighbours were tucked out of sight in their neat little bungalows and sprawling colonial houses, each content in this quiet corner of paradise. They ventured forth from their homes on a regular basis, meeting up for tennis parties, braaivleis and church. It was a tight-knit, small, but happy community.

Rose gripped the steering wheel of her old Morris Minor with two hands. She had little faith in things of a mechanical nature and was certain that if her attention lapsed even for one moment, the wretched machine would drive itself off the strip road and hurtle into the valley below.

One more treacherous turn at the top of the hill and Rose swung the car into her drive where it shuddered to a halt. She climbed out of the vehicle, dusted down her tartan kilt, and called for her house-boy, Taonga. There was no reply. Puzzled, Rose left the shopping in the boot of the car and went in search of her servant.

'Taonga! Where are you?'

The verandah ran along two sides of the house. It was wider at the far end to accommodate a table and eight wooden chairs next to the braai that had been set into the wall. Rose paused as she came round the corner. One of the chairs was lying on its side at the foot of the steps leading down to the lawn. Another had fallen against the sitting room door.

Suddenly, in spite of the warm morning, Rose felt a chill in her bones and she shuddered, pulling her shawl around her. She peered through the window. The sitting room was empty. The vacuum cleaner still stood in the middle of the floor and a duster lay crumpled on a chair. Something was wrong. Rose knew it and she called out again.

'Taonga!'

A flock of grey louries nesting in the syringa at the bottom of the garden suddenly took flight, and the air was filled with a cacophony of fluttering wings. The unexpected movement startled Rose and her shawl fell to the floor.

'Foolish old woman,' she declared, bending down to retrieve the crocheted garment. 'Frightened by a few little birds. Whatever next!'

Resorting to the pioneering spirit that had seen her through the toughest of times, Rose tucked her shawl under her arm and strode into the house. Courage was a commodity which this doughty woman possessed in abundance. It had been her constant companion through the difficult years and she did not expect it to fail her now. Her main concern, now that she had shaken off her earlier forebodings, was to find out what had happened to her useless house-boy.

'Taonga! For goodness sake, boy! There's a pile of shopping sitting out in the sun. Where on earth are you?'

'Taonga is not here, old woman.'

Rose's breath caught in her throat and she swung round to confront the intruder.

'Who are you?' she demanded. 'What are you doing in my house? And where is Taonga?'

'Taonga is not here, old woman. I have already told you this. It is just you… and me… and my comrade here.'

Another man appeared from the bedroom. He was carrying a knobkerrie made out of wood, the traditional weapon of the African warrior. Rose felt a knot of tension form in the pit of her stomach. Even so, she could not allow a couple of blacks to think that they had unsettled her and she fixed the man with a haughty gaze. 'What, may I ask, are you doing in my bedroom? How dare you come in here, brandishing your weapons! How dare you! Don't you realise the penalty for robbery? Now get out! The pair of you!'

She stepped forward, waving her hand in an imperious gesture of dismissal. But the gesture failed when her wrist, with its parchment skin and protruding blue veins, was seized in mid-air.

'We will not get out, old woman. This is our country and your home is our home. It is you, the whites, who should get out. We are fighting a war to reclaim our land. And you, old woman, are going to help us win this war.'

'Never!' Rose struggled to free her hand from the man's grip, but she was too weak. 'War, you call it? War! You're nothing but a bunch of tsotsis. You fools. Don't you know that it was the whites who brought civilisation to this country? We built your roads, sent your children to school, taught them the ways of the Lord. You'd still be living in the bush like animals if we hadn't come here.'

'We are still living like animals!' the man pushed his face close to hers and a fine rain of spittle sprayed against her cheeks. She recoiled in horror, but he twisted her arm behind her back and she was trapped.

'It is you, the whites, who live in the fine houses and own the cars on the roads. The African cannot afford such things. Not now. Not today… But soon.'

His breath was hot and fetid against her face. Never in her entire life had Rose Cameron been in so close to a black man and she was enraged by the indignity. 'You are bandits,' she cursed, summoning all her reserves of strength. 'Nothing more. You will never succeed in driving out the whites. Never! This is our country. We built it!'

Suddenly, the man slapped her hard and she slumped against the wall. Her lip was cut and she could taste blood in her mouth. She was panting now, her breath coming in short, sharp gasps and her chest was heaving. Again she felt a blow against her head and her world began to darken. Her legs felt weak and she sagged against her tormentor. The man loosened his grip and Rose sank to the floor.

'Now, old woman, tell us where your husband's weapons are kept.'

'I…I don't know. I have no husband… I am a widow!'

Her tormentor knelt down beside her and lifted her kilt high above her knees. He pressed his hand against the wrinkled flesh and grinned maliciously. 'Tell us, white woman … or you will regret it. I promise you!'

Rose recognised the threat, but still she refused to give in. 'You can't frighten me. I am a Cameron. My family have farmed this land for generations. We did not fear the Matabele savages. I do not fear you now.'

'Then you are a very foolish old woman.' The man pushed his hand between her thighs and forced her legs apart. His intention was clear and Rose knew now that resistance was futile.

'Please God! No!' she tried to pull back in disgust. 'For heaven's sake, no! Take the guns if you must. They are in the cupboard, in the study at the far end of the hall. Just take the wretched things and get out of my home.'

The man grinned and patted her shoulder. He nodded to his companion who tucked his knobkerrie under his arm and swaggered down the hall. Rose tugged her kilt over her legs and struggled into a sitting position. She was feeling sick and dizzy and her resolve was broken. Where was Taonga? If only he had been here to help her.

She could hear the two men crashing about in the study, prising the locks off the cupboard and her heart sank. Her husband's beloved 12 bore Phillipson shotgun, the one which Taonga had polished only last week, was in there. How Ewan had loved that gun. He would sit on the stoep cleaning it, caressing the exquisite craftsmanship with undisguised pleasure. Often, she had teased him about it. Now it would be stained by African sweat, broken, most likely, by clumsy African hands. It was too much to bear and, in spite of her resolve, a solitary tear began to roll down her cheek.

The men returned. They had discovered her housekeeping money and were busily stuffing loose cash into their pockets. One of the intruders had tucked her son's favourite .38mm revolver into his belt. The other was carrying the shotgun as he pushed past her into the kitchen. 'We must take food for our brothers out in the bush,' he called back over his shoulder. 'See that the white woman is silenced.'

The man with the knobkerrie towered over Rose. His eyes were bloodshot, yellowed at the corners, and there was an evil glint in them. His nose was massive, with nostrils that spread unevenly across his pock-marked face. In spite of her predicament, Rose could not help noticing how white and even his teeth were. They gleamed brightly against his coarse, ebony skin. Quite remarkable for a muntu she thought incongruously.

'Your time is up, old woman.' The man did not care for her scrutiny.

Rose glowered at him defiantly as his wooden knobkerrie came crashing down on top of her skull. For one moment, there was a flash of light. A soft, welcoming light that blinded her to all pain. She felt a second crack against the side of her head and then the light went out. She fell in a crumpled heap on the floor and lay there without moving. Somewhere, a floorboard creaked noisily and a door slammed shut. And then there was silence. Slowly the darkness crept over her, enveloping her in its warm, black mantle. She felt safe in the darkness. Safe and at peace.

The journey from Bulawayo to Inyanga was long and difficult. After Fort Victoria, the roads were often nothing more than strip roads. It was a test of a driver's skill not to depart from the two tarmac tracks and stray into the dirt and rubble on either side. Very occasionally, if the driver's attention wavered just a little, the car would wander from the tracks and the dissonant racket of the stones clattering against the undercarriage would quickly reclaim his attention.

Ralph stopped on the south side of the Birchenough Bridge so that Charlie could relieve himself in the bush. Ralph leaned against the concrete wall and looked up at the soaring silver structure. It was a fine piece of Italian engineering. He pushed his spectacles back on to the bridge of his nose and mentally traced the curves of the suspension bridge.

'It's the third largest suspension bridge in the world, you know,' Ralph turned to share this information with his brother who was heading back to the car. 'A fine achievement, if you ask me. A damn fine achievement.'

Charlie was still zipping up his flies, cursing when the corner of his shirt got caught in the zip. 'As long as it gets me across the Sabi River and into the Birchenough Hotel in time for a cold beer, I don't give a monkey's cuss what it is. Now come on boet. Look sharp! I don't want to be on the road come nightfall.'

The last part of the journey to Inyanga took them north along the Mozambique border and through the Bunga Forest en-route to the city of Umtali. Travelling through the blue-green mountains they crossed Christmas Pass, so called because Cecil Rhodes' pioneers had halted at the foot of the pass on Christmas Day in 1890. Beyond that, just past Penhalonga, the majesty of the Inyanga National Park unfurled in front of them.

Charlie did not notice the sweeping vistas beyond the car window. He had fallen into a doze in the passenger seat. His head lolled uncomfortably to one side and his mouth gaped open allowing a thin trickle of saliva to dribble down his chin. Occasionally, he would snore and snuffle in his sleep, startling Ralph who would then curse his brother under his breath. Thus, it was with great relief that the Mercedes lurched into second gear and began the final tortuous ascent to Rose Cameron's house.

The sight that greeted the brothers as they entered their mother's bedroom was alarming. Rose lay propped up on two pillows. Her cheeks were sunken and there were dark circles under her eyes. She seemed smaller somehow, shrunken, and both men were shocked. Their formidable mother, this tough woman who proudly hailed from pioneering stock, who had weathered the most appalling hardships in her early years, had been reduced to a shrivelled old lady surrounded by lace-frilled pillows and the remnants of a distant past.

'Mother...' Ralph approached the bed nervously. 'Mother, can you hear me?'

'Of course I can hear you. I'm not deaf!'

Ralph sagged with relief and perched on the edge of the bed. 'At least they didn't steal your wits,' he teased.

'Too right!' Charlie dragged up a chair, turned it round and straddled the seat. 'It would take more than a couple of kaffirs to defeat a Cameron, eh Ma?'

Rose smiled weakly and reached out a hand to Charlie. 'It's good of you to come so quickly. I know how busy you both are.'

Charlie took his mother's bony hands in his own. He gazed at it, marvelling anew at how thin and delicate the skin was. It seemed so fragile lying in his own ruddy paw that he could not help but be amazed that the old lady had survived such an appalling attack. He shook his head and muttered angrily under his breath.

'Now, now, Charles.' Rose soothed. 'Don't you go getting yourself in a state. What's done is done. At least I'm still alive.'

'Only just!' Ralph interjected, turning to the doctor for confirmation. 'Just how bad is she, Doctor Unwin?'

The doctor, an elderly gentleman with a shock of grey hair and half-moon spectacles, gestured to Ralph to follow him out of the bedroom. Ralph stood up, concern clouding his brow.

'Don't you listen to his death and doom stories!' Rose croaked from the bed. 'He'll have me in my coffin before the day's out given half a chance. These doctors,' she complained, turning back to Charlie. 'They're all the same. Always keen to make a drama out of nothing. Doctor Unwin! Don't you dare go filling my son's head with tales of terror! Do you hear me?'

Doctor Unwin shook his head and smiled. 'She's a tough old lady, your mother,' he declared as Ralph followed him into the hall. 'That blow would have finished anyone half her age. She's remarkable. No doubt about that. But ...'

'But?' Ralph heard the alarm bells ringing.

'Well, she was badly concussed and I think there may be internal damage, too. Obviously I can't tell just from looking at her, and she certainly won't admit to anything being wrong, but I need to get her into the hospital at Melsetter for tests.'

'What sort of tests?'

'I want to check that she hasn't suffered a contusion from such a serious blow to the brain. If the brain is bruised it could lead to a noticeable loss of functions.'

'So why is she still here, for God's sake?' Ralph was furious. His mother's life was at stake and she was still at home.

'It's not that simple. She's refusing to go. I've tried to persuade her that she should, but she will not budge. I need your help. She must have an x-ray and follow-up tests. I'm worried that she may even develop a hematoma, which could mean surgery to remove any blood clots.'

'Leave it to me, Doctor. I'll get her there even if I have to carry her to the ruddy hospital myself!'

'Mother ...' Ralph returned to the bedroom, aware that he had to tread cautiously. His mother, he knew from past experience, could be quite stubborn at times. 'Doctor Unwin tells me that you need to go into Melsetter. I want you to agree to do what's best for you. Will you do that?'

'Stuff and nonsense!' Rose tried to sit up, but she fell back against the pillow with a whimper of pain. 'I don't want to go into hospital. I will not go! I will not!'

Ralph and Charlie spotted the sudden deterioration in their mother at precisely the same moment. Her voice cracked in mid-sentence and she metamorphosed from the woman they both feared and respected, into a pitiful, petulant child, crying out in terror. Ralph felt a lump swell up in the back of his throat and he had to swallow hard to prevent tears forming in the corners of his eyes. He could not bear to witness the decline of such a splendid human being. Not yet. Not like this. His brother, however, always the pragmatist, seized the upper hand immediately.

'We'll be with you, Ma. No need to fret.' His voice took on a mildly bullying tone. 'You must do what Doctor Unwin suggests.'

'I will not go to Melsetter!' Rose Cameron had returned, vanquishing the feeble interloper who had momentarily overtaken her wits. 'I shall enter the gates of Heaven when I'm good and ready and not one minute before. Do you understand?'

'We're not carting you off to Heaven, Ma!' Charlie was exasperated. His patience was short at the best of times. 'It's Melsetter, for Christ's sake, not the goddam pearly gates! Jesus wept!'

'Don't you blaspheme, Charles Cameron. I may be laid up for now, but I'm not so feeble that I can't box my boy's ears if needs be.'

Charlie sighed and turned away to light a cigarette. He inhaled deeply, shrugging his shoulders at Doctor Unwin who had already accepted that defeat was imminent. The doctor took out a bottle of pills from his black, leather hold-all and handed them to Charlie.

'Give her one of these three times a day. They'll help kill the pain. It's all I can do.'

'It's okay, Doc'. You did your best. She's as stubborn as a mule when she sets her mind to it, and twice as stupid!'

Doctor Unwin chose not to dwell on the observation. 'She will need constant care. I'll arrange for someone to stay with her for the next few days. Also one of her neighbours, a widow, Mrs Mowbray, has kindly offered to help.'

'She would!' Charlie blew two thin lines of smoke down his nostrils. 'Old busybody! She'll do anything for a piece of the action!'

'Mother likes her,' Ralph came to join them. 'And she's a good sort at heart. She and Mother have been friends for years.'

'Friends!' Charlie snorted sarcastically. 'You ought to hear what they say about each other when their backs are turned. It's amazing! They're a right couple of old gossips.'

Ralph laughed. 'Well, the relationship seems to work for them. And we should be grateful that Mother will have someone to look after her. We can't stay here forever.'

Ralph and Charlie were sitting outside on the verandah when the house-boy, Taonga, arrived to set the table for dinner. His eyes were downcast as he greeted the Madam's sons and he seemed nervous. Charlie jumped up as the servant approached and his chair fell back with a clatter.

'Where the bloody hell were you, boy?' he demanded, angrily. 'Where were you when my mother got cracked over the head. Eh? Where were you?'

'I was in my kia, sah. I did not hear anything. I did not know the Madam was being attacked.'

'Didn't know?' Charlie echoed sarcastically. 'Didn't know? Come on, pull the other one. A couple of kaffirs just wander in here in broad daylight, when you're supposed to be on duty, and you claim you didn't know they were here.'

'No sah. I did not hear anything. My kia, it is down by the stream.'

Charlie laughed derisively. 'It's all a bit fishy, if you ask me. Well listen up, boy. If I hear one whisper, one little hint, that you know the munts who tried to kill my mother, I shall personally come and beat your ugly mug to a pulp with my own knobkerrie. Get it? And I shall enjoy every minute of it. You're a Shona, aren't you?'

'Yes sah.'

'I suppose you support these … what are they called …ZANU, that's it. This ZANU mob, eh?'

'No sah. I do not understand politics. I am just a servant.'

'That doesn't mean you don't dabble. You munts aren't expected to understand politics. You don't have the brain for it. But you like to play at politics. Give you a knackered old AK.47 and you fancy yourselves as US Marines, ready to slug away at anything that moves.'

Taonga shuffled uneasily from one foot to the other. He had encountered the Madam's fiery offspring before and he did not relish a repeat of his previous encounters. 'I am a servant, sah. Nothing more. Shall I lay the table for dinner?'

'Yes, lay the table, Taonga.' Wisely, Ralph decided to intervene. His head was aching and he did not want a scene. There had been enough horror for one day. He did not want Charlie to stir up more trouble. 'And don't make anything too elaborate. I'm not hungry. What about you, Charlie?'

His brother shrugged. 'I'll just have a beer and a couple of sandwiches. And make sure it's a cold beer!'

Taonga shuffled away and the brothers were left to themselves. 'You can't tell me he didn't know anything about it,' Charlie muttered. 'I wouldn't put it past him to have set the whole thing up.'

'We have no proof of that,' Ralph replied. 'I can't believe that Taonga would be that stupid. He wouldn't want trouble on his own doorstep. Besides, the day we start suspecting our own servants we've got problems.

Things are deteriorating here as it is. I don't want to start imagining that I'm not safe in my own bed anymore.'

The two men fell silent after that, each alone with their troubled thoughts. Quietly, efficiently, Taonga worked around them, taking care not to disturb their reverie. They hardly noticed him. To them, he was nothing more than a servant, there to make their lives as easy as possible.

This was the natural order of things in their small corner of the world. They had grown to manhood imbued with the principle of white supremacy, and it was hard to question that irresistible axiom now. Even Ralph, who prided himself on a tolerance far beyond that of most whites, and who had an innate respect for all Africans, could not truly endorse the precept of majority rule.

Deep down he could not really accept that Africans were capable of self-government. They needed guidance from the whites. Needed their superior wisdom and experience in matters of state. This quest for equality, admirable though it may be, was dangerous. It would upset the natural balance and bring about the destruction of this fine land called Rhodesia.

Ralph had a vision of the glorious civilisation, created by the Europeans, abandoned and left to crumble to dust. He foresaw tribal conflicts and divisions. He pictured the poor blacks growing poorer while the African intelligentsia creamed off all that the whites had once owned. He saw the breakdown of services such as education, transport and health provision. It was a horrifying prospect. One which Ralph prayed to God would never be allowed to come to pass.

Lydia Llewellyn stood on tiptoe at the edge of the swimming pool in her parents' garden, raised her hands above her head and plunged, smooth as an otter into the clear blue water. She surfaced, shook the sparkling droplets out of her copper-red hair, and smirked triumphantly at Miles. Miles shrugged and kicked away from the side of the pool, anxious to put as much distance between his own diving disaster and Lydia's infuriatingly smug expression. He cut a clumsy sideways path through the water in his bid to reach the far side of the pool, his ungainly breast-stroke creating a minor squall in the normally calm waters.

Above the splashes of the chlorinated water, most of which seemed to find its way up his nose, he could hear Lydia's throaty giggle accompanied by that of his traitorous sister, Beth. He ignored them as best he could and continued on his difficult journey. Having reached the other side, he pulled himself out of the water and shook himself dry like an eager puppy.

'Careful!' his mother cried. 'You'll soak everyone! Here's a towel. Go and dry yourself over there.'

Miles draped the towel around his waist and ambled across the lawn to pet the Llewellyn's dog, Buster. He squatted down on the grass and plucked distractedly at the sleeping dog's ear. Buster raised his head and promptly rolled over on his back, paws curled up on his chest, and assumed a suitably submissive countenance. Absently, Miles rubbed the large expanse of furry belly. Delighted by this unsolicited attention, Buster stared vacantly at the sky and lay perfectly still for its duration. Sadly, his pleasure was brought to an abrupt halt by the sound of a bell tinkling on the far side of the garden wall.

'It's the ice-cream boy!' Miles yelled, racing across the lawn and hopping from one foot to the other in front of the four adults. 'He's outside. I heard his bell. Can I have one, Mum? Please!'

'It's okay,' Dai Llewellyn patted Rachel's hand and reached into his pocket for the cash. 'They're on me.'

'Thanks Mr Llewellyn!' Miles grabbed the cash and ran in search of the ice-cream seller. He skirted the pool, vaulted the first flower bed and circumvented the huge, spiky aloe before hurtling at breakneck speed down the drive. He paused to unlock the wrought-iron gate and then was out in the street, hunting for the familiar bicycle with the large casket attached to the front.

Lydia and Beth had heard the bell, too, and they were only a few yards behind Miles. Lydia was still dripping from her swim and she left a dark, damp trail in the red earth. Her younger sister, Leah, trotted along behind them. At eight years of age, Beth and Lydia tolerated the irksome four-year-old with admirable stoicism. Leah, for the most part, accepted her inferior status with quiet equanimity and it was only at times such as this, when her little legs simply could not compete with her elder sibling, that she truly resented her subordinate position.

'There he is!' Miles pointed to the crest of the hill where the African had parked his bicycle on the grassy verge. 'Race you!'

Beth and Lydia tore after him with Leah bringing up the rear. Miles skidded to a halt in front of the bicycle, lifted the lid on the box and poked about, hunting for his favourite lolly. The African ice-cream boy waited patiently with an indulgent smile on his face.

'I have a new flavour today, Nkosizana,' he lisped through his teeth. 'Orange Lollies. Very cheap. You will like them.'

Miles took the orange ice-lolly and debated its merits. 'Okay,' he declared, satisfied that it would meet his requirements. He then turned to the girls. 'What do you lot want?'

Beth and Lydia dived into the casket, squabbling among themselves as to the merits of the various flavours. Leah, too small to see the treasures inside the box, with its distinctive blue and white stripes and famous "Dairy Board" logo, was happy to accept her sister's choice. Eventually, they settled on three choc-ices on sticks. They blew into the wrappers to separate the chocolate coating from the paper, mumbled their thanks to the African and skipped back to the house. Miles, as the man of the party, was responsible for payment. He discharged his duty with great aplomb, and only a small measure of self-importance, before pocketing the change and wandering back to the Llewellyns' house.

Once there, he climbed onto the tall gate and swung back and forth while he sucked at his swiftly melting lolly. Through the trees, he could just about make out the figures of his parents and the Llewellyns sitting on deck-chairs next to the pool. As always, they were deep in conversation.

The two families had been friends for years now, since before Leah was born, and they saw each other often. Miles enjoyed visiting their lovely home on the outskirts of Bulawayo near the bush. He liked their bungalow with its pretty Cape-Dutch façade, and he enjoyed swimming in their pool. They had a tennis court, too, though neither could play and it was abandoned and used as a centre for Mrs Llewellyn's pot plants.

He liked the doctor who made him laugh, and he liked the Doctor's wife who made wonderful cookies and treated him like a grown-up. Lydia was okay, he grudgingly conceded, when she was not showing off her many talents, and Leah was … well, Leah. Just a baby really. Not worth forming an opinion of her he decided, slurping a trickle of juice before it ran down his chin.

His character assessments were rudely interrupted by the sound of low-pitched growl behind him and he turned, still swinging on the gate.

He did not recognise the danger at first. He saw only a large, black dog swaying unsteadily on its feet. But there was menace in those yellowing, bloodshot eyes and he began to panic. The dog edged closer, snarling viciously with two thick strands of white mucus hanging from its mouth.

Rabies!

Miles screamed and scrambled up the gate. The movement unsettled the animal who moved closer, teeth bared, with an evil glint in its eyes. Miles climbed higher, desperate to get away from those huge jaws.

Suddenly, the dog lunged at the gate barking furiously. It leaped into the air trying to reach Miles' foot which was still dangling perilously close to the ground. Miles screamed again and felt the gate swing underneath him almost toppling him from his precarious perch. The animal, now almost insane with blood-lust, hurled itself against the bars in a frenzy of razor-sharp teeth and fetid breath. Miles felt himself slipping, losing his grip on the ornate castings. The skin was torn from his fingers where he had clutched at the cold metal. He called out again, piteously now, and began to sob.

And then a shot rang out, crisp and clear in the quiet Bulawayo suburb. The dog howled, then fell in a crumpled heap on the floor and was still. Miles stared at the creature with tears rolling down his cheeks. His tee-shirt was stained with orange juice and his mouth was still sticky from the ice-lolly which now lay melting on the ground.

'It's okay, lad' Ralph helped his son down from the gate. 'It's all over.'

Dai handed his gun to Myra and knelt down to examine the boy. 'Did he bite you anywhere? Did you get hurt, or come into contact with his saliva - anywhere?' His tone was anxious.

Miles shook his head, still shocked by his close encounter with the deadly virus, and snuffled into his father's handkerchief. Beside him, Beth and Lydia were wide-eyed with fear. Leah gripped her mother's hand and sobbed in sympathy with Miles. Even Buster had been roused from his slumber and was now barking insanely at the unknown enemy that lay at the edge of his territory.

'He had a pre-exposure vaccine recently,' said Rachel. 'He went on a bush camp at school. The teachers recommended that the boys be vaccinated.'

'Quite right,' Dai poked and prodded Miles, searching for minor wounds which could easily be infected. 'You can't be too cautious where rabies is concerned. And that wretched animal is certainly a carrier.'

They all turned to look at the carcass. Myra shuddered, gathering up the three girls and shepherding them back to the house.

'I'll call the council,' Ralph volunteered. 'They'll have to send someone out to collect the beast. Someone will have to watch over it until they get here. We can't risk anyone touching it.'

'Good idea. Well, looks like you're clean, son.' Dai gave Miles a hearty slap on the back and handed him over to his mother who took him to join Myra and the girls.

Dai rubbed his chin thoughtfully and stared at the dead dog. 'Strange that it should venture this far out of the bush. It must have been forced into the town by the drought. Poor bugger. What a way to go.'

Later, when the children were washed and dried and playing quietly, the four adults sat out on the stoep for Sundowners. They were subdued by the events of the day and by the recent attack on Rose Cameron. Even the sunset, a wild mix of blood-red and rose-pink, could not lift their spirits.

'I'm beginning to feel that nothing is safe anymore,' Myra complained. 'There was that dreadful business with your mother, Ralph, and all the terrible stories we hear about the blacks arming themselves in the bush. It's quite frightening.'

'I agree,' Rachel nodded. 'Sometimes I feel a little isolated out on the farm. It was awful when Ralph had to go over to Juliasdale. I felt quite vulnerable.'

'I don't think we need worry as long as we take care,' Dai offered a token reassurance. 'It's just a few isolated incidents as far as I can make out. A few hotheads intent on causing trouble. As for the dog... well, I guess this is Africa. Rabies is rife here.'

Myra sighed. 'Rabies. Terrorists. Drought. This country is packed with potential dangers everywhere you turn. The children can't even swim in the rivers without the risk of catching bilharzia. There's always some life-threatening disaster lurking round the corner. Sometimes I long for the security of the Welsh hills. You don't get bilharzia in Snowdon's rivers!'

'True,' her husband agreed. 'You just die from the cold instead! At least no-one ever died of frost-bite in Rhodesia. Africa may have its hazards, but it's nowhere near as perilous as Wales in winter. Take it from me - I grew up there!'

'Welsh farmers don't have to arm themselves with guns,' Myra chided. 'I hear some farmers here are putting up anti-grenade screens. Surely that can't be necessary, Ralph?'

Ralph took a sip of beer and shrugged. 'People are starting to get nervous. A couple of farms have had stock stolen and they're beginning to feel under threat. I'm trying not to panic myself. I don't want to turn Scarfell into a fortress.'

'Ian Smith had better hurry up and do something,' Myra said. 'I hear the British now have a chap called Edward Heath at the helm. Let's hope he has a little more understanding of our needs than Harold Wilson ever did.'

'Well they'd better sort it out quickly.' Rachel added. 'The Africans in the bush are mobilising by all accounts. Hundreds of them are already in Mozambique and Zambia, training in guerrilla warfare. At this rate, we'll all be living under threat of terrorism.'

'How's your mother, Ralph?' Dai sought to steer the conversation away from politics.

'Not good. The doctor tells me she may be losing her memory. We're going to take a trip up there next week. I'm worried about her, but there's nothing I can do.'

'Is she still refusing treatment?'

'The only way we'll get her into hospital is to strap her to her bed and carry her there unconscious! She'll never agree to go under her own steam. She's always hated doctors and hospitals - no offence, Dai! - but she's as bad as the Africans. Doesn't trust anyone except her own self-healing processes.'

'If she's losing her memory there could be damage to the temporal lobes - that's the area of the brain responsible for processing things like language, memory and hearing.'

'Ja. Doctor Unwin has said her hearing seems to be impaired, too. Christ! What's wrong with the woman. Why won't she help herself?'

Rachel reached across and laid a hand on her husband's arm. 'Because she is Rose Cameron, that's why. She's never needed anyone in her life. She's a fighter. She won't change now. And that's what we all love about her - remember?'

'I don't love her stubbornness,' Ralph stuck to his guns. 'Even if I do share that unappealing character trait myself!' he added with a guilty grin.

They all laughed, grateful for the break in the sombre mood. Their world was changing all around them. They did not know which way it would go, what would happen to the Rhodesia they all treasured. They feared the end of the idyllic existence that had drawn countless Europeans to this blessed land. Things were different now. Their lives were changing. But they did not know how, or why.

Night fell swiftly in Bulawayo, the darkness only slightly broken by the pink glow from the street lights. There were fewer lights in the distant suburb where the Llewellyn family lived. There, the night was almost impenetrable.

The Llewellyns' servant squatted on the grass verge in front of the gate waiting for the baas to finish telling the men from the Ministry about the dog. They had parked their white van on the other side of the road while they went into the house to discuss the shooting. They had arrived with a bundle of clip-boards, papers and leaflets telling people what to do if they came into contact with rabies.

The servant was not concerned with such matters. His job was to watch over the carcass until the men took it away. It was dangerous, he had been told. No-one must touch it. He looked at the dog which lay on its side a couple of feet away. It did not look dangerous now, but he remembered the crazed animals that had terrorised his village when he was a child. They had been clubbed to death by the village elders and burned on the edge of the kraal. It had been swift and easy.

Here in the town, men needed special vans and protective clothing to dispose of the carcass. They wrote things down, questioned people and talked at length about the killing. The servant was content to wait for the white man's ritual to be completed. Time was of no consequence. He was blessed with the seemingly infinite patience of his race. He had no concept of boredom, had never known the frustrations of inactivity. He was required to remain in his position until the dog had gone. That was all he needed to know.

Eventually, the men returned and gathered up the animal in a plastic bag with a zip. They bundled it into the back of their van so that it could be taken to a laboratory in Bulawayo for tests. He did not know why they needed to carry out tests. It was obvious that the dog was a victim of the madness. He could have told them that.

He stood up and watched the van drive off down the road. He waited until it had turned the corner before shuffling back to the house. He pulled the wrought-iron gates shut behind him and locked them carefully, shaking both gates to ensure that they were secure. And then he made his way silently down the path that led to his kia. His day's work was done. It was time to sleep.

5

'Do you think he'll like it?' Beth sat astride the wall overlooking the milking parlour. 'It took ages to make.'

'I'm sure he'll love it, sweetheart. Sixpence tells me he couldn't have made a better birthday cake himself. Now that's praise indeed!'

'It's got extra cherries and tons of marzipan,' Beth continued to detail her culinary accomplishment. Her main concern was that her brother may not appreciate, nor even recognise, her magnificent contribution to his forthcoming birthday celebrations.

'I shall look forward to an extra large slice,' her father declared, pausing in his work to kiss the tip of her nose. 'Now mind you don't fall. If you must sit on that wall, at least sit still!'

Beth rolled her eyes and sighed. Her father was such a fuss-pot. She and Lydia Llewellyn had pretended to be circus tight-rope walkers on the wall only last week. Luckily, her father was busy elsewhere on the farm, or their fantasy would have been rapidly curtailed.

Beth enjoyed sitting on the wall watching the herdsmen at work. She loved the warm, earthy smell of the cattle as they crammed their great bulks into the milking parlour. She loved the sounds they made, and the way their great, doleful eyes stared at her under those long lashes. They were such beautiful animals. Beth had adopted a number of them, giving them pet names from the day they were born and keeping a motherly eye on their progress through life. Goldie was here now, lumbering into position ready for milking. The young labourer in attendance knew that Goldie was miss Beth's favourite, and he turned to nod reassuringly at her before proceeding with his task.

'You'll need to tie a rubber band around her teat when you finished,' Ralph yelled over his shoulder.

'Why?' Beth wriggled round on her perch to face her father who was about to enter his office at the back of the milking parlour.

'Because her teat is leaking. You'll see if you look closely'

Beth turned back and peered down at Goldie's udder. Her teats did not look any different and the milk seemed to be flowing normally.

'They may look normal from a distance,' her father read her thoughts, 'but her orifice - her opening - is far too wide and she's leaking milk. The rubber band will help prevent that.'

'But won't it hurt?'

'Not if Jacob applies it properly,' Ralph directed the comment at the labourer with a mildly menacing tone.

'I will do a good job, baas. She will not know it is there.'

'And see that she's milked more often. That's the best cure there is.'

'Yes baas.'

'What happens if it's too small?' Beth was fascinated by all things connected with the dairy. She was quick to learn and eager to expand her knowledge.

'That's not quite so easy.' Her father leaned against the wall, happy to share the secrets of Scarfell Farm with the next generation of Camerons. 'We'd have to get the vet in to deal with it. He might try to expand the orifice with a pair of teat expanders, or he might even have to carry out an operation to sever some of the sphincter muscles.'

'Yukk!' Beth shuddered. 'It sounds horrid!'

'It's not something a farmer would want to do, it carries a risk of mastitis, and you know all about that. But it has to be done or the cow has a hard time milking. You wouldn't want that for Goldie, would you?'

Beth glanced at Goldie's teats and shook her head. 'They look so soft and squidgy. It's a shame they have to be used for milking.'

Ralph laughed and hauled himself up on the wall. 'That's precisely why they're soft and squidgy.'

'Tell me some more,' Beth snuggled up to her father and nestled her head against his chest. 'Tell me how the milk is made.'

'How the milk is made ...' Ralph mused. 'Well, let's see... a cow's udder has four quarters, as you know. These are attached by a strong central ligament, and each quarter contains lots and lots of milk-manufacturing cells. These are called alveoli.'

Beth mouthed the word then, satisfied with the accuracy of her pronunciation, she nudged her father with her elbow to encourage him to continue.

'Inside the alveoli is lined with cells, too, and these take all the goodness from the cow's blood supply and convert it into milk. The milk is then stored in the quarters rather like a sponge holds water.'

'That's why they're all soft and squidgy!'

'Precisely!' Ralph ruffled her curls. 'When the cow is ready to let down her milk, a special hormone is released from the pituitary gland and then carried to the udder in the animal's bloodstream.'

'What happens next,' Beth's journey into the wonders of a cow's physiology was motivated in part by a desire to prolong the moment alone with her father. She had always been a daddy's girl and resented any incursion into their special relationship by her tedious elder sibling.

'The oxytocin causes the small muscles which surround the alveoli to contract. This increases the pressure inside the udder and, when outside pressure is applied, the milk starts to flow. That's it in a nutshell. Simple really!'

'Tell me some more,'

'Not now, sweetheart. I've got work to do. Off you go. You've still got to put those candles on your brother's cake.'

Beth jumped off the wall and dusted herself down. Her father was not a man to argue with and she knew she had had more than her fair share of his attention in the middle of his hectic schedule. Besides, he was quite right. Miles' cake, although already elaborately decorated, could do with a few extra candles. Also, there was a bit of space around the base where she could try her hand at making flowers with pink icing. It was a large cake, there was plenty of room for creative experimentation.

Ralph climbed off the wall with slightly less agility than his nine-year-old daughter. He was forty five and, although in excellent shape, was prone to the occasional twinge in his left knee. It was a nuisance, but Ralph was not one to publicise his ailments, or solicit unwarranted sympathy from others. He had no patience with the limitations of the human body and had already decided that the most effective remedy for his aching joint was to try to ignore it. He was, after all, a Cameron, and the Camerons were not renowned for their tolerance of physical inadequacies.

He bent down and rubbed his knee, cursing inwardly at the gnawing ache, then stood up and straightened his back. In the distance, he could see a sparkle of sunlight on his daughter's golden curls as she skipped across the lawn. She was so like her mother. So beautiful and so very perfect. She bent down to remove her sandals and Ralph was greeted by a flash of frilly, white cotton knickers from under her skirt. He laughed aloud, proud of her youth and innocence and purity. He stood and watched her running towards the house, her hair cascading behind her and her sandals dangling in her hand. It was a wonderful sight.

The Camerons of Scarfell Farm. They were as much a part of this land as the wild animals who roamed the open savannahs. They always would be. And Ralph discovered a new and surprisingly youthful spring in his own step as he went back into his office, closing the door behind him.

Miles paced up and down the stoep, occasionally trying to peer through the curtains into the sitting room. He knew there was a birthday surprise in there, but he was forbidden to enter until his father gave the go-ahead. He had no idea what it was. He had tried to wrest the information from Beth, but she was in the dark too. He knew this for certain, because he had compelled her to swear to 'tell the truth and hope to die', threatening dire consequences for her favourite teddy if she lied. But she had still pleaded ignorance.

'It's no good jumping up and down,' his mother cautioned, moving her glass away from her son's flailing arms. 'Daddy will call you when he's ready.'

Miles leaped to her side and dropped into a squat in front of her chair. 'Is it a puppy?' he cried, sneaking a guzzle of lemonade from his mother's glass.

'My lips are sealed,' Rachel teased, pressing her lips firmly together and folding her hands neatly in her lap.

'Oh Mu-um!' Miles whined. 'Even Beth doesn't know what it is. It must be something super-special!'

'Okay! You can come in now!' Ralph called from inside the house.

Miles jumped up and bolted through the door, pushing aside his sister in his quest to be the first to uncover the mystery. Beth howled in protest, but her step did not falter and she skidded to a halt only a few seconds behind her brother.

A huge box sat in the corner of the room. It was covered in wrapping paper and secured with ribbons. All that could been seen were four wooden legs poking out from under the folds of paper. Miles frowned and looked at his father.

'What is it?' he whispered, awed by the sheer size of the item. He had not expected to receive such a big present.

'Open it and see,' Rachel came to stand beside her husband. She threaded her arm around Ralph's waist and smiled indulgently as her son ripped the ribbon with his teeth. 'Gently now!'

Miles allowed the paper to fall to the floor and his jaw dropped open in silent disbelief when he saw what lay beyond the folds. Beth, too, was momentarily silenced and her eyes widened like two shiny saucers.

'Wow!' Miles quickly recovered his voice. 'A TV set! Cool! Mark Hammond hasn't got one of these.'

'Nor Susie Shaw!' Beth added, moving closer to inspect the television.

Ralph beamed. 'They don't even have TV in South Africa, you know. You're two very lucky children.'

Rachel ran her fingers over the polished wood. 'It's beautifully made,' she said, lifting the catch on the front-opening doors and folding them back against the sides of the cabinet.

'Made right here in Rhodesia,' Ralph volunteered. 'At least the cabinet was.'

'I gather eighty per cent of Rhodesian households now have television sets.'

'Ja, I read that, too. Well, I think we can safely claim that the Cameron household has now joined that group!'

'We have, but Mark Hammond hasn't,' Miles persisted doggedly.

'Nor Susie Shaw,' Beth added.

'It's great, Dad. Thanks!' Miles beamed at his father. 'And you Mum!'

Ralph stifled the urge to hug the lad. Miles had now reached the sensitive age of eleven, and was already beginning to exhibit a desire for more manly conduct. Instead he ruffled his son's hair and grinned.

Rachel, on the other hand, flatly refused to acknowledge Miles' aspirations to manhood. She knew that she would resist the relentless march of time until the bitter end and, defiantly, she bent down and planted a large kiss on his cheek. Miles accepted the gesture passively, but Rachel could not fail to spot the stiffness in his shoulders and the way he surreptitiously wiped away her kiss as soon as he could.

'We have another little surprise for you, darling,' she said, brushing aside the realisation that, one day, she would lose the battle with her son's impending maturity.

Miles spun round to face his mother. 'Two surprises! Wow!'

'Two presents!' Beth wailed. 'I never get two presents.'

'Yes you do,' Rachel swiftly contradicted her daughter in an effort to quell any sibling rivalry. 'Besides, the television set was a present for both of you. Now then, if you sit nicely on the sofa, Miles, I'll ask Daddy to bring it in.'

Miles obeyed the command with unusual alacrity. Beth followed suit, eager to see if she might share in this second surprise as she would undoubtedly share in the delights of the first. The two children sat bolt upright on the sofa, hands pressed neatly at their sides, mouths agog with excitement. This, they both agreed, was turning into a very special birthday celebration.

Ralph returned to the sitting room clutching a basket. He placed it carefully on Miles' lap then gestured for him to open it. Miles had already guessed what it could be but, hardly daring to breathe in case his conjecture proved wrong, he cautiously lifted the lid and peered inside. His whoops of joy and huge grin confirmed that his guess had been correct and that he was thrilled with his gift.

'I want to see!' Beth was feeling left out. 'Let me see!' She leaned over and gasped with amazement. 'A puppy! A baby puppy! Oh, isn't he a darling. Oh, please can I hold him, Mummy? I know he's Miles' puppy, but please can I hold him?'

Ralph plucked the tiny honey-coloured pup from the basket and placed it in Beth's lap. The puppy whimpered a little, then nuzzled Beth's fingers. Beth was entranced. Still hardly daring to believe his good fortune, Miles reached out a hand to tickle the puppy's ear. It responded with a huge lick from a very pink tongue.

'Here, let me hold him. He is mine after all.'

Reluctantly, Beth allowed the adorable parcel of soft warm fur to be removed from her embrace and lifted into the arms of his new master. The puppy snuggled into this new alien territory, breathed a great, big sigh and then promptly proceeded to lick every available surface within reach.

'He's a Labrador,' Ralph said. 'Piet Bezuidenhout, the vet, tipped me off about him. He's no cross-breed, mind. He's the real McCoy.'

Rachel knelt in front of her son and teased the excitable little bundle. 'He certainly is a sweetie. What are you going to call him, Miles?'

Miles pondered this for a moment, rolling his eyes skywards in a gesture of concentration. 'England!' he declared at last.

'England!' Beth echoed. 'That's a stupid name!'

'No it isn't. Nana and Gramps live in England and Mum was born there. It's a good name. England.' He enunciated the name slowly. 'It's a great name!'

'England it is then,' Ralph confirmed, concealing the traces of a smile.

Rachel ruffled the dog's ear and pinched her son's chin. 'It's a fine name, my darling. And thank you very much. I shall be proud to have a little bit of England at Scarfell Farm and I know Nana and Gramps will be delighted.'

'You reckon?' Miles had not quite anticipated such a positive response. 'I'll write and tell them, shall I?'

'I think that's a super idea, but first we'd better give England some water and sort out his bed. He's going to take a lot of looking after. And,' she added, frowning at the puppy's rather strained expression as he blinked at the strange surroundings, 'I think a sheet of newspaper on the floor wouldn't be a bad idea!'

Beth followed them into the kitchen. She had already decided that she would use her brother's good fortune to press her own suit for a pony. If Miles could have a puppy she could see no reason why she should not have a pony. She brushed a corn-gold curl from her cheek and grinned at Sixpence who was waiting with a water bowl, a cushion and various other goods and chattels designed to smooth England's inauguration into the Cameron household.

'England,' Beth muttered to herself as she stood on tiptoe to turn on the tap and pour herself a drink of water. 'Stupid name!'

Miles leaned against the wall of the tree-house and plucked Mexican Marigold seeds from the hem of his trousers. Blackjacks, as they were known, were common in the bush and were the scourge of poor England who invariably returned home from his walk with clumps of the irritants caught in his fur. Even when Miles had patiently removed every seed, England would continue to scratch and worry his flank with an almost hypochondriacal fervour.

Outside it was dark, save for the glimmering moon, the light of the Tilley lamp and the luminous glow of the fireflies as they danced in the shadows below. The evening quiet was broken only by the call of the crickets and the tree-frogs tinkling in the distance.

Opposite Miles, his thick curly hair illuminated by the lamp, Julius was carving a woman's image out of jacaranda wood. It was meant to be his mother. The baas had agreed to take it to Moses on his next visit to Que Que. Julius was grateful. He did not want his father to forget how beautiful Bliss was. And she was certainly very beautiful. The sculpture, with its full, rich mouth and slumberous eyes had captured her charms to perfection. Julius was a talented artist.

'Want to see what I've got?' Miles did not like it when Julius was absorbed in his own, independent pastimes. And if Miles was unable to join in, he would apply more intrusive tactics.

'Depends.' Julius did not even raise his head. He was accustomed to these diversions.

'On what?'

'On what it is you have to show me,' Julius declared with irritating logic. He held up the carving and angled it against the light, viewing it with a critical eye for any imperfections. He nodded, satisfied with his efforts, and tried to imagine what Moses would say when he saw it. Would he like it? Would he be proud of his son's creative skills?

Julius laid the carving on the mat and sighed. Truly he did not know. He had not seen his father for five years and he could barely picture the towering giant he had loved and feared so completely. He could still recall the magnificent presence of his father, could still smell the warm, animal scents that clung to his clothes, but he could not picture his father's face.

For Julius, standing alone on the path to manhood, his father, his guiding light and cherished role-model, was nothing more than a shadow. A memory. And, untarnished by day-to-day concerns and the limitations of reality, Moses would never fall from that lofty pedestal in his son's mind. Julius idolised his father as only a thirteen year old boy can. His father was an icon. And each passing year reinforced that impression.

'Oh well, if you're not interested...' Miles made a great show of yawning and fiddling about with the flap on his satchel.

Julius laid aside his carving knife and crawled over to his friend. 'Okay. What is it?'

'A girlie magazine!'

Julius scrambled into a comfortable position. 'Let me see it then.'

Miles plucked the tattered magazine from his bag and lifted the corner of the front cover to prove his point.

'Where did you get it?'

'Oom Charlie. He doesn't know I've got it. I nicked it from his bin. He's got loads of them and he chucks them away when tante Clara goes on the prowl. Don't tell Bliss, or my parents, or I'm in big trouble.'

'I'm not stupid,' Julius was irked.

'I'm not saying you are. I'm just making sure, that's all.'

'I'm two years older than you are. I am old enough to know that men's things must not be shared with women.' Julius puffed up his chest to amplify his point.

'Okay! Keep your shirt on!' Miles called a truce. He did not want the moment to be spoiled by a fight. 'I'll show you my favourite first.'

He flicked through the well-thumbed pages until he arrived at a photograph of a young woman with hair the colour of copper and firm, well-rounded breasts. She was sitting astride a child's rocking horse and her buttocks were flattened against the saddle. Wisps of pubic hair could be glimpsed at the top of her thighs and they, too, were the colour of fire.

'Look at her pubes!' Miles was eager to share this unexpected insight into the wonders of the female form. 'They look great don't they?' He tilted his head from side-to-side in his appraisal of the young woman. 'She's nice, isn't she?'

Julius did not respond. He swallowed hard, trying to quench the dryness that had closed up his throat. He stared at the image, his gaze travelling swiftly over those creamy curves and pausing to rest on the red peaks that thrust pertly from her breasts. There was a tingling in his loins that was becoming uncomfortable and he shifted his position to try to alleviate it.

'Well? What do you think?' Miles was unaware of his friend's discomfort and he continued to press for a response.

'She…' Julius' voice caught in the back of his throat and he coughed dryly. 'She's a bit skinny.'

Miles shrugged and scrutinised the photograph. The woman looked pretty enough to him. Julius was obviously not playing the game properly. He licked his finger and proceeded to flick through the magazine at random until Julius placed a hand on his arm.

'Stop! Wait there! Go back a page… and again. That's it. Now that is a woman who will bear many sons.'

Miles glanced sideways at his friend, puzzled by the unusual huskiness in his voice, but Julius' eyes were fixed upon the image sprawled across the page.

The woman was large, fat by some standards, with huge, pendulous breasts and thick black hair. She was lying spread-eagled on her back with her knees raised and slightly parted. The angle of the photograph allowed full view of the mass of coarse, black pubic hair, which sprouted like a dense, forbidding bush between her legs.

Miles stared at the picture. The woman was so vast that her breasts hung over the sides of her rib cage and looked as though they might squash the life out of him if he were to get too close. The black matt between her legs was awesome, thick and springy and quite unlike anything he had ever imagined.

'She's fat!' he declared, vaguely unsettled by this vivid example of womanhood.

Julius did not reply. His breath came in short, sharp gasps and the ache in his groin grew more intense. He shuffled on the floor, searching for a way to ease the tension. He glanced at Miles who screwed up his face up in disgust. Julius could not share his friend's distaste. For him, the woman, with her big white buttocks squashed flat underneath her, and that challenging look in her eye as she raised her head to look directly into the lens, was beyond endurance. He felt hot and the sweat prickled on his brow. He wiped it away with the back of his hand and fought to regain control of his senses.

'What's up with you?' Miles queried, having spotted Julius' discomfiture at last. 'You look a bit weird.'

Julius lowered his eyes and fiddled with his carving knife. 'It's nothing,' he retorted irritably.

Miles turned the page. He was losing interest in the magazine, which had failed to provoke a satisfactory response from Julius. Miles' interest in sex was still confined to giggles and innuendo and he had expected at least that much from his friend. Miles was interested in the concept of sex, and he had already decided that he would like to try it out sometime, but it seemed a lot of fuss and bother for such a brief moment. He recalled the swift slams and grunts of the bull as it serviced the cows on the farm. There was lots of heaving and shuffling about, but very little to show for it in the end. Sex and all that went with it was not really up his street, Miles decided, but it was interesting nonetheless.

'My dad's going to have England castrated.' he said in an effort to brighten Julius' mood. 'What do you think of that?'

'Why?'

'He reckons it'll keep him loyal and he won't go berserk around Prince and the other animals. So old Bezuidenhout is coming round next week to chop off his balls. Scary, huh?'

Miles folded up the magazine and was about to replace it in his bag when Julius placed a hand on his arm. 'This is your uncle's book, yes?'

'It's oom Charlie's okay. Cripes! You don't imagine my Dad would have something like this, do you?'

'What's he like?'

'Oom Charlie? He's great. He's a brilliant tennis player and a complete nutcase.'

Julius stared at the wood shavings caught against his jeans and he began to pluck them off one by one. He had seen baas Charlie on a number of occasions. The man was strong and powerful with a hearty laugh. And yet there was something strangely menacing about him.

Julius did not like the way baas Charlie frowned when he saw the two boys playing together. He did not like the way he cracked the joints of his fingers. But most of all Julius did not like the way baas Charlie looked at his mother. He had seen that look before. It was a smouldering look - hungry and dangerous. Baas Charlie would follow her with his eyes, running his tongue over his lips if she bent down to pick something off the floor. Julius resented those moments and longed to protect his mother from the white man's scrutiny.

But he was only a boy. He had no power to thwart the intentions of baas Charlie. But one day he would be a man. And then no man would dare to look at his beloved mother in that way again. He would not allow it. He would protect her. He would be her champion against all the white men who might cause her pain. He would do these things when he became a man. And that day would soon come. He knew that now.

Every hour, on the hour, Rose Cameron's beloved grandfather clock filled the corners of the room with its faithful rendition of the Westminster Abbey chimes. A fine reproduction of Herschede's Duke of Marlborough masterpiece, the clock had been a gift from an old aunt and had been shipped out from Scotland when Rose and Ewan were first married. The precious timepiece had withstood treacherous seas, a perilous journey overland from Cape Town and the rigours of life in Africa to take pride of place at Scarfell Farm.

When her two young sons had finally grown to manhood, and Rose had moved to her beloved highland home, the clock had gone with her. After its departure, an eerie silence had descended upon Scarfell.

'Good riddance!' Charlie had muttered, having been startled by the clock's noisy chimes on more than one occasion.

'She's welcome to it,' Ralph had said, remembering the occasions when he had covered his ears in the middle of the night to muffle the clamour of no fewer than nine tubular bells.

And yet the brothers were saddened by the loss of the old clock with its cabinet of rich cherry solids, burl cherry overlays and exquisite carvings. The place where it once stood so proudly now seemed empty and forlorn. The hours came and went unmarked by its faithful report. Eventually, Rachel had replaced the clock with a beautiful Queen Anne tallboy, but it had been a poor substitute.

Now, as nine o'clock approached, Ralph and Charlie glanced at the clock, mentally preparing themselves for its intrusion. They looked at each other and smiled, each transported back to a time when they were young, just two small boys tumbling over each other in their eagerness to escape from the house before the clock announced the hour. It was a game, a brotherly contest, and one that they had played many times in those carefree years.

But now they were no longer boys. Their childhood had passed and they had become men. And Rose Cameron was no longer a young wife and mother, her days marked by the regular hourly chimes. Now Rose Cameron was an old woman. She had lived a long and useful life. She had raised two fine boys and had guaranteed future generations of Camerons in Rhodesia. But her time had come. Her own hour was upon her. Rose Cameron was dying.

She had been taken to the hospital at Melsetter, too weak for protest now, and it would be there that she would end her days. It was just a question of time, the doctors had said, and there was precious little time left for Rose Cameron. The cancer had spread, its pernicious tentacles reaching out to every corner of her emaciated body.

No-one could say for sure whether the 'incident' had contributed to the onslaught of the deadly disease, but many were prepared to speculate. Among the white community of the Eastern Highlands, there was little doubt that the blacks had killed Rose Cameron. Rose Cameron was a victim of terrorism. An innocent white woman snatched from their ranks by evil 'terrs' who had broken into her home. And their contempt for the African deepened.

Slowly, almost imperceptibly, they began to close ranks, retreating into an increasingly insular world of European values and European culture in the midst of an alien land. They did not like what was happening outside. The Africa they knew, the Africa that they had shaped and fashioned in their own image, was changing. It was different now. Threatening. A place where danger lurked in the darkness. And they did not like the transformation.

Across the border in neighbouring Mozambique things were moving at a far greater pace. The Portuguese colonial government was under threat from FRELIMO, the Front for the Liberation of Mozambique, led by Samora Machel. Already there was a steady trickle of Portuguese crossing the Rhodesian border to escape from civil unrest and the fear of rising black power. This would swell as Samora Machel led his people to wage war upon the whites.

The majestic calm and beauty of the Eastern Highlands was slowly being eroded by its unfortunate proximity with a country standing on the brink of war. Robert Mugabe, from the confines of his prison cell, was not slow to recognise the value of Machel's quest for power. An ally in Mozambique would enable his own ZANU warriors to train with FRELIMO. Then, armed and skilled in the tactics of guerrilla warfare, they would infiltrate Rhodesia using the old slave routes across the Chimanimani Mountains.

White farms in the Eastern Highlands were obvious targets. The attacks could be carried out at night and the perpetrators safely back in the camps in Mozambique by dawn. Mugabe had not underestimated the value of black liberation in Mozambique, and he was too astute a leader not to use it for his own purposes.

But things were changing closer to home, too. On 24th November 1971, Ian Smith and the British Foreign Secretary, Sir Alec Douglas-Home, signed an Anglo-Rhodesian Agreement. This required Smith to set up a commission to investigate racial discrimination in Rhodesia and to make more unoccupied land available to blacks.

Many whites were outraged, seeing the compromise as a sell-out and the first steps to the erosion of white supremacy. Others accepted that Smith was first and foremost a statesman who had been compelled to put interests of the state above personal preferences. Smith knew that Rhodesia needed the $100 million promised by the British if he agreed to end discrimination. He knew that the British would never tolerate apartheid. And he knew that things would have to change one day. His only hope was that he would be able to manipulate the changes to preserve the way of life he had always known and loved.

He was a politician. He knew that he must compromise his beliefs, and perhaps his popularity, to secure a settlement with the British. To this end, he accepted the rights of the British to secure the Africans' views on these issues. He had even agreed to call in Joshua Nkomo from his prison cell to participate in the talks. Nkomo arrived at Government House in a truck disguised with blackened windows and newspaper across the windscreen. Its camouflage was so ostentatious that the world's press, waiting at the gates to record this important event in African history, knew for certain that it contained the African revolutionary and made sure that photographs of the truck appeared back home.

With all signatures secured, a special commission was set up to elicit the views of black Africans on the proposed constitutional changes. And it was this commission that brought the Head of the United Methodist Church in Rhodesia into the forefront of politics.

Bishop Abel Muzorewa campaigned tirelessly for Africans to vote against any changes that were not in their best interests. He was a man of the church, a moderate by many standards, but he was to become engulfed in the winds of change that were sweeping across Africa. And his life would never be the same again.

Rachel was too preoccupied with her own domestic upheaval to pay much attention to politics tonight. Anxiously, she stood up from the Rose Cameron's table and glanced at her watch. 'Anyone hungry? I can rustle up a toasted cheese sandwich if you like. What about you Charlie? Fancy a bite to eat?'

Charlie reached for the crumpled pack of Gold Leaf cigarettes and shook his head. 'Not for me, thanks,' he replied, gripping the butt of a dog-end between his teeth while he lit the match. 'I wouldn't say no to a beer, though.'

'What about you, darling?'

Ralph glanced up at his wife and pushed his spectacles back on to the bridge of his nose. His eyes were heavy, darkened by purple shadows and bloodshot in the corners. He smiled wearily and cast aside the copy of the Illustrated Life of Rhodesia he had been reading.

'I'll just have a cup of tea, if that's okay sweetheart.'

Rachel left the two men alone with their thoughts and went into the kitchen. They could do little more than wait patiently for Rose's departure from this life. They had chosen to be here in the Eastern Highlands to say their farewells, but time hung heavily upon them. In some perverse way, Rachel wished that she could hasten the end so that she and her husband could go home to their children, to Scarfell and to life.

She fretted about Ralph who was clearly exhausted and who had left the farm at such a busy time in its year. Without Moses Khumalo, he was left to shoulder most of the burden, for few men could match the African's natural affinity with the animals, nor his power to command and win the respect of the farm labourers. Now, the sombre vigil in this house of death was taking its toll on the last of her husband's strength.

Charlie was no help. He could not be relied upon to organise the practicalities of death – and they were many. The administration was down to Ralph alone, and Rachel resented that fact. She was also cross with Clara for opting out. She knew that Rose and Clara had never been friends, had never accepted the family ties which should have drawn them together, but Rachel did not accept that as an excuse for shirking her wifely duty now that the end was upon them. If nothing else, Clara should have been there for Charlie. But perhaps that was wishful thinking Rachel decided, reaching up to take one of Rose's delicate china cups and saucers from the cupboard. Clara and Charlie were on opposite sides of a deep ravine, one that was as impenetrable as death itself. Their marriage was dead, had died long ago, and even a bereavement in the family could not rekindle the flames.

The telephone rang just as Rachel returned to the sitting room. All three adults stopped what they were doing to listen carefully. Two short rings and one long ring. It was not for them. One of the other households that shared the party line accepted the call and the telephone went silent.

'So what happens if the ruddy hospital wants to get through?' Charlie took the beer from Rachel and downed half the glass in one go. He belched quietly and wiped his mouth with the back of his hand. 'If that's Mrs Mowbray yakking on the other end, we could be cut off for hours. See if you can get her off the line, boet.'

'It's not Mrs Mowbray,' Ralph replied. 'She's three short...'

'Ha! Of course! How could I forget? Three short! Good old Mrs M. She gets more calls than the rest of the ruddy neighbourhood put together!'

'...but I will ask whoever's on it to clear the line. You're right. The hospital may be trying to get through.'

Gingerly, Ralph picked up the receiver. The party line worked well, provided that everyone behaved in a civilised fashion and adhered to certain unwritten rules. One rule, perhaps the most important, was that calls could be intercepted in an emergency and the original call terminated. Even so, it seemed to Ralph like an invasion of privacy, and it was with reluctance that he broke into the conversation between two neighbours.

Naturally, everyone knew of Rose Cameron's plight and all had rallied together to help where they could. A freshly-baked apple pie had been left on the kitchen table when Ralph, Rachel and Charlie first arrived and the cupboards had been stocked with groceries. Mrs Mowbray had taken over the supervision of Rose's house-boy, Taonga, who had been forced to work even harder than when his mistress was in residence. Terminating a telephone call was a small favour to ask for such a respected member of the community.

The telephone rang again before Ralph could reach his seat. Two short rings and two long rings. It was their code. The brothers looked at each other, unsure as to who would take the call. Inevitably, the responsibility fell to Ralph. It was the hospital.

Ralph nodded, muttered a couple of affirmatives and concluded with the words 'Thanks. We'll be there right away.' He replaced the receiver, turned to his brother and said quietly: 'We'd better get going. There isn't much time.'

Rose Cameron lay quietly on the hospital bed. Her eyes were closed, the paper-thin membrane scarcely covering her sunken orbs in their deep, dark sockets. She seemed to have lost all substance and her flesh hung limply over her bones. Her hair, always immaculate thanks to a 'shampoo and set' every Friday at ten o'clock, was now patchy and the shape of her skull could be seen through the remnants of her curls. She looked cold and pale. The side-ward was filled with flowers, glorious in their vibrant colours and heady scents. But their brilliant blooms served only to enhance her deathly pallor and the contrast was too crude, too cruel.

Above the bed a plain, white plastic clock ticked away the last moments of a long and worthwhile life. Occasional sounds filtered in from the corridor. Laughter, the rattle of a nurse's trolley, muted conversation. But they did not intrude. Life went on beyond the confines of Rose Cameron's room. It was a reassuring thought.

Her two sons sat on either side of the bed, perched uncomfortably on the vinyl seats. They each held one of Rose's hands in their own. Neither one spoke, although both glanced at the clock above the bed as it relayed the relentless march of time. It was almost midnight and Ralph wondered, incongruously, what date would be entered on his mother's death certificate.

'Ewan? Is that you, my dear?' Rose's voice seemed feeble.

'No Mother,' Ralph patted her hand. 'It's Ralph... Father's not here.'

'Oh...' Rose closed her eyes. 'I thought I saw Ewan .... just there ...' she stretched out her hand and pointed into the distance. Once again her eyes opened and she stared without comprehension into the light. But then her gaze fell upon Ralph and she smiled and nodded. 'Ralph.'

Ralph tipped his spectacles back on to his nose and glanced at Charlie who was rubbing his mother's hand with uncharacteristic tenderness. Rachel stood behind her husband, her hand resting lightly on his shoulder. She would be there when he needed her. She would be his comfort when the time came.

Rose breathed deeply and smiled at Rachel. Then she turned and looked at each of her sons. She did not speak, but both knew that she was lucid and that she recognised them. It was as though the veil of shadows had momentarily parted.

'Promise me...' she was breathless and her words were dragged from the hollows of her chest.

'Ma... save your breath. There's no need to talk.' Charlie winced at the old woman's agony.

'I have something to say.'

Briefly, the Rose Cameron that they both remembered had risen from that ghostly shell. Her rheumy old eyes glinted with the determination they both knew would brook no argument. They laughed quietly and shook their heads, knowing that even death itself would be a poor match for this remarkable woman. They bent down, their heads almost touching, to hear what she had to say.

'Scarfell Farm... don't let it go. The blacks... taking over... Don't let them take Scarfell ...'

'No-one's going to take Scarfell Farm, Ma,' Charlie whispered. 'And the blacks won't get their paws on this country, either. They're not capable of taking anything away from us. They're just savages.'

'Okay,' Ralph shushed his brother. 'She knows that, don't you Mother?'

Rose beckoned for Ralph to come closer. Her voice was hoarse, barely a whisper, and it was increasingly difficult to make out the words.

'We built this country. Camerons... we built it. Don't ever forget that... Scarfell Farm... promise me... don't let it go...'

'Take it easy, Ma. You should rest.' Gently, Ralph laid her head back on the pillow, but still she fixed him with that determined glare.

'Promise me…' she gripped his arm with surprising strength. 'Please… promise me…'

Ralph's eyes filled with tears and he bent down and kissed the old woman's forehead. 'I promise you, Mother. I will live and die at Scarfell Farm. You have my word on that.'

Rose sighed deeply and a shadow of a smile flickered across her face. Quickly, she scanned the room, barely able to make out Rachel and her beloved sons, and then her lucidity faded and she stared blankly into space.

'Ewan?' she cried. 'Ewan…? Is that you, dearest?'

Eventually, her eyes closed and her head lolled to one side. Her laboured breathing grew fainter until only the sounds of the clock ticking were audible. Slowly, inexorably, the midnight hour approached until, suddenly, a shudder engulfed the old woman and her breath rasped in her throat. Her final breath lasted no longer than a few seconds but to her sons, who sat watching their mother depart from this life, it seemed to last forever. Tears welled in the corners of their eyes and Charlie swallowed the lump in his throat.

'Has she gone?' he glanced up at Rachel.

'Yes Charlie. She's gone. It's all over. She's at peace.'

In the foothills of the Inyanga Mountains, nestling beneath Punch Rock, Rose Cameron's bungalow was shrouded in darkness. At the bottom of the beautifully manicured lawns, the stream tumbled over the rocks tinkling like sweet music in the quiet night.

But then the silence was broken and more strident tunes filled the air.

Inside the house, as it had done without fail since the beginning of its own time, Rose's beloved Herschede clock marked the hour with its imposing Westminster Chimes. One-by-one the resonant tubular bells heralded the approach of midnight until, when the clock struck twelve, it fell silent once more and was still.

The midnight hour had passed. A new day had begun.

With typical attention to detail, Rose had left precise instructions for the funeral. Surprisingly, she had chosen to be buried at Hope Fountain the graveyard of the early pioneers that sat on top of a hill just outside Umtali. Most people had assumed that she would be laid to rest at Scarfell Farm next to the grave of her husband, Ewan. They were wrong.

'There will be no need to cart my coffin all the way to Bulawayo,' she had written in her sprawling hand. 'We will find each other soon enough in Heaven.'

Rose had always scorned the mock solemnity of funerals and viewed with horror the mournful expressions of the undertakers with their 'sombre suits'. Her send-off was to be a cause for 'celebration' she had insisted. Ladies in cheerful hats and flowers were to be the order of the day - although flame lilies were definitely off the agenda. 'Too vulgar' Rose had declared in her final instructions.

And so there were no flame lilies at Rose Cameron's funeral, and the ladies sported their most colourful hats to celebrate the passing of such a fine member of the community. Unfortunately, a stiff breeze blew around the top of the hill on the day and most were obliged to hang on to their elaborate constructions for fear of losing them. The men were grateful for the breeze which cooled the sweat on their backs. They were farmers. Men who worked the land. They were not accustomed to standing under the African sun in suits with collars buttoned up to the neck and a tie knotted at their throats.

Jacob, the African wood carver from Umtali, had made the coffin. Rose had admired his simple craftsmanship and had commissioned him three years earlier to assemble and store the article until it was needed. Not for Rose Cameron, the chaos of last-minute preparations. Even at her own funeral she presided with an iron fist.

The coffin had been loaded on the back of a Land Rover where it hung precariously on the steep drive up the track to Hope Fountain. Several cars followed, muddy station wagons, a couple of old Mercedes and the ubiquitous Morris Minors. It had rained earlier and the red earth had been churned into mud that clung to the wheel arches and spattered the windscreens.

Behind the vehicles, trudging through the dirt in bare feet or plimsolls, the black African labourers, servants and townsfolk who had known and revered this great white lady, keened softly in the mid-day sun.

Slowly, the entourage wound its way through the bush until it reached the cemetery at the top of the hill. It was small and neat, carefully tended by members of the Pioneer Society who were direct descendants of the brave souls who had been laid to rest here. It was a measure of Rose's pedigree that she had secured a plot in this coveted ground. But then Rose was a Cameron. She had earned the right to lie with the country's oldest and finest families.

Hope Fountain was surrounded by a low brick wall, against which grew acacia thorns, clumps of mopani scrub, lemon and plum trees. A creaky iron gate led into the enclosure where gravel paths threaded their way past the graves. It was a quiet orderly place that symbolised the civilisation that these brave men and women had brought to a savage land called Africa. Now they were at peace. They had done their duty to God, to their children and to the British Empire.

And Rose Cameron, carried aloft by four local Afrikaners and two healthy sons, was ready to take her place among them.

The mourners gathered round the grave as Rose's coffin was lowered into it. In spite of his tears, Miles could not resist peering over the edge to see how deep the hole was. He was prevented from tumbling in to join his grandmother by a stern parental hand on the back of his collar and a gentle tug which returned him to an upright position.

Beth had brought her GoiGoi. It was not the original, indeed it was the fifth tea-towel to claim the title, but it had supplied the same important service as its predecessors. Now, at the age of nine, Beth was too grown-up to need such childish supports. But the GoiGoi still had a role to play. Today she had to say goodbye to Grandma Cameron, and the GoiGoi would be her parting gift.

When the prayers were over, Ralph moved forward to drop a clump of caked mud into the grave. It landed with a soft thud on the coffin. Charlie stepped up to repeat the ritual, although he paused briefly to whisper something unintelligible into the hollow.

Miles chewed his top lip and peered up at his mother. 'Can I do that, Mum?' he pleaded. 'I want to say goodbye to Grandma like that, too.'

'If you wish, dear. I'm sure no-one will mind.'

Miles stepped up to the grave, as close as he dared without actually falling in. He bent down and scooped a huge fistful of earth and lobbed it over the edge. It spattered noisily on the coffin below and Miles was satisfied. He wanted his Grandma to know that this was his own special farewell message to her. No-one else's.

And then it was Beth's turn. She crept to the edge of the grave and shuddered. It was so cold and silent in the depths of the pit. She turned back to her mother, eyes brimming with tears. 'It's horrid to think of Grandma all alone in there. It's really dark in the hole.'

Rachel lowered her eyes to conceal her grief and instinctively reached for her husband who also swallowed hard in a bid to fight back the tears. Even Charlie had turned away and was fumbling in his pockets for a cigarette. It was indeed dark in that gaping cavern, and Rose was definitely alone.

Tenderly, Beth rolled up her precious GoiGoi and kissed it before letting it float into the blackness. It came to rest on top of the coffin, its gay red and white checks seeming oddly out of place in such a sombre setting. But Beth was satisfied as she returned to her parents, saying simply:

'Grandma would have liked that.'

Eventually, the mourners trooped out of the cemetery and returned to their cars. One or two nodded, but most did not acknowledge the small group of Africans who had waited politely outside the walls before being allowed in to pay their respects. They had brought gifts for Rose Cameron's spirit to use in the afterlife. They were sensible things such as a plastic washing up bowl, a bicycle wheel and a chipped earthenware mug. These were all they could spare, but they were treasured possessions that would ease the transition into the afterlife.

'Jesus wept!' Charlie gritted his teeth as the group shuffled into the cemetery. 'What the hell do they think they're playing at? They'll litter up the place with junk before my mother's even buried.'

Ralph hushed him. 'Remember Mother's wishes. "The Africans should be allowed to pay their respects". We can't ignore that.'

'Pay their respects, fair enough,' Charlie groaned. 'But dumping their garbage wasn't part of the deal.'

'It's not garbage to them, Charlie,' Rachel intervened, whispering so that her children might not overhear the dispute. 'They believe that the spirit will need such possessions in the afterlife. These gifts are a token of their affection and respect. We can't deny them a chance to pay their respects, can we? After all, didn't your own niece offer her precious GoiGoi for similar reasons?'

Charlie grabbed the side of the Land Rover and hauled himself up into the passenger seat. 'That was different,' he muttered moodily. 'That was family. They're just a bunch of bloody muntus. You can't let a bunch of blacks wander into Hope Fountain. Jesus! They'll start thinking they've got rights. God knows this country's going to the dogs as it is. Start giving them rights and they'll think they can run the bloody place. And then where will we be, eh? Answer me that if you can!'

6

Bishop Abel Muzorewa was bitterly cold as he stood on a platform in London's Trafalgar Square. He shivered. His lips were frozen and the tips of his ears were sore. Someone, a stranger in the crowd, stepped forward and handed him a pair of gloves. He took them gratefully and tried to smile.

The London rally had been organised to press for a "No" vote to Rhodesia's proposed Constitutional changes. It was a huge gathering with colourful banners held high in the streets. The demonstration marked the growing antipathy of the British people towards the Smith regime, and many welcomed the opportunity to voice their concerns.

Muzorewa was in Britain to ensure that the views of black Africans were accurately interpreted. He had already had talks with the British Prime Minister and the leader of the Liberal Party, Jeremy Thorpe, and now he was tired. He wanted to go home, wanted to feel the warm sun on his face and to begin the next stage of the long journey to freedom.

The last few months had been hectic. Alongside his commitments to the church, Muzorewa was now chairman of the new African National Council. The party took its initials from the first nationalist movement, the African National Congress, and was formed to support the campaign against the changes.

Ndabaningi Sithole and Joshua Nkomo co-ordinated the fledgling party from their respective detention centres. Muzorewa's name was first mooted for the post of treasurer, but it was felt that, as a political novice, Muzorewa would be better suited, and more easily manipulated, in the role of chairman. Muzorewa accepted the position and thus began what Nkomo contemptuously called "poor Abel's illusion of leadership".

Muzorewa did not know then, and would not come to know for many years, that he was regarded as nothing more than a puppet in the eyes of these powerful African revolutionaries, and he would never rise much above that lowly estimation in the eyes of the whites either.

Blissfully unaware of these opinions, Muzorewa embraced his new responsibilities with relish. He was a small man, only five feet two, with bright eyes and a beak like a weaverbird's. He lacked the force and charisma of a natural leader, but he was full of enthusiasm and a belief that he had an important part to play in the emancipation of his people. His political career seemed to be blooming and he could smell victory in the air. He had been given a cause. And he would not be stopped until the cause was won.

And so it was that on a bitterly cold day in February 1972, Abel Muzorewa found himself singing "Zimbabwe will be free" with hundreds of British sympathisers in Trafalgar Square.

His crowning moment followed swiftly. On 23rd May, black Rhodesians voted overwhelmingly against the Anglo/Rhodesian agreement. The Prime Minister, Ian Smith was said to be enraged. He had already realised that this would be the last chance the whites had to achieve a settlement while they were still in a powerful bargaining position. Rhodesia's days were numbered.

Later, at a large gathering of his supporters back home in Salisbury, Muzorewa declared with pride: "We are not yet a nation, but we are struggling to be recognised as one people and one nation".

For many it was an impossible dream, but for others it was a song of Africa. The voice of a people waiting to be free.

Marc de Borchgrave had no reason to doubt the African worker he had employed to help build the extension to his home at Altena in Centenary. The chap seemed honest enough. There was no reason to suspect that he might be attached to a group of guerrillas who had infiltrated the area. There was no reason to think that his black comrades would empty their AK 47s into the bedroom where Marc's two daughters slept. The girls narrowly missed death, but one received a wound to the foot and thus secured a place in history as the first white casualty of the guerrilla war.

Two days later, de Borchgrave and his other daughter were sleeping at a neighbour's home when they were attacked by a rocket fired at the window. His daughter was seriously injured in the stomach and chest.

A few days after the incident, an Afrikaner living nearby declared that blacks were "completely useless" and could only "come here and shoot at children". On 24 January 1972, he was seriously injured and his wife killed in a grenade attack on their home.

After that the whites fell silent, fearing that they might be the next target.

In his regular contributions to the Sinoia News, a former Rhodesia Front Party chairman sought to reassure local whites that things were under control. Few were reassured, preferring the Government's pledge to introduce Emergency Regulations. They also took little comfort from reports that the police had closed all the beer halls, clinics, schools, butchers and shops in Chiweshe as a reprisal for terrorist activity in that area, and by the fact that the penalty for such crimes had been increased from five to twenty years.

They were no longer at ease in their homes. The attack at Altena marked the beginning of the guerrilla war in their eyes, just as the Battle of Sinoia, six years earlier, marked the start of the great chimurenga for black Africans.

At last, after many years, black and white Rhodesians were in complete agreement. Both sides had finally accepted that they were now at war.

Rachel had taken to wearing spectacles for reading and close work. She had recently celebrated her forty-seventh birthday and had noticed a slight deterioration in her eyesight in the last couple of years.

'I suppose I'm officially "middle-aged" now,' she murmured to Ralph, peering at her reflection in the mirror and deliberately accentuating the few fine lines that had begun to crinkle the corners of her eyes. 'What a perfectly ghastly thought! And just look at those wrinkles. I look like an old prune.'

Ralph lay on the bed with his hands clasped behind his head and roared with laughter. 'I like prunes!' he declared. 'They're good for the digestive system!'

Rachel pouted into the mirror and then sighed. 'Oh well! No use complaining.' She began to massage a handful of Pond's cold cream into the areas most affected by the onslaught of old age. 'Fat lot of good this will do. I'm fighting a losing battle!'

Ralph raised himself up on his elbows and studied the sweeping curves of his wife's slender body. Forty-seven years old she may be, but she was still a fine figure of a woman and those barely noticeable lines simply added to her appeal. He patted the bed beside him.

'Come here, sweetheart. I need to take a closer look at these wrinkles you've been complaining about...'

Later, Ralph and Rachel lay entwined in each other's arms listening to the creak of the corrugated iron roof and watching the moon outside their window. The call of the crickets and the accompanying chorus of insects were the only sounds that filtered into the bedroom and the air was sweet with night-time scents. They were hot and they had cast off the sheets so that their naked bodies were illuminated by silver moonlight.

'I love you, husband,' Rachel whispered against Ralph's chest.

'And I love you, wife,' he replied, kissing the top of her head.

'Ralph...?'

'Yes my sweetheart?'

'I'm worried.'

Ralph pulled his wife closer. 'What are you worrying about, sweetheart?'

'I'm not sure that we're safe here in Matabeleland any more. Even Smith's publicity campaign to encourage more whites into Rhodesia has been a huge flop. It's obvious that people are thinking it would be madness to emigrate to a country gripped by civil war.'

'Ja, the "Settlers 74" campaign never did get off the ground, did it?' Ralph leaned over to reach for a cigarette from the bedside table. He flicked the cigarette lighter and the golden flame danced before their eyes. 'To be honest, I never held out much hope for it. If Smith was hoping to encourage more whites into the country, he should have done more than simply send out brochures telling Europeans what a great climate we have here and what a fine place it is to live. What he didn't tell them, but what they already know, is that the country is falling apart. "Come to Rhodesia and you could be murdered in your beds and see your kids blown apart by landmines!" That's the impression the whites in Europe have. A few glossy brochures aren't going to change that.'

Rachel shuddered and nestled deeper into Ralph's arms. 'It's as though the rest of the world considers us social outcasts.'

'I suppose we are in many ways. And I don't blame the Europeans for preferring to remain in their own countries. We're living in dangerous times here. Things are particularly bad in the Eastern Highlands. They're hiding behind electrified fences and windows covered with steel mesh to repel grenade attacks up there. Some farmers have even converted their bedrooms into makeshift bomb shelters!'

'Oh Ralph, it's so horrible. Do you think Matabeleland will get to be as bad as that?'

Ralph drew on his cigarette and inhaled deeply, watching the silver smoke strands curl into the night. 'It could happen, though heaven forbid it ever should. ZANU are the main threat, not ZAPU. ZANU are backed by the Russians and the Chinese, so they'll be a force to be reckoned with when the times comes. Right now, they seem content to attack white farms along the Mozambique borders. They're not interested in Matabeleland.'

'There is one other blessing,'

'What's that?'

'Our son is too young to be affected by the new call up regulations.'

Ralph stubbed out his cigarette. 'Too young right now, but he's growing up fast. He's in his second year at Plumtree. Before you know it, he'll be taking his O' levels!'

Rachel pulled the pale lemon sheet over her husband's chest, her fingers lingering on his skin. 'Do you think he's happy at school, Ralph?'

'It's been a bit tough on the lad, no doubt about that. He hasn't settled in as well as I'd hoped, but he's happy enough and he'll cope. He comes from pioneering stock! Besides, it's a good school – the best in Rhodesia some say – and he'll thank us when he's older. Now stop worrying and give me a kiss goodnight. There's a good girl. We're going to need our beauty sleep. We've got a big day coming up tomorrow.'

Julius awoke with the call of the cockerel at dawn. He threw aside the coarse blanket and opened the curtains that divided his bunk from the rest of the kia. He had hardly slept and was too excited to eat the breakfast his mother had left on the table before setting off for her duties at the main house. He splashed cold water on his face and ran outside to greet the morning. This, he decided, was possibly the most exciting day of his life. He did not intend to miss one precious minute of it.

He bounded up the steps to the main house, taking them two at a time in his haste. He wore no shoes, but seemed not to notice the stones that bore into the soles of his feet. He could see the house behind the jacarandas and he quickened his pace. Mindful of his mother's stern warnings over the years, he took care not to stray into the Camerons' garden, but skirted it using the rough path that led to the back of the house.

His mother was in the kitchen rinsing out a pile of dusters. Sixpence was preparing breakfast for the Madam who rose promptly at seven o'clock each morning. The baas was already at work on the farm. Another busy day had started at Scarfell.

Julius crept under the kitchen window, avoiding his mother's eagle eye, and made his way round to the far side of the house.

The windows of Miles' bedroom were flung open to accommodate any breeze that might help lessen the heat of the night, but the curtains were drawn. Carefully, Julius parted them and peered inside the room to where his friend was sleeping.

'Miles!' Julius hissed. 'Wake up. The day has come. Miles!'

Miles was curled up in a foetal position with one hand dangling off the edge off the bed. He stretched lazily, murmured something unintelligible, and then turned over to resume his sleep.

'Miles! Wake up!'

Miles stretched again and rubbed his eyes with his knuckles. He yawned, pushed his hair out of his eyes and focused on the shiny, nut-brown face at the window. Suddenly, with the mental agility of the young, he was awake and he leapt out of bed and grabbed his dressing gown.

'Hell! I forgot!' He struggled with the sleeves of the dressing gown then tied the cord around his waist. 'I've got to get something to eat first.'

'There is no time,' Julius was eager to begin this very special day. 'We will miss him.'

Miles yawned again and shrugged. 'Okay. I'll bring something with me. Nip round to the kitchen and ask Bliss to make me a sandwich.'

'You know I cannot do that. She would kill me if she knew I had come up to the house. You know the rules.'

'Okay. Okay. Keep your hair on. Meet me down by the gate in ten minutes.'

'Five!' said Julius, ducking to avoid the missile which was aimed directly at his head.

'Okay. Five. Now give me back my shoe and clear off.'

Julius retrieved the shoe from the flowerbed and brushed away the dirt before returning it to its owner. 'Missed at point blank range,' he teased, chucking the shoe through the window before racing down the path and out of range of any return salvo.

Miles tugged on his jeans and tee shirt and made his way into the kitchen where Bliss was now buttering toast. She looked up when her young charge entered and frowned.

'I did not think Master Miles would be ready to join his mother for breakfast,' she declared, glancing with undisguised dismay at the unkempt boy before her. 'But I had hoped he would have time to brush his hair at least.'

'I'll brush it later,' Miles replied, running a hand through his sleep-tousled locks. 'I'm late as it is.'

He crammed a slice of toast into his mouth and accepted the glass of mango juice from Sixpence with a grateful thumbs-up and a wink. Still munching the toast, he gulped the juice and tried to avoid Bliss' attempts to restore order to his hair with her fingers.

'That's it,' he cried, wiping the crumbs from his mouth with the back of his hand. 'I'm done here. See you later alligator!'

Pausing only to grab a second piece of toast, he snatched up his rucksack and sped down the drive to where Julius was waiting. He could see his friend at the bottom of the hill, sitting astride the farm gates, and he waved. Julius waved back. The adventure had begun. The day had finally arrived.

'Your father is late!'

'Relax! He'll be here when he's ready.' Miles replied. 'And don't forget we have to stop off at Gwelo first.'

'Why do we have to go all the way to Gwelo when there is a factory in Bulawayo?'

'Miles shielded his eyes from the early morning rays and peered up the hill expectantly. 'I don't know. We'll have to ask him. Here he comes now.'

Julius followed the direction of Miles' finger to the top of the track where the milk wagon was making a slow and ponderous journey towards them. The urns shuddered and rattled with each bump on the way, and the old wagon threw up great belches of black smoke as it trundled down to meet them.

'All set?' Ralph leaned across and pushed open the passenger door. 'Climb aboard!'

Miles scrambled on to the torn vinyl seat beside his father and paused to lend Julius a helping hand as he squeezed into the corner beside him.

'Big day, huh?' Ralph checked that the passenger door was properly closed before double de-clutching and shoving the lever into first gear. 'First stop Gwelo, though. We have to make a delivery en-route.'

'Why do we have to go all the way to Gwelo when the Dairy Marketing Board has a factory at Bulawayo?' Miles turned to his father. 'It seems daft.'

Ralph swung the heavy wagon out on to the main road before replying. 'Because, unlike Bulawayo, Gwelo takes butterfat as well as whole milk. And that's precisely what I'm selling today.'

'Can we stop off for lunch at that hotel on the road to Zhombe?' Miles turned to Julius. 'They do fantastic vanilla milkshakes,' he added for emphasis.

'Good idea. Just as soon as I've dropped off this little lot.' Ralph gestured towards the urns roped together on the back of the wagon.

'I am worried we will miss him,' Julius whispered in Miles' ear.

'Julius is worried we'll miss him,' Miles instantly betrayed his friend's confidence.

'Don't you worry about that,' Ralph winked at the boy who was now squirming with embarrassment in his seat. 'His release time is set for two-thirty. We'll be there well before that.'

Julius breathed a sigh of relief. He had not meant to question the baas but was anxious to get to Que Que on time. He then shot Miles a scornful glance before turning to stare out of the window.

The wagon slowed down to accommodate a lop-sided bus that had stopped to cram yet more Africans on to its already overloaded suspension. Young mothers perched on the seats, sitting well forward to avoid crushing the babies strapped to their backs, men hung out of the doors and squatted on the roof of the vehicle alongside chickens, steel drums and the various other travelling baggage which invariably accompanied the African on his travels. It was a miracle the bus could move at all, but move it did in a burst of exhaust fumes and a heavy cranking of gears. Slowly, lacking the power to overtake, the milk wagon followed.

'It's a wonder there aren't more deaths on the roads with vehicles like that about,' Ralph kept well away from the bus, which was tilting at an alarming angle towards the centre of the road. 'It's a wonder he can drive it at all, let alone drive straight.'

Julius heard the words exchanged between father and son, but they hardly registered. He saw the roadside traders with their hand carvings, mangoes or lacework thrust out optimistically as each vehicle approached, but he did not acknowledge them. He saw beggars sitting forlornly on broken tree stumps, but he did not wave as he might normally have done.

Today his thoughts were elsewhere. Today was a special day. Today his father, Moses, was coming home.

After those long years in confinement, Moses Khumalo would walk away from Sikombela detention centre a free man. And he, Julius, would be the first to greet him as he left that cruel and desolate place.

Without its cargo the wagon was lighter and speedier, but it was still as noisy as ever. Perhaps even more so as it bumped and clattered over the rough dirt road that led to the prison gates. The two boys clung on to the dashboard as it bounced from side to side and they were thrown together in a fit of giggles. Julius' mood had lightened now that the delivery was complete and they were on their way to meet his father. Miles, too, sensed the air of gaiety and was making more of the rough and tumble drive than it truly merited.

'There it is!' Julius pointed into the distance. 'I can see it!'

Rising out of a featureless plain of sparse scrub and red dirt, the barbed wire fences of Sikombela loomed large and awesome. Nearby, the conical roofs of the detainees' rondavels reached up towards the scorching sun. Unlike the haphazard structures in an ordinary kraal, these stood in regimented rows. There were no children playing as there would be in an ordinary kraal, there were no old men chewing on biltong, reminiscing of days gone by, and there were no women gossiping and giggling as they hung their washing out to dry.

Here, there was only silence. Here, the dust lay undisturbed under the thorn bushes, and white men with guns paraded with menacing gait throughout the compound. And the black men were no longer proud warriors who had once strutted so arrogantly in their kraals. No indeed. These men were painfully thin, stooped by hard labour and little food, and racked with sickness. Some of these men were on the edge of madness and despair. This was a place where the white man broke the black man's heart and his spirit. This was a place where many Africans lay down to die.

But some men had overcome the rigours of life at Sikombela and had carved out a disciplined routine that would prepare them for freedom. Not all were prepared to lie down and die for their crimes against the white man. Some had clung to hope with tenacity of men who believed in their freedom and their right to life. These men had managed to survive the harsh regime at Sikombela and take that precious walk to freedom.

Back among their family and friends, they told tales of a fellow inmate who had helped guide them out of the darkness of despair and into the light of life itself. The tales were exaggerated, shamelessly embellished, but based on truth. The man had been a source of inspiration to all who felt the chill of imprisonment when the gates were first locked behind them. His name was Moses Khumalo.

And today, Moses Khumalo, would keep his promise to himself and to all those who believed in life. Today he would walk unaided through those gates and return to the world he had left behind so long ago.

Tall, black as wet coal and cruelly emaciated, Moses Khumalo walked past the armed guards with barely a second glance. His head was held high and his eyes burned fiercely with an almost fanatical light. He was gaunt, with bones that jutted from his flesh, and tight curly hair that was now tinged with white. But he was still a proud man. And his step did not falter as he passed beyond the gates and out on to the long dusty road that led away from that evil place.

'Baba!' Julius leaped from the cab and ran headlong into his father's arms. At sixteen, with a sturdy, muscular frame and a strong, square jaw, he was well equipped to take his place among the men of his tribe. He had already tasted the sweet moisture of a young girl's lips and knew how to assuage the secret longings that assailed him alone in his bed at night. And yet the years seemed to slip away when he hugged his father under the fierce African sun. He felt like a child again. He was the boy who could not understand why strange men had come in the night to take his father away for seven long years. He felt an unfamiliar urge to cry, but he knew his father would disapprove. Instead, he swallowed his tears and stood straight to look admiringly at the man he was proud to call baba.

'You have grown, my son,' Moses surveyed the handsome young man standing before him. 'You have grown into a fine warrior.'

Julius beamed with pride and followed his father like a doting puppy as he went over to greet Miles and Ralph who were waiting politely in the distance. Ralph held out his hand and smiled warmly. 'Welcome back to the world, Moses,'

'I am glad to be back in the world, baas. Although I am fearful as to what kind of world it has become.'

Effortlessly, he swung himself up into the back of the wagon. Julius scrambled up beside him while Miles and Ralph climbed into the cab. With much noise and a swirl of red dust, the milk wagon made its way back down the dirt track and away from Sikombela.

Moses did not speak. He seemed not to notice the young boy who sat beside him, unconsciously imitating his thoughtful gaze. His eyes were fixed like the points of two sharp spears at the barbed wire that had contained him for so long. He vowed never to forget that cruel symbol of the white man's oppression. Never again would he allow himself to be captured and confined like an animal. He would rather die.

But first there was work to be done. He did not know what kind of world lay beyond that barbed wire, but he knew it would be very different from the one he had left seven years ago. The struggle had already begun. The chimurenga was already being waged out in the bush. He had been idle for too long. Now he would play his part in Africa's long and bloody fight for freedom. He would take his rightful place at the forefront of the armed revolt. He owed it to his black brothers. He would fight, and where necessary, he would kill the white men who had come to claim his beloved homeland as their own. Then, when the time came, he would be ready to take his place among the fallen heroes. He would be ready to die a free man in a free Africa.

'Mummy says she wouldn't sleep soundly in her bed with someone like that around.' Lydia stroked England's ear gently. 'She says he scares her a little.'

'My mum reckons he's changed,' Miles replied. 'She says there's a "hardness" to him now.'

'Do you think Moses has changed, Miles?'

Miles pondered the question. He swung his feet up on to the bench beside Lydia and poked England in the head with his toe. Contentedly, the dog snuffled a little, turned his big, doleful eyes to Miles, and then snuggled his head deeper into Lydia's lap where the caresses were less rigorous. Miles pushed his toes under Lydia's legs and replied: 'He's tougher than he was, no doubt about that, but he's okay with me. Mind you, he doesn't lark around much any more, but maybe that's because I'm no longer a kid. Maybe he knows he has to treat me like a man.'

Lydia smiled and bent down to kiss the top of England's head. She had developed an infuriating habit of blushing madly for no apparent reason, and the curse was upon her now. She concentrated her attention on the dog who, delighted to be the focus of such unexpected pampering, promptly wagged his tail furiously and began to fidget and puff and pant. Grateful for the distraction, Lydia fussed over the animal who immediately became overexcited by the attention and started barking hysterically.

Miles watched the spectacle with a grin. He had not noticed Lydia's discomfort, had seen only a pleasing glow to her cheeks before she concealed them under that glossy mane of copper-red hair. He liked it when her cheeks took on that rosy hue. It accentuated the vivid colours of her cat-like eyes. And he liked the brilliance of her hair, which shone like fire in the mid-day sun. In fact, much to his amazement, he quite liked Lydia!

Puzzled by this unexpected revelation, he studied the young girl sitting on the bench beside him. He tried to recall the many times she had infuriated him as a child. He tried to picture the gawky girl who had pointed out his imperfections with such relish. Try as he might, he could not imagine why he had found her company so utterly irksome in the past. Neither could he explain why he enjoyed her company now. She was, after all, only twelve years old. But in spite of this massive two-year age gap, Miles did like Lydia. She made him laugh, she maddened him with her wicked taunts, she played a great game of tennis and she was pretty. Reasons enough, he decided, for seeking her company today on a swimming trip to the Hillside dams near Bulawayo.

Distracted by England's antics, Lydia recovered her composure. She had been unsettled by Miles' description of himself as a "man". She did not like to think of him as a "man". She preferred her comfortable, unthreatening relationship with Miles the boy, and dreaded the uncertainties that she felt sure would accompany a relationship with that alien being called "man".

Sadly, one of those uncertainties was assailing her right now. Dressed only in her swimsuit, she was acutely conscious of Miles' toes squashed under her thighs. The sensation in that one, small area was overwhelming and caused her cheeks to flare up again. Confused, she wriggled out of reach of the unnerving bodily contact and pressed herself into the corner of the bench.

'Mummy says we can't trust any African now.' Anxiously, she sought to steer the conversation away from her own discomfiture. 'She says she wouldn't trust him with a barge pole!'

'Who?' Miles plucked at the hairs on his legs. He was inordinately proud of the hairs on his legs. In fact, he was particularly proud of his bodily hair per se and made much of the ritual of shaving the soft, down from his chin and examining his underarms regularly for confirmation of his burgeoning manhood.

'Moses, of course!'

'Oh right, Moses. Hell, I don't know. He's been with us for years, since before I was born. He's like one of the family. Of course we can trust him. My dad says he's a brilliant herdsman. The best! Besides, he's

Julius' father, and Julius is my buddy. Anyway, that's boring stuff. Come on! Race you to the tree in the centre of the dam.'

Miles jumped down from the bench, hurtled down the steps and waded into the water. With a purposeful crawl, quite unlike his ungainly childhood splashes, he struck out for the old msasa tree poking out of the water. The rains had been good this year and only the top branches of the tree could be seen, the rest submerged in the clear, cool waters that were the lifeblood of Bulawayo.

In the dry season the old tree stood gaunt on the dusty bed, surrounded only by stones and red dirt. Vulnerable to Africa's cruelly inconsistent rainfall, the Hillside dams changed completely with each passing season. Occasionally, they were a children's paradise with deep reservoirs circled by a labyrinth of stony paths to explore. More often, they were dry and barren places where only lizards and white ants flourished. But today they were brimming with water, providing endless pleasure for Miles and England, who was now paddling furiously in pursuit of his beloved master.

Miles turned and trod water. 'Come on!' he yelled to Lydia. 'It's great!'

He waited while she removed her flip-flops, tied her hair into a ponytail and slipped into the water. He waited while she made her way towards him, wet and sleek, and then turned as she drew close. He knew she would remember his challenge to reach the tree first, and that she would gather speed when she drew near. He knew also that she was a formidable opponent and that she might even win the race. Losing any contest to Lydia Llewellyn was a miserable experience, as she tended to compound her victory with infuriating smugness. Unable to accept such a prospect, Miles hurled a few customary taunts over his shoulder, kicked out his legs and skimmed the surface of the water at a cracking pace.

The man had disappeared. The boy had returned.

Charlie wiped the gravy from his plate with a crust of bread and swallowed the tasty chunk whole. Satisfied, he patted his stomach and leaned back in his chair. 'A fine effort, Rachel, my girl. A damn fine effort.'

Rachel pressed the napkin to the side of her mouth and smiled. 'I can't really take much credit for it I'm afraid. Sixpence, here, is the one who deserves all the praise.' She turned and handed her plate to the house-boy who was hovering nearby.

'Thank you Nkosikazi,' Sixpence bowed his head. 'May I take this, sah?'

Ralph handed his plate to the servant who then made his way cautiously to the end of the table where the Nkosi's brother sat.

The table was vast, carved from the traditional mukwa tree, and easily accommodated Ralph and Rachel, their two children and guests, Charlie and Clara. Yet, in spite of the ample space available, Sixpence found it difficult to reach Baas Charlie's plate. He was reluctant to draw attention to himself, having been at the receiving end of the white man's volatile temper in the past.

Charlie rested his elbows on the table, cupping a glass of wine in both hands. He refused to acknowledge the servant's nervous attempts to take his plate, pretending to contemplate the swirling liquid in his glass, but he knew well enough that the house-boy was flustered and he took a perverse pleasure in being the cause of the little Malawian's distress.

'Sixpence wants to take your plate, oom Charlie,' Keenly aware of the sufferings of all her fellow creatures, Beth could not bear to see poor Sixpence so disconcerted.

'Well, he should speak up and say so,' Charlie leaned to one side and waved away the plate. 'No good just standing there, boy. How am I to know what you want? I can't read your mind!'

Sixpence cleared the table in double-quick time and beat a hasty retreat to the sanctuary of his kitchen. He would need a moment to compose himself before returning to the dining room with fresh paw-paws and sweet bananas for desert.

'So what do you think of our new national anthem, Clara?' With her usual tact, Rachel managed to turn the conversation away from a confrontation between her strong-willed daughter, Beth, and her equally strong-willed brother-in-law.

'I think it's quite beautiful,' Clara replied. 'She's a South African, Mary Bloom, did you know that? She lives in Gwelo now, but she was born in South Africa.'

Clara clung to her homeland, South Africa, with a tenacity that had not wavered during her unhappy years in Rhodesia. She yearned for the land of her birth. She had grown up there, safe in the bosom of the Van Vuuren family and other close-knit Afrikaners. She had been young then and happy. And she had not known the miserable fate which lay in store for her north of the Limpopo River.

Sensing the change of mood in her sister-in-law, Rachel pressed on with the conversation. 'It's odd to think that our national anthem was written as a competition entry. It's quite amusing really. I read that Mrs

Bloom had previously won an award for naming a cocktail bar in the town!'

'Ja.' Ralph interjected. 'Only this time, I think she got $500 for her winning entry,'

'Jeez! We've got petrol rationing, our guys are doing call up duties, and old Smithy decides to chuck away five hundred bucks on some bloody poem or other,' Charlie drained his glass and poured himself another. 'More money than sense if you ask me.'

'More wine, Clara?' said Rachel.

Clara placed her hand over her glass and shook her head. She glanced at her husband, who was happily downing the contents of his refill, and sighed. She would need her wits about her tonight. Charlie was bad when he was sober. He was far worse when he was drunk. 'I rather like having Beethoven's Ode to Joy as the tune, and I think Mrs Bloom's words fit it perfectly.'

'I gather there's been some criticism about that,' Rachel followed the direction of Clara's gaze, and understood at once the woman's concerns. 'The music critic in the Herald is amazed that we had the nerve to... what did he say...? Oh yes, to plagiarise a melody with "supra-national associations" for nationalistic ends!'

'Well he would bloody well say that, wouldn't he. The Herald is a Marxist rag if ever I saw one!'

Sensing that the conversation was teetering on the brink of politics, Miles and Beth begged to be excused from the table. Oom Charlie was great fun, but things could get a little heated once he was on a roll. Gratefully, they made their escape from the tedium of adult pre-occupations.

'I hear we've got the Salvation Army complaining about the state of these new protected villages,' Charlie poured himself another glass of wine and followed Ralph out on to the stoep. 'Apparently they reckon the conditions there are "inhumane". What the bloody hell do they expect? Five star hotels? Hell, it's no easy task shepherding thousands of kaffirs halfway across the country!'

'The whole operation was handled badly,' Ralph contended. 'The blacks were only given a couple of hours notice to leave their farms. The Government left themselves no time to install essentials such as running water and toilets. It must have been a pretty grim experience all round.'

Charlie grinned. 'You're too soft, little brother. You forget that your typical African doesn't need luxuries such as toilets and running water. He survived in the bush for centuries without them. It's only since the white man arrived that your average munt has given a moment's thought to such things. And it's not the blacks doing the whinging anyway. It's the do-gooders as usual. It's the bloody sally army imagining that the black man has the same needs as the white man!'

'Even so, I think it could have been handled better. I heard that almost 50,000 people were shifted out of their kraals on the Chiweshe tribal trust lands, and herded against their will into makeshift shelters in these so-called protected villages.'

'You say "so-called" protected villages, but let me tell you that it's for their own good. The Government's not just shifting the blacks to protect the white farmers. They're moving them to protect them from these press gangs we hear about - rebels who sneak across the border and grab innocent black children to train as soldiers in Mozambique. I'd like to know what the sally-bloody-army has to say about that. They'd have something to complain about if they were the parents of one of those nippers. And they're moaning about the fact that the blacks are only given fifteen metres for living space. How much more do they need. Huh? Tell me that. All they want to do with the land is plant a few mealies. How much more do they need?'

Ralph took that to be a rhetorical question and remained silent. He glanced up at the sky, grateful that many of the stars were hidden behind clouds. The rains had come early this year, he noted with pleasure, and it had been a good season so far.

He pushed his spectacles back on to the bridge of his nose and leaned back in the rocking chair. Charlie was right, in part, of course. The blacks were safer in the new PVs, especially since this new method of recruiting fresh troops for ZANU had emerged. Joseph knew of someone whose two young sons had been snatched in the night.

The war was turning ugly. There was no room left for compassion. Trust between the white masters and their black servants was gradually being eroded. No-one knew where it would all end. No-one knew who would survive to see the new Africa which was slowly clawing its way out of the dirt. Ralph glanced at his brother and sighed. Perhaps it was necessary to be tough, like Charlie, to survive.

Unlike Ralph, Charlie seemed unaffected by the tensions that were filtering down into the relative calm of Matabeleland. Unlike Ralph, he seemed to relish the opportunity to heap scorn upon the African. And perhaps, unlike Ralph, he would survive unscathed the bloody repercussions of a land torn apart by civil war.

Life inside the protected villages was harsh. Confined to only fifteen square metres, each family had to erect its own pole-and-dagga thatched hut and a toilet which, for most, was nothing more than a hole in the ground. Families had to remain in the PV from dusk until dawn, but could return to their own lands during the day. In spite of this, many Africans lost their livestock and their crops during this period of enforced dislodgement.

The village perimeter was illuminated all night by powerful electric lights, and African District Assistants armed with .303 rifles guarded both exits. Once inside, the area that housed the European Officer and his African assistants was separately fenced and protected by earthworks and sandbags.

And yet, in spite of this elaborate security, the rebels still managed to exert their power inside the compound and exact serious repercussions upon any who failed to support the cause and provide food and shelter to guerrilla fighters out in the bush.

To prevent this, the authorities took all surplus food away from the inhabitants of the villages, leaving them enough for only one meal a day. From these meagre rations, the women would put their own mealie-meal into a small packet, tie the bag up tight and squeeze it between their thighs. Each time they went through the gate, the guards would make them jump, legs apart, but their secret cargo, supported by two stout pairs of knickers, would remain hidden.

Back on their own farms, they would bury the bag in a hole for collection by their "comrades" out in the bush. The penalty for failing to support their comrades was harsh. Among other tortures, a husband might be forced to watch while his wife's top lip was hacked off. He would then be forced to eat it or face death. The loss of a day's food was a small price to pay for immunity from such retribution.

Bernard Mabeteya had survived the perilous thirty-day journey from his training camp in Zambia thanks to the sustenance provided by inhabitants of the protected villages en-route. He accepted their food without gratitude. He was a freedom fighter, a member of ZAPU, a man who would kill and torture his own people without mercy in his quest to set them free.

ZAPU shared the same cause as their northern allies, ZANU, and yet the ancient tribal conflicts between Matabele and Shona were never far from the surface. Although they were fighting on the same side of the same war, they could not co-exist without conflict.

Thus, while Mugabe's ZANU forces enjoyed the hospitality of Mozambique, Nkomo's ZAPU guerrillas were invited by President Kaunda to base their camps in Zambia.

Unfortunately for the Matabeles, the mighty Zambesi and Lake Kariba protected the frontier with Zambia. Infiltrators had to cross the pounding river first before being exposed to the deadly terrain of Matabeleland, which included deep ravines, high bare hills and wide expanses of open bush and semi-desert. In addition to these natural hazards, the Rhodesian forces had made the crossing even more difficult for terrorists by planting landmines at strategic points.

But Nkomo's men were highly trained, far more so than their ZANU counterparts, and most managed to survive the perils of the journey from Zambia to return to wage war against the whites in their homeland.

Now, it was not only the whites in the Eastern Highlands who were exposed to acts of terrorism. Matabeleland was swiftly becoming engulfed in the tide of hostility that was sweeping across the country. No-one was safe. Darkness was descending upon the wide open spaces of Matabeleland. And for some, it came in the shape of a man called Bernard Mabeteya.

Julius did not like the man who had emerged from the shadows late at night and entered their kia with furtive glances over his shoulder. He did not like the way his mother trembled as she handed him a waxed carton of Ingwebu beer, nor the heavy lines that creased his father's brow as the stranger approached.

The man was still here. Julius could hear him whispering with his father outside the kia, but he could not hear what they were saying. He lay quietly in his bunk, straining to catch the words, but it was no use. The African night was upon them and the men's muffled voices were lost in a chorus of insects and the distant howls of hyenas. Eventually, lulled by the deep resonance of male conversation, and by the ceaseless rhythm of nature, Julius closed his eyes, drew his knees up to his chest and drifted off to sleep.

Moses rested his head against the wall at the back of the kia. He, too, had closed his eyes, but he was not sleeping. He was thinking, mulling over the words that Comrade Mabeteya had said. In the moonlight, his profile was regal, still gaunt from his recent confinement at Que Que, but regal nonetheless. His cheekbones, highlighted by a silver lunar shadow, gave shape to his handsome countenance.

He seemed at peace, but in truth his heart was pounding. He had not expected to receive the call to arms so soon. He knew he would eventually take his place beside his brothers in Zambia, but he had only just been released from detention. He was worried that he might not be equipped for active duty.

Even so, he longed to hold a stubby, reliable AK47 rifle in his hands. The AK47 was favoured by ZAPU who believed it to be better by far than the long NATO rifles used by the Rhodesians. But weapons of all sorts were pouring into Rhodesia from the weakened border with Mozambique. The Soviet Union, China and Cuba were all backing the struggle for independence and were willing to invest time and money into securing victory for the blacks.

Bernard Mabeteya studied the Matabele sitting beside him. He took note of the powerful jaw, the lean, sinewy arms and the towering presence of the man. He had heard talk of this man called Moses Khumalo, and had sought him out as soon as he left Zambia. ZAPU needed men like Moses Khumalo. It was true that Moses was not yet ready for combat – seven years in detention had diminished his strength – but he would regain it with proper training and military discipline in the Zambian camps.

But first there was a job to be done, and Moses Khumalo had been elected to carry out the task. Moses Khumalo was to be given the honour of demonstrating the courage of the Matabele and their determination to win this war with the whites. After the deed was done, he would disappear into the bush and make his way across the border. It had all been planned. And Bernard Mabeteya was here to ensure that the plan was successful.

Moses sensed his companion's intense scrutiny and he lifted his hooded eyes to meet those which studied him so openly. 'What is it you want me to do, Comrade Mabeteya?' he asked, meeting the man's gaze steadily. 'You know I am here to serve the cause in any way I can.'

'I know that, Comrade, and so do the members of the ZAPU High Command. They have selected you for an important task, Moses Khumalo. They have selected you to teach the white man a lesson he will never forget. The whites sleep easily in their beds down here in Matabeleland. For them, the war is raging far away in the north and east with Mugabe and his Shona dogs. They believe that, if they keep quiet, the war will pass over their heads. After that, the white fascist, Ian Smith, and that fool, Muzorewa, will reach a nice, safe compromise. A compromise that will change nothing.'

'You are right,' Moses stared straight ahead. 'The whites in Bulawayo do not live in fear as do those in the towns of the Eastern Districts.

Perhaps the Matabele are not feared as the Shona are. Perhaps the whites do not know that the sons of Mzilikazi are more deadly than any Shona dog.'

'They must learn,' Bernard Mabeteya agreed. 'And you, my brother, will teach them. You will show them the might of the Matabele warrior. This, Moses Khumalo, will be your task.'

Moses did not reply. He finished the carton of beer and hurled it into the thorn bushes. For a while both men were silent. There was no hurry, no need for pointless conversation. Eventually, Moses turned to his companion and said: 'What must I do?'

Bernard Mabeteya looked deep into the eyes of the man who sat next to him. Moses felt a momentary chill, which he shook off swiftly. The man was assessing him, he could feel it, gauging his commitment to the struggle, probing his most private thoughts for signs of weakness. But then, satisfied with what he saw, Bernard Mabeteya leaned forward so the he could not see Moses' response when he whispered:

'You will kill the farmer, Ralph Cameron, and his wife and his children.' Moses inhaled, but he said nothing. 'And then you will leave this place, and your own family, and make your way to the border where you will be met by men who will know of your brave deed.'

'And then?'

'Then Comrade, you will begin to train for war. This,' he waved a dismissive hand at the land that was Scarfell Farm. 'This is nothing. When you return, you will be a great warrior and this… this will be nothing. All that will be left will be the dust that blows over the bones of the white oppressors who once claimed it as their own.'

Moses was troubled. Wearily, he climbed the steps that led to the main house. He stopped near the tennis court and turned to gaze upon the two kias that were home to his family, and to Sixpence and Joseph. And then he lifted his eyes to the top of the hill where the windows of the main house were illuminated with a soft, warm glow.

Somewhere in that house, the baas and his wife lay sleeping. Their daughter would be close by and so would Master Miles with his faithful hound at his feet. The task was simple. Moses had to supply Bernard Mabeteya and his men with a layout of the house and details of who slept where. He would then have to ensure that the doors were opened in the night for the assailants to enter. He would have to tell them which night would best suit the slaying. It would have to be a night when there were no guests present, but when all the Camerons were at home. He would be given an AK47, so that he could take his rightful place at the forefront of the slaying.

It would be swift and simple, Bernard Mabeteya had said.

But it was not that simple for Moses. Images of a young boy flashed into his mind. A white boy who trusted him, who turned to him for advice on how to be a man. A boy who had not yet fully understood that he was white and therefore a legitimate target. And Moses saw his own son, Julius, playing with that white boy as a child. He saw their heads together, wiry black curls pressed against soft brown strands, and he saw them laughing. It would not be easy to kill the boy who was a blood brother to his own son.

And the baas. Moses reached the top of the steps and wandered along the paths that led around the house. The baas had always been fair to him and to his family. Ralph Cameron liked the Matabele, Moses knew that - considered himself one of them having been born and raised in Matabeleland. Did he really have to die? Surely, Moses argued with his own conscience, there were other whites more deserving of such a brutal end. The Camerons were good people. White people, but good people, and they would need good white people in the years which followed liberation. Moses was sure of that.

'Hey! You boy! What are you doing creeping around the house, eh? Looking for something to nick, I'll bet.'

Moses hung his head low and adopted a cowed posture that was less likely to provoke a man like Charlie Cameron. He did not reply and took care not to meet the other man's bloodshot eyes as he pressed his face close.

'What are you doing, you sneaky kaffir? Eh? Up to no good, if I'm any judge.'

Moses could smell the alcohol on Charlie's breath and knew at once that the white man was drunk. Sober, the baas' brother was a dangerous man. Drunk, he was a time-bomb waiting to explode.

'I cannot sleep, sah.' Sensibly, Moses kept his eyes downcast.

'Can't sleep!' Charlie guffawed. 'Can't bloody sleep! You kaffirs spend your entire lives asleep! I'll bet you even service your women while you're asleep! I've never met a muntu who was awake, for chrissake!'

Charlie burst into drunken laughter and tilted towards Moses who reached out to prevent the man from falling upon him. Through his drunken haze, Charlie spotted the raised arm and his head cleared in an instant.

'Raise your hand to me, would you? Raise a hand to a white man? You filthy nigger!' Charlie sprayed Moses with a fine rain of spittle as he spat out the words. 'I'll teach you to raise your hand to your betters!'

Moses saw it coming, but he was not quite ready for the impact of Charlie's fist crashing against his temple. It was a good hit, Charlie was a strong, well-built man, and Moses reeled from the force. But he did not fall. He stood his ground, refusing to wipe away the blood that trickled into his eyes. Nor did he respond. It would be a futile gesture, for the white man would win in the end.

Instead, he gritted his teeth and stood with fists clenched at his sides until Charlie had staggered back to the house. Only then did Moses Khumalo stir. He lifted one of those clenched fists and rammed it into his mouth, biting down hard on his knuckles to quell the hatred which rose up like bile in his throat.

He stood in the dark, legs apart, eyes black with fury. The man would pay. This Moses swore upon the graves of his ancestors. The Camerons would pay for the insult they had visited upon this son of the house of Khumalo tonight.

Briefly, the clouds parted and the moon shone full upon the face of Moses Khumalo. It was a face contorted by hatred. A dark, cruel face of a man with revenge in his heart.

Moses Khumalo had been chosen to bring suffering to Scarfell Farm. He had been chosen to destroy the Camerons, who stood as a symbol of all who had come to claim his beloved Africa as their own. He would do his duty. He knew that now. He was ready.

Slowly, the clouds drifted across the moon once more, plunging Scarfell Farm into darkness. Moses paused to reiterate the oath that he would avenge his African brothers and then he slipped into the shadows and disappeared.

7

Clara sat on her verandah watching a column of flying ants rise from the nest at the bottom of the lawn and spiral into the setting sun. It was their nuptial flight and by morning the ground would be covered with a gossamer carpet of discarded wings.

She recalled the days when Miles used to feast on their butter-basted bodies and wondered whether he still did that. Probably not, she decided, reverting to her needlepoint, for her nephew was rapidly leaving his childhood behind and taking his place in the world of men. And a fine young man he was, too, she thought with pride. He would do well for himself, no doubt about that. He had inherited his Uncle Charles' good looks without, fingers crossed, his less admirable qualities. She would not wish Charles' dubious traits on anyone - certainly not young Miles.

Her thoughts were rudely interrupted by the clamour of a fire engine hurtling down the main road at the bottom of her garden. It was a common sound in the summer months when grass fires raged across the sun-baked bush. Even a good rainy season could not prevent fire damage when the sun rose to its peak during the day. Clara had heard that huge tracts of the Matopos had been burnt, and much of the bush to the north of the city.

She placed her needlepoint in her lap and closed her eyes, letting the coral pink sunlight filter through her lids. She paused until the siren faded before returning to her tapestry with its picture of snow-capped mountains and glacial lake. She threaded her needle with dark green cotton and focused on a patch of cloth that would eventually be transformed into a pine forest. Framed, it would make a lovely gift for Rachel who missed the snowy landscapes of the English winter. She studied the half-finished project and nodded. It was a lovely picture. Rachel would appreciate such a gift.

'Madam?'

Clara jumped at the sound and swung round to face the young girl who stood beside her. 'Matilda! How many times have I told you not to creep up on me like that? It's most alarming.'

'I am sorry Madam. I did not creep. I simply came round the side of the verandah.'

'Well you should announce yourself, girl. How am I supposed to know you are there if you don't announce yourself.'

Matilda dropped her eyes and stood with her hands limply at her sides. 'I am sorry Madam.'

'Well? What do you want, girl?' Irritably, Clara stuffed her needlepoint into the sewing box.

'The Nkosi will be returning from work shortly. Is there anything I must do to prepare for this?'

'You know quite well what you must do. Goodness, I must have told you a dozen times! You must set the table for dinner. Make sure the newspaper is folded next to the baas' cigarettes on the side table. Make sure there is a drink waiting for him. Oh heavens, girl! You've been here for two months. You must know the drill by now!'

'Yes Madam.'

Clara watched with growing agitation as the young Zulu disappeared round the side of the house. Matilda was the second replacement for Ibbo Tembani, their former house-boy, who had fled in the night with a bottle of Charlie's best brandy and a carriage clock. It was assumed that he had returned to live among his own people, the Shona in the north, and it was generally agreed that there was little point in trying to recover the stolen items. Instead, Clara applied herself to the task of finding a suitable replacement.

She had settled on a maid after convincing herself that African women were more trustworthy than the men. But the first girl had not lasted long. Clara had caught her "making eyes" at Charlie and wriggling her bottom a little too vigorously when she polished the table next to his chair. She had been fired on the spot. Servants were cheap and plentiful and Clara was not prepared to tolerate unseemly conduct.

It was not long before Matilda arrived to take her place. The young Zulu was tall and sturdy and, unlike many women of her tender years, unhindered by a brood of offspring. She was comely with the padded cheeks and large breasts that were typical of this ancient African tribe. Her skin was flawless, a perfect blend of coffee and cream, and her bearing was regal as befits a member of the proud house of Zulu. It was unusual to find a Zulu maid and Clara had been delighted with her luck, but Matilda had failed to live up to the Madam's high standards.

She was irritating, Clara decided as she got up from her chair and went into the house. A bit too full of herself. She would need to be brought down a peg or two before she could perform her household duties with any degree of satisfaction. The Zulus were a strong, healthy race, well used to work, but they were a proud people. And Clara had set herself the task of transforming this so-called member of the house of Zulu into a successful housemaid. It would be difficult, but she would not be daunted. It was for the best. The girl would thank her in the end when she was good enough to act as servant to any of the grandest white families in the land.

After dinner, Clara retrieved her needlepoint from the sewing box and settled into her favourite chair. She was determined to finish the pine forest before the weekend. After that, she could make a start on the snowy peaks.

Her husband lounged on the sofa opposite. He was reading the Bulawayo Chronicle. A half-empty glass of lager sat on the table beside him and a cigarette burned slowly down to the stub in the ashtray. Occasionally, he would grunt and bluster at some disagreeable item of news, but there was little or no conversation emanating from that quarter of the room. The spark that had once ignited the passions of Charlie Cameron and Clara Van Vuuren had long since fizzled out. Now their marriage was as cold and grey as the ashes of a winter fire at dawn.

Clara studied her husband covertly and wondered, yet again, why her marriage had turned out so badly. She could still appreciate the devastatingly good looks that had first attracted her to him, and she could still sense the smouldering sensuality that had so easily seduced an innocent Afrikaner girl. Even lolling on the sofa, he exuded a charm that, she knew to her chagrin, most women found irresistible. And yet in spite of his looks, Clara despised the man.

She despised him for making her believe that he was someone worthwhile, a man to be reckoned with in his homeland, Rhodesia. She despised him for taking her away from everything that she loved, everything that was safe and familiar, and bringing her to this distant land. Here, she had learned to suffer the ignominy of being married to a failure. She had to remain silent while other women boasted of their husbands' successful careers and accomplishments. And she knew the humiliation of being nothing more than a visitor at Scarfell Farm. She would never know the pleasures associated with the prosperous inheritance that Charlie had so foolishly turned his back upon.

Charlie was popular, no doubt about that, both men and women were drawn to his magnetic charisma, but few remained to bask in his radiant sunshine. They knew that there was little more to Charlie Cameron than a brief, bright sparkle of light. Beyond that he had little worth. And Clara hated him for it.

'Will you stop staring at me woman!' Charlie crumpled the paper into a ball and lobbed it halfway across the room. 'You should get your ruddy head looked at. You're going gaga in your old age.'

'And we all know why!' Clara leaned forward, picked up the newspaper and smoothed out the creases.

'Ja!' Charlie persisted. 'Because you take after your old man who also went off his rocker before he croaked!'

Clara pressed her lips into a thin, blood-red line and concentrated on the emerging outline of the pine forest. It was too easy to fight with Charlie. The hard part was walking away. Carefully, she folded her tapestry, wound the thread around the needle and replaced it in the sewing box before leaving the room. The pine forest would have to wait.

Matilda was in the kitchen. She paused when Clara entered and waited for orders. Irked by the girl's complete lack of initiative, Clara ignored her and went out into the garden.

Outside, the plum trees were heavy with ripe fruit and the marulas had already started to fall and ferment with their characteristic beery smell. Clara wandered among them, pausing to scrape the white ant tunnels off the trees with a stick. The termites carried the bark into their nests and if they ringed the tree it would die. Rachel had almost lost her beloved jacaranda to termites.

Alone in her garden, among the dahlias, Clara felt at peace. It was her territory. Charlie rarely spent time in the garden, preferring to fall asleep in front of the television or enjoy more manly pursuits of snooker and rugby. He could not understand why women were so preoccupied with their gardens. And he could not be bothered to find out.

It was dark outside, but the garden was illuminated by the soft glow from the full moon. Slowly, stopping only to dead-head the occasional rose, or smell the sweet scents of summer in Africa, Clara made her way to the bench that nestled among the dahlias against the perimeter wall. She fingered the blooms and made a mental note to stake and tie them the next day to prevent them from drooping, and then she brushed away the fallen petals and twigs from the seat and sat down.

From that position, she could scan her beautiful creation and survey the small, neat bungalow that she had transformed from an early pioneer's shack into a much loved, albeit loveless, home. She peered down at her feet to the collection of eggshells carefully placed to deter slugs from destroying the flowers. There were so many slugs and snails at this time of year and Clara was grateful to Rachel for coming up with such a simple remedy.

Her gaze swept across the wide expanse of lawn, now green and lush following the heavy rains, and continued up the stone steps of her verandah, its entrance flanked by mock Corinthian columns. Beyond that she could see the back of her husband's head as he sat watching television in the sitting room. The room was well lit and, from the darkness of her garden bench, Clara could see quite clearly the pictures and ornaments that she had collected on her visits home to South Africa. It was a lovely room filled with memories of her girlhood. An Afrikaner's room. In fact, the only item in the room that jarred her faultless symmetry was her husband. And she deeply resented his intrusion.

In the far corner she saw the door open as Matilda came in carrying a glass of lager. She moved to the chair where Charlie sat and leaned over him to deposit the glass on the table.

Charlie said something and the girl smiled and bowed her head in a blushing, maidenly way. But there was nothing maidenly about Matilda. Her breasts were full and firm and pressed against the thin white blouse so that her nipples protruded clearly. Clara ground her teeth and resolved to buy the girl a bra next time she was in Bulawayo. And a larger blouse for good measure!

Matilda was still quite young, but her hips were wide and welcoming and ripe for child bearing. And they swung provocatively when she walked. She was a Zulu and her sensuality was innate. She did not have to cultivate it, and she could never hope to conceal it.

Suddenly, unexpectedly, the scene began to change and Clara watched, appalled, as Charlie reached out to touch Matilda's thigh. Obviously, it was on the pretext of pointing out a stain of some sort, because Matilda glanced down at the spot where Charlie's finger rested and dabbed anxiously at the material. From her secluded spot, Clara could see quite clearly that the maid was unsettled by Charlie's attentions.

Clara swallowed hard and felt the bile rise in her throat. She wanted to turn away, to escape this unpalatable scene, but she could not move. She was mesmerised by it, even though she knew it could only bring torment and pain. She wanted to know the truth, no matter how hurtful. She wanted undeniable proof of her husband's disloyalty. And then she could truly despise him. She would be free of him forever.

Matilda was chewing her bottom lip, swaying gently as she plucked up the courage to leave the room. She stood straight and tall and her blouse buttons strained to contain their ample burdens as her breasts bulged and creased appealingly. Charlie was obviously unable to resist their ripe charms and he reached up and tweaked a tantalising nipple. Matilda stepped back in horror and made much of covering her breasts. She did not dare offend the baas, but she knew the consequences of such a liaison and, terrified, she scurried out of the room.

Charlie watched her go. And Clara watched Charlie watching her. It was a painful cycle.

Hot tears stung the corners of Clara's eyes and she wiped them away irritably with the back of her hand. Then, through her tears, she saw her husband rise from his chair and follow the maid out of the room. It was too much to bear and Clara buried her face in her hands and started to weep.

Hastily, she shook aside her grief and vowed to put an end to the humiliation once and for all. Hardly daring to acknowledge the consequences, and uncertain of her own actions, she made her way to the servant's quarters at the back of the house.

The neat paths gave way to rough stones and unkempt grasses as Clara approached the kia that was home to Matilda. It was a typical kia. A single room with a bunk bed and cooking facilities. In the fashion of kias across Rhodesia, it was painted white, but the paint had now turned to grey and was flaking in parts.

As she drew closer, Clara's nerve failed her and she paused. Her breathing was shallow and ragged and she felt sick. In her heart, she was not sure whether she wanted to know the full extent of Charlie's contempt for her. She did not know whether she could cope with the truth. Would it would free her … or destroy her? She did not know, but with the gritty determination of a true Afrikaner, she was prepared to find out.

Silently, she approached the door. She could hear Charlie's laughter from within, accompanied by Matilda's muffled cries. Summoning all her reserves of strength, Clara opened the door and stepped inside. What she saw horrified her, and she struggled to quell her cries of anguish.

Matilda was leaning over the table. Her skirt had been pulled up to her waist and her rosy-brown buttocks were exposed. Her blouse lay on the floor and she was naked from the waist up. Her breasts hung freely and Charlie had leaned forward to grip one of them in his meaty paw, while the other swung to the rhythm of his hard, uncompromising thrusts.

It was only a matter of seconds, but it seemed like an eternity to Clara as she stood and watched this crude display of raw, animal passion. She reached for the door handle to steady herself, and was just about to flee the scene when Charlie sensed her presence and turned to face her.

In that one brief moment, Clara saw the thin veil of civilisation slip from Charlie's countenance, and his eyes darkened into something evil and terrifying. His mouth twisted into an ugly snarl and his teeth were bared like a wild animal poised to kill. He swore loudly, pushing the servant girl away as he pulled his trousers up from around his ankles.

Matilda fell to the floor, uncomprehending at first, and then following her master's gaze to where the Madam stood. She screamed and tugged at her skirt with one hand, feebly attempting to hide her engorged nipples with the other. It was no use.

'Madam! I ...' her voice tailed off and she cried in pain when Charlie pushed her back to the floor with the heel of his shoe.

'If you will go creeping round the joint looking for trouble...' he hissed, glaring at his wife with a vicious glint in his eyes, 'you've only got yourself to blame when you find it.' With that, he zipped up his flies, stepped over the dishevelled serving girl, and elbowed his way past his wife out into the warm summer night.

Clara waited while Matilda struggled to recover her clothing and her dignity. She waited for the girl to stand up, pull her blouse over her head and wriggle her skirt back into place before she spoke.

'You will gather your possessions and leave this place tonight,' she said calmly. 'Do you understand?'

'Madam...I ...It was not my fault. Madam, please!' Matilda reached out with begging hands, but Clara stepped out of reach.

'You will leave my home at once.' Clara spat out the words through clenched teeth. 'Tonight! You are fired.'

Matilda began to cry, her loud sobs filling the dingy little room. With no references, she would be on the streets. A beggar. She would be a drain on the scant resources of her family's kraal. There would be no place for her to go. She would be destitute.

She looked up at the Madam with eyes pleading. What she saw there sealed her fate forever. She saw herself mirrored in the eyes of this white women. She saw a dirty black servant, clothes awry and smelling of sweat. She saw reddened eyes, wet with tears and fearful from looking into the abyss. She saw blotched cheeks and thin lines of mucus hanging from her nose. She saw a future without hope.

And then the shutters came down as the white woman, who held her fate in her hands, studied her with an icy calm. The Madam dwelt in a cold and unmerciful place. A place where compassion no longer existed. Matilda knew that there would be no pity in such a place. The young girl shivered beneath the older woman's scrutiny then winced when Clara laughed aloud. It was a cruel, brittle laugh and Matilda recoiled in horror.

Clara turned to go, pausing just for a moment as she opened the door to cast a disdainful glance at this member of the proud house of Zulu. And then she stepped outside, closing the door quietly behind her. The two women would travel different paths from now on, but they would arrive at the same place eventually. They did not know it, but both paths led to hell.

'Loosen up, lad! You're as stiff as a board!' Ralph sat at the side of the tennis court, issuing instructions to his son who was standing on the base line ready to serve. 'Sloppy spaghetti! Remember?'

Miles chuckled and shook himself free of the tension that invariably accompanied him on the court. He was a good player, but competitive like his father, and he did not like to lose. Worse, he did not like the ignominy of losing to a woman – even if that woman happened to be his mother.

'And reach for it! You won't serve Aces from that position!'

'You stay out of it,' Rachel admonished her husband. 'We don't want unruly, partisan crowds here, okay? Now can we please get on with the game? We're at 30-40 and I'm already one set up. I intend to claim the victory that is rightly mine!'

Miles frowned at his mother. For a woman, she was unacceptably competitive, quite unlike his friends' mothers who were far more … sensible. And she was a jolly good player, too, one who would not balk at giving her beloved son a sound thrashing. He watched her take her stand at the far end of the court, lean forward slightly and, racquet at the ready, sway gently in readiness to return his serve.

He would show her!

Taking a deep breath, he swung forward and then flung the ball high in the air, arching his back to obtain maximum height with his racquet. His forearms were strong, finely muscled and covered with a sprinkling of tight, curly hair. His dark eyes concentrated on the ball and he waited until it fell within reach of his racquet. Then, with supreme strength and co-ordination, he leaned into the shot and slammed at the ball with all the force he could muster.

The ball sailed over the net and hit the ground on the edge of the box with such velocity that it sprang up again and bounced well out of reach of Rachel's outstretched hand.

'Bravo!' Ralph leapt out of his seat. 'A masterstroke! That Ace brings us to Deuce, my dear Mrs Cameron … if I'm not mistaken!'

'No, you are not mistaken, Mr Cameron. Now kindly sit down and keep quiet. I've got to concentrate. My son seems to have gathered his second wind.'

Miles felt a warm glow of satisfaction. He did not like mediocrity, firmly believing that if a job was worth doing, it was worth doing well. And he applied that rigorous maxim to every aspect of his life. Miles had already decided that he was going to be one of life's winners, like his father, and nothing gave him greater pleasure than praise from the man he admired above all others.

Fortified by his recent Ace, and determined to equal his mother in this game, he drew upon his ability to exclude all external distractions, and focussed on his next shot.

After that, his game went from strength to strength and he went on to take the set with great panache. A perfectly respectable defeat in the final set did not dampen his spirits and he left the court with a big grin on his face.

'What's this dross?' he flopped down on the blanket next to his sister and flicked through the book lying next to her. 'Lady Chatterley's Lover! Hot stuff! I bet Mum doesn't know you're reading it.'

'Of course she knows, stupid!' Beth rolled on to her side and snatched the book from her brother who was waving it threateningly in the air. 'It's D.H. Lawrence. It's not some grubby magazine like the sort I see you reading. I bet she doesn't know about those!'

'Mum knows everything, my dears. That's what mothers are for, to keep a watchful eye on troublesome children. Now stop trying to cause trouble for your sister, Miles, and run and get me some lemonade from the kitchen. And you, young lady, should cover up. Sunbathing in a bikini in this heat is just plain silly. Look at you, you're already as brown as a berry. You'll spoil your skin if you're not careful. You don't want to end up looking like a wrinkled old prune, do you?'

Beth pulled a tee shirt over her head and grimaced at the deep tan on her legs. 'Oh Mum! I haven't gone too far have I? I must have fallen asleep. Look at me! My legs are like a pair of leather boots!'

Rachel laughed and ruffled her daughter's hair. 'Nonsense, you look perfect. I just don't want you to burn, that's all. Now don't be so sensitive, darling. Your legs look lovely.'

'No they don't!' Miles plonked himself next to his mother and handed her the glass of lemonade. 'They're scrawny.'

'They are not! See what I have to put up with? No wonder I'm so sensitive. Why did you have to give me a brother, Mum? Why couldn't I have a sister, like Lydia? It's perfectly loathsome having a brother.'

'It's not as bad as having a sister,' Miles slugged a gulp of cola straight from the bottle. 'This is great, Ma. I thought you couldn't get it in the shops at the moment.'

Rachel sipped her lemonade. 'For some reason, they're back on the shelves. Don't ask me why. Sanctions don't seem to follow a logical pattern. Last month it was toothpaste that was in short supply. Remember?'

'That was horrible. I hated not having nice toothpaste.' Beth wrinkled her nose and examined the tan on her arms. 'My arms are okay though, aren't they Mummy?'

'I'd rather go without toothpaste than Cola,' Miles persisted.

'That's no surprise,' said Rachel. 'You've never been keen on your ablutions.'

'Ablutions? What's ablutions when it's at home?'

'It means, dummy, that you're grubby and horrible. And that you pong, just like you do now! In fact, you pong so much that I'm going to my room to breathe in some clean air!' With that scathing attack, Beth jumped to her feet, picked up Lady Chatterley's Lover, and flounced into the house.

Rachel watched her go, dismayed by the sight of that pert, young bottom poking cheekily from beneath the tee shirt. Beth was growing up fast. And what a beauty she would become, Rachel realised with a gnawing anxiety in the pit of her stomach. She was already long and supple, with curves forming in all the right places. In fact, both of her children had inherited the good looks associated with the Camerons. Good looks which would serve them well in their adult lives.

Beth had inherited her mother's mass of corn-gold curls and flawless complexion but, surprisingly, she did not share her mother's blue eyes. Hers were a deep, chocolate-brown, again so typical of the Camerons. A truly beautiful child, Rachel thought with pride. And she would be a truly beautiful woman. A heartbreaker, too, with that wilful temperament and vivacity.

Rachel watched her daughter disappear into the house and she sighed. There was little she could do about it. It was the relentless march of time and she was powerless to halt it. Sometimes she wanted to stop the clock, to keep her beloved family exactly as they were today. Young, healthy and happy. She did not want her offspring to grow up and leave the nest. She wanted them here with her, always. The Camerons of Scarfell Farm. That was how it should be. That was how it had always been.

In the distance she heard a faint rumble of thunder and she glanced up at the grey clouds forming over Bulawayo. A storm was brewing and she calculated that it would reach Scarfell by nightfall. Suddenly, Rachel shivered. Nothing ever stayed the same, she realised with a heavy heart. Even a blazing summer sun could be obliterated within an hour by awesome storms.

But that was Africa. A land destined to be swept up by the winds of change and hurtled into the unknown. It was unsettling, frightening sometimes, but it was Africa. It was her home. And she loved it so.

'I wouldn't sleep with your window open, dear.'

'No, don't close it, Ma. This is going to be a cracker of a storm, isn't it, Dad? I don't want to miss it.' Miles was sitting up in bed, his pyjama top open to the waist. A pair of headphones lay in his lap. He would turn the stereo up loud when his parents had finally gone to bed.

Ralph sat on the end of his son's bed. 'Oh, it's going to be a cracker, all right. I hear hail is forecast.'

Rachel stood over him. 'Daddy tells me you're going to the club's swimming tournament tomorrow. Why aren't you entering?'

'I was down for the butterfly, but they've got a team together now. And besides, Philip's a much better swimmer than me. We're just going along to cheer the lads on, aren't we Dad?'

'You've never been one for the water, have you darling?' Rachel leaned over and kissed the top of her son's head. 'Ball games are more your forte, as that game of tennis this afternoon proves. If I wasn't such a skilful player myself, you might just have beaten me!'

Miles rolled his eyes then glanced at his father.

'Don't you worry, son. She'll dine out on this one small victory for months. You know what she's like. As far as I'm concerned, that Ace was worth a dozen victories. The mark of a true professional. You take after your old man for that, my lad!'

'Goodness! Will you listen to it! Such nonsense.' Rachel squeezed Miles' hand. She had learned to limit her motherly affections in the face of growing opposition from this burgeoning young man. Yet bedtime rituals still prevailed, albeit at a suitably moderate level, and Rachel never failed to make the most of them. 'Goodnight, my heart.'

'Night, Ma.'

'Butterfly's for wimps,' Ralph stood at the door and grinned. 'Give me a tennis player any day!'

'And rugby player!' Miles added. 'Don't forget I'm down to play fly half with the Under-15s next term.'

'Great position. Even I didn't make fly half. I'm looking forward to seeing you play. Rugby's a man's game. No doubt about that! Sleep well, son. See you tomorrow.'

Outside Beth's room, Rachel turned to her husband and whispered: 'I think she's asleep. She's been on the go since dawn. She's exhausted, poor girl.'

Carefully, they opened the door and stepped inside. Unlike her brother's pit, Beth's room was immaculate. Her books were neatly catalogued on the shelves and favourite dolls from her childhood sat smartly underneath. The walls were plastered with pictures of The Beatles, with pride of place given to her idol, Paul McCartney. The open sleeve of Sergeant Pepper's Lonely Hearts Club Band was also pinned up on the wall. It was Beth's first teenage rebellion. Lucy in the Sky with Diamonds, one of the album tracks, had been banned in Rhodesia because it carried a subliminal message about LSD and hallucinogenic drugs. Beth was too young to know or care about the many social hazards that lay in wait for teenagers world-wide. She just liked the song. And she loved The Beatles.

Rachel crept up to the bed and gazed down at her daughter. Beth was fast asleep. Her mouth was open slightly, and her breath was soft and warm against the pillow. Her hair framed her face and, in the eyes of her doting mother, she looked like one of God's own angels. Overcome, Rachel bent down and pressed her lips against Beth's peachy skin.

'Goodnight, my darling angel,' she whispered. 'Sleep tight.'

Miles waited until he heard his parents' bedroom door click shut, and then he donned his headphones and turned up the radio. It was Radio Jacaranda, his favourite late night show. With a head full of rock and roll, Miles didn't hear the sound of Julius' voice. It was the frantic waving at the window that first alerted him to his friend's presence. He took off his headphones and winced at the loud crash of thunder and the cacophony of fine hailstones against the corrugated iron roof.

'Miles!'

Miles peered at the face at the window and frowned. 'What's up?'

'Nothing's up. There is a storm on its way. Baba said it would make a fine spectacle from the tree house.'

'Baba said that?' Miles was accustomed to the same exaggerated caution from Bliss and Moses as he got from his own parents. Such an endorsement of a fairly risky activity was most unusual. And not to be sneezed at, he decided, jumping out of bed and hitching up his pyjama bottoms. 'Hang on. I'll grab my coat.'

'Hurry. I'm getting soaked.'

'Sshh! You'll wake my parents. You go on ahead. I'll follow.'

Silently, Miles padded along the hall and unlocked the back door. He glanced at England who was asleep in the middle of the floor and grinned. Stupid dog. He had a lovely soft bed to sleep in, but insisted on sprawling in the middle of the kitchen where he invariably got under everyone's feet.

Miles let himself out and left the key hanging on the inside wall. He would need to sneak back in the following morning and it would be easier if the back door were unlocked. He skirted the house and, tugging his coat over his head, raced down to the kopje at the bottom of the garden. There, its roots entwined around the massive granite outcrop, the ancient fig tree loomed large. At the top was the boys' pride and joy. The tree house.

'Come on!' Julius peered over the edge of the structure and urged his friend to hurry.

Already the rain was falling steadily, interspersed with tiny hailstones. The sky was heavy with dense black clouds, while flashes of lightning broke up the darkness and cast wild lights over Scarfell Farm.

Miles shinnied up the rope ladder and fell into the tree house with a yelp of pain. 'Ow! That was my ankle!' He rubbed the spot where a bruise would form later. 'Hey, are you sure that baba is happy for you to be here. My parents would go berserk if they knew. You know we're not allowed up here in a storm. Ma reckons it's too dangerous.'

135

The two boys looked at each other and grinned. Their faces were streaked with rain and their clothes wet through. They nodded conspiratorially. The prospect of doing something illicit and dangerous was exhilarating, and any concerns they may have had were pushed to the back of their minds as they clambered over to the corner to wriggle into their sleeping bags. Warm and cosy, they settled down to wait for the full fury of the storm to descend upon Scarfell Farm.

The thunder grew loud and awesome, the lightning more terrifying and the hailstones larger and more destructive. The tree house shook with the wind, and its branches creaked and groaned with the weight. Mother Nature demonstrated her mighty powers with stupendous clarity and the two boys were exhilarated. They were about to start another glorious adventure. What more could they possibly want?

The storm raged on through the night and Rachel was restless. On one occasion she thought she heard the sound of glass breaking and went to investigate, but it was only the hailstones clattering against the window. She peered out into the darkness and saw white lightning splinter the sky and cast weird shadows across Scarfell.

She paused to peep into Beth's room and was relieved, if a little surprised, to see that her daughter was still asleep. It never ceased to amaze her how her children could snooze their way through even the most horrendous storms. They took after their father who, she often teased, would not notice if an atom bomb landed on his pillow.

She was just about to return to bed when she heard banging in the sitting room. She went to check and was appalled to discover that Ralph had left one of the doors unlocked. It had been torn open by the fierce winds and was now knocking against the jamb. Rachel shook her head crossly, and went to close it. She locked it then gave it a hearty tug so that it was properly secured.

'What's up?' Ralph stirred from his deep sleep.

'You left the sitting room door unlocked.' Rachel climbed into bed beside him.

'Did I?' Ralph was puzzled. 'Are you sure?'

'Of course I'm sure. I've just locked it myself.'

Ralph yawned and stretched, still half asleep, and then shrugged and pulled his wife into his arms. 'Funny... I could have sworn I'd locked it....'

'What a terrible night.' Rachel snuggled into the comfort of his embrace.

'Mmmm…'

She glanced at her husband who was now slipping back into oblivion and smiled. Sleep came easily to him. It was as though he did not have a care in the world. She, on the other hand, would lie awake for hours pondering recent events or fretting over some domestic trifle. It was a tedious affliction. She heard the sitting room door rattle again, but she resolved to ignore it. She would be up and down all night if she responded to every little noise.

What Rachel did not hear, but what she would most certainly have responded to if she had, was the sound of hushed voices outside the house. She did not hear, nor did she see, the dark shadows that lurked in the darkness. Nevertheless, Rachel was troubled, and even when she fell into a fitful slumber she was not at peace.

Outside the house, on the verandah, the dark shadows transformed themselves into men. One was short and stocky with bad teeth and hairy hands. He was carrying a sharpened machete. His partner was taller, but with the same thickset features and heavy muscular frame. He sported a pair of British NHS spectacles and an AK47 slung over his shoulder. The third man was Moses Khumalo. He, too, was carrying a deadly assault rifle.

'You said it would be open,' the short man hissed at Moses.

'It was open. Someone must have locked it.'

The men stood there, uncertain what to do next. Things were not going according to plan and it had thrown their careful strategy into chaos. They were drenched from the rain and their boots squelched noisily on the Rhodesian teak floor. But any noise they might have made was deadened by the angry clamour of the storm raging all around them.

'It's no good. We'll have to smash a window. They won't notice. They'll think it's hailstones.'

Moses caught the man's hand in mid-air. 'No!' he cried. 'The baas keeps a weapon in the bedroom. We must not alert him. The back door may be easier to prise open. And it is further away from the bedrooms. Come. There is no time to waste.'

Moses led his companions to the rear of the house. They moved quickly, shielding their heads from the hailstones, some of which were more than an inch in diameter. When they reached the entrance to the kitchen, Moses tried the door handle and was startled to find that it opened immediately.

'You must have unlocked the wrong door,' one of the terrorists said with a touch of contempt in his voice. Moses silenced him with a scathing glare and the man kept quiet after that.

In the gloom they almost tripped over the inert furry body sprawled in the centre of the kitchen floor. It was England. The young dog lay on his side with all four legs stretched out in front of him. His glossy coat, so lovingly brushed by Miles only hours before, shone like gold in the moonlight. He looked peaceful and at rest.

But England was not resting. He was dead. Killed by a slow acting poison administered by Moses Khumalo when he had come to the house earlier. Moses recalled how the dog had bounded up to him, tail wagging and big pink tongue lolling out of the side of his mouth. He had been impressed when the dog had dutifully sat to receive the treat offered. He could still picture England gazing up at him with huge, trusting eyes, panting with excitement while waiting obediently for the next command.

England did not even taste the poison as he wolfed down the chocolate morsel given to him by Moses. He was overjoyed to receive this unexpected attention and he gave Moses one of his finest licks with a very wet tongue. When Moses turned to go, England sat down, his tail brushing the floor from side to side, and whined after the man whom he had not recognised as a carrier of death.

'You take the door on the left of the hall. It is the daughter's room.' Moses addressed the taller man after shoving England's body aside with his foot. He turned to the other man: 'You and I will deal with the farmer and his wife.'

'What about the boy?'

Moses paused. 'I will take care of him myself.'

Silently, the three terrorists crept through the house. Their muddy boots and soaking wet coats left a mucky trail on the normally pristine floors and brightly-coloured South African rugs. They did not care. They were unimpressed by the meaningless vanities of white women.

The door to Beth's room was ajar and the taller man made his way towards it. As he drew closer, he could hear the soft murmurings and snuffles of a young girl deep in slumber. Inadvertently, his breath quickened and he ran his tongue over his lips.

'A clean kill,' Moses warned. 'Swift and clean. Do you understand?'

Thwarted, the man acknowledged the command with a surly smile and lifted his AK47 into position under his arm.

The door to Ralph and Rachel's room was closed. Moses clasped his rifle to his chest and waited while his companion opened it by leaning cautiously on the handle. It clicked and the white woman stirred in her bed. Both men waited until she had settled once more before entering the room.

A sudden fork of lightning illuminated their features, contorting their facial expressions and throwing up ghastly shadows so that they resembled strange visitations from hell. The lightning caught the edge of the machete's vicious blade and it glinted cruelly in the darkened room. They stood motionless, each anticipating the moment when they would kill the white farmer and his wife. They had been charged with the task of stepping up the war in Matabeleland. Bernard Mabeteya had entrusted them with this awesome responsibility. They would not fail him. They would not fail their African brothers.

Suddenly, the night was pierced by the terrified cry of a young girl, followed swiftly by the sharp report of a rifle and a strangled scream.

Ralph and Rachel woke in an instant and were half out of bed before they realised that they were not alone. Two evil shapes loomed large at the foot of the bed and one held an AK47 aimed directly at Ralph's head.

'Moses? What the …'

Ralph's query died in his throat as the bullet smashed straight into his temple. It travelled right through his skull and exited out of the back of his head. Suddenly, the pillows were covered in blood and clumps of brain matter. The wall behind the bed was also spattered with gore and Rachel screamed aloud.

'Beth!'

With the strength of a lioness fighting for her cubs, she pushed the man with the machete aside and raced for the door. She did not feel the blade slice through her fingers and was completely oblivious to her own blood spurting copiously from the wounds as she struggled to save her babies.

She saw the terrorist emerge from Beth's room and she noticed only that he was tall. She did not see the African behind her. She did not see him raise his evil weapon high above her head, nor witness that curiously salacious grin as he bought the machete crashing down upon her skull.

What she did see was a fierce white light.

What was that light? Was it the storm?

Then, almost instantly, the light was extinguished and a dense black cloud descended upon her as she fell to the ground. The wall prevented her from falling directly on to the floor. Instead she slid down it slowly, leaving a sickly smear of blood on the fresh white paint. And then she came to rest in a grotesque sitting position, crumpled and broken and bloody, in a peculiar parody of life.

But there was no life left in Rachel Cameron. All that was left was a bloodied corpse. A corpse that had once been a beloved wife and mother and the mistress of Scarfell Farm.

'What about the boy?'

You go on,' Moses spat out the words. 'I will kill him myself.'

The two men left, disappearing into the night. Once they were gone, Moses went into Miles' room and stared at the empty bed with the poster of Olivia Newton-John above it. He glanced without emotion at the white boy's possessions. Calmly, he wandered round the room. He flicked open a scrapbook full of pictures and press cuttings of heroes from the South African Currie Cup matches, he fingered the half-finished model of a Samurai warrior and gazed at the deflated orange ball he knew was once called "Chuff". And then Moses raised his AK47, fired a single shot into the air and left the room.

There had been enough killing for one night. The war would come to Matabeleland soon enough after this night's deed. He did not need to kill the boy to bring terror to the white population of Bulawayo. They would live in terror from this day forth. And they would die in terror as victims of this chimurenga until the time came when the African was able to reclaim the land that was rightfully his.

Moses left the house and slipped into the shadows. Later that night he would cross the border into Zambia. He would wait there until the time was right and it was safe to return to his homeland. He had demonstrated great courage this night. He had accomplished his mission without cowardice, and yet had managed to spare the boy. The deaths of the others were necessary. They would serve the cause. In that matter, his conscience was clear.

Centuries before this night of the slaying, and in a land far from Africa, Niccolo Machiavelli, had issued a stark warning to all engaged in conflict. But Moses Khumalo had never heard of the great military strategist and so could not heed the wisdom of Machiavelli's advice that, if you kill Brutus, you must be sure to kill the sons of Brutus, too.

'Did you hear that?' Miles sat up and glanced around him.

'What?' Julius had fallen asleep. He now peered groggily at his friend's back and sighed. 'It is just the storm. There are many strange noises tonight.'

'It sounded just like a shot being fired. Just before that, I thought I heard a scream.'

'It was most likely branches cracking and falling from the trees. There will be much devastation tonight. I, too, heard the scream. Hyenas out in the bush. They're probably injured by hail and falling debris. You know how human they sound.'

Miles drew his knees up to his chest and pulled the sleeping bag up to his chin. 'It's one helluva storm,' he declared. 'Just look at the size of those hailstones. They're like golf balls.'

Fully awake now, Julius shrugged off his sleeping bag and crawled over to the wall of the tree house. The structure was sturdy and yet it rocked alarmingly in the gale. Julius peered over the edge, screwing up his eyes against the ferocious wind and rain.

He was completely naked and his back was curved and supple as he leaned over to see the ground. His buttocks were hard and firm, like two flat brown stones, and his legs were finely muscled. Julius had not inherited his father's ebony skin. His was a warm caramel colour.

Not a bad looking dude, Miles conceded as he lay there waiting for his friend's report on the storm's progress. A pity Julius was black and would probably end up paying some extortionate lobola, or bride price, for a maiden from the kraals. They would have loads of kids and Julius would grow fat and bored and probably drink himself to death outside his local shebeen.

Not the sort of future he would want for his friend, Miles decided, but one that was the destiny of many black Africans. Perhaps Julius would not need to tread the same sorry path as other Africans. There would always be a good job and a home for him here at Scarfell. And for his family, too. One day, Miles would be the master of Scarfell Farm. It would be his duty to protect those he cared about.

'There is much devastation,' Julius crawled back to his sleeping bag. 'It is not surprising that you are troubled by strange noises. Two of the marulas have splintered and I think the truck's windscreen might be shattered.'

'Do you think we ought to get down? It's pretty dangerous up here.'

Julius cast a scornful glance at his companion's uncharacteristic timidity. 'It will take more than a sprinkling of rain to destroy this old tree. This tree was here before you and I were born. It will be here long after you and I are dead. This much I know for sure.' Julius wriggled into the bag and pulled it tight across his chest. 'I would not miss this night for all of King Lobengula's diamonds. We will tell our children tales of this night one day.'

'That's if we survive to tell any tales at all,' Miles complained. 'Besides, it's cold. This old bag's lining's all chewed up and ripped inside. It's all right for you. Your bag's in much better condition.'

'You whinge like an old woman,' Julius chided. 'Yet you tell me you are a man. You would not be allowed to whinge like that if you were a son of Mzilikazi.'

Miles pulled a face and turned on his side. 'I'm not a son of Mzilikazi,' he grumbled against his pillow. 'I'm a son of the Camerons. And I'm bloody well freezing!'

Julius knuckled his friend playfully in the back of the neck and grinned as he lay down on the hard wooden floor. For a white boy, Miles was unusually daring and adventurous, but, like all white boys, he was soft. He could not cope with the rigours of the real Africa. He needed his European comforts such as feather pillows and a sprung mattress. But it was no matter. Miles was his friend. His blood brother. He would accept these occasional weaknesses for, apart from those, Miles was a fine warrior. And a fine friend.

Miles curled up into a foetal position and closed his eyes. He was cold and uncomfortable, and he began to regret his decision to spend such an inclement night outside the comfort of his own bed. His parents would be livid if they knew. He resolved to sneak back into the house well before the family rose for breakfast or he would never hear the last of it.

Fully awake, Miles lay listening to the torrential rain, to the mighty rolls of thunder and the animals' cries, and he shivered. He dreaded the desolation that he would find when the storm had finally passed for it was certainly wreaking havoc in its path.

Suddenly his hand began to ache. He opened his eyes and peered at the old childhood wound. It was a pale pink scar, which ran from one side of his palm to the other, just below the crease of his fingers.

He remembered at time when he and Julius were children and had indulged in an ancient ritual of friendship here in the tree house. Following that ritual, they had become blood brothers. This would never change, for the blood of each boy now flowed through the veins of the other. It was a comforting thought, Miles decided, attempting to shut out the raging tempest. It was good to have a brother.

Yet, in spite of this pleasing thought, he was troubled and could not rest. The palm of his hand throbbed uncomfortably and he rubbed it with his fingers. It was an old wound, long since healed, but it pained him tonight.

He glanced at Julius. The young Matabele had been a fine brother over the years and always would be. Such minor pain was a small price to pay for kinship. They were blood brothers, Miles Cameron and Julius Khumalo. And they had the scars to prove it.

What they did not know as they lay side by side on that terrible night, was that the scars of their blood brotherhood would pain them for the rest of their lives.

8

England was buried in a part of the garden where the manicured lawn met the open bush. His burial had been a simple affair. Miles and Sixpence had dug the grave together. They had made sure it was deep enough to thwart any scavengers that might choose to investigate it.

Miles had knelt down and smoothed the earth into hard cake, patting the mound with his bare hands until he was satisfied. It was hot in the noon sun and he paused to wipe the sweat from his eyes with the back of his hand. The movement left a trail of dirt across his forehead that gave him a curiously warlike appearance. But there was nothing warlike in his attitude as he knelt over the grave, manfully trying to conceal the sobs that wracked his body and caused his shoulders to shake involuntarily.

Sixpence leaned on his shovel and waited patiently for the boy to finish his task. Baas Miles needed to honour his faithful hound. Sixpence could respect that. He had taken it upon himself to watch over this son of the house of Cameron in the dark days ahead. Demons had visited Scarfell Farm under the cover of night and destroyed the safe world where the boy had once dwelt. Nothing would be the same again. There would be much suffering in the time to come, but Sixpence swore upon the graves of his ancestors that he would protect Miles Cameron from further harm, even if it meant sacrificing his own life to do so. Henceforth, he would be the guardian of a young man who had been dealt a cruel blow and was stumbling blindly on life's treacherous path.

Less than a week later, Miles stood once more beside England's grave. His hands were thrust deep into the pockets of his school uniform and he loosened his tie, pulling the shirt collar open at the top. The sun beat down mercilessly on his head and he pulled his cap over his eyes for protection against the heat. His mother would have been pleased with him today. She preferred him to wear a hat in the sun.

Absently, he pushed the loose stones back into place with his foot. Immediately, the red dust billowed around his shoes and dulled the shiny black polish that Sixpence had applied with such vigour only a couple of hours ago. Try as he might, Miles could not maintain a pristine appearance for long. His sister, Beth, on the other hand, was always neat and clean. Such clean hands, Miles observed. And clean fingernails, too. Even when she was just a little baby.

Her hands had been scrubbed clean the last time he had seen her. They had folded them across her chest in the shape of a cross. Beth would have liked that. Everything was neat and tidy in her little coffin. Beth was always very tidy. They had combed her hair and arranged it in thick golden curls across the satin pillow. She would have liked that, too. It made her look like Ophelia, the floating maiden in the Pre-Raphaelite painting by Millais.

Miles closed his eyes and swallowed the lump that lodged at the back of his throat. In spite of his efforts to concentrate on the image of his sister at peace, his thoughts were dragged elsewhere. His tortured mind refused to free him from the terrifying scenes that had awaited him as he crept back into the house the morning after the storm.

He had grinned when he spotted England bunched up against the kitchen cupboard in an ungainly heap. Briefly, he had wondered why the dog had chosen to sleep in such an uncomfortable position, but he quickly saw that England was not sleeping and he had called out for his mother in alarm. He had knelt down, hot tears spilling down his cheeks, and pushed hopelessly at the dog's lifeless belly with the palm of his hand.

"Mum!" He had yelled again.

But no-one answered.

At the time he had felt guilty about waking up the sleeping household. He was also worried about having to confess that he had slept outside in the storm. But then came the truth, which carried with it a far greater pain.

His beloved England lay dead at his feet and he did not know why. He cried out once more and then, panicked by the unnerving silence, he got to his feet and ran through the house.

He had stumbled across his mother first. She was sitting on the floor, her battered head lolling awkwardly against her chest. Miles was sickened by the smears of blood on the wall and the gruesome stumps where the tops of her fingers had been sliced off. He leaned against the opposite wall, overwhelmed by nausea.

He had been unable to look upon that gruesome image of the woman who was his mother. Instead, he had inched past nervously and hurled himself into Beth's room. His sister lay on her back with the lower half of her body still covered by a sheet. Her upper torso had twisted to one side and her head hung over the edge of the mattress. Miles stared in horror at the dark red blood on the floor. There was such a lot of blood. There was blood all over his sister.

He fell to his knees fighting for breath. He tried to cry out, but no sound came. Somewhere, in the far, far distance, he thought he heard a child screaming. It sounded like his voice, but he did not think it could be him. Surely he was too tired to scream. He felt desperately, unutterably tired. His head started to spin and he keeled over, embracing the opportunity to escape from this terrible nightmare.

'Are you ready, Miles dear?'

Miles patted the last clod of earth into place on England's grave and spun round to face his aunt. She looked pale and haggard. He knew that she had always been close to his mother, but he had not realised the extent of her loss.

'As ready as I'll ever be,' he shrugged.

In a rare display of emotion, Clara rubbed his cheek with her thumb then laid her hand lightly on his shoulder as they walked back towards the house. She did not speak, but Miles could sense her despair. She seemed to have shrunk in stature, her naturally slim frame now thin and gaunt. She wore the same black dress that she had worn to Rose Cameron's funeral. It was an ideal outfit for a funeral and it had fitted her well in the past. Now it hung from her bony shoulders and accentuated her pallor.

The drive at Scarfell Farm was crammed with cars and trucks, each parked bumper to bumper. Dozens of people were milling about the house, or huddled together in tense, miserable groups. Some were whispering, others shook their heads in disbelief or stared gloomily at the floor. Most were silent, not knowing what to say.

It was strange to see so many friends and neighbours dressed in black, Miles observed as he and Clara approached. It was a dismal colour. His grandmother had always hated it. He noticed that old Sandy Fitzgerald was wearing his maroon Rotary Club blazer with its international emblem sewn on to the breast pocket. It set him apart from the sombre citizens and he wore it with pride as a tribute to one of Bulawayo's finest families.

As he passed by, Miles could see tears in Sandy Fitzgerald's eyes. His normally florid complexion was even more blotched and reddened than usual. He was clutching a handkerchief and Miles turned away, anxious that he might have to deal with a grown man's grief. He could not bear to see a grown man crying. Men only cried when something truly awful had happened.

But something truly awful had happened here at Scarfell Farm. And today would always be remembered as a truly awful day in the life of Miles Ewan Cameron. For today was the day that he would be asked to bury his entire family in the dark, red earth of the land they had dared to call their home.

Grandpa George was staring out of the window at the far end of the dining room. Although surrounded by fellow mourners, he stood alone in the crowded room. Miles had not seen his grandfather cry and he was grateful for the senior man's strength. But there was something in the way old George Bentley held his head that hinted at the full awesome extent of his loss. Gone was the tall, straight back and squared shoulders of this former scientist and renowned academic. Gone was the kindly smile and the mischievous twinkle in his eyes that his daughter, Rachel, had inherited. George Bentley had metamorphosed overnight into a frail old man. An old man who had somehow survived to see his daughter and her family wiped out by hatred in a harsh and distant land.

Sitting beside him, lost in her own grief, was his wife, Doris. She could not conceal her pain and shreds of damp tissues lay in her lap. She fiddled with the corners of the tissues, winding them into little cones or tearing them into even smaller pieces. Sometimes she simply stared out of the window, twisting her wedding ring round and round on her finger until the skin underneath grew red and sore.

She glanced up as Miles and Clara approached, hastily wiping her nose and crumpling loose pieces of tissue into a ball. She smiled warmly at her grandson, this lone survivor of the massacre, and held out her arms to enfold the boy in a loving embrace. She nodded at Clara over her grandson's shoulder, but there was little warmth in their exchange. Doris had never been overly fond of the woman – too cold and haughty by far – but she was grateful for any kindness given to Miles at this terrible time. And there was little doubt that Clara had been a tower of strength in the days following the slaying.

Slowly, the mourners parted to allow the boy and his English grandparents to pass. It was time for him to bury his parents and little sister. And they all knew that there would be no avoiding this onerous responsibility.

Slowly, silently, the mourners climbed the hill beyond the milking parlour, crossing the top field that Ralph had finally managed to turn over to maize. On top of the ridge, in sight of the magnificent Blue Hills and in the shade of the old marula tree, the grave was waiting.

The mourners gathered together at the top of the hill to watch as the three coffins were carefully lowered into the grave. There they would lie, side by side, for all eternity. Beth's white coffin nestled between those of her parents. Miles had asked for that. He wanted his sister to be placed in the middle where she would feel safe.

He stared down into the gaping hole, and felt a tinge of envy. For Beth there would be no more suffering. She would never know the torment of loss and loneliness. She would lie here with their beloved parents in this quiet, safe place while he, Miles, would have to walk away and bear the agony of bereavement and a lifetime of tormented memories.

Hot tears rolled down his cheeks as he listened to the prayers for the dead. They were going to a better place, he was told, a place where they would be happy and at peace in the shelter of the Lord. A place where there was no war, hatred or pain. A place where they would be together forever.

Miles glanced over his shoulder. The house, the beautiful land of Scarfell Farm and all that was within it, was now his alone. It was a horrible, daunting prospect. His vision blurred and he closed his eyes wishing with all his heart that he, too, could rest in peace with his family.

He sighed deeply and returned to the task in hand. It was time to say goodbye. Time to leave the three people he loved most in this world and walk away. For Miles' destiny did not lie with them. His destiny was here in the world and his duty was to his father's cherished land and to the memory of the Camerons of Scarfell Farm.

He scooped up a handful of dry earth and held his closed fist aloft, crinkling his eyes against the glare of the African sun. Silently, he made his solemn pledge to the spirits of his mother, his father and his sister. He would find their killers. He did not know how or when, but he would not rest until someone was called upon to pay the price for this evil deed.

Slowly, he opened his fingers and released the red dust. As it drifted down to earth, it glittered like a million powdered rubies in the sunlight. Miles waited until a thin layer of dust had settled upon each of the three coffins before turning away and wiping his eyes with the back of his hand.

His job was done. He had buried his family. Now he had a promise to keep.

The African farm labourers and servants stood in a ragged bunch at the bottom of the hill. A couple of the women keened softly. The men stood with their heads bowed. They removed their hats as the mourners approached and lowered their eyes.

Bliss stood with her hand resting lightly on her son's arm. Her hair was hidden beneath a black scarf and she wore her black and white uniform with pride. She had washed and pressed it the way the Madam liked it and had repaired the tear in the apron that she had been meaning to deal with for some time. Her beautiful big brown eyes glistened with tears that she dried from time to time on the corner of her apron.

Julius stood at least a head taller than his mother. His hands hung limply at his sides and he stared at the floor, absently poking a chongololo with his toe. He was no longer a child, had long since lost the sweet innocence of the early years, and yet he felt like a child again. The sense of powerlessness, bewilderment and fear that had plagued him as a boy had returned to haunt him.

A terrible catastrophe had occurred on the night of the storm and Julius felt that in some inexplicable way he had contributed to it. He did not know why, but he was troubled by guilt and it would not leave him.

If he had not persuaded Miles to sleep in the tree house that night, then Miles would have been there to protect his parents from harm. But then, if Miles had stayed in the house, he, too, might have been massacred in his own bed. Julius would never know which of these possibilities was the most likely, but he felt sure that he would agonise over it for the rest of his life.

And then there was the question of who did the deed. Fingers were pointing at his father who was not here to defend himself. The police had already been to their kia and ransacked it in search of evidence. They found nothing, but that did not free his father from the shadow of suspicion.

Even Julius, who could not bring himself to associate his own father with such horror, could not understand why Moses had disappeared during the night of the slaying. No-one knew where he had gone. No-one knew for certain why he had left so hurriedly. But most were ready to hazard a guess. And few believed they were wrong.

Julius had been the first to hear Miles' cry for help and he had rushed into the house to find his friend unconscious. Bliss, too, had heard the screams as she arrived to begin her breakfast duties. She had burst into the kitchen to find England dead at her feet and she had buried her face in her hands in fear of what more was to come.

'Where is Baba?' Julius had demanded.

'I do not know,' she had replied. 'He was not with me when I woke up this morning. I do not know where he is.'

'Well find him quickly!' barked Julius. 'Something terrible has happened here!'

Bliss had hurried off to search for her husband. But she did not find him. Moses Khumalo had fled in the night and was well on his way to the Zambian border. The fight for freedom had taken precedence over the love he bore his own son. He had committed himself to the cause irrevocably. Family affections did not count. He had made his choice. There was no turning back.

Bliss was also thinking of Moses as she stood there watching Miles make his way down the hill ahead of the mourners. She did not really miss her husband. He had always been a distant figure in her life. The responsibilities of a home and children had always fallen on her shoulders, as was the way in Africa, and she did not fear the burden of loneliness. What she did fear was poverty. The Camerons had given them a home, an income, and had paid for schooling for Julius. Without the Camerons there would be no money or security and, although Bliss did not fear the prospect of destitution for herself, she could not bear to expose her beloved son to the same ignominy.

And then there were the whispers. People were saying that Moses had killed the Camerons. Why else would he disappear? Bliss shuddered at the thought. It was not possible that the man she had lived with all these years, the man who was her husband and father to Julius, was responsible for the deaths of the Madam and her family. Miss Beth had been killed in her own bedroom. It was inconceivable that her husband would dare to enter the young Madam's bedroom at night. It was not possible. He could not have been the killer. Besides, he would never have left his own family to face the cruel accusations alone. Would he? And surely he would not put their home and their livelihood at risk. It simply could not be true. It was not possible.

She was worried about master Miles, too. She loved him dearly, had nursed him as a baby and watched with pride as he grew into manhood. She could not bear to see his distress. She wanted to ease his pain and, turning to her own son, she whispered: 'Baas Miles will need our love and support now, my son. He is alone in this world.'

'I am his blood brother, Mama,' Julius replied. 'He will never be alone in this world as long as I am alive.'

'That is good,' Bliss stroked the sinewy forearm. 'For even though his family are now safe in the hands of the Lord, I fear that there is more to come. I do not know why, but I see great suffering ahead for our young Master.'

'We will all suffer from the consequences of this day, Mama.'

'Yes, but there is darkness about baas Miles now. Do you not see it? Do you not see how it hangs heavily upon him?'

'No Mama,' Julius patted his mother's trembling hand. 'I do not see it. But I do not doubt that it is there. My brother is lost in the valley of the shadows, but he is not alone. I am with him, for I am lost too. If we stay together, we will find our way out into the light. I am certain of that.'

Julius watched the mourners making their way down the hill. Miles led the way, followed closely by his grandparents. Julius saw them reach out to steady him when he stumbled, but he walked alone. There was an invisible wall around their grandson. They tried, but they could not penetrate it. They could not ease his grief.

Julius drew a deep breath and swallowed hard. It was hard to witness such pain. He loved Miles as a brother. He had rejoiced with him in his childhood victories and commiserated with his childish woes. But nothing could compare with this. Nothing had prepared them for this. Julius shook his head angrily. He knew he could not take away the pain his friend was feeling, but he could most certainly share in it.

Miles approached the group of servants and labourers who were waiting to pay their respects and he lifted his head and straightened his shoulders. Hastily, he brushed the hair from his forehead and wiped the tears from his cheeks. He could see them all waiting for him, watching him, and he felt sick.

He knew it was his duty to thank them for their tributes, for their loyal service to his father and mother, but he did not think he could do it. They were African and his entire family had been slaughtered in support of black Africa. Miles did not know who he could trust any more. An innocent family had been wiped out, people who had cared for black Africa. A young girl who had grown up among them not knowing that she was destined to die at their hands. He could not smile at the faces that watched him now. In his eyes, any one of them may have contributed to those horrible crimes. He could not now be expected to smile and thank them for standing there while he buried his family.

Even so, his resolve weakened a little when Joseph stepped forward with his head bowed and his eyes downcast.

'Go well, baas Miles.' It was all he had to say, but it spoke volumes.

'Stay well, Joseph.' Miles paused and whispered in response.

Miles also had to acknowledge Bliss who stood sobbing in the crowd. He did not bear her ill will. He knew how devoted she was to his mother, and how she adored young Beth. And then Sixpence appeared at the back of the group and Miles smiled weakly for the first time. He turned to face them, slipping unconsciously into their native Sindebele.

'Thank you for coming to pay your respects today.'

There was a murmur of approval from the men and audible sighs from the women. Satisfied that he had done his duty, Miles turned to go, but a movement to his left caught his eye. He swung round to face Julius who had stepped forward from the group and was now standing before him.

'I share your pain, my brother,' Julius said quietly. 'And I want you to know that I am ready to travel this hard road at your side.'

Miles said nothing, but his eyes darkened and his teeth clenched. Instinctively, his breathing grew shallow and his hands formed tight knotted balls at his sides. He drew himself up to match Julius, who stood an inch or so above him, and then their gaze locked, shutting out all else, and there was silence.

Neither boy spoke. Neither boy smiled. The tension became so intense that one of the women cried out in fear. But neither boy heard.

Julius had managed to penetrate the valley of the shadows where Miles had walked alone, and he knew now that he was not welcome there. It was a private place. And he was an intruder.

'My pain is my own,' Miles hissed. 'You do not share it with me. I'll never let you share it with me. Your father caused this pain. We both know that. Your father killed my family.'

'But you are my blood brother...'

'No!' Miles shouted in anger. 'You are not my brother. You are my enemy. And your father is my enemy.'

'I am not your enemy,' Julius replied calmly. 'I am on your side. I am also a victim of these crimes. I, too, need answers.'

Miles was shaking now. 'I can give you all the answers you need. It's simple. Your father killed my family and you knew about it. You knew, damn you! You thought you would save my life by persuading me to sleep in the tree house that night. Didn't you? You needed at least one of the Camerons around to keep you and your family in work. Huh? Well you'll rue the day that you let me live, you bastard, because I'm going to make you pay for this shit. You'll be sorry you tricked me out of my bed that night. I swear it!'

The words shot out into the crowd and Bliss broke down and collapsed in a heap on the floor. The women fussed around her as she sobbed uncontrollably into her apron.

Miles ignored her and turned to leave. Pausing to look over his shoulder, he added: 'Don't give me that crap about walking the same road as me, Julius Khumalo, because that road only leads to one place. It leads to your father's death. Understood?'

It was Charlie who took Miles' arm and led him away from that awful confrontation, but not before Miles had pledged his revenge: 'As God is my witness, Julius Khumalo, son of Moses, your father will pay for this bloody deed. And I will live to see him pay!'

Doris Bentley adjusted the fold of her blouse and sat down. She was grateful for the elasticated waist on her Marks & Spencers skirt that gave a little as she moved and accommodated her increasing girth. Anxiously, she patted her silver-grey curls then sat, straight-backed in the chair, twisting her wedding ring on her finger. Her husband, George, was watching her and his heart went out to her. She was nervous. It was plain for all to see.

In spite of those additional inches, which she bemoaned on a regular basis, George still saw the sweet, vulnerable creature he had fallen in love with all those years ago. Her creamy complexion was now etched with lines, and there was a fine down on her cheeks, but he loved her all the more for that. She had been a wonderful wife, and a truly good woman. Surely, she did not deserve the appalling agony she was now being forced to endure.

Charlie and Clara sat opposite on the sofa. In spite of their physical proximity, there was a deep, unassailable chasm between them. Clara leaned forward, perched awkwardly on the edge. Charlie sprawled in the other corner, one arm draped over the back of the sofa, the other lolling over the side with a cigarette dangling from his fingers.

'Thanks for coming,' George began. 'Doris and I feel that we have a lot to talk about so it might be better if we got started straight away.'

'None of us could think clearly yesterday,' Doris added. 'We all had … other things on our minds, I'm sure.'

'So what is there to talk about?' Charlie tipped the ash into his saucer. 'Scarfell goes to Miles, lock, stock and barrel, you can be sure of that. You won't find any loose ends in my brother's will. Everything shipshape, that's how he liked it. He's always been like that. Even when we were kids …'

Charlie paused and looked away. He swallowed awkwardly and drew on the butt of his cigarette. Clara glanced at him. She understood that he was grieving for his brother, even though he would never show any emotion, but she did not feel any sympathy for him. He had devastated her mentally, destroying all compassion in the process. She could not pity him now. She barely had the strength to despise him.

'We're not querying our grandson's inheritance,' Doris retorted. 'It's his well-being we're concerned about!'

'Hush now, dear.' George intervened. 'You mustn't upset yourself. Charlie is simply confirming what we already knew. Ralph was a fine father who would never leave his affairs in disarray. I'm sure we are all grateful for that.'

'So what is there to talk about?' Charlie stood up and went to pour himself a drink. The Bentleys seemed to think that a cup of tea would solve everything. He, on the other hand, needed something a little stronger. Filling the tumbler, he turned and strode over to the fireplace. He did not want to sit down, preferring to tower over old George Bentley and thus gain a minor psychological advantage. That, coupled with the glass of courage in his hand, would help him to deal with whatever the old man had to throw at him.

He had no idea what to expect, or what it was they wanted to talk about, but he felt sure it would be critical. He had never liked Rachel's parents, wasn't too keen on the British in general, barring Rachel of course, and felt sure that they didn't really like him either for one reason or another. He would listen to what they had to say, for the boy's sake if nothing else, but he was not going to change his ways. He would look after Miles as his appointed guardian. It was his duty, and a privilege for he had always been fond of the lad, but he did not have to change in order to take care of his own nephew. He was not going to become a saint. His brother would not have wanted him to. He was certain of that.

'We would like to discuss Miles' future,' George said softly, aware of the other man's agitation. 'Doris and I think it would be better if he came home with us, to England. As his guardian, we wanted to hear what you think. Obviously, we want what's best for our grandson.'

'I can tell you what's best for your grandson,' Charlie snorted. 'What's best for your grandson is that you leave well alone and don't go uprooting the boy and dragging him off to that godforsaken place.'

'We shan't be "dragging him off" as you put it,' Doris was offended. 'We are simply trying to do the right thing. My daughter is dead. The boy's mother is dead. You can't expect him to stay here and fend for himself.'

'Who's letting him fend for himself? I'll be here to keep an eye on him. She'll be here,' Charlie nodded at his wife. 'He won't have to "fend for himself" as you put it!'

'What about the farm?' George tried to steer the conversation into a more practical domain.

'I'll run it,' Charlie declared flatly. 'I'll give up my job and I'll run it.'

'You don't know the first thing about farming,' said Doris. 'How on earth do you expect to run a farm and bring up a young lad when you don't know anything about either responsibility? It's madness!'

'I was born and raised on this farm,' Charlie snarled, slugging the last of the brandy. 'And so was Miles. We're Rhodesians born and bred. There's no way that a Cameron would want to walk away from all this to live on your damp little island!'

'There are opportunities in England for a young man with his talents.'

'Opportunities? Are you telling me that he can own twelve thousand acres of prime farming land over there? Not a hope in hell and you know it. This is where he belongs. And this is where he is going to stay!'

'Perhaps we ought to ask Miles.' Clara's hushed tones cut through the tension and the others swung round to face her.

'That sounds like a good idea. I wouldn't mind having a say in my own future.' Miles entered the room and went to stand beside his grandmother's chair. 'I know you've got my interests at heart, Nana, and that you and Gramps want what's best for me, but Charlie is right. I belong here. It's my duty to look after Scarfell Farm just like my dad and his dad did before me. I don't want to leave the place to rot. I owe it to my parents to stay and keep Scarfell alive. And if oom Charlie will help me, then so much the better, although I'll do it on my own if I have to.'

'You don't have to worry about that, lad,' Charlie grinned at the boy. 'We can move back in here, Clara and me. Clara's always fancied herself as a farmer's wife, haven't you? So you see, you won't be on your own. I can promise you that. We're Camerons, you and me. We're part of Scarfell Farm, and it'll take more than a bunch of kaffirs to get rid of us. Eh?'

Doris squeezed her grandson's hand and looked up with him with anxious eyes. 'Please don't make any hasty decisions, Miles. Take a few days to think about it. Gramps and I aren't leaving today. There's no need to make your mind up immediately. Just think about it, darling.'

'Your grandmother's right, son,' George agreed. 'Take your time. You don't want to make the wrong decision. Rhodesia is on the brink of civil war - your uncle will be the first to agree with that, I'm sure. It's just not safe here any more, and it's going to get worse. You're young. You're white. You're an obvious target. If you come back with us, you can finish your schooling in Shropshire and maybe go on to agricultural college. You know yourself that white farmers here choose to send their sons to study in England. You'll simply be following a tradition.'

'If I leave now, Gramps, I might never be able to come home again.' Miles frowned at the older man, pleading with him to understand. 'I couldn't bear that. Don't you see that I have to stay? This is my home. This is where I belong.'

George Bentley looked at his grandson without saying a word. For a few seconds he was transported back in time. It was Christmas 1965. Victoria Falls. A young boy was patiently explaining the Camerons' family history to a rather dim old Gramps who was clearly getting confused between the various African tribes. But Miles had persevered, certain that Gramps would be able to grasp it in the end. And, sure enough, in spite of being perfectly ancient in the eyes of a five-year-old child, Gramps had understood.

He had understood that the boy was proud to belong to such an old and distinguished family. He understood that, although they were a white family, the Camerons were first and foremost Africans. "White Matabeles" as Ralph had often said. The Camerons had lived in this part of Africa for generations. Now it was Miles' turn to keep alive that proud tradition.

And the boy would not fail in his duty. George understood that now. Miles believed that he owed it to his parents to carry on where they had left off. It may be a foolish undertaking, dangerous even, and so very difficult, but this was something the boy had to do. He did not have a choice. He was a Cameron, after all.

On 25th June 1975, the Portuguese colonial government in Mozambique handed over power to FRELIMO, the Front for the Liberation of Mozambique, led by Samora Machel.

The country was in chaos. The Portuguese had fled in droves, fearing the consequences of black majority rule. On the day that Samora Machel celebrated independence, only thirty-six doctors remained to serve a nation of more than twelve million people. The whites had deserted the country, taking their expertise and their cash with them. FRELIMO inherited a country devastated by years of civil war and bankrupt of all the necessary skills to repair it.

Fearing a backlash from the Rhodesia crisis on their doorsteps, President Vorster called for urgent talks with the Zambian President Kaunda. Both were leaders of front-line states with Rhodesia, and both could see the value of easing the tension across their borders before it escalated beyond their control. With this in mind, Vorster called for urgent talks with Ian Smith's government and members of the ANC.

It was not easy to draw the two sides together. The whites had refused to attend any talks which took place in Zambia, and the blacks would not agree to a meeting held on Rhodesian soil. Eventually, a compromise was reached whereby the conference would take place on the railway bridge that spanned the Zambesi River and linked the Zambian border with that of Rhodesia.

The railway carriages were donated by South African Railways and were positioned at the exact centre of the bridge. A white line was drawn across the table in the central coach, so that neither delegation would inadvertently set foot on hostile territory. It was not an auspicious beginning.

Kaunda and Vorster opened the conference together with talk of immediate majority rule. Smith refused to participate in the debate, claiming that he would not negotiate with terrorists. Muzorewa, leader of the ANC delegation, then raised the complex issue of immunity. Again, Smith refused to participate. Finally, Joshua Nkomo, frustrated by the attitude of the white delegation claimed that nothing could cross the white line 'not even ideas'.

The conference was abandoned.

Miles spent the 'Rhodes and Founders' holiday weekend at the Llewellyns' home in Bulawayo. He had grown closer to the family in the weeks following the tragedy and welcomed the chance to spend a few days with them.

Scarfell Farm was full of tragic memories and it was still too early for Miles to feel completely at ease there. Charlie and Clara had moved in and, although Miles welcomed the company, he was acutely aware of the friction that came with them. Try as they might to conceal their marital difficulties, the atmosphere between them was cool and served only to reinforce the air of gloom that clung to the house.

Life at the Llewellyns' was happier, more reminiscent of the family life he had once known. Here, he could cope with the tormented thoughts that plagued him at night alone in his bed. Here, he could rest his troubled mind and be a boy again.

The annual Rhodes and Founders holiday was in honour of the early pioneers who had first settled in Rhodesia. Known colloquially as "Rogues and Bounders" weekend it occurred on the second Monday and Tuesday in July. It was a popular four-day break in the middle of winter and was celebrated by adults and children alike.

This year, the early morning frost had given way to unusually hot sunshine and a clear blue sky. Miles had taken advantage of the fine weather to enjoy a swim in the Llewellyns' pool. Having completed twenty lengths, he hauled himself out and grabbed a towel from the back of the chair. He shook the excess water from his hair and then proceeded to rub himself dry.

At five feet nine he was not tall, but his body was lean and muscular with a natural tan. The dark curly hairs forming on his chest, arms and legs emphasised his burgeoning manhood and the manner in which his swimming trunks clung to his hips merely enhanced to his appeal. Miles Cameron was a handsome young man. He had inherited his uncle's chocolate brown eyes and almost girlishly long lashes, and he had the Camerons' nose. But the determined set of his jaw and the sideways grin was his father's. There was no doubt about that.

In spite of his physical attractions, Miles, like his father before him, was a quiet, unassuming fellow. He was modest, too, almost to the point of self-deprecation. It was a quality that had already begun to intrigue Bulawayo's female society who had been quick to spot the combination of a rugged masculinity and boyish insecurity. Unbeknown to Miles, he was often a topic of conversation in St Hilda's school dormitories at night, and an audible sigh would ripple through the female contingent at the local tennis club when he took to the court in his white shorts.

But such matters were of little interest to Miles as he draped the damp towel over the back of his chair and sat down. He crossed his legs underneath him and reached for his copy of 'The Taking of Pelham 123'. The film told the story of the hijacking of a New York subway train and it had been a huge box office success in Salisbury. Rhodesia's censors, anxious to protect young people from its graphic violence and subversive message, had banned the paperback version on the grounds that teenagers were more likely to have access to it. Although it was illegal to buy, sell or display the cheaper copy, the hardback version was available to

Rhodesians of any age and Miles had been able to borrow Charlie's copy quite easily.

He settled down to read and was quickly engrossed in the story so that he did not hear Lydia approach. She was barefoot and wearing a bright red swimsuit with a halter-neck top. Her step was light and dainty, like a kitten, and she pounced on him with a squeal of delight.

'Boo!'

Miles ducked to avoid any missile that might accompany the attack then flicked the top of her head as she dropped on to the ground in front of him.

'What are you reading?' Lydia sucked on the peach she was carrying. Tilting her head back, she swallowed a mouthful of fruit and then wiped the juice from her chin with the back of her hand. Miles showed her the front cover of his book. 'Wow! Did you buy that?'

'No,' Miles closed the book and put it on the table. 'It's oom Charlie's.'

'Does he know you've borrowed it?'

'No, but I don't think he'd care if he did.'

'I don't suppose he would,' Lydia agreed, finishing the peach. 'He's not a stickler for rules and regulations, your uncle!'

'He's good at breaking them,' Miles replied with a wry smile.

Lydia paused and let her gaze drift across the sparkling water. 'What's it like up at the farm now, Miles?' she asked tentatively.

'It's okay. Charlie and Clara ignore each other, Sixpence hides in his kitchen and Joseph is complaining about all the extra work he has to do. The farm workers are wandering around like lost souls and our accounts are getting in a mess. Charlie doesn't know a cow's udder from a pig's ear and Clara's finding it hard to cope with all the muck. Things are great. Just great!'

'And Bliss? How is she? And Julius …'

Miles stared into the distance and his expression hardened. 'They're okay,' he replied. 'As far as I know.'

Lydia glanced up at him and caught a fleeting glimpse of the resentment that was beginning to gnaw into his soul. She wanted to reach out to him, to soften the sharp edges of his grief, but she did not know how to deal with such complicated emotions. The pain that Miles was suffering was way beyond anything she had known or could ever imagine. And she was too young and inexperienced to alleviate it.

Her inadequacy troubled her, for Lydia did know one thing. She knew that she loved Miles Cameron. She had always loved him, even when she was a little girl. And she loved him more now that he was lost and vulnerable. She did not know how to show it, and doubted whether he would ever return it, but it was a fact which, in spite of her tender age, she had accepted without question.

And it was a fact that made her task now so very much harder.

'Miles...' she set aside the peach stone and swung round to face him, kneeling in front of him.

'What?' He smiled at her.

'Miles... there's something I have to tell you.' A bee buzzed noisily around her head. She moved closer to Miles to avoid it, but it followed her persistently.

Miles swatted it with his book and it zigzagged away in protest. 'What is it? Judging by the look on your face, it must something big!'

'It is. Miles... Daddy says we're leaving Rhodesia.'

Miles felt a churning in his stomach. 'Define "we"? Who's leaving Rhodesia?'

'All of us. Mum and Dad, Leah and me. We're going to the UK.'

'But why? I mean, why now?'

'My Mum's been desperate to leave ever since your ... well ... you know what I mean. She says she can't relax here and she's worried sick about us all. We never go anywhere or see anyone because of the fuel shortages, and she hates that. But even if we did have petrol she wouldn't want to go anywhere because of all the landmines. One of our teachers has just lost his leg in a car accident caused by a mine.'

'It's only a few roads that are mined.' Miles persisted stubbornly. Not all of them.'

'I know,' Lydia lifted her lashes to look at him and her eyes were brimming with tears. 'And I don't want to go. I really, really don't want to go, but I have no choice. What is it they call the whites that take the Yellow Route?'

'Dismal Jimmies.'

'Well I don't want to be another Dismal Jimmy.'

'But your dad wouldn't want to be one either, would he? He loves it here. And what about his work? Rhodesia needs doctors! He can't walk out now!'

'He says he doesn't have a choice. He has to do what's right for us. I think his mind was made up when the Vic' Falls Conference fell apart. He reckons that the problem can never be solved amicably. And he was concerned about the assassination of that black lawyer, Herbert Chitepo …'

'Chitepo! He's ZANU! What's that got to do with us? Everybody knows that it was ZANU themselves who planted that car bomb – no matter what that bloke Mugabe claims.'

'That's the point!' Lydia protested. 'Although Mugabe is saying the whites killed him, everyone knows that ZANU did it. Daddy says that if things are so bad that they've started killing their own, it won't be long before all the whites are massacred.'

Miles held his head in his hands and his shoulders drooped. His hair, with its glorious flecks of gold and curiously disobedient fringe, fell forward. He flicked it away irritably and stared at Lydia with a terrible haunted look in his eyes. 'When will you leave?' he muttered.

'At the end of the month.'

Miles groaned and snatched up her hand, holding it to his cheek in an unprecedented show of affection. 'Can't you make him change his mind?'

Lydia shook her head, the tears rolling freely now.

Miles sagged with defeat. He knew that Dai Llewellyn was doing the right thing. The whites were leaving in droves, flocking to safety in South Africa, Canada, Australia and the UK. Treasured possessions were packed into boxes and shipped out of the country. Those that were too heavy or expensive to export, such as books, were tagged and offered for sale to friends and neighbours who would probably sell up and flee themselves eventually.

'So where will you live?'

'In Wales. My Dad has a job at a hospital in a place called Bala. Apparently, we've got loads of friends and family there.'

Miles looked up as one of the fruits fell from the paw paw tree. It landed on the other side of the pool, spilling thick milk all over the flagstones. The jacarandas were also shedding their autumn foliage and the lawn was now covered in a blanket of bright yellow leaves. High above them a grey lourie cried out its strange song. Miles scanned the branches to locate the bird and he smiled ruefully. 'It's the "go-away" bird,' he whispered. 'Seems appropriate somehow.'

Lydia began to sob quietly. Her world was collapsing around her. She was a part of Africa. This was her home, her land, and now she was being forced to leave against her will. She was too young and helpless to struggle against the madness and heartbreak in an adult world.

She turned to Miles with huge, frightened eyes and pleaded: 'You won't forget me will you Miles?'

'Oh God!' Miles groaned and bent down to hug her. 'What the hell is happening here? And where will it all end?'

They clung to each other, tangled up in wisps of Lydia's fiery mane that burned so brightly in the noon sun. All around them, the smells and sounds of their beloved Africa filled their hearts. But the winds of change were swirling around them and they were like the jacaranda leaves, spinning helplessly in a world gone mad.

They gripped each other tightly, their tears mingling, oblivious to everything except the dreadful knowledge that they were to be torn apart and that the world they knew and loved had finally been destroyed.

9

It was the end of term and the Plumtree boys were eager to start their school holidays. They hung around the platform of Plumtree Station in small, animated groups waiting for the train that would take them back to Bulawayo. Their school uniform, grey trousers, green blazer and distinctive red and green striped tie, brought a splash of colour to the quiet country railway station.

It was a common enough scene, but there was something that set these youngsters apart from schoolboys elsewhere. The seniors were sporting FN7.62 mm automatic rifles and many of the other boys, the sons of farmers, were carrying guns brought from home. Even the masters were issued with army weapons. For Rhodesia was a country at war. And death lurked in the dense scrub that lined the remote African railway tracks.

Miles sat on the floor with his back against the wall. He was grateful for a place in the shade. His shoes were scuffed from walking, and the seat of his trousers was covered with dust, but he wore his school uniform with an easy style. He had almost completed the transition from boy to man and it suited him well.

'Here she comes!' Andrew Turner-Woods nodded in the direction of the approaching train. 'And about time too!'

The diesel engine was painted bright yellow with "Rhodesia Railways" emblazoned on the side. It drew to a halt and a human tidal wave surged towards its doors. The boys knew the value of boarding early. Plumtree School reserved a number of second class carriages for its pupils and there was always a mad scramble to secure the best compartments.

Seniors could claim their seats without a fight but fourth formers, such as Miles and his friends, might find themselves evicted from a compartment if the others were occupied. They, in turn, would have to turf out the younger boys until the smallest juniors were reduced to standing in the corridors. Such was the hierarchy of public school life. Everyone was in their place because everyone instinctively knew and accepted their place. It could be hard, especially in the early years, but it seemed to work quite well.

Andrew Turner-Woods had begun to enjoy the privileges of age and status, and he did not want to have to forfeit his seat to seniors. He was lucky. The first compartment he opened was empty and he announced his territorial claim with determined optimism.

'In here lads!' He slung his rucksack on the overhead bunk and flopped down on the green vinyl seat. 'Bags being by the window!'

The twins, Balfour and William Coker, loaded their gear on the bunk opposite and grinned in unison. There were windows on either side of the washbasin and Balfour tugged one down and poked his head out, yelling to one of the boys in the next compartment.

'Spottie, my man! You look even uglier from here!'

'Simon Spicer, otherwise known as Spottie because of a persistent adolescent affliction, prepared a ball of spit and aimed it at a small boy standing anxiously on the platform, dressed in a blazer that was far too big for him. 'So says Coker the Clown!' he scoffed, pleased with his direct hit. 'The guy with the biggest conk in Christendom!'

'You mean the biggest cock in Christendom' Balfour countered merrily.

'In your dreams, Coker! In your dreams'

The good-natured banter continued for a few minutes until both boys had exhausted their repertoire of insults and the stationmaster blew the whistle for the train to depart. Balfour ducked his head inside and collapsed in a heap as the train lurched forward. His brother, irked by the tangle of arms and legs across his lap, shoved him aside roughly and Balfour was sent tumbling to the floor.

'Watch out moron!' he cried. 'You'll break my bloody neck at this rate!'

Fortunately, all-out sibling war was interrupted by Miles, who pushed open the door with his foot and said: 'Refreshments gentlemen?'

'Holy shit!' Balfour struggled to his feet. 'How'd you get hold of that little lot?'

Miles distributed the Carafino wine and grinned with pride. 'It's impossible to sneak a drink out of the dining car while the masters are on the prowl. I figured I'd get in early while they were still loading their gear. We'd never get anything past them now they're on board.'

'Wow!' Andrew picked up a glass and held it up to the light. 'Nice one, Miles!'

'And the Af' served you without question?' William slugged his wine greedily and licked his lips.

'Naturally. He's hardly likely to question my age. I can easily pass off as eighteen.'

'You don't look eighteen to me,' Andrew grumbled, acutely aware of his own patchy stubble and embarrassingly youthful complexion.

'You look like a pratt to me!' Balfour added, anxious to redress the imbalance and reclaim the upper hand now that his initial gratitude had waned.

'Thanks for those kind words, gentlemen. I now propose a toast to the looting, pillaging and burning to the ground of Plumtree School for Boys while we're on hols.'

'I'll drink to that!' William laughed. 'Here's to freedom from poxy old plummers!'

The boys leaned back against the hot, sticky vinyl to enjoy their wine. It would be a long journey, one plagued by the threat of ambush, but they had grown accustomed to the rigours of life in Rhodesia. Many of them had already experienced tragedy in some way or another, but they were young and resilient. They would see it through.

'You've left this a bit late, haven't you?' Miles glowered at the farm labourer. 'It should have been done at two weeks.'

'I am not the one, baas.' The boy offered the traditional African response to criticism. 'Baas Charlie. He did not tell me to do it.'

Miles rolled his eyes skyward. 'You've worked here for two years and you're telling me that you don't know when to dis-bud a calf?'

'I know when, baas. But baas Charlie. He did not tell me to do it.'

Miles held the anaesthetic injection against the calf's skull ready to guide the needle in with his thumb. 'Hold her steady. I can't find the groove.'

Gingerly, he ran his finger over the bony skull in search of the groove between the eye and the horn bud. Having located it, he injected the area and ruffled the top of the animal's head to reassure her.

'Okay Bella. You won't feel a thing soon.' Then, turning to the boy, added: 'It'll take about fifteen minutes to freeze the nerves. You can clip back some of her hair while we wait. It'll give us better access with the iron. Not that we need to worry about that. Her horns are already starting to mature.'

Miles spun round on his heels and made his way up to the house. He was irritated that Charlie had let the farm deteriorate in his absence. He had found milk-stone deposits on the tanks and too much barley in the meal, and the farm buildings and pastureland were in a poor state. Miles had every reason to feel disheartened.

As he approached the back door to the kitchen, he heard Charlie's voice raised in anger. This was followed by a squeal of protest from Sixpence and the sound of cutlery crashing to the floor. Miles burst in to find Bliss cowering against the stove and Sixpence on his hands and knees gathering up the scattered knives and forks.

'What's going on?' he demanded, glowering at his uncle.

'Just a little domestic incident,' Charlie replied breathlessly. 'Sixpence here needs a little more house-training. Don't you boy?'

Miles decided to ignore the altercation. He had other things on his mind. 'You're late with the dis-budding. Bella's are almost through.'

'A week or two won't make any difference. There's no point in making hard work of everything.'

'It's not a question of making hard work. The jobs have to be done. It's as simple as that. You can't just leave everything until the last minute. This is a farm. We need to stay on schedule.'

'I know it's a goddamn farm, son. I lived here before you were born, remember? You don't have to tell me about running a bloody farm. I grew up here!' Charlie did not take kindly to criticism in front of servants.

Miles clenched his fists and his eyes narrowed. Under normal circumstances he would ignore Charlie's volatile temper and avoid making a scene in front of the servants, but not today. 'Being born here doesn't make you a farmer.' He retorted angrily.

'And it doesn't make you a farmer either.' Charlie was provoked. 'So don't try playing the big landowner with me, buster. I'm sweating blood day-in-day-out to keep this joint going while you ponce about at school. I've never worked so bloody hard in all my life! And you!' Charlie swung round to face Sixpence who was still scrabbling about on the floor. 'You can shut that bloody racket up right now. Got that? I can't hear myself think!'

Unable to control his anger any longer, but loth to give vent to it on his nephew, Charlie lashed out at Sixpence with his foot. It was a misdirected shot, a simple case of aggression diverted, but it caught the house-boy off balance and the little Malawian was sent sprawling across the floor.

'Back off!' Miles yelled at his uncle. 'We don't hit servants in this house. My mother would never have allowed that!'

'Your mother isn't here, sonny,' Charlie snarled. 'I'm the number one honcho here now, okay? I'm the one breaking my back to keep this place afloat. That means what I say goes. And if I say one of the muntus needs a good hiding, that's what they get. You can call the shots when you're out of school and grafting like everyone else. But not before. Not while I'm in charge. Okay?'

Hot tears of frustration pricked the back of Miles' eyes, but his pride would not let Charlie see his momentary weakness. Instead, he helped Sixpence to his feet and then slammed out of the house.

He made his way back to the dairy where Bella was waiting. Things had changed so much in his life, and Scarfell no longer felt like home, but there was always one constant. The animals would always be here. They would always need care and attention. And they would always give him a reason for coming home.

'Ready Eli?' Miles took a deep breath to calm himself and then checked that the de-horning iron was red hot. 'Grip her with your thighs. That's it. Now bend her neck this way. Got her? Okay, now hold her tight.'

Expertly, having watched his father on many occasions, Miles ensured that the horn bud was fully enclosed in the burning ring before pressing down firmly. His job was made more difficult by the size of the horns that had been allowed to grow beyond that normally treated. But with dexterity and patience, he managed to enclose the bud completely. He rotated the iron to speed up the burning action and prevent any build-up of singed material before pausing to check whether he had reached white cartilage. Satisfied, he reached in his pocket for his knife and cut out the bud. It was a clean and efficient operation that had managed to burn away the top layer of skin and skull without damaging the actual flesh. Two neat bud sockets were all that remained. Miles wiped his hands on his apron and winked at his willing assistant.

'Nice job, Eli. Now don't forget to dust the wound with the sulphanilamide powder over there, and keep an eye out for bleeding. I'm going to take a shower.'

Miles shrugged out of his apron and hung it over the post. The earlier quarrel had left a sour taste in his mouth and he was anxious to wash it all away. He was angry with Charlie for leaving Bella too long. It had made the de-horning process more difficult. And Bella was special. She was descended from Goldie, the beautiful golden beast that had been Beth's favourite. It was not right that the animals should suffer because of Charlie's laziness. But everyone was suffering at Scarfell Farm. It had been transformed from a wonderfully happy home into a house of tears and bitter recriminations. A house haunted by its past.

But the past was already haunting the present right across the vast continent of Africa. Decades of colonial rule were being challenged by a people crying out for freedom and fair play. Their cause was just, and their resentment justified in many cases, but the horror of war was spreading and the heart of Africa was sorely wounded.

A number of African nations had begun to lose patience with white Rhodesia, believing that Ian Smith's Government would never accept black majority rule. They agreed that that there could never be a peaceful settlement to the crisis, and each began to assess the potential of Robert Mugabe as a war leader.

The failure of the Victoria Falls Conference was regarded as yet another sign of Smith's intransigence. Frustrated by the breakdown in talks, Samora Machel of Mozambique decided that he had no alternative other than to place his country on a war footing with white Rhodesia.

Rhodesia's assets were seized while fuel and other essential supplies blocked. White Rhodesians, alarmed by tales of Russian T55 tanks and SAM-7 missiles across their borders, began to contemplate failure for the very first time. With Russian, Cuban and Chinese backing, there emerged a very real and very frightening possibility of victory for the black African.

To add to their alarm, they heard stories of fully-trained guerrillas infiltrating Rhodesia along the old Chimanimani slave routes. Whites who got in the way were maimed and killed. Black labourers were threatened with torture if they continued to work on the sugar and wheat farms in the area. Company buses were ambushed, roads were mined and the mills and pumping stations bombarded by mortar shells. The whites were afraid.

Smith responded to the crisis by increasing the Rhodesian armed forces and tightening call-up regulations. He also introduced measures to prevent teenagers leaving the country for further study abroad. Rhodesia was at war. She could not afford to deplete her stocks of fit and healthy soldiers.

In an attempt to bolster public morale and demonstrate their military muscle, the Rhodesians carried out a full-scale raid into Mozambique. They attacked a camp at Nyazonia, about thirty-five miles from the border. They were able to penetrate deep into enemy territory by posing as members of the Front for the Liberation of Mozambique. They had FRELIMO insignia on their trucks, wore FRELIMO uniforms and even sang FRELIMO songs. When they reached the camp at Nyazonia, they opened fire indiscriminately. Hundreds of men were killed.

Samora Machel was outraged, claiming that Nyazonia was a refugee camp and that the Rhodesian forces had massacred innocent civilians. Later that month, he invited Robert Mugabe, Jason Moyo, Ndabaningi Sithole and James Chikerema to Maputo. He wanted them to see for themselves the extent of the massacre.

The delegation visited the hospital at Chimoyo and saw the injured lying critically ill with bullet wounds to their chests and stomach. They followed the path trodden by Smith's men and saw the spot where the telephone wires had been cut. They were also shown the beautifully engineered bridge over the Pungwe River that had been blown up and destroyed by the attackers. And finally the spot where the "racist soldiers" had murdered a white priest and nun.

When they reached Nyazonia camp itself, they saw how people had perished in buildings gutted by fire. The bodies of the victims were heaped together in mass graves. There were more than 675 Zimbabweans buried at Nyazonia.

At home, the whites knew that they could no longer rely on in-fighting among the blacks to strengthen their position. In spite of disagreements with Muzorewa, Joshua Nkomo and Robert Mugabe were encouraged to put their tribal conflicts aside and agree to a merger between ZAPU in Matabeleland and ZANU in Mashonaland. The war against white imperialism should come before tribal conflicts they said, and on 9th October 1976 in Dar es Salaam, the new Patriotic Front party was formed.

With no common philosophy, strategy, trust or friendship, it was an uneasy alliance. But both sides realised that they needed the strength that came with unity, and both were prepared to tolerate an unhappy marriage for the time being.

With Kaunda pressing for trade routes to be re-opened, the American, Gerald Ford, hoping to notch up points in his election campaign by orchestrating a settlement in Rhodesia, and the British desperate to rid themselves of the last colonial thorn in their side, the war was escalating into global proportions.

And the world, it seemed, was on the side of black Africa.

'Looks like Kissinger's joined sides with the blacks,' Charlie read aloud from the Bulawayo Chronicle over dinner. 'The Yanks have suddenly decided that they want an immediate solution to the "Rhodesia problem"! What the hell do the bloody Yanks know about anything? They ought to try living here. If they want a solution to the problem, they should come right on in and nuke the kaffirs. That's what I call a solution!'

Miles nodded, but he did not reply. He was still smarting from the altercation earlier that day. He knew that Charlie would have forgotten about it by now. Charlie's fuse was easily lit and swiftly extinguished, but Miles was different. Miles could not forgive and forget so easily. He could not forgive Charlie for failing to respect the inheritance that his parents had worked so hard to provide. He cursed the fact that, at sixteen, he was too young to have any real say in the way things were run. He was away at school and did not even know what was happening at the farm most of the time. But it would not be forever. He would not be sixteen forever. And then things would change. He would work to rebuild Scarfell Farm and repair the damage caused by Charlie's mismanagement. He would remodel the milking parlour, plant cash crops and extend the herd. It would be a home once more.

Outside, silhouetted against the pale silver moon, Bliss was busy sweeping the path. Her hair was tucked up beneath her maid's cap and she was wearing a thin cotton dress. One of the buttons had popped at the top revealing a deep cleavage that jiggled with each thrust of her broom.

She was humming a song that her mother had taught her in the kraals outside Tshotsholo. It reminded her of happy times when her parents and siblings would gather around the central hearth in the kitchen hut to sing hymns and read aloud from the Bible.

The village where Bliss grew up was a cluster of thatched rondavels. Bliss' father had only one wife and so was allocated four huts for his family. The Great Chief Dzingai had five wives and a grand total of twenty-five huts.

But numbers did not mean much to the children who grew up in the kraals. They knew only that these small, conical structures, and the land upon which they stood, belonged to their family and to their tribe. The rondavels were painted on the outside in bold bright Ndebele colours and the kraal was kept scrupulously clean and tidy.

The focus of each home was the kitchen. The hearth was built around three flat stones to support the cooking pots. There were no windows or chimney and the smoke had to find its own way out through a gap between the walls and the roof. Bliss' mother had stuck ears of grain into the cracks so that the smoke could cure them against weevils. It was an effective remedy.

But that was long ago. Things had changed.

Bliss leaned on her broom handle and stared into the distance where the streets of Bulawayo glowed pink along the edge of the horizon. The happiness she had known as a child in Tshotsholo, and later here at Scarfell Farm, had evaporated like perfume in the heat of the sun.

Her own mother had died long ago, her husband had fled under the cover of the night and her son had withdrawn into himself. The Madam was dead, killed, some said, by Moses Khumalo, and her beloved Miss Beth was also gone. Master Miles seemed to despise all members of the Khumalo clan and the farm had been taken over by the Nkosi's vicious and unpredictable brother. Bliss had never imagined that things would turn out so badly, and it was painful to recall the way things used to be. Hot tears welled in the corner of her eyes and she lifted up the hem of her skirt to wipe them away. The movement afforded a brief glimpse of her broad, sturdy thighs.

The gesture had not gone unnoticed inside the house.

The flicker of the white cotton dress in the moonlight had caught Charlie's eye and he had paused in his diatribe against the iniquities of Henry Kissinger's foreign policy to watch the woman outside. Unconsciously, he licked his lips and his breath quickened.

Miles had not noticed Bliss. He was too busy watching his aunt. As usual, Clara was neatly turned out in a high-necked blouse and beige pleated skirt, the colours of which did little to illuminate her sallow skin. Her hair was dragged back into a tight little bun, and there were deep frown lines in her forehead. She ate little, choosing to pick at her food like an injured bird. Sixpence had served up his favourite meal of lamb bobotie with apricots and almonds, but nothing could tempt Clara's palate.

Although she did little to endear herself to people in general, Miles could not help but feel sorry for his aunt. He knew now that Clara's life was hard, and that not even the temporary occupation of a beautiful farmhouse, set in twelve thousand acres of hills and glorious savannahs, could make up for the things that were lacking.

For now, having lost the blind innocence of youth, Miles was able to recognise his uncle for the man he truly was. He was lazy, volatile and cruel. He was also charismatic, the sort of man who would easily fit a young boy's criteria for hero-worship, but his charm belied the selfishness within. Miles knew now that Clara was imprisoned in a cold and miserable marriage, with a husband whose temper could cause him to lash out at anyone who happened to be within reach - including his own wife.

Tonight, however, Clara seemed even more remote than usual. Her food was untouched on her plate and she avoided meeting Miles' eye. Nothing was said, but Miles knew that she felt responsible for the deteriorating state of the farm. He knew also that she was powerless to stop the rot. To try to make up for her husband's neglect, she had thrown herself into the care and maintenance of the house itself with an enthusiasm that bordered on obsession. Miles was grateful for the fact that his shirts were always ironed and his shoes polished, and he could tolerate the almost clinical levels of cleanliness, but her obsessive housework had somehow robbed the house of its heart. Now it was simply a well-organised shell. It was no longer a home.

No matter how hard she tried, Clara could not make a home. She did not know how. Miles understood this now. She had left her family in South Africa to come to a land full of hope with a handsome husband and the promise of children of her own. But those dreams had long since died. Now she had nothing, other than this farm, and this was the legacy of a terrible murder and the loss of a beloved sister-in-law. It was too great a price to pay.

Miles watched her quietly. Her gaze was fixed on Charlie and there was an expression of inconsolable sadness in her eyes. The lines of her mouth drooped downwards and her body seemed to sag under the weight of a great burden. Miles glanced at his uncle who was obviously transfixed by something that was happening outside.

Charlie's brow was furrowed in an effort of concentration and he chewed at his bottom lip. Puzzled, Miles followed his gaze to where Bliss was working under the jacaranda.

For the first time in his life, Miles no longer saw his nanny, mother to Julius and loyal servant, he saw Bliss the woman. He saw a big, good-looking woman in her prime, with wide hips and a full round breasts. Unaware of her audience, Bliss paused to rest her chin on top of the broom handle. The gesture, although innocent enough, was unconsciously provocative and Charlie ran his tongue over his lips.

Miles could not bear to watch his sad and lonely aunt watching her lascivious husband watching the woman who was once his nanny. It was an ugly scene - one which did not belong in the magnificent teak-panelled dining room of Scarfell Farm. It belonged in a bar, or a shebeen on the outskirts of Bulawayo. But not here.

Miles pushed his plate away and dabbed at the corner of his mouth with his napkin. There was nothing he could say. Nothing he could do. He was not the master of Scarfell Farm. That man was dead, brutally murdered along with his wife who was once the mistress of this wonderful house. Charlie had taken his place. But as far as Miles was concerned, Charlie had not earned the right to sit, albeit temporarily, at the head of the splendid mukwa dining table. He had not earned the right to be the guardian of this fine enterprise.

Desperate to blot out the grim reality, Miles stood up and dropped his napkin on to the table. He said nothing. There was nothing to say. He simply left the room shutting the door quietly behind him.

Esther's kraal was approached by a single dirt track rutted with potholes and strewn with tumbleweed. The people in the village kept to themselves. They knew that a fierce battle was raging in the world beyond the borders of their meagre plot, but they did not understand it and they did not want to play any part in it.

They knew only that they did not support the black man's cause. They did not think the African was capable of understanding the complex machinery of Government. That was for the white man. And they had no truck with the white man.

They were simple farming folk. They measured their wealth, as did all the Matabele, in heads of cattle. They did not need big cars and big houses in the white man's world. That was an alien world. They belonged here on their land with their cattle. It was the Matabele way.

In spite of its rural isolation, the white man had managed to impose himself upon even this most primitive of kraals, but it was an imposition which could be tolerated. In the early days, the old Chief, Esther's father, had been puzzled by the white man's passion for registers, lists and big books crammed with unintelligible symbols. But he had learned not to question these strange rituals.

He knew, for example, that the other headmen resented the weekly call to herd their cattle into one of the collective dip tanks set up by the District Commissioner, but he did not feel the need to follow their example and devise ways to avoid this responsibility.

The dip tanks were constructed at strategic sites in a bid to control disease among the native herds. Dipping took place weekly in summer and fortnightly in winter. Owners were charged one dollar a year for dipping, but few could accept the value of the exercise and many tried to avoid payment altogether. There arose in Matabeleland a series of "ghost herds"- magical beasts that were never seen at the dip tanks and thus were never included on the cattle registers.

The District Commissioners spent a great deal of time and effort in combating the various tactics employed by the natives to hide their cattle. They would even hire in spotter planes to swoop down on unregistered herds if they felt it would help them meet their collection targets.

Esther's father did not feel the need to question the procedures laid down by the white man. Every week he would dutifully lead his cattle to the dip tanks and, after a while, actually began to enjoy the event, which provided an opportunity to meet neighbours, exchange goods and give his bulls a chance to sow their wild oats.

He had just paid his dipping fee for the year and was now on his way back to his kraal at dusk. His daughter was with him, as was her young admirer, Julius, son of the House of Khumalo. The young buck's attentions were honourable, the old Chief could see that for himself, and it was fitting that a child of his should bond with one from the House of Khumalo. But he knew that it would not be wise to leave the youngsters alone for too long. Julius had already crossed the borders into manhood, and it was clear that he sought a man's release from his cravings. Julius could not be expected to contain his seed within his aching loins for much longer.

The old Chief decided that he must speak with the boy's maternal grandfather as soon as possible. Julius' father, Moses, had disappeared after the Night of the Slaying and he could not negotiate a suitable lobola, or bride price, with Julius' mother. This was a matter for men to decide. He would travel to Tshotsholo after the next rains.

Esther leaned against the old msasa tree and pursed her lips in a girlish pout. 'Stay awhile Julius. We have so little time together.'

Julius glanced up at the moon. 'I must get back in case I meet one of the patrols. I have broken the curfew as it is.'

Esther fondled the wooden beads at her throat and let her fingers trail down the swell of her breasts. Julius followed the line hungrily with his eyes and his breath quickened. Esther was still a virgin, but she understood the power that she could wield over a young man such as Julius Khumalo.

'A kiss at least,' she purred.

Julius groaned and pulled her close, feeling her curves and squashy bumps against his hard flesh. A fierce heat gripped his loins and he could not ignore its demands. Roughly, he pushed her back against the coarse bark and crushed her lips with his own. He heard her murmur and squeal beneath him, and the mewling kitten sounds served only to fuel his lust. As always, he was maddened by his own urges and his thoughts were focussed on the throbbing sensation in his groin.

Esther lifted her arms above her head and the smell of her sweat drove him crazy. He kissed the hollows under her arms and ran his tongue down the side of her lovely young body. With one hand he gripped her braided hair and tugged her neck back into an arc. The other hand sought the warmth between her thighs. Instinctively, her legs parted and, she cried aloud.

'Take what is yours Julius! I beg you!'

'No!' Julius pushed her aside and struggled to calm his laboured breathing. 'You know I cannot! I cannot dishonour you and your father!'

Esther fought hard to regain her composure. 'I am so sorry Julius. Please don't be angry with me.' She gathered up her loose cotton top and held it against her breasts. It failed to conceal those fleshy mounds and Julius had to force himself to look away.

'I am not angry,' he explained, staring gloomily at the ground. 'It's just that I must not think of you as I would other girls. You are not some whore from a local shebeen that I might straddle in a hurry and abandon after I am spent. You will be my bride one day. This has been agreed by our families. I have no right to dishonour you and claim your virginity before it is my right and duty to do so.'

'But no-one will know,' Esther persisted stubbornly. 'I will not tell anyone.'

Julius turned to look at her and his eyes were burning brightly. 'I will know,' he hissed. 'I will know that, although I am a son of the House of Khumalo, I am as lowly as an animal rutting in the bush. I will know that I had no respect for my bride's purity and that I have acted without honour. There is already a cloud of shame that hangs over our family. My father is... No! I will not add to our shame.'

Esther knew better than to try to persuade Julius to change his mind once it was settled. Her power over his sexual urges was immense but, ultimately, he was the one with the greater power. She could never compete with the inner strength of a man like Julius Khumalo. And she knew that she could never conquer the terrible demons that tormented his soul. He was confused and angry. Her womanly charms could only hold sway for so long. After that, he was his own man.

'Will you come and see me again soon?' she whispered, compliant now.

'I will come when I can,' Julius sucked in a deep breath and lifted her chin with his thumb. 'When you are my wife... I will claim your virginity as is my right. And you will be mine.'

Esther did not reply. She watched silently as Julius stole away into the bush. For a while, she could hear him moving through the long grasses. But then there was silence. He was gone. He had disappeared into the bush and she was left with her appetite unassuaged. But he would be back. She did not know when, but he would be back. She would have to wait patiently, as was the way of Africa. And she could. It was in her blood.

Julius found his bicycle beside the mopani tree where he had left it earlier. Carefully, without making a sound, he wheeled it through the scrub until he reached the open road. Wild animals and predators roamed the bush, but the roads that led from the towns and villages were far more deadly. Man lurked in the shadows and, black or white, man was the most dangerous predator of all.

Many of the roads were mined making travel a risky undertaking. In some cases, drivers who survived a blast would stagger out of their vehicles and stumble straight into the sniper fire from a nearby ambush. So common were these occurrences that Rhodesia's armed patrols had traded their Land Rovers for special mine-protected vehicles. These were painted in camouflage colours and contained devices such as v-shaped metal floors to deflect the blast, armoured glass windscreens and slits for gun ports.

Julius was also afraid that, if a patrol convoy spotted him, he might be kidnapped and roped to the front of the lead vehicle where he would be forced to act as a human mine detector. The theory was that if there were mines ahead the civilian would know this and, fearing for his life, would bang on the roof to beg the convoy to stop. The authorities frowned upon this tactic, but the patrollers were loathe to relinquish their unique method of insurance and the practice continued. Of course, in some cases, the African genuinely did not know whether the road was mined and his life, along with members of the convoy, would be lost. But in the main it was an effective counter-measure and many lives were saved by these reluctant lookouts.

Overhead the moon hung heavily in the night sky, casting its silver rays far and wide. Julius did not want to be seen, so he kept to the shadows of the thorn bushes and scrub as best he could. Only when he felt certain that the road was truly deserted did he feel confident enough to push his bicycle out into the light.

Casting an anxious glance over his shoulder, he jumped on his bike and pedalled furiously towards Scarfell Farm. He recalled the tale of the old man who had been shot in the back and killed by a patroller. It was shortly before curfew and, as rumour had it, he had been shot simply because the patroller did not think he could cover the five miles to his kraal in the time available. He was guilty because he was going to break the curfew. And blacks who broke the curfew were shot. The law was as simple as that.

Charlie clutched a half-empty bottle of wine and staggered drunkenly down the steps that led to the servants' kias. He belched loudly and a fog of evil smelling breath momentarily obscured the sweet perfume of the white jasmine and citrus flowers. He shook his head to clear his thoughts and leaned against the lemon tree to take another swig of wine from the bottle. He wiped his chin with the back of his hand and leered drunkenly at the shimmering candlelight in the window below.

The black sow was in her sty, Charlie grinned, ready and waiting to be serviced by her white master.

Bliss was standing over the stove, stirring a huge pot of mealie meal. It was hot and she had opened the top buttons of her frock to cool the sweat between her breasts. It was a warm, sticky night and she made a feeble attempt to dry herself with a towel from time to time, but it was a pointless exercise.

She was anxious. It was dark outside, long past curfew time, and Julius was still not home. She knew that he could be shot on sight if found breaking the curfew. Blacks were compelled to remain in their homes from six o'clock in the evening until six o'clock the following morning. The whites claimed that they were acting in the best interests of the black African who might be murdered or kidnapped by terrorists roaming the bush. But Bliss was not so sure. She did not fear the terrorists as she waited for her son to come home, she feared the white man with his pistol and his gung-ho attitude. These were dangerous times and it was not safe for a young black man to be abroad after curfew.

Bliss rubbed the towel down her legs and was just about to bend over to wipe her feet when she spotted someone pass by the window.

'Julius!' she whispered. 'Thank the Lord!'

The door creaked open and Bliss turned to stir the mealie meal again. 'You are late,' she admonished, not looking over her shoulder. 'You know your mama worries when you are late.'

'There's no need to worry, little black bunny. I'm here now.'

The voice did not belong to Julius. It was baas Charlie's voice. He was here, in her home. She spun round to face him and gasped, dropping the wooden spoon on the floor as she backed towards the window. The master was drunk. She could smell it on his breath even from this distance, and she could see it in the way he lurched towards her.

'Master!' she cried. 'You must return to the house. It is not right that you should be here.'

Charlie sniggered. 'Who says it's not right? You? Who are you to say what's right? You're a goddam kaffir. You don't have any rights. Now come here, my bouncy black bunny. Baas Charlie's got a little job for you…'

Bliss tried to scream hoping that maybe Sixpence would hear next door, but he was not home and, besides, her cries were stifled by Charlie's hand over her mouth. With the other hand, he tore the front of her dress from neck to waist and, grabbing one of her breasts, tugged it out of the flimsy cotton.

'That's better,' he gasped. 'Baas Charlie wants to see what you've got.' He held one heavy, fat breast in his cupped hand and licked her nipple greedily. 'Nice… nice little black bunny. Now just you lie back on that dirty little bunk of yours. That's it. Nice and quiet. I'm going to show you what a white man feels like.'

Bliss screamed and pushed against his chest. 'No! Please! Master! Please!'

Charlie laughed and pulled out his erect member. Bliss screamed again.

'Too big for you, huh? I thought you would be used to this. I thought your black bucks were supposed to be a well-hung bunch? Not as heavily hung as this though, eh?'

Clumsily, he struggled out of his clothes and forced his knee between her legs. Bliss was hysterical now. She was strong, but her strength was no match for the white man's.

Charlie thrust himself deep into her body, grunting like an animal. It was a cruel invasion and the pain tore at her flesh. Yet still Bliss fought on, punching and sobbing beneath him.

And then the door to the kia burst open and the shadow of a man was silhouetted against the moonlight. Bliss clawed at the air, desperate for salvation, before the darkness crashed in on her and she became a limp and lifeless figure shoved back and forth by the merciless thrusts of her attacker.

Henry Kissinger had been in West Germany for talks with South Africa's Prime Minister Vorster. They agreed that Rhodesia would have to accept the principle of black majority rule or face the threat of total isolation. At the same time, Ian Smith was adopting a more defiant stance.

"After the tremendous effort of the past ten years to preserve western civilisation, Rhodesians have no intention of handing over to anyone. We are not that kind of people."

His resolution changed when, on 19th September 1976, he met Henry Kissinger, in Pretoria. He was told in no uncertain terms that the situation was deteriorating rapidly and the West would no longer support them. Either the Rhodesians accepted the principle of black majority rule, or they would be completely alone.

To soften the blow, Kissinger promised that sanctions would be lifted immediately after the concession and that terrorism would cease. An injection of foreign capital into the country would bolster the economy and there would be financial provision to secure the confidence of the whites.

Smith came out of the meeting convinced that Kissinger had been decent, and that the South Africans were now the real villains in the destruction of white Rhodesia. In October of that year, he addressed the nation with what became known as his "surrender speech".

"It was made abundantly clear to me, and to my colleagues who accompanied me to Pretoria that, as long as the present circumstances in Rhodesia prevailed, we could expect no help or support of any kind from the free world. On the contrary, the pressures on us from the free world would continue to mount."

He added that race relations in their country "remained friendly and relaxed" and that Rhodesians had built up a magnificent country where the prospects were second to none in Africa. He concluded by borrowing from Winston Churchill:

"Now is not the end; it is not even the beginning of the end; but it is, perhaps, the end of the beginning."

What Ian Smith did not say as he uttered this convoluted quote, and what few Rhodesians could bear to imagine, was that he was actually talking about the beginning of the end.

Meanwhile, another battle was being fought in the capital of Rhodesia. The members of Salisbury City Council were about to vote on the thorny issue of rubbish collection.

In a bid to keep costs down, one group was suggesting that the rubbish bags should be left outside the gates of white homes in the suburbs. The opposition, supported by the vast majority of residents, declared that if the rubbish were to be left outside each week it would look unsightly. They were determined preserve their basic right to have their rubbish collected from inside their gates.

The war of words raged on and some began to wonder if an agreement would ever be reached on this delicate issue. But then, suddenly, the matter was resolved. The city's rubbish, it was decreed by Members of the Council, would, henceforth, be collected from outside the gates of residents' homes.

The local white population, much to their astonishment and bitter disappointment, had lost this crucial battle. Whatever was the world coming to!

10

Julius could tell from his mother's cries that something was wrong. Even so, he was shocked to see such horror when he kicked open the door to the kia. He heard his mother's strangled sob as she tried to call out his name. He saw her terrified eyes pleading for help.

Snapped out of his momentary paralysis, Julius sucked in his breath and bellowed a mighty roar that filled the tiny hut and echoed far away into the night. He lunged at Charlie and grabbed the older man by both shoulders. He hauled him off his mother and slung him against the far wall. Bliss shook pitifully, pulling at her tattered skirts to cover her nakedness.

Julius saw her pain and it maddened him still further. His liquid-brown eyes narrowed and an evil glint shone in the corners. Never before had he known the blood-lust that had fuelled his Matabele forefathers and driven them to conquer this vast terrain. He had never known the wild rage that had given the Matabele warriors their fearsome reputation. But he knew it now.

His lips curled back against ivory polished teeth and his breath came short and sharp as he approached his prey. The impact against the wall had stunned Charlie and he recovered his wits just in time to assess the awesome power of that muscular black body towering over him, and to smell the dank sweat upon it.

The sight of Julius bearing down upon him with the strength of youth and hate on his side might have cowed a lesser man, but Charlie was a fighter. He had sparred many times in local bar-room brawls and he was tough. Before Julius could stop him he grabbed Moses' old hunting knife from its peg on the wall and hurled it directly at his adversary.

The knife was huge with a ten inch blade and a rough handle carved from bone. The steel blade peaked to a crest halfway along and then curved down again to a sharp point. A slim channel had been gorged out of the blade along the side so that the blood could drain swiftly and the steel penetrate more deeply.

Julius raised his left hand to ward off the knife, but it caught his arm and tore the flesh. Julius was undeterred by the sight of blood, especially his own. Indeed the sight of it inflamed his passions still further and, using his entire bodyweight, he charged into his opponent.

Charlie took the full force of the impact and the air was knocked out of him as he doubled up in shock. The boy hugged him round the waist and both men crashed into the cooker sending mealie meal flying to the floor. The hot contents scalded them both and the shock broke their deadlock.

Charlie seized the moment and, bringing both arms under Julius' chest, he prised open the grip and knocked Julius to the floor. With his opponent now vulnerable, Charlie aimed a vicious kick at the young man's belly. Julius gasped and curled up in agony while Bliss cowered against the wall. Charlie grunted with the effort of a second kick, this one aimed at Julius' head, but his opponent was too quick for him. Julius rolled out of the way and grabbed at Charlie's foot, toppling him to the ground.

Now they were equals.

The two men rolled over, straining to remain uppermost, their bodies covered with blood and remnants of the mealie meal. Their blows were cruel, knuckle against bone, and the flesh was torn from their faces.

Charlie was tough and his tactics matched Julius' strength and youth. But Julius had one extra weapon in his arsenal. Hate. Charlie represented all those white men who had come to claim Africa from its people. Suddenly, like countless generations of Africans before him, Julius felt the resentment swell in his heart and the anger and frustration boil up inside him.

Bliss recognised the murderous intent in her son's eyes as he eyed the discarded knife and she cried out in fear: 'Julius! Kwete! No!'

Julius glanced at her and Charlie immediately took advantage of the distraction. Swiftly, he rolled over and pinned Julius to the floor with his knees. In his rage, Charlie had lost all sense of reason as he rained cruel blows upon the face of his adversary. Charlie's own blood and sweat mingled with that of Julius and gave them an evil look. Julius' cheeks were badly bruised and the sight of the injuries he had inflicted further inflamed Charlie's passions.

'Lay a hand on a white man, would you? You black fucker!' he spat out the words. 'I'll show you who's boss, you bastard!'

182

'No you won't!' A different voice, a clear authoritative voice, rang out above the heads of the two fighting men. 'Not while I'm here.'

Charlie turned to check the source and his mouth twisted into a grimace. He rolled off Julius and struggled to his feet while aiming one last vicious kick against the boy's ribs. Bliss cried out and rushed to her son who lay gasping for breath on the floor. Charlie dusted himself down, still fighting to regain his breath, and wiped the blood from his mouth with the back of his hand.

'Got a bit too cocky for his own good, nephew,' Charlie examined the stability of his front tooth with his thumb. 'Had to give him a bit of a talking to as you can see.'

Julius ignored his mother's ministrations and he pushed her aside as he got to his feet. He turned to face Miles who was standing, ashen-faced, in the doorway.

'Your uncle tried to rape my mother. That is the only truth you will need to know.'

Miles looked at Bliss and then turned to Charlie who was still only partially dressed. He looked at the torn sheet and scraps of clothing on bunk in the corner of the kia and then regarded Charlie with bile rising in his throat.

'Dear God! Is this true? Please don't let it be true.' How he longed for it not to be true, for he did not know how he would bear it.

'Depends what you call rape,' Charlie muttered. 'The black bitch was asking for it. You saw her flashing her tits outside the window. She was crying out for it.'

'Liar! You raped my mother! You dog!' Julius grabbed Charlie's arm, but Miles stepped in between them.

Bliss hung her head in shame and hot tears rolled silently down her cheeks. She did not feel strong enough to state her case for there would be little point. The white man always won in the end. There would be no justice for a black woman here in Rhodesia. But at least her son knew the truth. She was soiled and exposed before him, but Julius knew the truth. She would be satisfied with that.

Miles looked down at his former nanny and his heart broke at the sight of her shoulders now wracked by silent sobbing. Bliss was a big, strong African woman with eyes that danced with love and a smile that could light up a little boy's life. She had been his light once. He could still see her bending over the bathtub, threatening him playfully with soap and flannel, and he could still feel the warmth of her arms and smell that strangely comforting aroma of Vaseline as she rocked him to sleep. He saw a brief glimpse of Beth as a toddler, lurching unsteadily across the room, clutching a rag-dolly that she had made with the help of her nanny, and clinging on to the outstretched hand that was always there to guide and comfort.

And now, a member of the Cameron family had reduced Bliss to this pitiful creature, had transformed her into this pathetic, feeble victim trying desperately to conceal her bruised body with scraps of torn clothing. He could not bear to see Bliss thus shamed and helpless anger tore at his stomach.

He glowered at his uncle. 'You're disgusting!' He spat out the words.

'Easy to see whose side you're on nephew.' Charlie zipped up his flies. 'Surely you're not going to take the word of a couple of kaffirs against your own flesh and blood?'

Miles swallowed hard. 'I have no choice,' he said hopelessly. 'The truth is staring me right in the face. I have to take their side.'

Julius pushed his mother behind him and flared up at Miles. 'I do not want you to take my side, Miles Cameron. My battles are my own. All I ask is that you and … that white dog leave my home.'

Charlie swung round angrily. 'Who are you to go calling the shots mister? Huh? You're just a bloody servant here! You only live in this hovel because we say you can! Without Scarfell Farm, you and your slut of a mother will just be a couple more homeless kaffirs out in the bush. Get it?'

Charlie brought his face up close to Julius, but the younger man spat a neat ball of saliva directly into Charlie's eyes.

'White trash!' Julius snarled. 'You whites are only living in our country because we "kaffirs" say you can!'

Charlie grabbed at Julius' shirt and tugged him closer. 'Listen up boyo. Your whore mother was gagging for it. Gagging for it she was. She's been flashing her pussy at me since I got here. And a fine piece of pussy it was,' he added, grinning lasciviously at Bliss.

Miles pushed himself in between them and shoved Charlie towards the door and turned to Bliss.

'I… I'm so sorry, Bliss!' he stammered, unmanly sobs unexpectedly choking the back of his throat. 'I'm really so very sorry.'

Bliss looked up at him with forgiveness shining through her tears. She put out her hand, but Julius pushed it away furiously. 'No Mother. We do not forgive. We do not forget this night. The House of Khumalo has been shamed by a member of the Cameron family. We do not forgive.'

Miles spun round on his heels and then stopped suddenly. Clara was standing in front of him, small and frail and wan. Alarmed by the commotion, she had followed him and had seen the outcome of her husband's deeds for herself. She saw the wretched woman who had been raped by Charlie. And she saw how the woman's own son, Julius, had risked all in defence of his mother's honour.

And then Clara's shoulders sagged and she began to weep. It was not a stifled, ladylike weeping, but great gulping howls that threatened to tear her heart out. Clara knew that there was no-one who would defend her honour, tend to her injuries or fight her battles. She had no son to love and protect her. All she had was a husband who was capable of raping an innocent servant and bringing shame upon his wife and family without a second thought. And there was no doubt in Clara's mind that Charlie had shamed each and every one of them tonight.

Weakly, she fell against the wall as Charlie elbowed his way past her. Swearing loudly, he made his way along the path to the main house. She turned and watched him go and then stared again at the misery he had left behind. She sighed, but she did not speak. She simply turned to follow her husband back to the house.

It seemed such a long and arduous climb back to the main house. All the while her thoughts were racing. She knew now that she would never be able to call Scarfell Farm home. It did not belong to her. She had merely occupied it temporarily after the night of the slaying. She and Charlie should never have come to Scarfell Farm. They did not belong here. They were not fit to look after this beautiful place and the rich land that surrounded it. It was not right.

Charlie was lying on the steps of the stoep when Clara reached the house. She stepped over the drunken form and he muttered something unintelligible, but the whisky bottle in his hand put paid to any meaningful communication that night. Charlie was vaguely aware that his knuckles were bleeding and his jaw was throbbing, but the memory of the past hour was gradually fading from his alcohol-fuzzed brain and he was on the verge of passing out completely into an alcohol-induced oblivion.

Clara crossed the teak floor in the sitting room, pausing only to straighten one of the rugs and glance at Rachel's oil painting that still hung above the stone fireplace. It was a painting of the Matopos, that fertile place where the Semukwe and Tshatshane rivers bring fresh water to the foothills all year round. Clara smiled. Rachel had captured the staggering displays of light and colour perfectly. She remembered helping her sister-in-law choose the frame.

'It's a magical place for the Matabele, you know,' Rachel had once told her as she stood admiring her efforts. 'They believe that the Umlimo - a kind of oracle or wise man - lives in the Matopos Hills. It's fascinating stuff. I can lend you a book on the subject if you like…'

Clara remembered the conversation as though it was yesterday, but she had never been able to share Rachel's respect and admiration for black Africans and their ancient customs. Clara was an Afrikaner. She could trace her lineage back to the distant voortrekkers – those proud Dutch settlers who had moved their people north when the British Government took over the administration of the Cape Colony.

The Dutch, or Afrikaners as they were known, were dependent on black slave labour. When the British abolished slavery in 1834 they considered the act a provocative attack upon their customs and their revered way of life.

Rather than confront the mighty British Empire, the leading Afrikaners decided to move their people inland, away from Cape Town, in what became known as the Great Trek. The voortrekkers – those who move ahead – took over the empty tracts of land vacated by Mzilikazi in his flight from Chaka Zulu less than a decade earlier and, within a few years, had occupied most of the present Transvaal and Orange Free State where they set up independent republican governments.

Many Afrikaners had died in the Great Trek and those that survived had fought many battles. In 1836 when they first crossed the Vaal River, they unknowingly breached Mzilikazi's ruling governing entry to Matabeleland from that direction. Incensed, his impis attacked the voortrekkers who immediately responded by putting their wagons into the tight, defensive circle of a laager. They lashed them together and fortified the laager with thorn bushes. It was an impenetrable circle and in the bloody battle that followed hundreds of Matabele impis died, but only two Afrikaners were killed.

It was God's will, the Dutch cried in unison. The Great Trek had become a divine mission entrusted to God's chosen people. They had been given the task of moving their people north, and when the good Lord asked them to exact a terrible revenge on Mzilikazi and his sinful tribe, they had been ready to obey

Clara had been born and raised as an Afrikaner and had inherited the belief that blacks were inferior beings. They were primitive and dangerous and had been put upon this earth solely as beasts of burden to serve the white man.

But today Clara's feelings had changed. As she stood beneath Rachel's painting of the Matabele nation's mighty granite kingdom, with foul images of her husband's immorality still at the forefront of her mind, Clara felt an overwhelming sense of shame and an unfamiliar empathy with the suffering of black Africa. It was an unexpected and uncomfortable revelation.

'Are you okay, tante Clara?' Miles came up behind her and rested his hand lightly on her shoulders.

Clara reached up with both hands and took hold of her nephew's fingers, clinging to their warmth and strength like a lost soul. The table lamp illuminated the strands of silver in her hair and drained her complexion of its last remaining colour. Her fingers were thin and cold against Miles' and her shoulder bones jutted through her blouse. There was precious little left of the aunt Miles had once known. It was as though she was wasting away before his eyes.

'Your mother was a gifted artist, you know.'

Miles looked at the vast oil painting with its subtle shades of gold and grey. 'I know,' he whispered. 'But I'm more concerned about you. How are you?'

Clara pointedly ignored the main question. 'It's not just her talent for reproduction, this scene is so ... lifelike, but she could also capture its mood, its essence. Do you know what I mean, Miles?'

'I know what you mean.'

'I could never do that, you know. That's why I always stuck to embroidery and cross-stitch. I need to follow a pre-set pattern. I'm not very good at seeing things for myself. I'm afraid I never quite shared your mother's vision, nor her courage. I would be terrified to tackle such a large blank canvas without someone else's guidelines to follow. I'm rather a coward at heart.'

'I don't think you're a coward, tante Clara,' Miles threaded his arm around her waist and drew her down on to the sofa. 'It's not easy to make the first mark or set a trail. Look at me. I'm no leader. I reckon I was born to follow.'

Clara plucked a tissue out of its box on the table and blew her nose softly. 'Not you, Miles dearest. Not you. You were never born to follow. You are a leader in my eyes.'

Miles chuckled softly. 'I don't know about that! I'm not sure too many people would see me as one!'

'Perhaps not a leader in the ordinary sense of the word. Not a leader of men…' Clara agreed, 'but you have the courage of the Camerons in your heart. You're not weak or foolish. You will go where you have to go and do what you have to do. It's your way. You are proud and strong … like your father. I envy you your strength and determination. They are good qualities and they'll serve you well in life.'

Miles shrugged and leaned forward, resting his arms on his thighs so that his hands hung limply in between his knees. 'I guess I must be fairly tough. I seem to have coped with what life's chucked at me so far and I'm still here! I feel I've had a lifetime of pain crammed into the last seventeen years. There can't be much more to come surely.'

Clara laid her hand on her nephew's forearm and rested her head against his shoulder. 'I doubt there will be much more to come. You've suffered enough. One thing I do know, though, is that you will cope with whatever life deals you. You are a Cameron and you draw your strength from Scarfell Farm. As long as you remain on this precious soil, you'll be safe. I'm sure of that, Miles. This is your home.'

'And it's your home, too, tante Clara. For as long as you need it.'

Clara shook her head and pressed the soggy tissue into a ball in her lap. Tears had gathered in the corners of her eyes and they rolled down her cheeks unchecked. The sharp lines on her bird-like profile were etched with grief and her skinny frame sagged against Miles.

'I'm afraid I can't stay here any longer, Miles. I don't belong here. I must leave.'

'What for?' Miles swivelled round to face her. 'You don't have to go anywhere. This is your home. Don't let …him drive you away. We can work something out! I know we can!'

'No Miles. I know what I have to do. I can't remain downtrodden all my life. I can't stay on the farm any longer and … I can't follow the path that Charles has mapped out for me any more. It's time to make my own path. It's time to go home.'

'Home? Where are you calling home?'

Clara stared at the floor, tears falling freely into her lap now. Gratefully, she accepted another tissue from her nephew and she dabbed at her cheeks. 'I'm going back to South Africa. I have family there. I'll have to accept the humiliation of being a woman without a husband, nothing can be done about that, but I can no longer accept the shame of living with your uncle.'

Miles could think of nothing more to say. He looked at his aunt's expression and could see by the determined set of her jaw that this was something she had to do. This was something she would do, no matter what the cost. No matter what the pain.

'I think I understand,' he whispered.

'Do you?' Clara seized at the words. 'Do you, Miles? Oh I do hope so, because I don't fully understand it myself. It will be so hard for me to return to South Africa as a failure for everyone to see, and it will be so hard to hide the truth about my departure, but I simply don't have a choice. I have to go. I can't stay here with that … man out there.' She gestured in the direction of the stoep where Charlie was now snoring loudly. 'For the first time in my life, Miles, perhaps the only time knowing me, I shall start with a blank canvas....'

'And paint your own picture?' Miles whispered.

'And paint my own picture,' Clara agreed.

Later, when his aunt had gone to her room, Miles went outside to breathe in the sweet, clean air and to watch the clouds drifting across the face of the moon. He had to step over Charlie's inert body where he paused to remove the whisky bottle from his uncle's fingers. It was almost empty, its contents either helping to deaden Charlie's brain, or seeping through the floorboards on the verandah. Charlie's snoring had settled into a ragged deep breathing. He was out cold for the night, Miles decided. He would leave him where he was.

It was a warm, still night with the darkness illuminated by the silver rays of a magical full moon. Miles made his way down the garden, soothed by the whirr of insects and the occasional lowing of the cattle. Suddenly, a giant bullfrog leapt out on the path from behind the aloe. Its eyes reflected the moonlight like two luminous dials and it stared at Miles, frozen in fright.

'Hello old chap!' Miles greeted the frog and then stood still, waiting until it had plucked up the courage to hop into the safety of the bushes on the other side of the path.

But another movement caught Miles' eye and he peered into the clearing just beyond the aloes. Julius was at the edge of the garden where the garden lawns met the open bush.

The sight of Julius making his way out into the bush was common enough, the two boys had used this path many times as children, but tonight was different and Julius' presence seemed suddenly out of place. Surely Julius did not believe he still had the right to wander freely in the gardens of Scarfell Farm? He could not expect to consider this place his home after all that had happened, could he?

Miles felt his heart sink in his chest as a yearning for the carefree days of his childhood threatened to overwhelm him. How he longed for those halcyon days when he and Julius had fought the battles of the Boer War together, when their only dispute had centred on ownership of the coveted cardboard assegai.

But Miles knew that those memories were too distant to be relevant now. They belonged to someone else, to a different place, a different life.

Miles trod on a dry twig and it snapped beneath the weight of his foot. Julius heard the sharp crack and he spun round on his heels. For a brief second his eyes were like those of the bullfrog, two sharp twin points of light.

Miles' heart thumped solidly in his chest.

The twin beams shot through the darkness and fixed themselves upon Miles. Silently, the two young men glared at each other with an intensity that left them both shaking.

Beneath that withering stare, Miles felt a stab of fear, but he held his ground. This was his home, his land. Julius would not unsettle him now.

Back on the verandah, Charlie regained consciousness and he pulled himself into an upright position before being sick upon the steps.

Julius glanced beyond Miles at the man who had raped his mother and his eyes narrowed. He ground his teeth together, muscles working against jaw, and clenched his fists. He looked again at Miles and felt the bitterness consume his entire being and gnaw into the last vestiges of his compassion. Anxiously, as if in fear of what he had become, Julius turned and ran into the bush.

For the first time in his young life, he had experienced a hatred so pure that it felt like the grip of cold steel. He would never again be that innocent child who had loved and trusted his friend, Miles Cameron, as his own blood brother. He was a man now. He could never go back.

Panting heavily, Julius kept on running until he reached the open savannah and he could no longer hear the sounds of Charlie Cameron retching on the stoep.

Well away from Scarfell Farm he stopped and waited to regain his breath. He glanced up at the moon and spun round to take in the wide and distant horizons. He did not know which way to go that night and he did not care. There were no well-trodden paths out here on the plains, and he was free to follow the stars.

What Julius did not know was that he had reached one of life's invisible crossroads and that a heavy burden lay across one of the roads. Unknowingly, Julius chose to pick up that burden and make his way down that particular path. It was a heavy weight to carry, but he did not sense it at first, so he could not possibly have known that he would have to bear it for many years to come.

For the burden was revenge.

Sandy Fitzgerald had lost a lot of weight. Many said it suited him, made him look younger, and certainly there was a spring in his step that was not there before. His well-worn maroon Rotary blazer with its frayed emblem on the pocket was at least one size too big for him and his buckle-belt was on its last notch.

'Looks like the widow Barnett suits you well, old friend!' Charlie laughed, slapping the other man on the back. 'She's taken years off you.'

Sandy Fitzgerald blushed furiously and cast his eyes over the room. Two club members paused in their game of snooker listen to the exchange and the chaps at the bar were already smiling in his direction. He shuffled uncomfortably in his over-sized blazer and greeted Charlie with an embarrassed cough, fumbling in his pocket for his wallet.

'Charlie, old chap! Good to see you! Can I get you a drink?' Sandy turned to the barman, anxious to divert attention away from his recently rekindled lovelife, and ordered a Scotch and soda for his tormentor.

'Cheers!' Charlie raised his glass and, certain now of centre stage, turned to his fellows in the Bulawayo Club. 'Here's to Mrs Barnett. Long may she continue to serve old Sandy well!'

'Hear! Hear!'

Sandy gulped his cider and nodded uncomfortably at the chorus of good-natured ribaldry. He had recently formed an acquaintance with Robbie Barnett's widow, Norma, and thanks to Charlie the news had spread across the city like wildfire. Sandy did not mind Bulawayo's society knowing about his new relationship. Norma was a very respectable widow of an old friend. He just did not like Charlie turning it into something smutty. It was humiliating, and he did not want to jest about his courtship while standing at a bar. But that was Charlie Cameron for you. The man was totally insensitive, always had been. Not a patch on his late brother, Ralph!

'So how's life up at Scarfell Farm?' Sandy was determined not to enter into any further discourse on the subject.

'Couldn't be better,' Charlie replied.

'You're one of the lucky ones, you know, being too old for call-up duty. I hear they're extending the age limit to thirty-eight. It's already creating havoc on the farms with women left running the place on their own. Running a farm? That's no job for a woman! It's a recipe for disaster.'

Charlie finished his drink and slammed the glass down on the bar.

'Put another one in there will you buddy? And one for my friend here.' He turned back to Sandy. 'It's bad news all right. The terrs are swarming all over the place like flies on shit. The women are having a tough time of it. No doubt about that.'

'At least the crop farmers are exempt from call-up.'

'Ja, but only until the end of the growing season. Mind you, that's just common sense if you ask me. We're all going to bloody well starve if our boys are too busy fighting in the bush to see to food production. We'd be finished in less than a year. You mark my words, Sandy old boy.'

Sandy ran his finger under his collar. He was sweating, not so much from overweight as in the past, more from a close proximity to Charlie Cameron. The man was a minefield likely to blow up at any minute and Sandy was acutely conscious that he had to choose his words carefully in an effort not to upset him after his second whisky.

Besides, Sandy had heard that all was not well up at Scarfell Farm. There had been an altercation with one of the servants, so he had heard. Something to do with Charlie, people were saying, but no-one knew for certain what had happened. All they knew was that, with Miles now back at school, Scarfell Farm was once again starting to look shabby and neglected.

The people of Rhodesia had grown used to the sight of desolate farms abandoned by their owners after terrorist attacks. They recognised the signs. Tractors stood idle and rusty in the fields, weeds were left untended and in the kitchens there was a smell of burnt grease and milk going sour. Dogs piddled in the doorways and cockroaches crawled over the surfaces. It was a familiar sight in the north and Eastern Highlands, but not so much here in Matabeleland. And certainly it was not a sight you would want to associate with occupied homesteads.

Sandy prayed that Scarfell Farm would not be allowed to deteriorate to the point of dereliction, certainly not while a Cameron was at the helm.

The Camerons had farmed at the foot of the Blue Hills for generations. Surely one of their own would not stand by and allow that fertile land to fall into disrepair. Charlie owed it to his forefathers and to his brother Ralph to keep the farm functioning properly. He also owed it to young Miles, his nephew. Charlie had been appointed guardian of Scarfell Farm. It was his duty to guard it well for it was Miles' inheritance. And Miles was family.

'Anyway it'll take more than a couple of muntus with spears to see us off. The whites built this bloody country and we have a darn sight more right to stay here than the munts. Left to themselves they'd still be living in mud huts and shitting in holes. They'd never have had the intelligence to put in roads, running water, phones and everything. They've got the white man to thank for that. Not that they do thank us! Bloody ungrateful they are. But it's like I always say, you can take the black man out of the bush, but you can't take the bush out of the black man. They're savages plain and simple. They don't understand good manners. As far as they're concerned, if you don't give it to them on a plate they'll steal it from you. Simple as that. Savages! Blood-sucking, lazy, thieving savages!'

Sandy gulped his cider and looked about the room in hope that someone might come to his aid. He had never been overly fond of Charlie, in spite of his connections with the Cameron family, but now, without Ralph to rein him in, the man was like a mad dog straining at the leash.

'Are you linked up to agric-alert yet?' Sandy muttered in a bid to steer the conversation into calmer waters.

'My brother saw to all that just before he died.'

I suppose he would have,' Sandy nodded his approval. 'Ralph was always on the ball when it came to keeping things shipshape. And a damn good thing the system is, too, although you'll know that better than I.'

The agric-alert radio link had been established as a security measure in the Centenary area in 1973, Farmers who were connected to the network of sets could listen to each other's calls, and the central station could tell which particular set had raised the alarm. It was a radio communication network that reduced the feeling of isolation in the distant farms and gave neighbours the chance to arrive at a scene in time to save lives.

It was particularly reassuring for the hundreds of women left alone on the farms while their men were off fighting in the bush. Alone, and in danger from ZANU infiltrators coming across the border from the training grounds in Mozambique, it was a lifeline for this unrewarded community of women who were fighting to maintain the agricultural prosperity of their beloved country.

The value of agric-alert was immeasurable and soon the network had spread to other farming communities in Rhodesia. Ralph, ever conscious of his duty to protect his wife and family, had been one of the first farmers in the local area to subscribe to it. But it had served no real purpose at the end. For there had been no call for help from Scarfell Farm on the night of the slaying, no indication that lives were threatened and an entire family about to be extinguished. The radio set had remained silent on that night and people slept in their beds unaware that Death Most Vile had visited one of their own.

'I suppose you're lending your support to the Bright Lights at least?'

Charlie shook his head. 'No time for that. Too busy looking after my own farm to volunteer to patrol other people's. Now don't get me wrong, I think it's a damn good idea and I salute those chaps who volunteered to join, but I simply don't have the time myself. You understand, don't you? Scarfell Farm is a big responsibility and it's my job to keep it safe for my nephew when he comes of age. My priority is to look after everything my brother worked for and, although I wouldn't wish to see my neighbour's farm in trouble, I haven't got the time to go off and fight for him. The Camerons have had our share of troubles. The others have got to look after themselves now.'

'But members of the Bright Lights guard the entrance to your farm at night, don't they? I've seen them.'

'Oh sure. And very welcome they are too. It's a comfort to my Clara that they're prepared to sit at the front gates for hours on end. Helps her get to sleep at night. Do you know, a couple of guys even went with her to the top field last week to check out a couple of fences. Figured it's too isolated up there for her to go on her own, even during the day. Bloody good eggs. That's what they are.'

'And, of course, members of the Police Reserve are also patrolling your patch, aren't they?

'They sure are,' Charlie finished his drink and pulled a cigarette out of the crumpled pack from his pocket. The choice of forty different brands had recently been reduced to eight and the Government had begun selling them in unlined packets in a bid to save money. Rhodesians claimed they reminded them of rationing in wartime Britain and protested vigorously. Eventually, the Government gave in under pressure and agreed to forgo part of the anticipated savings by lengthening the filter tip and reintroducing foil wrapping. To many beleaguered Rhodesians, fighting a civil war they did not understand, this was seized as a victory over bureaucracy.

Charlie tugged out the cigarette with his teeth, lit it and dropped the match into the ashtray while it was still burning. Both he and Sandy watched as the orange flame wormed its way down the stick before extinguishing itself in a drop of beer that had fallen into the base of the ashtray.

'You must be reassured, though, that other people are prepared to risk their lives for you. I suppose it's that selfless spirit that sets us whites apart from the savages. We don't operate on a selfish basis. We look after each other.'

'That's it in a nutshell, Sandy my lad! In a nutshell!' Charlie lifted the empty glass in a gesture of salute before nodding to the barman for a refill.

He could not quite put his finger upon it but, in spite of the air of bonhomie, there was something in Sandy Fitzgerald's manner tonight that had begun to get up his nose. The little man's shoulders were just a little too square and his stance just a shade too self-confident, military even. He had even met Charlie eye-to-eye for some of the time, unusual for this squat little bloke. No, there was something about old Sandy Fitzgerald tonight that had begun to irk Charlie.

Irritably, he snatched his third Scotch and soda from the barman and threw the payment on the damp surface. He glanced once more at his companion who seemed to be watching him with a vaguely melancholy expression. By the look on his face anyone would think that he, Charlie, was responsible for the bloody mess they were all in.

Well that's just fine, Charlie mused over a long draft on his cigarette, the silly sod can act all high and mighty if he likes, but Charlie did not have to stay and put up with it. He scanned the room and spotted a poker game in the far corner. His eyes lit up and his handsome face creased into that famous grin that had captured so many female hearts in the past.

'Deal me in boys,' he yelled across the room. 'Sandy, here, has got to get back to his good lady, the widow Barnett.'

He pushed across the room and pulled up a stool, glancing back over his shoulder to where Sandy Fitzgerald still sat with his half empty glass of cider.

'Jesus!' he snorted in derision. 'Just because the guy's getting laid for the first time in God knows how many years, he thinks he's some kind of wise guy who can go telling everyone else how to run their lives. He's turning into a right superior so-and-so!'

With that, Charlie sucked in a deep breath, fanned the cards in his fingers and frowned over the hand he had just been dealt. It would be a winner, little doubt about that. Charlie's luck at cards never failed him.

Change had come upon the people of Rhodesia and they did not like it. In his surrender speech, Ian Smith had promised that a new Council of State would be established with an equal number of black and white representatives. Decisions would be reached by consensus, but the ultimate decision-making power would rest with a white chairman. It was viewed with suspicion on all sides.

The repeal of the Land Tenure Act was one such item on the complicated agenda for change. The law, which had been rushed through Parliament back in October 1969, with little or no debate, was responsible for allocating 45 million acres of land to a mere five per cent of its inhabitants. The rest, most of it infertile bushland, had gone to the blacks who constituted the remaining ninety five per cent of the population.

What had started out as a welcome policy of segregation in the eyes of most whites proved a mixed blessing in the mid-1970s when many European homes were left standing empty and vulnerable. Whites were not prepared to pay the exorbitant prices demanded, while blacks with money were willing to pay over the odds for the privilege of moving into districts that lay north of Salisbury's railway tracks.

Local tradesmen hit hard by the escalating war were also keen to welcome new customers, black or white! At the same time, however, few whites were willing to tolerate black neighbours living nearby. That was too much to ask and when members of Salisbury City Council voted to evict a local family in the European suburb of Prospect, purely on the basis that they were coloured, the white residents were relieved.

Ian Smith, keen to negotiate a favourable settlement with internal African leaders, had begun looking at ways to repeal the fundamental apartheid of the Land Tenure Act so that black Africans who could afford it were able to move into white areas without the risk of eviction.

One such prominent African, Ndabaningi Sithole, Mugabe's predecessor as leader of ZANU and a powerful force in the settlement talks, was pleased to accept the opportunity to experience life on the white side of the tracks. However, when Sithole was unexpectedly threatened with eviction, it did not augur well for Ian Smith's delicate diplomatic talks.

Clearly, the internal settlement was still a long way off but, in spite of the entrenched views of whites, Smith knew that the Land Tenure Act had to be repealed if Rhodesia was to achieve a successful transition to majority rule.

Derision greeted the Prime Minister's first tentative steps towards opening up white agricultural land for purchase by members of other races and adopting a non-racial housing policy in residential areas. He was accused of violating basic Rhodesia Front principles and no fewer than twelve Members of Parliament left the caucus over the issue.

The amendments, although contentious, were mainly symbolic as very few blacks could afford to buy land in white areas, but the debate was still heated. One Minister declared that the policy of land segregation had been responsible for Rhodesia's "excellent race relations" while others invoked the memory of the country's founding father, Cecil Rhodes.

The government won the vote on a knife-edge.

If urban blacks were still feeling the repression of old laws designed to protect white interests, the rural poor were under even greater pressure.

The Protected Villages (PV's) programme, first introduced in 1974 to "protect" the rural black population from terrorists, had expanded in spite of fierce opposition from African leaders, the Salvation Army and other human rights groups. The government's Internal Affairs Committee had set up Civil Action Teams to locate and prepare new sites into which thousands of Africans would be herded in the months to come. Members of the Committee stood accused of destroying the traditional agricultural system of black Africa and setting up the barbaric and inhumane PV's without giving any consideration as to how they intended to replace the cultural, social and economic structure of rural black Africa.

Such was the unpopularity of the PV's that a new protective unit, Guard Force, had been created to maintain order. The PV's were loathed by all and this was exacerbated by reports of brutality among the Guard Forces. The blame was shifted on to boredom, isolation and the low morale that invariably accompanied such a thankless and unwelcome task.

Hundreds of black farmers had lost their livestock and their crops and now had little choice other than to obey the regulations which stipulated that they could return to their land during the day but must remain under guard from dusk to dawn. Resentment simmered and the PV's became fertile territory for freedom fighters. For the people packed into those compounds had lost not only their livelihoods, they had lost their essential right to freedom of movement across the vast terrain that was their home. And the freedom fighter was promising to return to them that precious commodity.

Yes, they would fight for freedom. And, yes, they would die for freedom.

Night had fallen over Scarfell and an eerie quiet encircled the house. The servants had finished their chores for the day and Charlie was out drinking at the Bulawayo Club. Even the cattle were quiet on this night.

A party of moths and beetles swirled and danced beneath the light of the porch lanterns. The rest of the house, save for the main bedroom, was in darkness. Through the open window, a small, thin figure was moving back and forth.

Two suitcases lay open on the bed, neatly packed with clothes. On the floor, a cardboard box had been filled with books, photographs and other personal possessions. Clara squashed the contents into the larger suitcase and leaned heavily on the lid to close it. She arched her back and rubbed the base of her spine where a twinge of lumbago had begun to bother her. She then snapped the other suitcase shut and dragged them both off the bed. They were heavy and it was a long haul to the station wagon parked outside, but she would manage. Besides, there was no-one here to help her. She was alone.

She lugged the huge suitcase through the sitting room and down the steps of the verandah, pausing for breath before summoning the strength to hoist it into the back of the vehicle. The other case was lighter.

She returned to the bedroom to shift the cardboard box and, fearful that it might break if she tried to lift it, she pushed it along the floor with her foot. Once outside, she bent down and circled it with her arms before pulling it up to waist height. Almost swooning from the strain, she staggered with bent knees to the open trunk and shoved it inside, bending over it for a moment to gather her breath.

She closed the car door and went back inside the house to take one last lingering look at Scarfell Farm. The sitting room was in darkness. The lights were switched off and the only illumination came from the lanterns outside. Strange shadows danced in the corners of the room and the walls appeared to move as if by some unseen force. Clara closed her eyes and was transported back to a time when this room was bright and warm and colourful, alive with the sounds of children laughing, dogs barking and people going about their daily lives.

It was silent now, but the spirits of those who had loved Scarfell Farm lived on in the nooks and crannies of the magnificent old house. The Camerons would always be a part of this beautiful land. Generations had been born and raised here in Africa. They had built this farm with their bare hands and had shared their prosperity with the many black Africans who had lived and worked here with them.

Ralph and Rachel had been good, honest folks. They cared for each other, for their children and for the rich red earth of Africa. They had not expected to be sacrificed in the bloody quest for freedom. Their African workers were already free. The Camerons provided well for their employees who were well fed, well paid and their families well housed.

Did they really have to die?

Clara wiped away a tear and closed the doors quietly, locking them and leaving the key in its appointed place. She stood on the stoep and drew a deep breath before making her way down to the car and climbing into the driver's seat. She switched on the engine and the station wagon roared noisily into life, its headlights forming a new magnet for the dozens of flying insects outside.

The vehicle made its way down the drive, that was now pitted and potholed, until it reached the main gate. The car stopped for a moment with its tail-lights burning ruby red in the dark night. And then Clara shoved the engine into first gear and turned to join the main road that would led to Beitbridge and the South African border.

She was going home.

11

Miles was seventeen on 20th April 1977 and his powerful physique was proof that he had already crossed the line from boyhood to manhood. His muscles were lean and strong, honed from years spent outdoors, and his chest and forearms were covered with a sprinkling of dark hair. His skin, tanned by the African sun, was toughened by hard labour. His hands, with their unusually short, stubby fingers, were covered with calluses and dry from working the land at Scarfell Farm. In short, he was typical of hundreds of white Rhodesians from good farming stock.

Like his father before him, Miles was a quiet, thoughtful young man given to long periods of intense introspection. He was shy, and content to sit on the edge of a group and listen rather than meet the demands of centre stage. And he was modest, too. Surprisingly so, since Miles had inherited more than his fair share of the Cameron good looks.

His unruly mop of hair, the colour of polished bark, was tinged with flecks of gold that caught the sun, and his eyes were so dark they were almost black. But it was that lazy, lop-sided grin that tugged at the heart-strings of most young girls, and that casual wink that was guaranteed to leave hearts pounding. Miles was unaware of the impact he had on Bulawayo's female population. So much so that he did not even know that he had swept the board in the St. Hilda's Girls' School "Most Gorgeous Guys" competition! But it would not have made much difference if he had known. Miles was Miles and he was not prone to vanity. He was his own man.

But an innate modesty and genuine lack of guile did not prevent Miles from seeking the pleasure of female company at the popular MacDonalds Club disco in Bulawayo on his rare weekends at home. On those occasions, he would be seen with other lads of his age sporting a bottle of Lion lager and a hopeful smile on a Saturday night.

Max, as it was commonly known, was a local sports club in one of Bulawayo's affluent suburbs. It offered a range of sports including cricket, tennis and squash. It also had a well-stocked bar where guests could gather after a game to chat or mull over the latest news and affairs. But the Saturday night disco was by far the most popular activity and one that provided a lucrative source of income for the club's owners.

Every week, crowds of youngsters would queue outside the main gates. Once inside, the boys would push and jostle to get to the bar while the females grouped themselves around the tables along the wall. The dance floor was in the centre of the room, illuminated by flashing lights. In the corner, surrounded by cardboard boxes stuffed with records, was the DJ. It was no different from Saturday night discos the world over.

Miles was in a good mood. His seventeenth birthday had coincided with Plumtree's rugby match against St. Paul's in Bulawayo. In keeping with tradition at most boarding schools, boys were allowed the privilege of a stop-over if the event took place in their home town. As a result, Miles was able to celebrate his birthday at Max with some of his pals. He had been invited to stay with the Coker brothers. Their family home was in the same suburb as the club so everything had worked out perfectly.

The disco was already in full swing when Miles downed his second bottle of beer. The music was loud, and he and his companions were already feeling the heat from the dance floor and that heady mix of perfume and girlish perspiration.

True to form, the boys were standing by the bar with their beer bottles prominently displayed in front of their chests. It was not good to give the impression that you were a soft drinks kind of guy. Far better to let the girls know they were dealing with a real man - a man who could handle his beer! They stood with their feet planted firmly apart, laughing loudly at Balfour Coker's ribald anecdote. Although seemingly engrossed in the story, each boy had one eye fixed firmly on the activities out on the dance floor and even Balfour's renowned wit could not divert their attention completely away from that tantalising, swaying throng.

The girls had left their handbags under their table and were now pretending to ignore the attentions of the boys up at the bar. But a sophisticated communications network was in place, which guaranteed that any tacit signals were well and truly received.

Miles took a slug of beer and cast his eye over the dance floor. He did not know it, but he had already been singled out as prey for Mandy Shaw. In fact, Miles was regularly singled out by the girls, but few had plucked up the courage to make the first move. Miles always seemed so remote, and most girls were intimidated by his apparent indifference.

But tonight was going to be different, according to Amanda Shaw.

Each week, the girls would meet in the toilets to discuss strategy and to mark out their chosen partner for the night. This helped prevent potential rivals from encroaching on another female's territory. It was also the place to share news of recent conquests and to commiserate over failures. And it was in front of the mirror, halfway through a layer of lipstick, that Amanda Shaw announced her intentions.

'You'll never get Miles Cameron!' the other girls chorused.

'Yes I will!' Mandy pursed her lips with determination and smiled at her reflection. 'You watch. I'll have him eating out of my hand before the end of the night.'

Her sister, Susie, grinned. 'Not a chance. Miles Cameron is too cool. He's not going to bother with you! He's probably having a passionate affair with some glamorous married woman up in Harare. He's not going to be interested in you!'

Mandy thrust out her pert little breasts and tugged her top down a notch or two. 'Want a bet?'

Susie surveyed her sister with a critical sibling's eye. Tall and sporty, with a shock of blonde curls and thick, sensuous lips, Mandy was certainly well-equipped physically to wheedle her way into Miles' group, but what she did when she got there was quite another matter. Miles was a quiet, thoughtful guy. He could easily be put off by Mandy's girlish chatter.

'You might get a quick dance with him, but no more. You're not his type.'

Mandy tugged a hairbrush through her glossy locks and spun round to face her sister. 'I suppose you know who is, huh? You? No way!' She brandished the hairbrush menacingly in her sister's face. 'I reckon I've got more to offer Miles Cameron than any of the girls round here.'

'That's what we all think,' her best friend, Jane, interjected. 'I could offer him some fun myself, but I haven't got the nerve to talk to him when he's on his own. I reckon he still holds a torch for Lydia Llewellyn. They were really close before she and her parents upped sticks and moved to the UK. He's not approachable like the other guys. A bit too difficult to get through to for my liking, even though he is gorgeous. No, Balf Coker's more my type. He's much easier to deal with!'

Mandy peered at her reflection and examined her complexion for minor blemishes. It was clear and creamy, with sun-kissed cheeks and dazzling blue eyes. She was not going to waste her assets on easy targets like the Coker brothers. She deserved better. And they did not come much better than Miles Ewan Cameron.

The girls filed out of the toilets and dropped their bags under the table before sashaying out on to the dance floor. The music was loud and conversation was impossible, so they concentrated all their efforts on making the right moves at the right time. They all knew, and had practised at length, the latest dances that were the rage in England or America, and they followed the steps with self-conscious precision. Most disliked the Pogo that had accompanied bands like The Jam or The Clash, preferring dances that showed off their femininity and emphasised the feline grace that they had worked so hard to acquire.

For some, like Mandy Shaw and her sister, Susie, the moves came easily. They had a natural rhythm that suited most types of music. But Susie could not match her sister's self-confidence and she spent most of the time on the dance floor looking down at her feet. Mandy, on the other hand, gazed about her with deliberate nonchalance. But there was nothing nonchalant about Mandy Shaw. She was constantly on the lookout for a potential male admirer across the sea of bobbing heads. And, if she spotted one, she would deliberately turn to allow him a better view of her long, shapely legs or tight, little bottom.

Mostly, the boys would grin widely and elbow their mates before slamming their beer bottle on the bar and swaggering out to join her for a dance. Others would return her provocative smile with the promise of much more later.

There was little doubt that Mandy was a flirt, but she was a good sport and popular with both boys and girls. Tonight, however, Mandy was not interested in the lascivious attentions of her usual admirers, and she avoided meeting their eyes in case they mistook her glance as an invitation to join her. On this particular Saturday night, Mandy had set her sights on a much more difficult target. Tonight, Mandy had eyes only for Miles Cameron and, in spite of previous failed attempts, and the rumour that he still harboured a secret passion for Lydia Llewellyn, she was determined to win more than a dance with Bulawayo's Most Gorgeous Guy.

Miles was leaning back with both elbows resting on the bar. A half-empty bottle dangled from his fingers. Unlike his friends, Miles was not laughing aloud at Balfour's joke. He was frowning into the distance in a concentrated effort to remember the name of the song on the turntable.

An imitation diamond necklace, bought that very day for five dollars from the local store, sparkled in the light of the rotating mirror ball and caught his eye. Inadvertently, his gaze travelled up the long, creamy neck of its owner to those wet lips and big, blue eyes. Mandy spotted his appreciative inspection and immediately capitalised upon it by pursing her lips. Embarrassed, Miles looked away and gulped the last of the beer, but there was a sudden, nagging ache in his groin, and he could not stop his treacherous eyes from turning back to that lovely, young siren out on the dance floor.

Mandy was still watching him, her body swaying gently to the music. Unlike Miles, Mandy was far from embarrassed as she let her hands slide provocatively over her hips. In spite of his discomfiture, Miles followed the slow path of those hands and his breath quickened with every inch covered. He could feel his jeans growing tighter and he shifted uncomfortably against the bar, hoping that no-one would notice the swelling in his pants.

'She looks like she's up for it!' Balfour jutted his chin in Mandy's direction. 'I'd say you were in there buddy.'

Miles swore under his breath and looked away. He had not quite mastered the art of sexual ribaldry with other lads, and he was uneasy in the market-place atmosphere of the disco. Some of his pals would brag openly about their sexual encounters, often within earshot of the girl herself, but Miles could not bring himself to compete with the other young stallions. He guessed that most of their boasts were either fiction or fantasy. He knew that most of his contemporaries were as anxious as he was about actually "doing it" and there had been a number of speculative conversations on specific techniques or protocol in the school dormitories at night.

But most of his peers were not hampered by the irritating shyness and self-doubts that assailed Miles. Most were perfectly aware of their status as desirable mates and all expected to be in a position to speak with authority on carnal matters in the immediate future. Miles, on the other hand, was irked that he might have to wait for some time before he could pluck up the courage to rid himself of the powerful urges and that ache in his groin that invariably accompanied the sight of a pretty girl. Little did he know that he could have the pick of Bulawayo's female society, and that one smile from him could render most of them speechless. But then, even if he had guessed, he would probably not have believed it.

'Fancy a dance?'

Miles felt the warm breath against his ear and it tickled. He turned to discover its source and was pleasantly surprised to find Mandy Shaw crushed up against him. He took one last slug of beer before turning to her with a nervous, lop-sided grin.

'Sure.'

Fearful that he might change his mind, Mandy grabbed his hand and led him on to the dance floor with a proprietorial air. A superior smirk was delivered in the direction of her friends who were clearly impressed at the sight of Mandy Shaw with Bulawayo's "Most Gorgeous Guy" in tow.

As the evening drew to a close, the tempo slackened, the mood changed and the flashing lights were replaced by warm colours that swirled through the darkened room. It was hot, and hormone levels were high. Youngsters who had been staking their claims during the course of the evening now moved in on their quarry. This was the time for slow dancing, for the close physical contact that would establish exactly how far they and their dancing partner were willing to go.

Mandy opened her eyes wide and waited with feigned innocence for Miles to make the first move. Miles breathed deeply and drew her into his arms where she wriggled closer and moved her body in time to the music.

Miles was wearing a white capped-sleeve tee-shirt that accentuated his darkly tanned biceps. Mandy gripped his upper arms and her breath quickened. She could feel his heart beating as he threaded his arms around her tiny waist and pulled her against his chest until her breasts were squashed against the damp cotton. She let her hips gyrate a little and Miles groaned, inwardly struggling to prevent an erection. But Mandy was an expert in such matters and she knew at once the full extent of his arousal. It was a thrilling sensation and Mandy found herself overwhelmed by the heat, the husky smell of sweat and his lean, hard body.

'Take me home Miles' she whispered as the music faded to a close. She could barely stand, such was the intensity of her passion. 'I don't want to be here.'

Miles adjusted his crotch surreptitiously and, without saying a word, he pushed his way through the crowd and led her outside to the car park.

'You off somewhere nice, buddy?' Balfour Coker was leaning against his Mazda with a young girl pinned to his chest.

'I'll catch up with you later,' Miles hissed.

'Oh right!' Balfour spotted Mandy Shaw in tow and grinned. 'Say no more, old chap. You take as long as you like. I'll leave the key on the stoep. Hi there Mandy!'

'Hello Balfour,' Mandy dismissed Balfour with a disdainful look and then clambered into Miles' car. Her skirt was so short that it rode up to her bottom as she did so. Balfour, rewarded by a glimpse of two fleshy mounds, was more than happy to forgive her earlier haughtiness.

It was only a short journey, but Miles' and Mandy's fervour had reached boiling point by the time they pulled into her parents' drive.

'Park here,' Mandy gasped. 'Mum and Dad won't see the car and we can sneak in without being seen.'

'Won't they hear us?' Miles pulled the Morris Minor off the drive and left it under the branches of the old syringa. The tyres crackled on top of the fallen leaves and stones and Miles panicked.

'It's okay,' Mandy opened the car door and placed one long, shapely leg on the ground. 'They're probably fast asleep at the back of the house and besides …. the guest cottage is empty….'

Miles felt his erect member throb as she climbed out of the car. Perfectly content to be led to his doom by this enchanting female, he followed her along the path to the cottage at the side of the main house.

It was a typical guest cottage. Most Europeans had friends and family abroad who came to visit on a regular basis. Although they could stay in the main house if they chose, most preferred the independence of their own little holiday home. Servants were used to extending their duties to cater for extra visitors and guest cottages were rarely empty, even in these unsettled times.

The Shaw's cottage was a long, single-storey building, painted white with black leaded windows. The roof was thatched. A verandah ran along the front of the house and it was a short walk through the garden to the main house for breakfast. Although the cottage had its own kitchen and dining room, few guests used these facilities, preferring to join their hosts for meals and entertainment.

Mandy fumbled in her handbag for the key. Briefly, she lost her balance and she fell against Miles in a fit of giggles.

'Sshh… you'll wake your parents!'

Mandy pressed her fist against her mouth to stifle her laughter and then she held the key aloft with a triumphant wave. 'Got you! You naughty little key!'

Still giggling, but quieter now, she prodded the door in a vain attempt to locate the lock. 'Blast! Where is that wretched hole!' Her unintentional innuendo reduced her to hysterics and she sank down to the floor in a heap. 'I think I've had a wee drop too much to drink!' she declared solemnly.

Miles took the key and helped her to her feet. He pushed the door open with his foot and followed her inside.

'Don't put the lights on,' he said as she turned to the switch. 'The moon's bright enough.'

'Bright enough for you to see me?' Mandy whispered, letting her cotton top fall to the ground.

Miles stared at her half-naked body. The swell of her breasts, with their taut, rosy nipples, glimmered in the light of the moon and he swallowed hard. 'I reckon so….'

Mandy moved closer and helped him pull his tee-shirt over his head. She stood back, impressed by his physique. 'You're so… so handsome,' she said running her hands over his chest. 'You're not like the other lads. You're a real man.'

'Let's hope so,' Miles felt the first stab of terror in his stomach. Suddenly, he was going to be "doing it" for real and he was not sure he was fully prepared. It was one thing to be chatting about it in the dormitory, or reading one of Charlie's magazines, but Mandy was a flesh and blood female and he was expected to perform to a certain standard. It was a sobering thought.

'You're not serious?' Mandy gasped.

'What do you mean, serious? Serious about what?'

'Miles Cameron, is this your first time?'

Miles blushed and looked away. 'First of many, I hope,' he replied, trying in vain to recover his manly status.

'Oh wow! So I'll be your first! Oh Miles, that's fantastic!'

'It is?'

'Of course it is. That means you'll never forget me. You never forget your first love, you know.'

'First or last…' Miles said gruffly, pulling her back into his arms. 'I doubt I'll ever forget you, but you might need to give me a bit of coaching here and there.'

Completely naked now, the youngsters lay down on the quilted bedspread. Mandy had assumed an almost motherly protectiveness as she leaned over and kissed the tip of his nose. Slowly, she left a damp trail across his chest as she let her tongue wander freely down his body. Miles breathed deeply and threaded his fingers into her hair, willing her to complete her journey.

Mandy let her fingers play with the hairs at the top of his groin and she marvelled at the way his manhood quivered under her touch. She wanted this to be special, something that Miles would remember for the rest of his life, but her own passions were threatening to overwhelm her.

The two young bodies were entwined, lit with silver strands of moonlight, and glistening with their own sweat and lovemaking. The silence was broken by their ragged breathing and by the occasional murmur of shared pleasures.

Miles had fought to subdue the desire to abandon all etiquette and simply enter that warm, wet place that so beckoned, but now he was losing the battle. His head was at bursting point and the heat inside his body was too intense to quell much longer. It was time to let nature takes it course.

Mandy responded effortlessly, letting her legs slip apart and guiding him inside with experienced hands. It seemed so easy, so natural that all Miles had to do was follow his own instincts. After all, men and women had been successfully doing this for centuries. There was no reason why Miles Cameron should not join their ranks.

'Was that okay?' Miles leaned on his elbow and brushed a hair from Mandy's forehead.

'Perfect,' she murmured, snuggling closer. 'You were perfect.'

Miles leaned back against the pillow and allowed a smile to flicker across his lips. There had been a niggling doubt at the back of his mind as to whether he had done what was expected of him. After all, he had no way of knowing for certain whether Mandy had enjoyed their encounter as much as he had. He may have overlooked some crucial element or simply been unaware of his carnal duties. It was a worry, but reassured that Mandy had enjoyed his lovemaking, his overriding emotion was one of relief. He had 'done it' at last and he had done it properly without making a hash of things or making a complete fool of himself. Finally, and without mishaps, he had managed to rid himself of his virginity and he would never again have to worry about what the "first time" would be like.

He glanced down at the pretty young girl beside him. She opened her eyes wide and smiled. Immediately, he felt that familiar stirring in his loins and he pushed her back into the pillows, crushing her lips with his own.

He had no need for guidance or reassurance now. He had crossed the line from boyhood to manhood. And it was a great place to be.

'You don't have to go, you know. No-one's forcing you to go.'

'I know that, baas Miles,' Bliss smiled warmly at the young man who was once in her charge and unshed tears pricked the back of her eyes. 'It is for the best.'

Miles leaned against the edge of the table in the centre of the kia and stubbed the hard floor moodily with his toe. As was often the case, he was barefoot and his feet were stained with red dust. He no longer noticed the numerous cuts and scratches acquired during his daily walkabouts, and his soles were as tough and hardy as the wild animals who roamed the bush. A chongololo wriggled across the ground and Miles poked it gently until it rolled itself into a defensive ball.

'I wish I could do that,' he mused. 'It must great to be able to just curl up and let all your troubles disappear.'

'Perhaps, for the chongololo, they do disappear,' Bliss replied. 'And for you, too. If you cannot see the trouble, how do you know for certain it is still there?'

'Because I can feel it,' Miles persisted.

Bliss nodded. Perhaps, for this lonely descendant of the ill-fated Cameron family, trouble would never be far away. And even in times of joy, there would always be those cruel memories. Bliss looked at the handsome young man lounging against the table in front of her and her heart went out to him.

She did not want to leave Scarfell Farm. She did not want to abandon her beloved boy in his early years of manhood. But she had no choice. She felt threatened and vulnerable when baas Miles was away at school. It was a fear that had been compounded when baas Charlie's wife left. There were times now when Bliss was alone in the house with her tormentor, and she could bear it no longer.

Her son, Julius, had begged her to leave Scarfell Farm in the wake of Charlie's assault. He wanted to see her back in the relative safety of her family kraal at Tshotsholo, but she had fought against giving up her home and her independence. But, in the end, she knew he was right. It was impossible for her to stay at Scarfell Farm. Miles Cameron was a man now. He no longer needed her. There was no reason to stay at Scarfell any longer. She had completed her task and she could look at him with pride, for he was a fine young man. She knew that his parents, if they had lived, would have been proud of him. But, sadly, they had not survived to see their son grow into manhood. And they had not lived to see the destruction of the wonderful world they had created at Scarfell Farm.

The bittersweet memories were shattered by the presence of a dark and menacing figure at the door. 'What do you want?'

'I am here to say goodbye to your Mother.' Miles replied coldly.

Just like his father before him, Julius blocked out the light as he stood in the doorway, his towering frame edged with gold from the sun. And then he stepped into the room and glowered at the two plastic carrier bags and brown cardboard suitcase that contained his mother's meagre possessions. He could see the spout of the Queen's Coronation teapot jutting through the side of the plastic bag and he was angry that a proud African woman should want to burden herself with such Colonial frippery. The sight of it brought the memories flooding back and he swallowed hard to dispel the image of that scene of rape and degradation.

'Do you have everything packed?' Julius ignored Miles and spun round to face his mother.

'Yes.' Bliss could no longer choke back the tears and they rolled freely down her cheeks, leaving wet traces on her dust-smeared face.

'Then we will leave this place.' Julius swept up the cardboard suitcase and grabbed both the plastic bags with one hand. He did not glance at Miles, did not take one last lingering look at his boyhood home, but simply stepped outside into the mid-day sun.

Bliss made to follow him, but she paused as she drew level with Miles and they stared at each other for a moment. Miles moved to hug her, but resisted knowing that Julius would resent such familiarity. Bliss saw the move and, briefly, she lifted her arms to enfold him in the warm embrace that had so often comforted him in his childhood years. But she saw his hesitation and she drew back, fearful of stepping beyond the confines of her station. Instead, she simply dropped her eyes and her shoulders sagged.

Tentatively, Miles held out his hand and she looked at him through her tears. She wiped her own hand on her skirt before clasping Miles' outstretched palm in a clumsy imitation of British formality.

'Goodbye Bliss.'

'May God bless you and keep you safe, Nkosi.'

Miles watched as she turned to go and his heart was heavy.

'Thank you for loving me, Bliss' he whispered.

But Bliss did not hear. She was already too far away.

1978 was a year of change in Rhodesia. The Prime Minister, Ian Smith, had been locked in talks with Bishop Abel Muzorewa. Their priority was to find an internal settlement that would help smooth the way to black majority rule. Smith, wearied by years of conflict and fruitless negotiation, had agreed in principle to Muzorewa's demands, but had insisted that certain safeguards be built in to the settlement to protect the country's white minority. Tortuous negotiations followed where the thorny issue of white parliamentary representation was debated. With perseverance, Smith managed to secure an agreement to his proposed safeguards. There were guarantees about property and pension rights, an independent judiciary and Civil Service, and the security forces and prison service would be free from political interference. None of these provisions could be changed without the support of at least six white representatives.

Smith knew that black majority rule was inevitable. His task was to preserve the safety and well-being of Rhodesia's white population. Testament to this despair, was when Smith said:

'I love this country above all else and it breaks my heart to see it falling apart. I know I could retire to my farm if people think I am in the way of a settlement, but I just can't throw my country up in the air and hope someone will catch it.'

On a more militant note, Robert Mugabe christened 1978 as the Year of the People's Storm and his battle cry resounded across black Rhodesia:

'The enemy is battered and dazed. Let us now move towards him with all our mustered reserves, remembering always that ours is a people's war, fought by the people and for the people.'

On the 15th August, the Rhodesia Herald was renamed simply "The Herald" and the word "Rhodesia" was dropped from the name of the state lottery. In September, the Salisbury Chamber of Commerce appointed its first black African vice-president. This was followed by the Red Cross who appointed a black chairman in November. In the same year, the Education Department introduced compulsory courses in Shona and Sindebele. White schools complained that they were unable to implement the new policy due to a shortage of language tapes and machines. Their protest was ignored in a country where there were millions of Shona-speaking people.

The whites fought to stem the tide of black equality, but the political changes were relentless. With the white safeguards in place, the settlement, known as the Rhodesian Constitutional Agreement, was finally signed and a Transition Government formed that would prepare the way for majority black rule. The settlement, which clearly favoured the whites, was viewed with suspicion by the Patriotic Front, and both Joshua Nkomo and Robert Mugabe opposed it.

In spite of the opposition, the emancipation of black Africa was becoming more and more apparent in everyday life. Blacks were appointed to help in white hospitals and medical care was extended to cover increased numbers of black Africans.

It was a long and painful process, fraught with indecision, mistakes and dishonesty on both sides. But each step had to be taken. They were hesitant steps, teetering steps, but each and every one would lead to the emergence of a new Africa. Whether the new Africa would survive to take its place in the democratic world, or whether ancient conflicts and bitterness would lead to its destruction, no-one knew for sure. For that was the future.

September was known as the Blue Month when the jacarandas lining the wide avenues of the towns and cities were rich with blue and purple flowers. Gardens, too, were coming into bloom after the cold winter months. At Scarfell Farm, Rachel's beloved syringas were in full flower and their perfume mingled with that of the white jasmine and wild citrus flowers. Dawn was tinged with a magical blue mist that draped itself like lace across the landscape until the early morning clouds had been burned away by the sun.

Miles had been up since dawn and had already tended to the animals and made sure that the workers had their pay packets in time for the weekend. Charlie had overslept and had missed the milking, but Miles refused to waste his energies on fruitless anger. He had long since recognised his uncle for the man that he was, and had accepted that there was little he could do to change him. Charlie was a lost cause. The main concern was how to stop him dragging Scarfell Farm down with him.

Miles had toyed with the idea of leaving school early and devoting his time to the farm, but he knew that was naïve. He did not know enough about modern farming methods to bring Scarfell back to a level where it could sustain itself for any length of time. Miles knew that, to survive, Scarfell Farm would need to move forward. Major investment would be needed and a constant, reliable presence there to oversee its progress. After discussions with his friends' parents, and lengthy letters to and from his grandparents in England, Miles had decided to study agriculture in the UK. Only that way would he have sufficient knowledge to nurture the land that was his birthright.

The sound of car horns reminded Miles that he and his friends had planned a trip to the Matopos that day. The thought cheered him enormously and he ran to the top of the drive. A battered pick-up truck was tearing along the track leaving clouds of dust billowing in its wake.

Even from this distance, Miles could hear girls squealing as they bounced about in the back of the open wagon.

'Come on Cameron!' Balfour Coker leaned out of the driver's window and yelled at Miles. 'Look sharp! I've got a truckload of lovely ladies to deliver to the Matopos and I haven't got all day!'

Miles swung up on to the back of the vehicle. The Shaw sisters were there, together with Lizzie Partlow and Jane Bowler. William Coker, who had designs on Lizzie Partlow, had managed to squeeze himself into the space next to her and was now savouring the pleasant sensation of those long legs pressed against his. He also seized the opportunity to thread a supportive arm around her shoulders when the rough road threatened to send her sprawling into his lap. Balfour had borrowed his father's truck and was now sitting with Nina James on the passenger seat beside him. He glanced appreciatively in her direction and was rewarded with a flash of bare skin as she crossed her legs to avoid the scorching heat of the vinyl seat.

'These seats can get pretty hot.' He winked at her mischievously before yelling at the rear: 'All aboard?'

Without waiting for an affirmative, Balfour let out the clutch with such ferocity that the truck sprang forward. Miles, who was not yet fully on board, was pitched face first against Susie Shaw's chest.

'Sorry Susie!' Miles stuttered.

Susie blushed as she tried to conceal her pleasure at this unexpected encounter with Bulawayo's "Most Gorgeous Guy". Her sister, Mandy, however, did not share that pleasure and she glowered at Susie through gritted teeth.

'Sit here, Miles,' Mandy instructed, proprietarily patting a space beside her. 'You can squeeze in next to me.'

Miles squashed himself into the tight space between the Shaw sisters and was uncomfortably aware of the vague sibling rivalry. However, such subtle sensitivities were quickly dispelled by the more urgent sensations of Mandy's wriggling bottom next to his and the distinctly sweet smell of female perfume. The sun was high, it was hot and the silence of the African bush was broken by girlish giggles and the laughter of young people on their way to one of Rhodesia's magnificent historical sites. Life was good.

The Matopos Hills formed the southernmost region of the early Matabele kingdom that had been established by King Mzilikazi. When the old king died, his body was interred in the Nthumbane Cave in the north of that region. His son, Lobengula, had also chosen the Matopos as his final resting place. It was a place fit for kings.

'World's View! Park over there!' William Coker tapped on the back of the driver's window and gestured at a shady corner in the parking area. Balfour looked over his shoulder and nodded.

World's View was a high peak in the Matopos where Cecil Rhodes had elected to be buried. It was a favourite spot for tourists who happily tackled the arduous climb to reach the plain, marble slab that marked the grave of this famous son of the British Empire and the founder of Rhodesia. From there, visitors were rewarded with a panoramic sweep of a vast, rocky terrain, broken by huge granite kopjes and gnarled acacias.

'Let's not climb up to World's View,' Mandy Shaw whispered in Miles' ear. 'Let's just potter around down here by ourselves. It'll be much more... interesting.'

Mandy placed such emphasis on the last word that Miles was left in no doubt as to her meaning. He glanced at her from under his lashes and grinned that devilish lop-sided grin. 'I'm up for "interesting" if you are,' he murmured, returning the pressure of her thigh.

Balfour dropped the truck into second gear and swung it round into the shade. The tyres kicked up a minor dust storm as they shuddered to a halt, and the passengers in the back covered their eyes until it had abated.

Miles jumped down from the back of the wagon and then reached up to help Mandy. Hastily, she brushed the dust from her shorts and then smiled cheekily at Miles. 'I'm all yours now, Miles. I hope you know how to look after a girl when she's all alone in the bush!'

'Well you'd better stay close to me for a start,' Miles teased. 'Unless you want the dreaded Umlimo to get you!' He lunged at Mandy who squealed delightedly and edged just out of reach.

'Don't talk like that,' she begged. 'Not when we're alone or I'm sure I'll scream!'

'Then you'd better be a good girl and do exactly what I say. Okay you lot! We're going to hang around here for a while. We'll meet you back at the truck.'

Susie Shaw leaned over the side of the wagon and frowned at her sister. 'Are you sure that's wise?' she asked, nervously. 'Mummy would be furious if she knew we had separated. You know the rules. We're supposed to stick together.'

Mandy threw back her head and her golden curls danced. 'What's there to worry about? We're only going to potter about a bit. It's not as though I'm on my own. Miles is with me.'

The latter was added with a smug little grin, but Susie was not convinced. 'Miles? Do you think it's okay to split up? We're supposed to stay together when we're out in the bush. Mummy says ....'

'I don't care what Mummy says!' Mandy stamped her foot. 'I'm not a child. I'm old enough to make my own decisions.'

'Maybe your sister is right,' Miles interjected. 'Maybe we should stick together. The place could be crawling with ZAPU terrs for all we know.'

Mandy spun round to take in the vast panorama. A solitary black eagle hovered silently against the empty blue sky before swooping down upon some unexpecting prey. She watched in awe as the mighty bird soared upwards again, its victim dangling from its beak, and then circled lazily before disappearing behind one of the distant hills to some remote eyrie. There were no sounds. All was still, and the ground shimmered mysteriously in the noon-day sun.

The Matopos was a magical kingdom. A place where spirits roamed and the echoes of the dead reverberated. The Matabele believed it to be the home of the all-powerful Umlimo, while the Kalanga worshipped their own god, Mwali, among its forbidding hills. The more practical white Rhodesians believed it to be a hiding place for black guerrilla fighters who crossed the borders from the training camps in Zambia.

'See!' Mandy's voice crashed into the silence. 'Nothing! Not a sausage! The only danger we face is sunburn if we don't get going!'

Balfour laughed and winked at Miles. 'Up to you, buddy. If that's what you want, we can meet up in two hours.'

'We're fine. You go on. You're not scared to be alone with me, are you, Miles?' Mandy lifted her eyebrows, and her eyes smouldered.

'Should I be?' Miles pulled her closer.

'Who knows? Strange things can happen to a handsome young man out here.'

'Then we'd better get going and find out just how scared I can be!'

In spite of Mandy's bravado, she was well aware that Rhodesia was a country in the grip of civil war, and she was perfectly happy to keep the roadside tracks in view as they made their way through the bush.

An accomplished coquette, Mandy faltered deliberately on the uneven terrain to give Miles an opportunity to help her over obstacles. On one occasion she genuinely slipped, but Miles caught her before she fell. She smiled, safe in those sinewy arms, and lifted her chin up for a kiss, closing her eyes in sweet anticipation. Miles happily obliged and they clung to each other for a moment until Mandy shook herself free and admonished Miles with a breathless giggle.

'Not now. Wait until we find some grass. The ground is too hard here.'

Miles held her tighter, needing to feel her skin against his, and unable to quell the throbbing in his groin. 'The ground will be soft compared to this!' he moaned, thrusting himself against her. 'Now this is what I call hard!'

Mandy giggled and threw her head back so that he could kiss the curve of her throat. Then, with renewed will-power, she pushed him away again. 'No, let's wait awhile. I want to savour the moment.'

Reluctantly, Miles sighed deeply, adjusted his crotch and followed her into the bush. He was keeping his eyes on the ground, anxious not to break any bones in the treacherous crevices.

'Sometimes I hate Africa, you know' Mandy moaned as she picked her way across the dry earth. 'It's so dangerous here. Nowhere is safe any more. I hate it here.'

'No you don't. You just think you do because life's a bit hard here right now. Africa is your home. You belong here. You don't hate it.'

'It's all right for you. 'You'll be gone soon. You'll be nice and safe living in England, far away from this miserable place. I'll be stuck here until I finish school, and even then my parents won't let me leave. They almost went when the Llewellyns left, but that was as far as we got. My father reckons we have every right to be here and that we're going to stay here come what may! He doesn't listen to my opinions, nor Susie's for that matter. Do you know, I really envy Lydia. At least she managed to get away. I do miss her, though, don't you?'

Lydia....

Suddenly, as if by magic, the sound of the name transported Miles back to a place of peace and laughter and freedom from care. And, standing in that magical place, was a beautiful young girl with emerald eyes and hair that shone like fire. She smiled and reached out to him. Miles could almost feel himself being drawn into that warm, welcoming embrace and he was overwhelmed with a love so strong it took his breath away. The girl was so real, so close that he was sure he could smell her peach perfume and feel her sweet breath fanning his cheeks.

Lydia....

And then, as quickly as it had come, the vision faded and Miles found himself staring vacantly at the distant horizon. Maybe it was the special magic of the Matopos, but he could swear that the air was scented with peach and that the tops of the trees sparkled like rubies.

'Lydia,' he whispered her name and sighed deeply, adding simply: 'Yes. I miss her, too.'

Gently, Mandy reached for his hand. It was as though a window had opened in his heart and she could see quite clearly the gaping hole that Lydia Llewellyn had left behind. She knew now why he always seemed so lost and so alone. Not only had Miles Cameron suffered the loss of his entire family in his young life, he had also lost the girl he loved.

It was plain for all to see that Miles' feelings for his childhood companion had never really left him. He was in love with Lydia. He knew it and Mandy knew it. And there was nothing either one could do to change that.

'You'll see her when you get to the UK, won't you?' said Mandy.

Miles shrugged. 'I don't know. She's living in Wales with her parents. Her father works at a hospital near Bala. I'll be in Shropshire with my grandparents.'

'Shropshire's on the Welsh borders, isn't it? Surely that's not too far to travel to see an old friend.'

'I guess not, but she may not want to see me. I'll write to her when I get there and see if she wants to meet up. I don't want to push myself on her. Who knows, she may have a boyfriend...'

Mandy laid her hand on top of his. 'Even if she has, I'm sure she'll still be pleased to see you. You were so close before she left. You simply must meet up.'

Miles stared at the distant hills. He did not know whether he would have the courage to contact Lydia when he got to the UK. He did not know whether she would want to hear from him. He did not know what they would have to say to each other after all these years. So much had changed. He had changed. It was unlikely that she would still have feelings for him. And he was afraid that neither he nor Lydia would be able to make the leap from an innocent childhood friendship to a more complicated adult relationship.

Even so, he knew now that the image of Lydia Llewellyn was woven with invisible threads into the very fabric of his life, his happiness. She was a part of his past, nothing could change that, but was she a part of his future? He could not possibly know.

12

'Oh my!' Bliss cooed with delight and rocked back and forth on the stool outside her rondavel. She held the transistor radio at arms length and turned it from side to side, laughing aloud like a child.

Julius squatted beside her and smiled. It was a small, second-hand gift, yet it had guaranteed his mother the respect and admiration that befits the proud owner of such an indisputable status symbol. Bliss would be only the second person at Tshotsholo to own such a coveted item, and she was acutely aware of the privilege.

'It belonged to one of the whites who have chosen to take the "Yellow Route" out of the troubles,' said Julius. 'They sold their entire house contents, books, cooker, everything. I found it after the other whites had picked their way through the contents like vultures. It did not cost much.'

Bliss beamed and stroked the transistor radio with her fingers. 'It is a very fine radio.'

Julius was pleased to see that his mother had settled in so well at her childhood kraal. But then, as a daughter of Tshotsholo, there would always be a welcome for her here.

Tshotsholo was a large kraal by African standards, with well over thirty rondavels housing a loyal, tight-knit community. It was situated well away from the road, deep in the bush and, in the days of Bliss' childhood, had been a happy, thriving village with enough land to graze the herds and plant healthy crops of mealies. But those days were gone. Now the inhabitants lived in fear of white police patrols, or much worse, the gangs of freedom fighters who roamed the bush at nights looking for supplies and new recruits. Tshotsholo even had its own mujibas – children who were specially trained to be the eyes and ears of local terrorists – but on the whole it was a quiet, unspoiled place. Julius knew that there was nowhere for his mother to hide from the horrors of the liberation war that had gripped the country, but this village was as far away as she could possibly hope to get. Indeed, sitting by the smoky open fire, beneath a twinkling canopy of stars, Julius could almost believe that nothing had changed.

He cast his eyes around the kraal. Two children were sitting cross-legged in the dirt nearby, picking off the blackjacks that had snagged on their dog's mangy coat. They were chattering incessantly, giggling and paying little attention to their task, while the scrawny animal stood before them with his ears pressed flat against his skull and his head hanging low.

Two other boys were heading out of the village into the bush. They had been assigned to baboon duty for the night, and both relished the thought of camping out on their own. They were proud to have been given the responsibility of protecting the fields from baboons who could reap havoc overnight. They were also immensely proud of the guns they carried, though few baboons were fooled by the sight of a gun in a child's hand. The baboon's quick intelligence soon realised that a gun never went off in the hands of a child, and that an animal would have more to fear from the rocks that were lobbed at him as he approached.

Julius watched as they crossed the black-water stream before disappearing into the shadows on the other side. 'I will fetch fresh logs,' he said, unfurling his legs.

Bliss nodded, watching her son as he made his way down to the water's edge. He was a powerful, handsome young man, a true member of the Khumalo clan. She could see traces of his father, Moses, in the way he moved. Julius' caramel skin was lighter than his father's, but those luminous black eyes and proud set of the jaw were definitely Khumalo. He was a beautiful boy and Bliss' heart swelled with love.

She knew that he had not come all this way simply to bring her a radio. He wanted to talk. She did not know what he wanted to say, but her mother's instincts knew that he needed to talk. He was troubled. It was obvious in the way he creased his brow and in that haunted, faraway look in his eyes. She would wait until he was ready to tell her what was on his mind. It was not her place to pry. The boy had become a man. He would tell his mother only what he felt she needed to know.

Julius carried two wattle logs back to his mother's rondavel. He tucked one under each arm and his biceps bulged with the weight until the veins stood proud. He knelt down and placed them carefully into the heart of the fire. The flames crackled into life and sent a blaze of orange sparks shooting into the air as the fresh wood crackled. Julius rubbed his hands together and sat back on his haunches.

He was silent for a while, watching the firelight, but then he turned and said simply. 'Mother, they want me to register for call-up.'

Bliss' hand flew up to her mouth and she gasped aloud, but Julius sought to reassure her and gently coaxed her hand back down to her lap.

'What does this mean, my son?'

'It means,' Julius replied, 'that, when I do get called-up, I will have to fight for the whites against my black brothers. It means that I will have to kill, and perhaps die, so that Ian Smith and his colonialists can retain white supremacy.

'Do you have to go? Can you not refuse such an order?'

'If I refuse, I shall be breaking the law and I will have no choice other than to join the gangs of freedom fighters out in the bush. I do not want to do that. I want to complete my law degree at the University of Rhodesia. That is my dream. If they gave me nothing else, the whites gave me one thing: they gave me an education. They showed me how much can be achieved with knowledge. I will not waste my education. I will not waste my place at university. I can do more for my black brothers through the powers of justice and the law than I could ever hope to do out in the bush.'

Bliss wiped a tear from her eye with her sleeve. 'I am so proud to think of you studying at the University of Rhodesia. It is such a great honour. Surely the Government can see that. Surely they will not expect you to give it all up to take part in their war?'

'It is my war, too, Mother. Never forget that. But I have chosen to fight the whites using their own weapons. I do not want to kill my African brothers who are ready to die for my liberation, but I truly believe that we cannot hope to win real freedom, real independence, unless we adopt some of the ways of the white man when our time comes. I believe that the law will be a powerful weapon in the years ahead. And it will be a weapon that I shall be proud to wield.'

Julius took a deep breath and stared into the distance. He could slip away into the bush and join ZAPU. He could wage his own private war against the whites, stealing upon unsuspecting farms and settlements across Matabeleland, massacring the inhabitants in the name of freedom. Thousands of young black men had already made that choice. Or he could study the law, and when the black man finally won majority rule, he would be equipped to help his country find its post-independence identity.

'You will do what is right, my son,' Bliss laid a hand on his arm. 'God will help you to do what is right.'

'I hope so, Mother,' Julius capped her hand with his own. 'I hope so.'

The Rhodesian Prime Minister, Ian Smith, had resigned himself to the inevitability of black majority rule. His own blacks demanded it, the rest of Africa demanded it and, more importantly, the western world demanded it. He could not hope to hold out against the rest of the world forever.

Robert Mugabe was already receiving weapons from Russia and China. Even when the supply of arms and ammunition from China began to dry up, following the death of Chairman Mao, help continued to pour in from countries such as Romania and Iraq.

Smith knew that things had worsened when Fidel Castro agreed to send Cuban advisers to train Robert Mugabe's ZANU forces in Mozambique. It was a worrying development and one that sent alarm bells ringing throughout the civilised world.

Smith tried to tackle the flood of heavily-armed and well-trained guerrillas into his country by increasing his Rhodesian forces by fifty per cent, and by tightening call-up regulations. It was not popular move. White families did not want to see their sons dying in a bush war, the blacks did not want to fight for a white cause and businesses suffered when huge numbers of their skilled workforce were absent on call up duty.

On top of the international pressures, Smith was conscious of mounting criticism at home. His party's decision to end racial discrimination was met with horror as the whites conjured up images of their children sitting alongside older, less intelligent blacks in multi-racial schools. Hospitals would be serviced by under-qualified staff who knew nothing of hygiene regulations, and the clean, neat, white-only suburbs would be transformed overnight into filthy, noisy ghettos populated by dirty children, slovenly matrons and menacing layabouts.

Smith also understood the shortcomings of his own armed forces. The typical white Rhodesian male was a tough, outdoor creature. Hale and hearty, kindly and sociable to his fellows, but perhaps a little slow-witted some might say. 'Rhodesia born, Rhodesia bred, strong in the arm and thick in the head' said the popular little ditty. In comparison, the military wings of ZANU and ZAPU were leaner, hungrier and more determined - and they had world opinion on their side.

He knew also that many whites disagreed with, or completely misunderstood, his motives and saw him as the perpetrator of their doom. Some truly believed that they could win the war, or even that they could exist in complete isolation from the rest of the world, provided white privileges and supremacy were preserved. Smith had enemies on both sides, but there was nothing he could do to court popularity. All he could do was to try to ensure that the whites were protected from the dangers inherent in black majority rule and that there was a place in the new Rhodesia for them and their families.

With this goal in mind, he held secret talks in Lusaka with Joshua Nkomo. Smith genuinely believed that Nkomo and Bishop Abel Muzorewa would be more sympathetic to the whites than the militant Robert Mugabe and his Marxist followers in the north of the country. With a new transitional government in place, Smith hoped to effect a ceasefire and bring an end to racial segregation without harming the rights and freedoms of the white minority. He was certain that they could find a way forward if the whites could be persuaded to join hands with the more liberal blacks. Smith truly believed that it would be a partnership formed with the interests of both sides at heart.

He was wrong.

The Zambian side of Lake Kariba and the Zambesi River was home to large numbers of itinerant fisherfolk who built their crude shelters on its banks. They lived a simple life, following the moods of the great river over the seasons. They also followed the shoals of tilapia and tiger fish which were their staple diet, dismantling their rude huts and leaving smouldering ash fires in their wake when they moved camp. They were a poor people, but even these wretched souls had something of value that could be used in the war of independence in neighbouring Rhodesia. They had the means of crossing the Zambesi.

Poachers would often force the villagers to ferry them across to the Rhodesia National Park in search of ivory, but it was the ZAPU guerrillas, who had fled their native Rhodesia to train in the Zambian camps, that were the greatest threat.

The men would sneak upon them in the night and demand to be ferried across in the fragile fishing canoes. The boats were fashioned from a single log of the kigelia tree and could accommodate six or seven men for the crossing. But three nights ago, when the last group had emerged from the shadows, it had taken three canoes to carry them over the Zambesi because one had been taken up almost entirely by a long and mysterious weapon.

'Manheru Baba.'

The Zambian headsman had been staring at the smoking fire with rheumy eyes. He had seemed to be far away, deep in thought, but he was not startled by the tall black man who emerged from the mopani forest. He had heard the bark of the baboons warning of a potentially dangerous predator, and had heard the screech of the grey louries disturbed by an unexpected presence. The bush had told him that something was heading towards his village. It may be an animal. It may be human. Whatever it was, the headman knew it would come. He could not stop it.

'Good evening old father,' the stranger towered over the withered old man. 'My men and I are in need of your help.'

The old man shrugged his shoulders and tugged on his pipe. Racks of smoked fish dangled above his head. At his feet, the fire belched smoke into the air as the damp logs struggled to catch fire.

The stranger squatted down on his haunches so that his eyes could look directly into the thick, yellowed orbs of the village headman. The silver moonlight cast a glossy sheen on his skin so that it shone like polished ivory. 'I need three of your men to carry my warriors across the river in your canoes. Will you help your black brothers in their fight for freedom?'

The headman nodded. He had no choice. The alternative was death and the loss of his precious craft. Slowly, he tipped the contents of his pipe on to the fire and stood up. An old hag was skinning a fish and she looked up as they passed and cackled cheerily.

'Manheru, Old Mother,' the stranger whispered, and she cackled louder.

As they made their way through the bush to the water's edge, they were joined by the rest of the gang. They were a fit, disciplined bunch who had pledged their lives to the fight for freedom. Lean and strong, they trotted behind their leader with two men at the rear carrying their precious weapon.

The canoes were moored with their points nestling into the clumps of papyrus stems that formed the reedbed. Their leader inspected the fragile craft and nodded his approval.

'These will do, but I will need three of your best boatman to navigate the craft across the river. They will remain under armed guard on the Rhodesian side for two days and then they will ferry us back here to Zambia. If you keep your mouth shut, all will be well. Do you understand?'

The headman nodded and his solitary tooth wiggled in his gums.

If you keep your mouth shut, your men and your craft will be returned in one piece within two days. If you do not keep your mouth shut....' The stranger fingered the knife that hung from his belt, 'You and your people will pay a heavy price for your folly.'

Silently, efficiently, the Matabele warriors climbed into the rickety canoes and sat with their AK47 assault rifles on their laps. Their leader climbed into the last canoe with one other man who carried certain death in his callused hands. Unbeknown to the innocent boatman who had been dragooned into playing a part in a war on his borders, he was carrying a 9M32 "Strela" missile, commonly known as the deadly SAM-7 missile.

The surface-to-air weapon was capable of bringing down a low-flying aircraft with deadly accuracy. It was a weapon of awesome ferocity and it was now in the hands of ZAPU guerrillas who were trained to exploit its lethal capabilities.

Two of the gang had remained on the riverbank to guard the boatmen who might otherwise flee back to their village and disappear into the bush. Their homes were temporary structures. The Zambians moved with the river. It would not be easy to follow them. As a precaution, two men with AK47 rifles were left behind, ready to ensure that the escape route was clear, and that the boats would still be there to carry the men away from Rhodesia.

The Matabele guards sat back-to-back, knees brought up to their chests, smoking. For the most part, they sat in silence, but now and again they broke out into friendly conversation. They were young, one was in his teenage years and the other had only just reached his twenties. They still enjoyed the exuberance of youth and the promise of a long life before them. Also, with their leader out of earshot, their tensions had given way a little and they were more relaxed.

'Comrade? I have a question.'

'What is it?'

'It is this,' the younger man paused to exhale a perfect ring of smoke. 'I do not understand why we are doing this.'

His comrade shuffled round on his backside to face him. 'What is it you do not understand little brother?'

'The planes that travel from Rhodesia's Kariba airport carry only civilian passengers.'

'White passengers,' his companion corrected him.

'Black or white, they are civilians. Families with women and children. Is it right to shoot women and children out of the skies? The planes from Kariba are not military targets.'

'But we have heard that they carry military personnel,' his companion interjected. 'Armed paratroopers travel on the civil flights. Our leader says this is so.'

'How do we know that this particular plane will be carrying armed soldiers,' the younger man persisted. 'How can we be sure that we are not using a SAM-7 missile to kill children and innocent civilians?'

'We cannot be sure, but it is of no matter. We know for sure that the plane will be carrying whites. The whites have taken our land, have subjected our children to servitude and deprived us of our freedom. Yes, there will be children on board that plane. And yes, they will die. But you must remember that those children are the sons of white people and that, one day, they will grow into men and then they will play their part in the destruction of our beloved Africa. We cannot allow that to happen. They are innocent now. If we kill them now they will always be innocent. They will not live to sully that innocence with the blood of black Africa. They die for our future. Remember that, little brother. Their death is Africa's future.'

His comrade nodded and drew heavily on his cigarette before stubbing it out on to the ground. He did not like the thought of murdering innocent women and children, but he was prepared to do his duty for Africa, and for his leader, Comrade Moses Khumalo.

Rhodesia's Urungwe Tribal Trust Land was fifty miles west of Karoi, close to Kariba airport. Often, its quiet little villages would have their peace shattered by the roar of aircraft flying low for take-off or landing. But the villagers did not fear what they saw in the skies. They feared what they met at ground level. In particular, they feared their black brothers who stole upon them in the night demanding food and shelter and threatening the villagers with cruel retribution if they did not comply.

The old African, Thomas, had seen much suffering in his long life. He had seen a man with his penis hacked off and his wife forced to eat it as punishment for helping the whites. He had seen a mother wringing her hands in anguish at the loss of her son, snatched from the safety of the kraal under the cover of darkness. He had seen grown men, warriors, in tears. Indeed, old man Thomas had witnessed far more than he needed to see over the years.

Generally, the villagers simply did as they were told. They did not care whether the invaders were black guerrillas, or white police patrols. Both groups could wreak havoc. Instead, the villagers clung to a simple policy of supporting whichever group descended upon them at any particular time.

This prudent policy had worked for the last two nights while the ZAPU warriors, who had crossed the river from Zambia, were with them. The freedom fighters had left the village now and the villagers were safe. Things had returned to normal. It was time to give thanks. They had been spared.

Thomas sat with his wife, Jetina, on the bench outside their hut. Together they watched the plane from Kariba flying low above their village. Thomas had made the bench with his own hands. It was old now, bowed in the middle, and the wood was warped from the rains and the heat. But Thomas and Jetina did not count their blessings in material terms. They were poor, even by African standards, but they were alive.

They had no sons, only daughters. Three of their daughters had watched their husbands disappear into the night to join the fight for liberation. Two of these young men had since died in the bush war and the third had lost both his legs when a landmine planted by his own people had blasted him into pieces on the main road into Kariba.

Thomas still had all of his limbs, and he had outlived all of his contemporaries, but he had lost all his teeth, and he sucked with withered gums on a stick of biltong as he and his wife sat in the warmth of sundown. Beside him, Jetina whistled tunelessly, seemingly oblivious to the roar of the aircraft.

Both knew that they were lucky to have survived the last two nights when the ZAPU warriors had first emerged from the shadows. They were burned black by days of direct sun and they were dirty from living rough. It was always the same. Zambia lay across the green waters of the Zambesi River, and there were many places where it was possible to cross before the rains came. The simple fisherfolk on the Zambian side would be coerced into sneaking the terrorists across in the canoes under cover of darkness. The freedom fighters would then set out to accomplish their mission in Rhodesia before returning to Zambia the same way that they had arrived.

Even so, Thomas could not help thinking that this group seemed more dangerous than the others, more disciplined, more determined. They did not take the children away, did not pleasure themselves with the women, did not threaten the locals with death or mutilation, but there was something in their eyes that was far more menacing than mere threats, and the villagers were more than happy to give up their meagre stocks of fish and water to accommodate them.

One of the group stood apart from the others. He was taller and his eyes were dark and fathomless in his finely chiselled face. He had a natural authority that the others tacitly acknowledged, but there was a hint of cruelty that seemed to lie beneath the handsome smile.

He had not made any threats, nor engaged in idle chat, and he prowled about on the edges of the main group like a dominant male in a pride of lions. Thomas had watched him carving a piece of wood into the shape of a woman's torso. He had looked up on one occasion, and Thomas had seen a strange light in his eyes. Thomas did not smile in greeting, his mouth had shrivelled back into his gums and it was impossible for him to effect such a muscular contortion, but he held the other man's gaze. "They were evil eyes," Thomas had whispered to his wife that night as they lay under the stars, having given up their beds to the intruders. This was not a man to be trifled with.

And so he had said nothing when the men stripped his old scotch cart of the few remaining tomatoes from the harvest. His wife would have lugged them down to the roadside the following day in a bid to sell them to passers-by. Few would buy them of course. Their cherry skins were spoiled with white patches from the drought and they were poor fare.

But the men from ZAPU did not care about quality. They cared only for their mission. Thomas did not know what that mission was. He knew that they carried with them a formidable weapon, the like of which he had never seen before, and that it had been concealed in the donga outside the village and guarded by at least one of the group at all times. But he did not know what they intended to do with that weapon.

Thomas knew only that he could smell death in the air. He turned to his wife, Jetina, who was still whistling on the bench beside him, and he wondered if she could smell it, too. Death was in the air. He did not need to know more than that.

With the roads mined, and the ever-present fear of ambush from terrorists, the whites believed that the safest way to travel around Rhodesia was to fly. One of the popular routes with civilians was the daily scheduled flight from Lake Kariba to the capital, Salisbury.

Despite its close proximity with Zambia, Lake Kariba, with its water-skiing and fishing, remained a popular destination for tourists. There had been rocket and mortar attacks at Kariba, but these were not enough to deter hundreds of white Rhodesians from flocking to the area for weekend breaks and family holidays.

It was a particularly fine September day when the Air Rhodesia flight, RH825, took off from the resort en-route for Salisbury. It was late afternoon and the sun was already low in the sky. Passengers pressed their faces to the windows to enjoy the views and snatch a last glimpse of glassy surface of the lake. To their delight, the wild birds nesting at the edges of the lake took off in their own flight of fantastic colours, their wings shining in the sunlight.

RH825 carried a crew of four with Captain John Hood at the controls. More than fifty civilian passengers were on board and they quickly settled into their seats for the relatively short journey home. The children chattered excitedly as the four-engine Viscount gained altitude and swept them up into the skies.

After clearing the lake, the plane was set to follow an easterly direction which would take it over the Urungwe Tribal Trust Lands. It was just after five o'clock on the afternoon of 3rd September 1978.

The four year old girl sitting at the back of the plane beamed at the man who came to take his seat next to her while her mother adjusted her seat belt for comfort.

Cecil McLaren was returning to Salisbury after a spell of duty as a visiting dentist at the Central African Generating Authority, whose staff were responsible for running the Kariba Dam. He was one of the last to board the plane and he was happy to take the seat at the rear of the plane next to the woman and her young daughter.

The plane took off smoothly, It had crossed the sparkling waters of Lake Kariba and was heading over Urungwe, a vast area of sparsely-populated, hilly bushland west of Karoi, when Captain John Hood switched off the no-smoking signs. Cecil McLaren reached for a cigarette. The two young air hostesses began their flight duties.

Near the front of the plane, a couple were discussing the recent announcement that their Prime Minister had held secret talks with the leader of ZAPU in Lusaka. They were concerned. It was like doing a deal with the devil, one had said. No good would come of it, the other agreed. Blacks could not be trusted.

The man sitting in the seat in front of them overheard the conversation and he turned to join in the debate. He, too, had heard the news. He, too, was dubious about doing business with the blacks. But what choice did they have? Nkomo was a far safer bet than that madman, Mugabe, and his Shona thugs. After all, Mugabe was a Marxist who would not listen to reason. There would be no mercy for the whites with him at the helm. Black majority rule with Mugabe as leader was unthinkable. Maybe Smith was right to try to broker a deal with the lesser of two evils.

He offered the couple a cigarette and they accepted, unsure of their opinions in a world which was changing from day to day, where loyalties could be shattered overnight and where the enemy lurked in dark places. They did not know whether their fellow passenger was right or wrong. Nothing was certain in these unstable times. They would have to place their faith in their Prime Minister, Ian Smith, and his Rhodesia Front Party. After all, he was their leader. He must know who they could trust. And if "Old Smithy" felt he could trust ZAPU and the chubby, Joshua Nkomo, who were they to question his judgement?

The plane was heading directly towards the range of granite kopjes that stood tall and proud among the other hills of the Urungwe, but Captain John Hood did not see the small group of terrorists lying low on the top of the highest peak. He did not see one of the terrorists swing round and steady the powerful shoulder-held SAM-7 missile as the plane approached. He saw only the vivid rays of the sun colouring the sky before him.

On top of the hill, the young Matabele knew that he would get only one chance to alter the course of history. He knew that his comrades were waiting for him to accomplish his deed. He knew also that, tomorrow, the entire world would be shocked by this savage blow against colonialism.

He must not fail.

The Soviet SAM-7 portable missile launcher was designed to be fired at low altitude. The high-explosive warhead had its own heat-seeking system that could target the plume of an aircraft engine's exhaust. The terrorist knew that SAM-7s could be affected by the sun. He also knew that he must be sure to fire behind the target so that the warhead could chase the tail of the aircraft.

The noise was deafening as Flight RH825 approached the kopje, and the Matabele swallowed hard to lessen the pounding in his ears. His mouth was dry and his eyes were watering, but his hand was steady. No matter that his heart beat fiercely in his chest and there was a bitter taste of blood in his mouth. The death lust had come upon him and he was insensible to all else but the need to bring down the aircraft as it roared above his head.

Time seemed to come to a halt as the man aimed the shoulder-held missile launcher at the tail of the plane and fired. Within seconds the lethal warhead had identified its target and homed in for the kill. Its passenger was Death.

Suddenly, the plane lurched and an almighty bang was followed by the inner starboard engine bursting into flames. Ground Control received a distress call from Captain John Hood who called out: "Mayday! Mayday! I have lost both starboard engines. We're going in…"

Flames and jagged metal flew past the windows and the passengers screamed. The aircraft turned a full ninety degrees, from east to due south, and then plunged into a rapid descent. Panic spread like the fire that was raging at the side of the plane. Men and women began to cry and the bewildered children clung to their mothers. One man ran up and down the aisle in panic, crying out for help. Others sat with their heads between their knees, holding on to their ankles in the traditional crash position.

Captain John Hood was thirty-six years old. He had been married for three months. For a full, five minutes he managed to control his stricken aircraft in an attempt to bring her safely down to the ground. With remarkable skill, he managed to steer the craft towards the huge cotton field that he could see in the Whamira Hills in front of him. The field was the size of two football pitches and he was certain he could effect a successful landing.

He could hear the treetops whipping against the wings and fuselage and he yelled over the intercom: 'Brace yourselves for impact!' Manfully, he grappled with the controls and then, miraculously, he felt the wheels touch down smoothly. He had done it! He was alive! His passengers and crew were alive!

What he did not know, however, was that the cotton field was divided in half by a wide donga, an irrigation ditch that was easily two metres deep and four metres wide. The plane hit the ditch and cartwheeled after impact. It then exploded, scattering parts of its wings and fuselage in every direction.

The captain was killed instantly, as were most of the other passengers. But, thanks to his heroic efforts, eighteen of the fifty-six people on board survived the crash. All were sitting at the back of the plane which, by now, was an inferno. With ears and noses full of sand and earth, the pathetic survivors struggled to free themselves from the flaming wreckage.

The dentist, Cecil McLaren, was still alive, along with the woman and her daughter who had been sitting next to him. He saw a gap in the wreckage and took the little girl through with him. Her mother followed.

His first instinct was to help get the injured survivors as far away from the plane as possible. With the uninjured, mostly women and children, tearing up their clothes to make bandages for the wounded, McLaren gathered together a small group and ploughed into the bush to find the nearest village where they could get water. There would be plenty of villages scattered about the Urungwe Tribal Trust Lands.

The first village they came across was inhabited by terrified villagers who huddled behind closed doors, alarmed by the sight of the bedraggled whites in torn, blood-stained clothing. They had heard the loud bangs and had seen the tail of fire sweep across the sky, but they did not want to see more than that. They were afraid. The terrorists' vengeance would know no limits if the villagers gave aid to these white people. Anxiously, they cloaked their fear for their lives in sullen hostility.

Cecil McLaren had to beg for help. Eventually, an old woman took pity on the wretched group and offered them water. Tired and frightened, they hurried back to the crash site to help their fellow passengers.

It was then that they heard voices and the zip and hiss of tracer bullets flying over the tops of the trees. The light was fading and there was the unmistakable stench of charred flesh and dry, acrid smoke in the air, but they recognised the sounds of gunfire and the deep timbre of agitated African voices.

'Buia lapa!' Moses Khumalo spat out the words. 'Come here.'

Cecil McLaren and his party dived for cover in a nearby donga. They covered themselves with grass and earth to hide their pale skins. They heard an elderly European, lying injured on the ground, challenge the ZAPU terrorists: 'What do you bastards want now?' and then a long burst of gunfire followed by screaming. Some of the other survivors scattered, fleeing for their lives. Ten did not make it. Ten women and children and elderly civilians had suddenly and unexpectedly found themselves caught up in the reality of the war that had devastated their country.

Moses Khumalo and his team herded the others together, using the points of their bayonets to prod them into a huddle. He saw a little boy crying over and over again 'Mummy! Mummy!' His mother never answered. She was one of the victims who had died on impact. Moses watched the little lad, but he felt nothing. The red mist had descended and he saw everything through a haze of blood-lust and fury.

Tall and menacing, he kicked a teddy-bear and white leather handbag out of his path. He was not troubled by these pathetic remnants of lives now lost. He was oblivious to everything but the need to kill, and die if needs be, for Africa. He saw the wailing, pitiful group who cowered before him as the evil oppressors of his beloved people. They were not innocent. They had lived well by the sweat of the black man, and enjoyed the privileges of Ian Smith's racist regime. This was Africa. There was no place for innocence here.

Moses glanced over his shoulders. Two of his men were raiding the aircraft wreckage, hunting for booty in the suitcases that were strewn all around. One man ran off into the bush with his hands full. Moses watched him go, but he made no effort to follow him. He had accomplished his task. He was of no consequence now.

Moses turned back and nodded at his men. There was a pause, broken only by the shrieks of an injured woman and the tears of a child. And then came the signal and the deadly circle of men with AK47s opened fire on the few remaining survivors. Most died instantly, but their killers coldly stepped over the bodies to seek out the injured. They drove their bayonets into the limp bodies time and time again in a frenzy of killing until each and every one of the whites lay still and silent with their flame of life brutally extinguished.

For most of the night, Moses and his murderous gang hunted for the handful of stragglers who had managed to escape. Cowering in the donga, Cecil McLaren and the other escapees listened in terror to the hoarse voices of the killers hunting them down, intent upon their murder.

Suddenly, Africa had ceased to be a place of sundowners, tennis and barbecues. It was no longer a warmer, more colourful imitation of Surrey, the Lake District and other places that the whites had once called home. Swimming pools, servants and lush bougainvillaea had no place out here in the bush. Out here in the dark, alone at night, they were in the black man's territory.

This was the real Africa. Raw, uncompromisingly cruel and savage, and yet undeniably awesome in its beauty. The real Africa would not be beaten. It would not lie down and die. In the end, even if it brought about its own destruction, Africa would win.

Eyewitness accounts from Cecil McLaren and his fellow survivors confirmed the details of the ill-fated flight and the subsequent slaughter of innocent men, women and children. The public outrage that followed was compounded by a BBC television interview when the leader of ZAPU, Joshua Nkomo, was asked to comment on the alleged brutality. When asked how the aircraft was brought down, Nkomo was reluctant to admit to owning Soviet missiles, claiming instead that his men had brought the aircraft down by "throwing stones". Chortling at his own evasive answer,

Nkomo inadvertently became the heartless slaughterer of innocents in the eyes of the world.

Five days later, the Rhodesian Ministry of Transport confirmed that the Viscount had been brought down by a SAM-7 heat-seeking missile.

For Ian Smith, who had met with Nkomo in Lusaka only three weeks earlier, it spelled political disaster and the condemnation of white Africa. He had hoped to make a deal with Joshua Nkomo and his ZAPU followers, believing them to be more pliable than Robert Mugabe. He had hoped that such a deal would secure white interests in the transition to black majority rule. Instead he stood accused of making a pact with the devil. In the interests of expediency, or perhaps because of sheer stupidity, he had inadvertently linked arms with the perpetrators of what the world's press were now calling 'a murder of the most savage and treacherous sort'.

Julius was sitting on a bench on the university campus near Salisbury. It was hot, almost thirty-six degrees, and he was sweating. He had rolled up his white cotton shirt sleeves to just above the elbow and loosened his collar, but there were still dark, damp patches under his arms and between his shoulder blades.

The lecture theatre had been dry and airless, and he was glad to escape the confines of the stark room with its blank magnolia walls and high windows. A pile of heavy textbooks were stacked on the bench beside him with a notebook and biro resting on top. He had planned to spend his lunch break catching up on notes for his essay on corporate law, but he could not concentrate.

Under normal circumstances, Julius was a model student. He was bright and conscientious, and he was determined not to fritter away the opportunities that the Camerons had given him by investing in his education before they died. He had reconciled himself to the fact that he was benefiting from their legacy by telling himself that, as a lawyer, he would be in a better position to fight for the Africans' cause in the future. It was reassuring counsel and he was comfortable with his decision.

Today, however, he could not concentrate on the legal issues governing selected case histories. He had other things on his mind. He was about to join hundreds of students who had agreed to take part in the demonstrations against conscription to military service imposed upon them by the Smith regime. The announcement had said that specified Africans must register for National Service by 1st December. The order applied to black men aged between 18 and 25 who had completed at least three years' secondary school education. Once registered, they would then receive their call-up papers ready to start their compulsory twelve months' service in January 1979.

Julius could understand the urgency of the white government. They were still reeling from the shooting down of the Viscount over Lake Kariba. Julius had not condoned the deed. The casualties were civilians, mainly women and children. He could not accept that, but he sympathised with the need for dramatic action to hasten a conclusion to the long, drawn-out struggle for independence. The perpetrators, whoever they were, had fled the country and were probably back in their training camps in Zambia leaving white Rhodesians living in fear of further acts of terrorism.

But young black men in Rhodesia did not feel the same sense of urgency, and most were not prepared to fight their black brothers out in the bush simply because Ian Smith had said that they must. How could they accept their freedom if they had killed their fellow Africans to achieve it? It was too high a price to pay.

The following day, Julius joined his fellow students in the protest against conscription. Undeterred by the scale of the resistance, the Smith Government issued over 1500 call-up papers to those who should have registered. Julius received his papers just before Christmas.

Only 300 recruits turned up on the 10th January 1979, the day that their call-up was due to start. In spite of his opposition to the ruling, Julius Khumalo was one of those who did turn up. He had made his decision. He would fulfil his call-up duties, so that he could resume his law studies after his twelve-month spell of duty. Then, in the future, armed with a knowledge of the law, he would fight his battles in his own way.

Across the border, safely back in one of the Zambian training camps, Moses Khumalo heard the news of the massive boycott and nodded his approval. What he did not know was that his own son was one of the 300 young men who had turned up for duty on that hot, sunny day. Had he known, it would not have troubled him for long. Julius was a Matabele, a descendant of the great King Mzilikazi. Moses knew that a son of his could never fight the white man's war in his heart. If he did, he would have his own reasons for doing so. Julius would find his own way to freedom. Moses was sure of that.

He sat cross-legged beside the fire, fashioning a branch of mukwa into the shape a curved dagger. He, like his son, had his own war to fight. He, like his son, had already chosen his road to freedom. And for Moses Khumalo it would always be a long and lonely road.

13

Lydia Llewellyn sat on her parents' rose-patterned sofa with her legs tucked underneath her. She was wearing a black velvet smock, decorated with tiny black sequins, and a pair of tight black denim jeans. She had kicked off her shoes to reveal a pair of vivid crimson and black striped socks. Her long red hair was tied back and held at the base of her neck by a silver scarf. As always, she looked stunningly and effortlessly beautiful, as the young man sitting next to her was all too painfully aware.

'Is it bad news?' he asked, nodding at the letter in her hand.

Lydia stared out of the picture window and her emerald eyes were misty with unshed tears. Far below, through the trees, she could see the street lights of Bala.

She had grown to love the little Welsh town. She adored her parents' hillside home, with its views of the lake and its easy access to the walks through Penllyn Forest. During the summer she and her younger sister, Leah, would climb the hills to watch the tourists gathering round the lake below. She delighted in the stark splendour of her parents' native land, but there was a place in her heart that even the beauty of Wales could not fill.

Africa.

Today, a letter had arrived out of the blue that had filled the empty space in her heart with warm and wonderful memories of magenta sunsets, wide open savannahs and wild, untamed animals.

Africa. The land of her birth. The place she still called Home.

'It's from an old friend of mine,' Lydia blinked away the tears with a curtain of long dark lashes and turned to Philip with a smile.

'From Africa?' Philip fiddled with his earring. 'Is it from that guy you were telling me about?'

Lydia nodded.

'What does he want?' A note of irritation crept into Philip's voice. He felt vaguely threatened by the note in Lydia's hand.

'He wants to see me. He's over here studying agriculture at a college in Shropshire. Oh Philip, just think – that's only a short drive away away! He wants us to meet up.' Carefully, she unfolded the Basildon Bond paper and scanned the contents once more. 'He says it would be good to talk over old times.'

Philip rolled the silver hoop through his ear lobe and brushed his hair out of his eyes with the back of his hand. 'Are you sure that's a good idea?' he said, conscious that his heart was thumping against his ribs . He felt a deep and unexpected resentment against the author of the letter. 'After all, you haven't heard from him in years.'

'True,' Lydia replied. 'But I feel I should see him. He is a family friend, after all. Our parents were really close before …. before it happened.'

Philip sighed and struggled to quell the anxiety that gathered in the pit of his stomach. He knew it was unreasonable to assume that Miles Cameron was any kind of threat, but he was unsettled. He knew he could not compete with a childhood full of love and trust and years of shared hardships, joys and pain. He knew he could not compete with Africa.

'Maybe I should come with you?' the words were out of his mouth before he had chance to realise how he would feel if his proposal were rejected.

'I think I'd rather go on my own,' Lydia reached across and squeezed his hand. Her eyes glimmered in the soft lamplight and Philip knew that his actions at this exact moment might affect their relationship in the future. Nevertheless, he felt hurt that she should want to keep him out. They had been dating for almost a year. Surely that gave him the right to be concerned when she wanted to go off and meet someone else? Especially when that guy held such a special place in her memories.

Philip struggled silently with his demons before accepting that, although he had the right to voice his concerns, he certainly did not have the right to tell Miss Lydia Llewellyn what she could or could not do. She was a strong-willed young lady who knew her own mind and was not afraid to speak it. And it was precisely this fiery spirit that had drawn Philip to her in the first place. Now he found himself hopelessly entangled in her innocent, but utterly enticing, web. He was left with no other option than to subdue his jealousy and play it cool.

'Okay,' he shrugged his shoulders with a nonchalance he did not feel. 'It's up to you. I guess it would be a bit awkward having to sit there while you two relive your childhood. But if he's turned into some boring old fart, or worse, an insufferable racist like most of the whites out there, then just split. Okay? You don't have to stay longer than necessary, and you certainly don't have to sit and listen to garbage about the good old British Empire if you don't want to.'

An image of eyes as dark as liquid chocolate, and a lop-sided grin leapt into Lydia's mind and she smiled. 'You don't have to worry, Philip. I doubt very much that Miles has become a bigot. If he's half as lovely as his parents were, I'm sure I'll have a wonderful time. All I want to do is catch up on news of Africa and all my old friends out there. It's years since I set foot in the place, but I still miss it so much. I suppose you can take the girl out of Africa, but you can't take Africa out of the girl. And it's still in me, Philip. Africa is in my blood.'

Philip stood up and pulled his leather jacket over his torn tee-shirt. 'That's what worries me,' he said simply. 'How the hell am I supposed to compete with that?'

'Right! Books open! I want you to give me the main factors to be taken into consideration when designing a farm's layout. Let's kick off with you, Michael.'

'The size of the herd,' the young student sitting in the front row volunteered.

'Exactly!' the tutor spun round on his heels and scrawled "SIZE OF HERD" in big letters on the board. 'Another one please!'

'The farm management policy, things like breeding patterns, calving patterns…'

'Good!' John Edwards scribbled the words on the board while another student called out from the rear of the class: 'Feeding policy, whether it's going to be hay, silage or self-feed for example.'

'Anything else,' the tutor peered over the rims of his spectacles and surveyed his class of aspiring young agriculturists. 'What about you, Miles. What else would you take into account in your farm layout?'

'Cow shit!' Miles offered with a cheeky grin. The rest of the group giggled.

'Precisely!' John Edwards nodded enthusiastically and proceeded to plaster the words "WASTE MANAGEMENT" on the board. 'Never underestimate the value of proper waste management. Now class, I want you to go away and consider the pros and cons of bringing all the dairy functions, housing, feeding, milking operations and so on, under one roof. We'll debate your findings next week.'

The students gathered up their books and papers and filed out of the lecture room in a noisy huddle. They were a particularly bright and lively year, their tutor noted with pride, and they carried the usual quota of students from Africa. Shrewsbury College was one of the country's leading agricultural institutions and many white farming families sent their sons to the UK to learn how to run the vast African farms when their time came. Miles Cameron, was one of them.

'Coming to the pub?' one of the students yelled across the corridor as Miles crammed his books into his rucksack. 'They're organising a table football competition. With your wrist action, you ought to enter!'

'I might just do that,' Miles grabbed a can of Coke from the drinks machine and tugged off the ring pull before gulping down half the contents. 'I have to get home first. I'll catch up with you later.'

'I'll put you on the list of entrants – maybe we could go for doubles?'

Miles nodded, swinging his rucksack over his shoulder as he pushed open the big double doors that led into the car park. A bitterly cold north wind tore into him as he loped with easy strides across the car park and flung his bag into the back seat of his grandmother's Mini. He jumped into the driver's seat, switched on the engine and made his way out of Shrewsbury. Halfway down the A49, the rain turned to sleet that blotched and splattered against his windscreen. He reduced his speed to cope with the wet conditions.

His grandparents, George and Doris Bentley, lived on the edge of Church Stretton in south Shropshire. The picturesque town nestled peacefully among the majestic hills of Long Mynd and was a haven for walkers and tourists alike.

Their house had been built into the curve of a steep hill alongside one of the tracks that led to the top of Long Mynd. Visitors had to climb steps to reach the front door and the back garden rose higher than the house. George had toyed with the idea of moving into a bungalow further down the hill, and Doris had welcomed the idea of a manageable lawn and no steps, but they had never done anything about it. Doris might call into the estate agents in Church Stretton when a particularly attractive bungalow for sale had caught her eye, and she and George would discuss the merits of moving with enthusiasm, but then the little piece of paper would be left on the coffee table, or used to build a fire in the morning, or simply thrown out with the rubbish. And the Bentleys would remain in the beautiful home that they both loved so much.

Miles parked the Mini in the drive and, shielding his face from the harsh winds, he climbed the steep steps that led to the front door. His grandmother was there to open it.

'Come in! Come in!' she cried, helping him out of his coat. 'Look at you! You're soaked through just from leaving the car. My word! Is the weather that bad?' Doris peered out at the winter storm. 'Go on through and get warm, darling. I'll bring you some tomato soup. That should fix you up nicely.'

Miles dropped his rucksack in the hall and made his way into the sitting room where his grandfather was reading The Telegraph. The old man looked up when his grandson entered and his eyes twinkled mischievously.

'I was working in the garden this afternoon. Damn near caught my death, but not so much as a whisper of sympathy from Mrs Bentley. You come in, strong as an ox, and she's fussing over you as though you're a half-dead fledgling. No justice in this household, and that's a fact.'

'Just ignore him,' Doris settled Miles into the big armchair and placed a tray on his lap. The steaming bowl of home-made tomato soup was accompanied by a hunk of fresh bread, thick with butter, and a crisp, white napkin. 'He's just jealous. You're turning into a grumpy old man, Mr Bentley. Heaven knows why I married you. I just hope this dear boy has inherited my genes and not yours!'

George chuckled and returned to his paper, mumbling: 'You'll turn the boy soft if you're not careful!'

Doris waved an irritated hand in his direction then turned to her beloved grandson with a huge smile. 'Ignore him. He doesn't appreciate what it's like to be raised in a hot climate. You're not used to our English weather. Would you like a hot water bottle for your feet? It'll warm you up nicely.'

'I'm okay thanks, Nana.' Miles grinned and cast a guilty, sideways glance at his grandfather. George Bentley rolled his eyes in comic exasperation. 'I like the winter weather. It's different. Exciting.'

'Talking of exciting,' Doris went over to the sideboard and shuffled among her papers. 'A letter came for you today. It's postmarked Bala. It must be from that young girl you wrote to.'

Miles' heart missed a beat and he paused with a spoonful of tomato soup midway between his bowl and his mouth. He dropped the spoon, laid the tray on the coffee table and took the white envelope from his grandmother's hand. The handwriting surprised him. It was small and neat with the address written in capital letters in green biro. Miles stared at it and turned it over in his hands as though expecting to see the contents through the gummed strip.

'Aren't you going to open it?' Doris was beside herself with curiosity. 'It must be from her. Oh how exciting. What do you say, George?'

'Very exciting,' her husband dryly observed.

'But then what am I saying?' Doris scooped up the tea-tray. 'You'll want to read it in private. What a fool I am! Finish your soup and then you can go up to your room for a bit of peace and quiet.'

Miles knew how his grandmother loved to fuss over him and he dutifully finished his soup, but that white envelope, with the neat green handwriting, absorbed his every thought and he practically choked on his soup in an effort to finish his supper and escape to the privacy of his own room. Once there, he flung himself on the bed and tore open the seal. In his haste, he accidentally tore a tiny strip off the page itself and he swore under his breath. He settled a pillow against the headboard and lay full length on the bed to savour the moment.

It began: Dearest Miles.

Miles devoured every word, hungry for news of the girl who had once been such an important part of his childhood, desperate to see how she had fared so far away from the land of her birth. But Lydia did not say anything about herself in the letter. She was more anxious to find out about Miles, and to learn what had happened to all her old friends in Africa. At the end of the short note, she included an invitation to visit the Llewellyn household in Bala. Mum and Dad would love to see you again, she had added, saying nothing of her own feelings on the matter. Miles was disappointed but his spirits rallied when he read the end of the note which said simply: Lots of love from Lydia with two little crosses that stood as kisses underneath.

Miles had no idea what to expect, and he certainly had no idea what he wanted from a meeting with Lydia Llewellyn, but he knew that he had to see her again. If only once, just to talk about old times and to see what kind of person she had become. He would accept the invitation to visit Doctor Llewellyn and his family in Bala. And his heart skipped a beat at the prospect.

On 12th February 1979, Ian Douglas Smith gave his last public address as the Prime Minister of Rhodesia. He looked pale and his eyes were tired. He spoke falteringly in his flat nasal tones, angrily accusing the British of "treachery" and "vindictiveness" in their betrayal of Rhodesia. He had done his best to protect the white man's position, but the winds of change that had blown across Africa were too strong, too swift. Now, black majority rule was imminent.

Smith knew that the Rhodesia that thousands of whites had made their home, had loved and nurtured, was no more. Henceforth, even the name would be changed. The land would be called Zimbabwe-Rhodesia. It was a clumsy compromise that united blacks and whites in a chorus of derision. The new Zimbabwe-Rhodesia would be governed by a Transitional Government of National Unity.

Smith was hoping that Bishop Abel Muzorewa would be elected to the Transitional Government. His party was more moderate than Mugabe's ZANU in the north or Nkomo's ZAPU in Matabeleland. The whites were convinced they would have no place in a country governed by such militant forces. They hoped that Muzorewa, foolish, deluded man that he was, would be more pliant.

Robert Mugabe and Joshua Nkomo were scornful of this alliance. As far as they were concerned, it was simply another ploy to retain white supremacy. There was little doubt that the way forward lay with ZANU and ZAPU fighting the election together as the Patriotic Front.

In spite of his natural aversion towards the Shona, Nkomo believed that an alliance under the banner of the Patriotic Front would strengthen ZAPU's position and secure the future for Zimbabwe-Rhodesia. It was a logical, strategic step, but ancient tribal mistrust and an inborn antipathy prevailed and the Patriotic Front was weakened by disunity. But they were united on one point. They were angered by the pact between Muzorewa and the whites, and both agreed that the Patriotic Front should boycott the Transitional Government elections. There would be no compromise with the whites.

Dai Llewellyn was exactly as Miles had remembered him - tall and gangly with a prominent nose and wide, welcoming smile. He was quick to laugh and, when he did, his sea-green eyes sparkled merrily and he threw back his head with gusto. He was not exactly good-looking, even Miles could see that, but he had great charisma and few could resist his easy-going charm.

Leaving Africa had been difficult for the Llewellyns, especially the two girls, Lydia and Leah. But Dai had his roots in Wales and the family was happy here. Dai Llewellyn had been welcomed as a surgeon at the hospital in Bala, and he was now a popular member of the community. His daughters were enrolled at local schools and his wife could rest easy in her bed knowing that the dangers that lurked in the dark corners of Africa could not touch them here.

'It's so good to see you again lad,' Dai said with that appealing lilt in his voice. Miles noticed that the doctor's Welsh accent was more pronounced than he remembered. It sounded nice.

'I couldn't agree more,' Myra Llewellyn sat next to Miles on the rose-patterned sofa. 'I can't get over how much you've changed. Look at you! You're a young man now. How time has flown.'

Miles blushed and avoided catching the eye of the two girls opposite. He tried to think of a witty retort, but none came. He felt gauche and dull in their presence and no matter how hard he tried, he could think of nothing to say. In fact the more he tried, the harder it became. The problem was that, although Lydia's parents seemed more or less as he remembered them, their daughters had changed beyond recognition. As far as Miles was concerned, Lydia was a complete stranger. And a very composed and beautiful stranger at that.

He had been taken aback by her appearance as soon as she opened the front door. She was taller of course, but as slim as a reed with obvious curves in all the right places. They stood in the porch, momentarily at a loss for words. Both had expected to hug, they were childhood pals after all, but an invisible wall had sprung up between them in the intervening years and neither could pluck up the courage to make the first move. Luckily, Lydia's mother had taken charge of the situation and both were grateful to escape from the tense atmosphere.

Miles was pleased to see that neither Dai nor Myra Llewellyn had changed and that he was still at ease in their company, but the other teenager, perched on the edge of the armchair sucking a string of red liquorice, was quite another matter. Miles could hardly believe that it was Lydia's younger sister, Leah.

'Wow! You look different!' Leah jumped up, rolled the liquorice round her forefinger, and gave Miles a quick peck on the cheek. 'Doesn't he look great, Lyds? She was wondering what you were going to look like, weren't you sis?'

Lydia nodded, but her eyes were firmly fixed on the floor. At this precise moment, she would gladly have allowed the earth to open up and swallow her whole. Either that, or some painful mishap befall her tactless sister in the not too distant future. Blushing furiously, Lydia took the seat opposite without saying a word. She found it hard to join in the conversation after that. Instead, she had to sit dumbly while Leah and her parents chatted away as though she was not even in the room. She sighed and chewed her bottom lip. It was all going horribly wrong.

Leah was right, of course. Lydia had been excited at the prospect of seeing Miles Cameron again. She had dressed with care that morning and had brushed her hair until it shone like burnished copper. She had twisted her body from side to side in front of the full-length mirror and had to admit that she looked "okay". She had so many questions to ask, so much to tell her childhood chum, that she wondered if this one, short day would be long enough.

Now, instead of impressing Miles with her transformation from a silly child to a sophisticated seventeen-year-old, she looked and felt like a complete idiot. He must find her such a dull companion compared to the sun-tanned lovelies he knew in Africa. She glanced at her hands. Her skin looked pasty in comparison with his. Even Leah looked prettier with her animated expression, girlish giggle and natural good humour. Certainly Miles was finding Leah easier to talk to. Lydia saw herself in his eyes and she saw a boring teenager from the Welsh valleys who would have little appreciation of the excitement, danger and glamour of everyday life in Africa.

'Your father would have been proud of you,' Dai ran a hand through his unruly mass of ginger hair. 'Shrewsbury College is a splendid achievement. It's one of the finest agricultural colleges in Britain. So what happens next. What are your plans?'

'I'm going to finish my studies… and then I'm going home,' Miles said simply.

Lydia heard the words and her breath caught in her throat. She looked up and her eyes met his. For one brief moment the two teenagers looked at each other without embarrassment, liquid chocolate melting in a sea of emerald green, and an unspoken agreement seemed to hover between them.

Africa was home. Home was Africa.

'So Scarfell Farm will benefit from everything you pick up over here? You'll carry on where your father left off, will you?'

'I will,' Miles nodded, losing his inhibitions in his desire to talk about Scarfell Farm. 'But I'm going to change lots of things. Farming is moving forwards. There are lots of new ways of increasing productivity and I can already see room for improvement in the way things are run out there. Farming methods have changed beyond recognition since my dad ran the farm. I've learned so much on this course already. I just can't wait to get the next three years over so I can go home and start putting it all into practice.'

Dai laughed. 'Don't go wishing your life away. Mind you, I have to admit that I know how you feel. I was a bit like that with my medical studies. I just couldn't wait to get going on the real thing.'

'Yuck!' Leah interjected. 'The "real" thing for you would be people and dead bodies. Vile!' she sucked the red string into her mouth in a series of tiny nibbling movements. 'At least Miles is only talking about fields and green grass…'

'And mud and muck and animals dying, giving birth and all those "real" things that happen on a farm,' Lydia joined in the debate. 'It's not some fantasy farm, you know. It's a real farm. It has real problems and real pleasures.' She paused before adding in a whisper: 'Scarfell is…it's a real home.'

Dai and Myra both glanced at their daughter. Myra frowned, but Dai shook his head almost imperceptibly. Wisely, Myra said nothing, but she recognised the chemistry between her daughter and the handsome boy from Bulawayo. She had noticed it when they were children, when they were too young to appreciate such things. They had been drawn to each other then, and the years had done nothing to break those invisible bonds.

Secretly, Myra had hoped that Miles Cameron would turn out to be a plain, rather dull young farmer from the third world. The kind of boy who would never appeal to her daughter's imaginative, artistic nature. But the fates had deemed otherwise. Myra was forced to admit that Miles Cameron had grown into a roguishly handsome young man. He was also lean and fit with strong forearms and hint of manly stubble on his chin. He was far more than the simple soul she had hoped to meet. And she was worried.

With an effort, Myra shrugged off her sense of impending gloom and passed a slice of fruit cake to Miles. She had come to hate living in Africa. She had feared Africa and could not wait to bring her precious girls home to the safety of Wales – to a place where they could grow up without the threat of being murdered in their beds, or struck down by some unspeakable foreign ailment. But Myra knew that Lydia still thought of Africa as home. It was in her blood. And now, this dashing young man from her past had fuelled the fire of Lydia's romanticism. Myra could not bear to even think of losing her daughter to that dark continent, even though Lydia had often talked about returning. This was her eldest child. Myra was determined to keep Lydia here in Wales where she would be safe and happy.

'Lydia's been offered a place at art college when she finishes her A' levels, haven't you darling?' Myra wanted to break the spell between the two.

'That's great!' Miles grinned at Lydia, genuinely interested in her plans. 'So you're going to be an artist?'

'Something like that, but I'm not sure what I want to do. I thought it might be nice to teach.'

'Africa always needs good teachers,' Miles blurted out. 'You should bear that in mind when you start to make your plans.'

Myra stood up and tugged her chunky home-knit down over her hips. 'I think Lydia has plenty of time to think about her future, Miles. Wales needs good teachers, too, remember. Besides, you'll want to chat about it with Philip, won't you dear?'

'Philip?' Miles took a swift intake of breath.

'A lovely boy,' Myra replied. 'Lydia's boyfriend. They've been dating for a year now, haven't you darling. He's training to be an architect at Manchester University. We're hoping Lydia will get into Manchester Art College. It's such a wonderful city. You must go there while you're here Miles.'

Miles nodded and dropped the slice of cake back on the plate. Of course she had a boyfriend. She was beautiful, young and lovely and living in one of the most fantastic countries on earth. A broken-down farm in Bulawayo must seem very primitive in comparison with the social whirl of Manchester. And Philip, Lydia's boyfriend, sounded very cool. An architect studying at Manchester University. Can't compete with that, Miles told himself.

But then he was not here to compete with anybody. He deliberately shook away the gloomy thoughts. He was here simply to catch up on old times with a family friend. He had not expected more than that from this visit. He did not want more than that from this visit. Lydia belonged in his childhood. He had to accept that.

Maybe it was foolish to visit her. Too much time had passed between them and she was a different person now. A stranger. And a stranger with a boyfriend at that. But no matter, Miles told himself sternly. He would be going home soon. He simply wanted to meet her again and chat about old times. That was his only reason for coming to Bala. Nothing more.

'It's a good job you brought a pair of wellies,' Lydia teased as she and Miles traipsed through the mud at the edge of Bala Lake. It gets worse up there.'

'Shropshire is pretty muddy, too,' Miles laughed. 'But I guess we're asking for trouble if we choose to go walking in the pouring rain.'

Lydia glanced up at the sky. It was heavy, like sheet metal, and the droplets ran down her cheeks. Giggling, she pulled her hood around her face. 'I just wanted to get out of the house. I didn't want you to leave without…talking to you… properly.'

'I wasn't sure your mother approved of you going out in this weather.'

'Oh it's not that. I'm always out in weather like this. You should see me when the snow comes. I spend hours in Penllyn Forest in the snow. I love it. No, I think Mum was more worried about me being on my own with you.'

'With me? Why?'

'Because you're a part of my past. Because you're a part of Africa. And she knows what Africa means to me.'

Miles' foot had become stuck in the thick mud at the water's edge and he tugged his boot against the suction. Lydia watched with a broad smile on her face. 'Careful you don't pull your wellie off!' she warned.

Having retrieved his boot, with his foot still in it, Miles followed Lydia to a fallen tree trunk that had been brought down in last year's storms. Lydia sat on top of it so that her feet were dangling among the soggy leaves. The rain was steady and her face was wet and shiny.

'So what does Africa mean to you?' Miles leaned against the trunk and turned to face her.

Lydia paused and stared out across the lake. 'I don't really know. It's hard to explain. You have to remember that it was home for the first thirteen years of my life. I feel I know Bulawayo better than I know Bala. It's weird, but I still think of Bulawayo as home. When you said that you were going "home" I felt jealous. I don't know why. All I know is that I have to see it again. I'm thinking of trekking across Africa when I finish college. I may even work there for a while.'

'I'd like that,' Miles whispered.

Lydia looked at him. Her long lashes were sparkling with droplets of rain, and she smiled. 'I could come and visit you at Scarfell Farm…if you're still there.'

'Oh, I'll be there,' Miles grinned. 'No doubt about that.'

Lydia jumped down from the tree trunk and kicked a path through the leaves. 'Of course, you'll probably have a wife and ten kids by the time I get there...'

'Perhaps,' Miles followed her and took her coat sleeve to halt her in her tracks. 'But I doubt it. I can't explain things any better than you can, but something tells me I'll be waiting when you get there.'

Lydia blushed and shook herself free of his grasp before skipping off along the lakeside path. 'You say that now, Miles Cameron, but anything can happen between now and when I finish my studies. Who knows what fate has in store for us.'

Miles shook the rain out of his hair and smiled wistfully. 'Well, I guess it doesn't really matter whether I'm there or not. What matters is that Scarfell Farm will be there. Scarfell Farm will always be there.'

George Bentley peered over the tops of his spectacles to watch the BBC news on television. Zimbabwe-Rhodesia was very much in the public eye following the Commonwealth Conference in Lusaka. For it was from this platform that the newly-elected British Prime Minister had announced in connection with African affairs: 'I will not be bullied.'

Margaret Thatcher had come to power on 3rd May 1979. White and black Africans now waited anxiously to see how Britain's first female Prime Minister was going to deal with their deepening crisis. The common view, especially among white Rhodesians, was that she would favour Bishop Abel Muzorewa's Transitional Government. After all, it would reassure the right-wing members of her own party that the British Government still favoured what was best for Ian Smith and the whites, and that they did not support the Marxist madman, Robert Mugabe and his allies.

But Margaret Thatcher astonished the world when she flatly announced that the proposed coalition gave white Rhodesians powers which were disproportionate to their numbers in the country. She also added that the British Government would refuse to recognise Zimbabwe-Rhodesia until Mugabe's Patriotic Front had been brought into the fold. Her aim, she declared, was to secure a solid position for the whites in a government of genuine black majority rule.

The front-line African presidents, Kenneth Kaunda of Zambia, Julius Nyerere of Tanzania and Samora Machel of Mozambique had their own reasons for applauding Thatcher's proposals.

'Kaunda wants sanctions lifted so that he can get his South African maize supplies across Rhodesia,' George Bentley observed. 'His people are starving. He can't hold on to power much longer if Rhodesia remains at war.'

Miles leaned forward on the edge of his chair and nodded. 'Nyerere can't afford war much longer either, and poor old Machel's revolution will be in tatters before long if things don't improve soon.'

'I'd say Machel has the most to lose,' George Bentley agreed. 'He's saddled with thousands of refugees, and he's a target for the Rhodesian armed forces with all those ZANU training camps dotted around his northern borders.'

'The Telegraph reckons that people are crowding into the towns to escape the Rhodesian raids. It's causing havoc with Mozambique's infrastructure.'

'There can't be much infrastructure left in place,' his grandfather muttered, draining his coffee cup. 'Most of the whites have gone now. Mozambique is already crumbling. All it needs now is one major assault by Rhodesia and the country's finished. Machel must be desperate for Mugabe to reach an agreement with the British this time round.'

Miles turned to watch the live television coverage of the ZANU delegation arriving for talks at Lancaster House. The talks were designed to find a way to break the deadlock between members of the Transitional Government and Robert Mugabe's powerful ZANU party. The British had accommodated Mugabe and his ZANU delegation in a prestigious five-star hotel in Kensington High Street. But Robert Mugabe was not remotely interested in the luxuries of one of the world's most exciting capital cities. He was here for a purpose and he made that purpose crystal clear when he said:

'We have not come here to negotiate with Smith or Muzorewa. We have not come here to negotiate the principle of majority rule. We have come here to negotiate with the British the transfer of power. Nothing else is for discussion'.

But too many people had too much invested in the future of Africa to allow Mugabe's intransigence to prevent a lasting agreement in Rhodesia. The Foreign Secretary, Lord Carrington, was determined to broker a peace. And the way forward, in the eyes of the British, was to remove the major obstacle to black majority rule, which everyone accepted was white political power!

Lord Carrington's proposal was to remove the "safeguards" for whites, originally agreed with Smith and Muzorewa, by giving a new Prime Minister extra powers. Carrington was fully prepared to sacrifice concessions for white Rhodesians if it helped smooth the path to black majority rule. And he was fully prepared to ride out the backlash from the Conservative Party's right wing if needs be. Africa was too important to lose. There was no room left for political niceties.

Muzorewa was delighted with the proposals giving him tough new powers. They belied his weak image by making it look as though his party had triumphed over the whites in the Transistional Government. Sensing this, Ian Smith poured scorn on Muzorewa describing him as "the most inept politician I have ever met" and dismissing him as "wet putty" in the hands of the British.

Robert Mugabe, on the other hand, distanced himself from these crude machinations. He did not trust anyone, least of all Margaret Thatcher, and he dismissed the entire Lancaster House Conference as a sop to the Conservative right-wing.

The conference, like all other conferences before it, was getting off to a bad start. But there was a new and very different ingredient in the political mix. The British Prime Minister, Margaret Thatcher. The "Iron Lady" as she would come to be known. An iron lady who was determined not to lose this battle.

The Lancaster House Conference struggled on for ten long weeks. Bitterness and a mutual mistrust caused any fragile accord to be dashed time and again by unrealistic or unworkable demands on all sides.

Robert Mugabe and Joshua Nkomo had joined forces as the Patriotic Front to boycott the elections for the Transitional Government, but Mugabe was emerging as the most powerful negotiator of the two and a major stumbling block to peace. He had already fought for, and won, recognition for his men so that, henceforth, black freedom fighters would no longer be classed as terrorists, but legitimate armed forces. He was also demanding that South Africa withdraw their military personnel from Rhodesia.

Lord Carrington, who had expected to see the agreement signed and sealed fairly quickly, was forced to admit that Mugabe was a man of fine intellect and a formidable opponent. All sides were tantalisingly close to an agreement, but Mugabe was not prepared to budge on the South African issue. The whites, on the other hand, were not prepared to leave themselves vulnerable or without allies in the fragile peace that followed. Carrington was too astute to risk losing everything at this late stage in the conference, and he was relieved when the Secretary General of the Commonwealth provided a compromise with a carefully worded document: "There will be no external involvement in Rhodesia under the

British Governor. The position has been made clear to all the governments concerned."

Tired, but beaming with unashamed delight and relief, he told the world's media the following day:

"We have a Constitution, we have a transition and now we have the terms for a ceasefire. That's not bad, is it?"

Christopher Soames, the son-in-law of the late Winston Churchill, was chosen to act as British Governor during the next phase of the transition to black majority rule. Unlike Lord Carrington, he had never worked in Africa, but his ability to handle a crisis with good humour, patience and fairness proved critical. His job was to keep the momentum going, to keep the front-line Presidents happy by preventing raids into their countries and to bring the Patriotic Front fully on board. And Bishop Abel Muzorewa, the Prime Minister of the Transitional Government for such a short time, was instructed to hand power over to the British until full elections, which included the Patriotic Front could be held.

Unfortunately, Lord Carrington chose to announce the terms of the ceasefire on the day of the new Governor's departure for Rhodesia, and the optimistic event was immediately overshadowed by the contents of the document. In it, Lord Carrington had given forty seven operational bases to the white armed forces in the country, while ZAPU and ZANU military units together were allocated no more than sixteen. To add to the insult in Mugabe's eyes, the African bases had been located well away from key areas such as the main transport routes, white settlements, industry and the larger towns.

Mugabe feared that, if he were to try to move his men away from these strategic areas by herding them into far-flung camps, they would look like a defeated army. He did not think it would be possible to persuade them to give up their positions and abandon the strongholds they had fought to secure. Also, he was concerned that such large concentrations of black military personnel would make the camps sitting ducks for the Rhodesian forces if they chose to attack.

He refused to agree with the conditions.

Lord Carrington was infuriated by Mugabe's last-minute refusal to sign the crucial peace treaty. Angrily, he imposed a deadline of eleven o'clock on Saturday 15th December 1979, at which time the Lancaster House Conference would close, he warned, "with or without Robert Mugabe".

Mugabe responded through a statement read by his lawyer, Eddison Zvobgo: "Carrington can go to hell. Thatcher can jump in the Thames. Further more, Thatcher is in concubinage with Satan Botha." Brandishing maps which highlighted the unequal distribution of base camps, Zvobgo told the cameras "The answer Lord Carrington is NO...NO...NO."

Deadlock loomed, but a timely intervention by President Samora Machel saved the negotiations at the eleventh hour. Machel was fearful that his own fledgling revolution would flounder under constant pressure from Rhodesia and its allies. He warned his old friend that he refused to sign the agreement, his troops would no longer be welcome in Mozambique.

Robert Mugabe knew that he would be lost without the support and resources of neighbouring Mozambique. He knew also that the whites would find their own case strengthened if Mozambique, under black rule, were to flounder. He was quashed at last. But he was not subdued by a superior strength, nor by superior numbers, nor by a lack of commitment to the fight for freedom. He was subdued by his reliance on an old friend and comrade in arms and to his loyalty to black Africa .

He knew that he could not allow Mozambique's revolutionary success to be destroyed by his own intransigence, and he knew he could not win the war for independence without Mozambique as an ally. He was left with no choice other than to sign the historic Lancaster House Agreement. He knew that the agreement would bring his country to peace, but he did not believe that it would bring it to victory. And there were tears in his eyes when he finally agreed to allow Zimbabwe-Rhodesia to take this one final step towards black majority rule.

'Wow! Is this for me?' Lydia took the Christmas box from Miles and surveyed it from all angles. 'What is it?'

'You're supposed to open it,' Miles laughed. 'That's why I wrapped it up. So that you could open it!'

Lydia sat cross-legged on the floor in front of the roaring log fire. The golden flames leapt and danced behind her head while her hair, piled loosely on top of her head, glittered with ruby lights against the fire. Her cheeks were ruddy from the heat and her eyes glowed. 'Am I supposed to open it now, or wait until Christmas Day?'

Miles shrugged and leaned forward with his elbows on his knees. 'It's up to you.' He had not had time for a shave that morning and the rough stubble made him look darkly handsome. 'It's not much.'

Lydia reached across and touched his hand. 'It's from you. That's all that matters.'

Miles felt an jolt of pleasure in the pit of his stomach and he shifted his backside on the floor. He had seen a lot of Lydia in recent months and their initial awkwardness had quickly faded, but there was a tension between them that would flare up unexpectedly from time to time. Usually, it involved a brief physical touch, something that was said, or a chance look, but it was enough to unsettle them both until it had passed.

'Mother won't like you buying me presents,' Lydia said. 'Maybe I should open it now.'

'What does your mother have against me,' Miles asked, puzzled by the cold reception he had received from Myra Llewellyn.

'Oh, it's nothing personal.' Lydia smiled reassuringly. 'She just thinks you're going to whisk me away to the dark continent and she's worried. She hates Africa. It terrifies her.'

'I can understand that.' Miles conceded.

'That's why I wanted to come and see you in Church Stretton this time. I thought it would be less hassle to visit you here. Mum's pretty anti-everything to do with Africa, you know.'

'And you?' Miles leaned closer. 'How do you feel about Africa?'

Lydia turned and gazed into the fire. It was one of those troublesome moments when she had to confront her feelings, and voice her hopes and dreams. She felt afraid. Now was not the right time for Africa, she knew that, but she also knew that her future lay in that wild and wonderful place. She did not know how, nor why, but she knew that she would go back there one day.

'I love Africa,' she whispered into the fire. 'I love the sounds and smells of Africa. I have to go back there one day, because it's my home and because …. because you're there.'

Miles breathed deeply and took her hand, pulling her into his arms. She was hot from the fire and soft. So soft. Her hair smelled of peach. He hugged her closer, tighter, as though he feared she would fade away in a wisp of smoke. She did not resist. Gently, he lifted her chin with his thumb and tilted her head towards his.

'When will you come home, Lydia?' he whispered.

'I don't know,' she looked deep into his eyes. 'I truly don't know when I will come. But I will come back to Africa, Miles. I will come home.'

Miles looked long and hard into those emerald eyes that swam like the ocean tides before his gaze. He lifted a wisp of hair from her cheek and leaned towards her. He kissed her forehead, her nose and, when she pursed her lips to meet his, he kissed her warm, wet mouth. And it was the sweetest moment he had ever known.

14

With Robert Mugabe finally on board, the Lancaster House Agreement paved the way for the country's first elections to full and independent black majority rule. But the country's first steps towards democracy, where every one of its people had a voice, were not easy.

The campaign to elect a new, permanent government had already swung into action when the fragile unity between Nkomo and Mugabe, under the banner of the Patriotic Front, was finally broken. Without forewarning Nkomo, Mugabe registered his own party with the name: "ZANU (PF)". Angry, but undeterred, Nkomo stood for election as the "Patriotic Front (ZAPU)".

Christopher Soames, and the Commonwealth peace-keeping forces drafted in to ensure the country's first free and fair election, where all parties were fully represented, waited anxiously for tensions to erupt. They did not have to wait long.

Nkomo complained that his party could not campaign in Manicaland because of threats from ZANU (PF) supporters. The British election monitors agreed that a "free and fair" election would not be possible in some electoral districts due to intimidation by Mugabe's supporters. Mugabe counter-claimed that his people dared not go into Matabeleland.

The election campaign was a shambles, but the British knew that they had no choice other than to press on with it. The alternative was civil war. Even after the election, if ZANU (PF) were defeated, the prospect of reprisals loomed large.

The results of the elections would be announced on 4th March 1980. White people waited nervously in spite of the fact that Robert Mugabe's stance had been softened by his friend and mentor, Samora Machel.

Machel had called for pragmatism and moderation. He had warned Mugabe that talk of Marxism would alarm the whites. Mugabe heard the warning and he agreed to fight his campaign on a manifesto that owed its key principles to this wise counsel.

"ZANU wishes to give fullest assurance to the white community, the Asian and coloured communities that a ZANU government can never in principle, or in social or government practice, discriminate against them. Racism, whether practised by whites or blacks, is anathema to the humanitarian philosophy of ZANU. Let us work together and build a nation united and strong."

The whites did not believe his rhetoric. Now, as he stood at the door to power in their beloved Rhodesia, they feared him. Promises made in a campaign manifesto did not necessarily translate into government practice, and they were horrified when the final results were announced on television.

4 seats to Muzorewa's UANC

20 seats to Nkomo's Patriotic Front (ZAPU)

57 seats to Mugabe's ZANU (PF)

Robert Mugabe had been given just four weeks to win this crucial election, but his preparations had taken twenty years. He had finally given all black Africans a voice. He had fought inequality and injustice. And he had won. The future of Zimbabwe, as it would henceforth be known, was in his hands.

That night, on television, a white woman introduced the new Prime Minister Elect as Comrade Robert G. Mugabe. Few were prepared for what followed. Mugabe had chosen his words carefully.

"There is no intention on our part to use our majority to victimise the minority. We will ensure that there is a place for everyone in this country".

There would be no sweeping nationalisation, he promised, and white citizens would keep their jobs and their pensions. Furthermore, white farmers and house owners would keep the rights to their property.

The following day, resignations were withdrawn and houses taken off the market. White Zimbabweans did not want to leave their homeland. Many were third and fourth generation Africans. For many, this was the land of their birth and they knew no other way of life. If their new Prime Minister asked them to "Forgive and forget" and to "Join hands in a new amity", they would hear his pleas.

They had fought a long and bitter war with the blacks. They had lost that war. Now, they would stand side-by-side with black Zimbabweans, so that they and their children might know peace at last.

Julius had excelled in his studies at the University of Rhodesia. He had chosen to follow the law so that he would be well equipped to serve his country when his time came. He was a brilliant student, quiet and conscientious, with a mental discipline far beyond his years. Everyone who knew him said that he would make his mark in the new Zimbabwe. It was an emerging nation and it would need young men like Julius Khumalo to carry it into maturity.

His mother, Bliss, had wept when she watched him stride on to the platform in cap and gown at his graduation ceremony. She could barely believe that her son had come so far. She sat among the other happy parents, splendid in her yellow and white polyester suit, with a brand new hat decorated with orange flowers, and she felt proud.

Julius had accepted his mother's tearful hugs with a smile. He was a serious young man, not given to overt demonstrations of affection, but even his normal reserve gave way to laughter when confronted with his mother's unabashed exuberance. It was one of life's special moments and Julius was content.

The sun had not yet risen when Julius jumped off the bus at the main station in Salisbury, but he was not surprised to see hundreds of people pushing through the shanty towns. He kept his head down and followed the crowd. They were all heading in the same direction. Rufaro Stadium. The place where Zimbabwe would formally and finally be declared an independent nation.

It was 18th April 1980.

Independence Day.

Julius was one of the lucky ones. He had a ticket for the event. He was a member of the Khumalo family, son of Moses Khumalo who had played such a key role in the chimurenga. He knew that his father would be there, but he did not expect to see him. Moses would stand with the ZAPU freedom fighters – those Matabele warriors who had fought and died alongside the Shona to help liberate Zimbabwe.

Moses and his men had been recalled from Zambia following the Lancaster House Agreement. Many were angry to find themselves herded into cramped base camps alongside the Shona. Their resentment festered and fights broke out. The Matabele did not trust Mugabe to honour his pact with ZAPU.

Julius did not agree. He had been pleased when Joshua Nkomo accepted the position of Interior Minister for Home Affairs in the new Cabinet. He was certain that it signalled a new accord between the two tribes. He understood why Nkomo was not entirely happy with the position, and why he still resented the way Mugabe had abandoned the Patriotic Front to fight the election independently, but Joshua Nkomo was too astute to reject the position, and Julius applauded his stance.

Julius had also supported the appointment of a white man as Commander of the Armed Forces. It would reassure the whites that Robert Mugabe was a man of his word. White people began to warm to their new Prime Minister, and their opinions were further reinforced when the President of the white farmers' union was awarded the agriculture portfolio.

But black Africans were enraged by this decision. They had fought and died for the land and many had expected see white farms seized immediately and handed over to landless peasants. Few could understand Mugabe's argument that the land should be fully utilised, and most refused to accept that a white man should be appointed to the task.

Mugabe ignored their protests. It was an unpopular decision, but necessary. And, more importantly, it was a clear indication that Robert Mugabe intended to secure a place in history as one of the world's great statesmen.

Julius understood his reasons and approved of the appointments. Like Mugabe, he realised that Zimbabwe needed the white man's expertise. He was prepared to put aside his personal feelings in the country's interests. For Julius had only one aim, and that was to see Zimbabwe succeed as an independent nation. He wanted Zimbabwe to be free, and strong.

Rufaro Stadium was a blaze of colour when Julius arrived. The stalls had been painted bright blue with one stand set aside for visiting dignitaries. The concrete seating that surrounded the football pitch was decorated with flowers and flags, and there were streamers blowing in the breeze. A green and white canopy fluttered above the main stand to shield the guests from the heat of the noonday sun. The celebrations were scheduled to last all day. Schools had sent drum majorettes who marched proudly on the grassy pitch. African dancers pranced in rainbow colours and there was singing and marching and colourful pageantry.

But the highlight of the day was when the British flag was lowered and a new flag raised. The flag of Zimbabwe. The colours were symbolic. Green represented the land, gold was for the minerals that had made the country rich, black was for the people of Zimbabwe and red was for the blood of its people.

And there, at the forefront of it all, was Zimbabwe's first black Prime Minister, Robert Gabriel Mugabe. Prince Charles was the guest of honour, and the people clapped approvingly, but the loudest cheers were for Mugabe when he said:

"If yesterday I fought you as an enemy, today you have become a friend. If yesterday you hated me, today you cannot avoid the love that binds you to me and me to you."

Julius stood in the packed auditorium and loosened his collar. He swallowed hard and fought back the tears. Mugabe's words had struck a chord. He was a Matabele, but he could not avoid the love that would bind him to the Shona people. He was certain that the way forward lay with unity between ZAPU and ZANU. Together, they would rid themselves of the bitterness of their colonial past. Together, they would form a new nation that was recognised throughout the world. Zimbabwe would be the standard bearer for a new Africa. And he, Julius Khumalo, would be a part of it.

He cast his eyes around the stadium. People were laughing, crying and clapping their hands with joy. Some simply sat on their concrete benches in a daze. And then, just before midnight, Bob Marley, the world famous reggae star, entered the arena to sing the Zulu national anthem "Zimbabwe". It was a crowning moment and even Julius could not prevent a tear from falling.

On the opposite side of Rufaro Stadium, sitting among the gnarled and battered ZAPU freedom fighters, the chiselled features of Moses Khumalo were furrowed in concentration. Unlike many others at the Independence Day celebrations, he was not smiling. His brooding glare was fixed on two people who sat on the benches behind the podium, at the back of the saluting base. They were sitting behind the radio commentator's box, where the television cameras would not see them and where they could not be singled out for applause.

Moses watched the faces of Joshua Nkomo and his wife, MaFuyana, and his heart bled for them. He clenched his teeth and the muscles worked along his jawbone. He was angry that Mugabe had failed to recognise the contribution that the Matabele people had made to the war effort. He had placed Joshua Nkomo and his wife in a grossly inferior position and Moses could see that Nkomo felt the humiliation keenly.

At one point, scores of people outside tried to force their way into the stadium. The police repelled them swiftly with tear gas. Those sitting at the back of the stadium suffered from its effects, and Nkomo and his wife had coughed and spluttered throughout the ceremony.

Moses watched all this with rising resentment. He listened to the speeches, and he heard the words of reconciliation uttered by Zimbabwe's new Prime Minister, but he was not ready to celebrate Zimbabwe's independence until all its people were free. He was not prepared to exchange white colonial masters for Shona dogs.

The Matabele people had fought the Shona since the days when King Mzilikazi had fled north from the wrath of Chaka Zulu. The Shona and the Matabele were enemies. Reluctantly, they had joined forces in the liberation struggle, but only to help defeat the whites. The Matabele had fought and died for freedom, side by side with the Shona, and Moses Khumalo could not stand by and see their efforts ignored. He had always believed that that total power was evil, and he was afraid that ZANU (PF) might be far more ruthless in power than the whites ever were.

He had hoped to catch a glimpse of freedom on the day when they claimed their independence from white colonial rule. But freedom was not there. Freedom was nothing but a shadow passing in the distance. Today, Zimbabwe celebrated its independence, but its people had yet to know freedom.

Grimly, Moses Khumalo swore upon the spirits of the dead Matabele freedom fighters that, for him, the luta continua. The war continues.

On that same day, the parents of a young white soldier mourned the death of their beloved son. They posted these words in memoriam in the local newspapers.

"Killed in action one year ago today. What it meant to lose you no-one will ever know. We often wonder why. Was it all for nothing?"

Months later, an old taxi cab turned off the road from Bulawayo and swung into the entrance of Scarfell Farm. Slowly, the vehicle made its way up the drive, crunching gravel and loose stones under its tyres as it did so. Huge acacias lined the drive and stretched into the azure sky. In the distance, the magnificent Blue Hills stood silent and timeless.

The taxi ground to a halt outside the house. The driver, a wiry Matabele sporting a brown paper floppy hat, scurried round to the back of the car and opened the boot. With remarkable ease, he lifted two suitcases out and deposited them on the verandah. He then turned to his passenger with a broad smile.

'You want me to carry them into the house, baas?'

Miles Cameron stood in front of his childhood home and gazed about him with awe. It seemed bigger than he remembered. The stoep, with its Rhodesian teak floor, stretched the entire length of the house. Surprisingly, although the building looked tired, neglected even, the wood still glowed in the warm sunlight and the windows sparkled in the sunshine.

'You need me for anything else, sah?' the little African bobbed beside Miles with boundless energy.

'No thanks. I can manage.' Miles rummaged in his wallet, delighting in the feel of the crisp Zimbabwean dollar notes. He fished one out and gave it to the driver who raised his brown paper hat with comical solemnity before jumping back into his car and heading back into town.

Left alone, Miles savoured the moment. Home. He had come home.

The air was filled with a sweet perfume and the day was warm and still. The rains had been plentiful last season and the grass was still green. Even without his mother's tender ministrations, Miles could see that her garden had bloomed in the summer months. It pleased him that nature's cycle had continued unabated. Nature was tough, he mused, and Scarfell Farm had survived.

Anxious to prolong this pleasure, he wandered across the lawn, pausing to snatch a fruit from the marula tree. The skin was soft and he tore off a chunk with his teeth. He let the juice trickle through the hole in the pink flesh and then squeezed out the pip. As a child, he often pottered around the garden chewing on a marula pip. He was a man now, but the fruit tasted as sweet as ever.

Miles had not known what to expect from his homecoming. Clara had written to him to say that Charlie had died from cirrhosis of the liver. Miles had toyed with the idea of returning to Africa at that point, but his grandparents had persuaded him to stay and complete his studies. He would need an agricultural qualification to run Scarfell Farm, they said, and he knew they were right.

It had not been a difficult decision - the joy on Lydia's face when he told her the news was justification enough - and it had been the right choice. He had learned a lot about farming at Shrewsbury College and, more importantly, he had learned a lot about Lydia Llewellyn.

He had learned that the girl with the emerald eyes, who had played such an important part in his childhood, was still, and always would be, an important part of his life. He had learned that she was kind and generous, quick-witted, and that her heart was warm and loving. He had learned that he was as special to her as she was to him. She loved him with a passion that had transcended the affections of childhood and was now poised at the gates of a lifelong devotion. He knew this because she had told him so herself. She had told him as they stood at the barriers at Heathrow Airport. Somehow, through her tears, she had managed to say the words 'I love you' and Miles had pulled her closer and hugged her while they both wept. And then she had stayed at the gate and waved until he was out of sight. A vulnerable, crumpled young girl with tear-stained cheeks and a brave smile.

Miles had said goodbye to Lydia with the promise that he would be waiting for her when she came home. He understood that she needed to complete her studies. He did not mind the enforced separation. They were young and Miles knew that their passion was strong enough to endure the passing of time. For Miles loved Lydia completely and unconditionally. He had always loved her and he always would.

Now, with the sun shining in his eyes and the familiar smells of Africa in his nostrils, he knew he would have the strength to wait. Besides, he had work to do. Scarfell Farm needed the care and attention that his parents had once lavished upon it. His responsibility was to restore it to its former glory.

Buoyant with youth and optimism, he ran back to the house and threw open the front doors, leaving his luggage outside. Charlie had let the place deteriorate after Clara had left. Broken ornaments had not been replaced and the gaily-coloured rugs on the sitting room floor were threadbare. There were stains, presumably whisky, on the chairs, and cigarette burns on the traditional mukwa furniture. But, in spite of the neglect, the old house still felt like home. And there, as if to prove it, in pride of place above the hearth was his mother's favourite oil painting. She had signed it at the bottom. Rachel Cameron. She would have been a young woman then. A wife. A mother. She would have been full of joy when she created this vivid painting of the Matopos.

Miles breathed slowly. The house was silent and he could feel the spirits of the past moving gently all around him. If he closed his eyes tightly enough he could still see his father sitting in the armchair reading the Bulawayo Chronicle. He could still picture his mother on the sofa knitting. Miles and his sister, Beth, had never run short of woolly jumpers while his mother was alive. Rachel liked to knit!

Old family photograph albums were stacked on the coffee table. Clara had stored them in neat piles and had dusted them regularly. They were an historical record of Scarfell Farm and they were precious. Miles picked one up and leafed through it. He chuckled at the way his parents would try to capture every little detail in every photograph. There was one which included the house, the Morris Minor, Prince, their old Rhodesian Ridgeback, Beth and Miles in their Sunday best and most of the garden! Consequently, the main subjects, the children, had been reduced to minute figures in the corner of the frame. It was a typical family snapshot.

Miles' smile disappeared when he saw the photograph on the next page and he frowned. He and Julius were hanging over the wall of the newly-built tree house. Ralph had taken the picture to celebrate the moment when the boys had first claimed it as their own. He had captured the exact second when they had waved and, briefly, their fingers had locked in mid-air. They were laughing. They were just children then. Just two little boys with their whole lives in front of them. The photograph had recorded one of the many happy days in a childhood spent at Scarfell Farm. But Miles did not feel happy now. He felt the joy drain out of him as he recalled that distant memory. He carried the album over to the sofa and sat down with it open on his lap. Salty tears rolled down his cheek as he held his head in his hands and wept.

Many years had passed since Scarfell Farm had been a home, but the memories were still alive in the old house. Generations of Camerons had lived and died here. But now, a son of the Camerons had returned. And Scarfell Farm would be a home once more. Miles stared at the photograph and made a solemn promise through his tears. Scarfell would be a happy home once more. He would make it so.

Suddenly, Miles heard a soft, shuffling noise behind him. His skin prickled and his nerves were taut. Someone, or something, was sharing his solitude and he jumped up and spun round, half-angry, half-afraid, with his jaw set and his fists clenched.

'Welcome home, Nkosi.'

'Sixpence! Oh my God!' Miles' shoulders sagged and he hastily tried to wipe away his tears. 'Sixpence Dube!'

The faithful servant had aged considerably over the years. His woolly black hair was now silver and his pleasant face was crinkled like old shoe leather, but his eyes still twinkled when he smiled and his few remaining teeth shone like pearls.

He did not know where to go when baas Charlie had died. He thought of going back to Malawi, to his wife and family, but he believed that his duty was with Scarfell Farm. He did not doubt that Miles Cameron would return to claim it one day. He would watch over the farm until then. He would not shirk his duty, for Sixpence Dube was a man of honour.

It had not been a difficult task. His wife had joined him and they had planted mealies around their little kia. Together they kept the main house clean and tended to the graves at the top of the hill. They looked after the garden and did their best to maintain Scarfell Farm. For it was their home, too.

'Sixpence. What can I say?' Miles shrugged his shoulders and held out his hands palm upwards. The tears were running freely again, and he felt as though he might break down completely. 'Thank you. Thank you, Sixpence. I don't know what else to say.'

'There is no need to thank me, Nkosi,' Sixpence replied, using the traditional Zulu term of respect. 'I had to stay until you returned.'

Miles shook his head and stumbled towards his old servant like a lost child. They embraced. Miles towered over the little Malawian and it was an awkward, clumsy hug that lasted but a few seconds. But it was enough to seal the bond between these two old friends and strengthen their resolve. They had a job to do, and it was a job they would do together, no matter how long it took.

The months that followed were the hardest that Miles had ever known. There was much to do, but with the help of Sixpence and his kindly wife, Grace, Miles was equal to the task.

His father had built up one hundred head of cattle. It had been a good stock of Friesland-Holsteins and Jerseys with a high milk yield, but they had long since been killed or stolen. Miles was not yet ready to bring in new livestock. He was too busy experimenting with the modern farming methods he had studied in England. And he was not alone. Many old family friends were still farming nearby and they rallied round to help whenever they could. Many were interested in the developments taking place in agriculture and were keen to see how they would work in Africa. But some of the ideas that had looked so good on paper were not suitable for this unforgiving land, and Miles soon became adept at mixing traditional and modern techniques.

It did not take him long to realise that many of the automated systems would not work at Scarfell Farm. He had toyed with the idea of a circular milking parlour, but saw at once that it was far too complicated for the average farm labourer. Also, there were too many things that could go wrong with automation, and Miles was mindful of the costs of spare parts locally.

His naïve enthusiasm was replaced by pragmatism and the goals he set himself became more realistic and achievable. He would keep the milking parlour in the same area as before. It had worked well for his father's herd. It was close to the grazing land, so the cows would not have to waste energy walking to the milking unit, and his father had already taken into account drainage, so that they would not be dragging their teats in mud during the rainy season.

Standing on top of the hill, feet apart and with his sleeves rolled up to the elbow, Miles surveyed the 12,000 acres that were now his responsibility. It was ironic that, in spite of the advancements in agriculture, there was little he could do to improve upon the farming methods his father had used before him. There were a few labour-saving tricks that he intended to introduce, and one or two modern innovations, but, on the whole, Scarfell Farm would continue as it had always done. Ralph Cameron had always been ahead of his time and he had learned how to couple this with Africa's strengths and weaknesses. Now, Miles would reap the rewards of his father's management skills. As he stood there, his boots covered in dirt and his hands rough from daily toil, it was clear that he was his father's son and that he would honour this legacy. Before his eyes, with help from local people, government grants, his own inheritance and money invested by his grandparents, Scarfell Farm was rising from the ashes. And it was a glorious sight.

Miles tipped his hat back on his head and thrust his hands into his pockets as he made his way back down the hill to the house. The smell of fresh koeksisters greeted him as he drew closer and he knew that Sixpence had been busy. Newly-washed sheets billowed on the line at the back of the house and, once again, Miles was thankful that Sixpence had chosen such a generous, hard-working wife. Between them, they had transformed the house into the warm and welcoming home it had always been.

Miles entered the kitchen and scooped one of the sticky pastries off the plate. He stuffed it into his mouth with grubby hands and then grinned at Sixpence who frowned quietly over the mixing bowl.

'Don't go using up all your creative talents before the festive season, Sixpence,' he teased, brushing the crumbs off his chin. 'This is going to be a great Christmas. You understand what I'm saying? Save your energies for Christmas!'

'I am certain that a few koeksisters will not rob me of my ability to provide for your guests when they arrive, Nkosi.'

'I know! I know!' Miles grabbed another pastry and bit a chunk off the end. 'I'm sure you can cope, but… well… it's got to be special. Do you understand? This will be the first time that Nana and Gramps have been back here since ….well …. it's just got to be special.'

'It will be special, Nkosi,' Sixpence placed a new tray of pastries into the oven and then wiped the flour from his hands on his apron. 'I will not let you down. I will prepare a banquet that would have pleased even the great Queen Nandi. Your grandparents will be pleased to see how well you are doing now that you are the master of Scarfell Farm. They will not be disappointed in you. Trust me, Nkosi. This much I know to be true.'

In the former capital city of Salisbury, now renamed Harare, Robert Mugabe was dealing with threats on all fronts. He was mindful of the economic problems that would follow a white exodus and yet, in spite of his reassuring rhetoric, white people were leaving in droves. He was also troubled by rivalries between his own party and ZAPU ministers.

Their leader, Joshua Nkomo, had already argued that Mugabe's new Cabinet favoured the Shona. He had also accused ZANU (PF) ministers of favouring ZANU ex-combatants and their own families when negotiating resettlement deals. He claimed that his position as Minister for Home Affairs was not worthy of his status as the leader of the Matabele nation. But his complaints were dismissed.

Mugabe had more pressing concerns. The war had ended, but he still had to decide what to do with the thousands of ex-combatants roaming the streets. These battle-weary men had fought a bloody war for freedom, for a better quality of life and for their share of the land. So far, they had yet to receive the rewards they had been promised and to claim the land that they felt was rightfully theirs.

Nkomo was adamant that the soldiers loitering in the towns would be less trouble if they were confined to camps out in the bush. ZANU ministers disagreed, claiming that they could not shut up healthy young men in remote areas forever. Ignoring Nkomo's protests, and those of the white residents, the Government proceeded to set up resettlement camps close to the major towns. The policy, as many had predicted, was a disaster.

ZANU and ZAPU ex-soldiers did not want to be pushed into the new resettlement camps and their resentment festered. They had risked their lives in the liberation war, they had struggled to survive and bring their country to glory. Now they were bored, confined like wild animals, and they were angry. There had been no attempt to integrate the two tribes and Matabele and Shona rivalries, subdued in part during the war, bubbled to the surface.

ZANU, too, felt uneasy at what they saw as a betrayal by their own people. They blamed the Matabele for the pressures faced by the

Government. They believed that Joshua Nkomo, backed by the whites and the western world, was forcing Comrade Mugabe to withhold the redistribution of land until the Matabele claims had been satisfied.

The atmosphere inside two of the camps was volatile and fights broke out from time to time. It did not take long for the fires of discontent to be fuelled. A ZANU rally at Bulawayo's White City Stadium gave speakers a perfect platform to voice their feelings about the Matabele, and to make disparaging remarks about Joshua Nkomo.

News of the insults spread to the men at the Entumbane camp where Moses Khumalo was confined. When the news reached him, he stuffed his fist into his mouth and bit down hard. Lines of blood trickled down his knuckles and his eyes narrowed.

'Are we going to stand by and allow these attacks upon our Leader?' he growled at his men. 'Are we prepared to let the Shona dogs insult the Matabele?' He stood up, knocking into the man sitting next to him, and towered above the group. 'We are soldiers, and we must now behave like soldiers!'

The men caught up his battle cry and grabbed their weapons. They had been waiting for a chance to release their pent-up anger and frustration and the ZANU rally had given them a reason to take up arms. Suddenly, the evening calm was shattered by the sound of bullets firing from Entumbane. Those in the ZANU camp opposite had been expecting reprisals, and they were fully armed and spoiling for a fight. The howls of the dying and injured pierced the night.

The bloodbath that followed gave the Government an excuse to insist upon the removal of all weapons from the camps. It was not an easy task. ZANU officials were accused of turning a blind eye to their comrades' weapons and concentrating upon those held by the Matabele. Joshua Nkomo was incensed when members of his party were arrested without his knowledge and charged with weapons offences. As Minister for Home Affairs, he refused to sign the orders for detention, claiming that no-one had told him why they had been arrested. The orders were signed in his absence and, when he returned, he discovered that Robert Mugabe had demoted him to a position with little or no authority.

Moses Khumalo lent his voice to those clamouring for Nkomo to resign in protest at his demotion, but Nkomo was first and foremost a statesman. He knew that, if he were to resign, ZAPU members would follow suit and there would be no Matabele representation in Parliament. Robert Mugabe would then be free to deliver his pre-war promises to the Shona, and the needs of the Matabele people would be ignored.

Moses lay on his bunk in his cramped quarters, and pondered the current state of affairs. The coalition Government was a sham. Mugabe was under pressure from his own people to remove Nkomo from power. To achieve this, he was attempting to discredit Nkomo in the eyes of the whites so that, when the time came to be rid of ZAPU completely, world opinion would be on his side.

Moses sighed and rose from his bed. He wandered outside and gazed up at the moon. The silence was broken by the town dogs barking and the occasional wagon rolling by. He thrust his hands into the pockets of his combat trousers and stood alone in the dusty compound.

He thought it ironic that he and his men were still wearing their military uniforms even though the war was over. But then, in reality, Moses knew the war was not really over. His war would never be over. He would never know peace and contentment. Moses had suffered all his life and he would die suffering. He understood that now. He had fought and won the war against white oppression. Now he would be called upon to fight a different war. There, alone in the moonlight, he finally realised that there could never be peace between the Matabele and Shona nations. There would be a fragile unity at times, and a hopeless attempt at democracy, but he did not believe that there could never be trust, honour and truth between the two nations.

Moses pulled his hands out of his pockets and chewed at the skin on his gnarled fingers. He had travelled a long and lonely road, but perhaps the end was in sight. He stood tall and menacing beneath the moonlit sky and offered a silent pledge to his ancestors. He would give his life for freedom. His country had celebrated independence, but the Matabele nation still did not know freedom. Perhaps they never would. Perhaps the vast open plains of Zimbabwe were not big enough for two tribes, whose bloodlust and hatred ran so deep, to exist in harmony.

Moses returned to the hut where his men were still sleeping. He roused the nearest body with the toe of his boot. The commotion aroused the other men. They were hardened war veterans. Their senses had been finely tuned over the years and, within seconds, every man was fully alert. They gathered under the light to hear the words of Moses Khumalo. One man knocked the hanging light-bulb with his head as he pushed his way through the squatting figures.

'Listen to me, my brothers.' Moses lifted a hand to steady the light bulb, but still it rocked back and forth casting strange shadows on his face. 'We have been betrayed by Mugabe and his Shona dogs. We fought and died beside them in the struggle for liberation, but now we are abandoned. There are those who say the Shona are suffering, too, but this is not true. ZANU ministers are already making sure that they are given the best jobs and land under the resettlement programme.

'I have not seen my wife and children for five years,' one grizzled war veteran muttered. ' I do not know if they are alive or dead.'

'My wife is dead,' his comrade replied. 'I sent her to Gwelo, to stay with my mother and sisters. They are all dead. Killed by the Rhodesians. Now I am alone.'

Moses' eyes glinted in the swaying light and, for a moment, the hard angles were softened. He smiled at the man and his teeth shone like polished pearls. 'You are not alone, my brother. You are a part of the great Matabele nation. But your labours are not yet over. Mzilikazi brought us here to flee the wrath of the Zulu King. He wanted to find a home for his people. That home is here in Matabeleland, but we must continue to fight for the right to call it our own. The Shona will try to take it away from us. Already there is talk that Comrade Nkomo is to be expelled from the Government. Without true representation, the Matabele voice will be silenced forever. There will be no future for our people. We will never be free.'

'What must we do, Comrade?'

Moses paused for a moment and searched deep into their eyes as though probing their very souls. 'You must keep your weapons. ZANU will try to force us to disarm, so that we will be weak. That cannot be allowed to happen. You must go out into the bush now. You must never give up your arms. Then, when we are called upon to fight again, we will be ready.'

Julius pulled the blinds shut and sat at his desk. A copy of The Herald was open in front of him, but a pile of papers were strewn across its centre pages. He picked up a biro and chewed the plastic top thoughtfully. Although the blinds had shut out some of the sun, the heat still penetrated the glass and made the back of his neck damp with sweat. He ran a finger between his neck and shirt collar and loosened his tie.

His office was in the centre of Harare, on the top floor of modern office block just off Tongogara Avenue. It was small, only three rooms, but he was determined that his fledgling law firm would grow in time. It would be renowned for its honesty, its dedication to truth and justice for the citizens of the new Zimbabwe. This was Julius' dream.

Julius' intelligence, integrity and patriotism had brought him to the attention of central figures in Harare, and had earned him the respect of both ZAPU and ZANU Government officials. Both parties could see that he was a man who genuinely believed in unity between the two tribes. He believed in Zimbabwe. And, unlike many of his African brothers, Julius was fully prepared to put aside his personal feelings to secure its future. But there were obstacles on the way.

'What do they think they can gain from all this!' Julius waved a hand at the papers in front of him and frowned at his assistant, Eli. 'It is madness!'

'ZAPU say they have been abandoned,' Eli proffered. 'They believe that retaining their weapons is the only way to claim what is rightfully theirs.'

'I know all that!' Julius was brusque, 'but this... this will not help the black man's cause. These arms caches are huge. They must have been dumping illegal weapons for months. What were they planning to do with them? They have enough in these arsenals to fight another chimurenga. Anyway, I need facts. Sit down, Eli, and let us get started.'

Eli sat on the other side of the desk and flicked open his notebook. 'Government ministers have discovered more than thirty arms caches on two farms near Bula.'

'These are resettlement farms for ZAPU ex-combatants?'

'That is correct. The government claims that they are part of a plot to overthrow the Prime Minister.'

Julius rolled up his sleeves and scribbled some notes on his pad. 'I do not believe that. The Matabele people would not be so naive. Do not forget that I am a Matabele. These are my people. I know them.'

'Yes Sir. Joshua Nkomo has denied the allegations. He claims that the story was invented in a bid to discredit him. He claims that one cache was purported to contain enough electronic equipment to jam Zimbabwe's entire security forces. He says this is not possible. He claims that they were simply camera parts and fittings for a dental surgery given to the people of Zimbabwe as part of Zambia's Humanitarian Aid programme.'

Julius shook his head. 'And the second discovery, near Gwelo? What does he say about that?'

'He says that many weapons were not collected when the forces were disarmed. He claims that the weapons were found near assembly points for soldiers, and that it is likely that some were left over or abandoned. He also claims that ZANU exaggerated the number of weapons found.'

'And what about the deaths of the white farmers? How does he explain those? Does he deny that the arms stores were used to murder white civilians in Matabeleland?'

'He denies this, too, Sir. He says that he is a victim of a campaign of intimidation orchestrated by the government. He says that they want to discredit him and his party. He claims that the killings, beatings and rape of black Africans were carried out by "gangsters" acting for Mugabe. He denies any ZAPU involvement in the murder of the white farmers.'

Julius finished taking notes and looked up at the young clerk in front of him. He felt tired and weary and hot in his office suit and tie. He leaned across and poured himself a glass of water from the decanter on his desk. This was going to be a difficult case and, in some ways, he would have preferred it to go to another firm. But he knew that he was probably the only lawyer in Harare that both sides could trust, and the government wanted to be seen to be using the proper legal channels. In his heart, Julius was angry that ZAPU had been so foolish as to undermine the fragile accord between the two tribes, and he could picture the scorn on the faces of the whites. They would laugh at this crude demonstration of the black man's inability to govern himself, let alone an entire country.

Julius was extremely sensitive to the derision of white people. He was keenly aware of the black man's inadequacies and he deeply resented any action that might subject black people to ridicule. The whites were expecting his people to fail. They were expecting to see ancient tribal conflicts re-emerge. Julius did not have any sympathies for the whites, but he could not condone murder. Surely there had been enough blood shed. Surely, it was time for all the people of Zimbabwe to work together.

'Get me all the information you can on this, Eli. I have been asked to fight this case on the government's behalf. If ZAPU continue to ignore the rulings on weapons abandonment, they will jeopardise Zimbabwe's future. Dissident acts such as these will unsettle the very fabric of the society we are trying to build. This cannot be allowed to happen.'

Miles leaned back in his father's old chair with his legs resting on the footstool. He had just finished a superb lamb boboete - one of Sixpence's finest culinary delights. He was tired and he was glad to put his feet up with a glass of wine and a copy of the Bulawayo Chronicle.

The newspaper was unopened. Miles had been too busy re-reading Lydia's letter. In it, she had told him about her studies at art college. The course was excellent and the students were nice, she had said. She had already become good friends with two other girls with whom she was now sharing a flat. Miles tried to picture her in her student digs, but it was difficult. He was glad that she had found a couple of flatmates, but he could not prevent twinge of jealousy when he pictured her with other men. No doubt her flatmates would have boyfriends, but would Lydia be tempted? She was a beautiful young woman. How long would it be before some handsome student swept her off her feet? Miles took a sip of wine and pushed the unwelcome thoughts to the back of his mind. He read the end of the letter once more.

"I miss you so much, Miles," she had said. "I miss Africa, too. I will come home soon, I promise. I'm counting the days until we can be together again. Remember that." And she had signed it "With love and hugs and kisses from your own Lydia."

Miles put the letter back into its envelope and picked up the newspaper. There was a picture of Joshua Nkomo's podgy face on the front page with the words "THE FATHER OF ZIMBABWE" written in capital letters above it. The accolade had been coined after Independence Day. It was a tribute to Nkomo's part in the struggle for freedom. At the bottom of the page, underneath the picture, was the strapline "NOW THE FATHER OF THE DISSIDENTS"

Miles sighed. He refused to believe that ZAPU were responsible for the killings that were now taking place in Matabeleland. He was more inclined to believe the rumours that the government was trying to oust Nkomo from office. Miles did not trust Robert Mugabe's rhetoric.

It was true that the Prime Minister was under enormous pressure to appease all sides and to meet many conflicting demands, but ZANU (PF) had no sympathy for the Matabele nation and old wounds ran deep. Miles did not trust the new National Army that had been formed to police the country, and he certainly did not trust the newly-created Fifth Brigade who answered only to the Prime Minister himself. Fear had returned to Matabeleland, but it was the Fifth Brigade who caused the most fear. Even the Catholic Church had accused the Fifth Brigade of "brutality and atrocity". Now, with Nkomo being hounded out of office, his home searched and ZAPU party officials under arrest, it was difficult to know what lay in store for the country. They were at war again. This time, the fight was between the two tribes, with white people dying in the cross fire.

Miles skimmed the article and his heart skipped a beat when he read the last paragraph. It told of a young lawyer, one whose integrity and credibility was beyond question. It spoke of the man who had been commissioned to fight the government's case against ZAPU, who were claiming that the illegal arms caches were a threat to the national security. The lawyer's name was Julius Khumalo.

Miles was shocked. Julius was a Matabele. Surely he could not fight his brethren in a court of law? Surely he had not disowned his own people in the quest for wealth and power. There were reports that many of the black intelligentsia were creaming off lucrative contracts, homes and jobs for themselves and their families. Was Julius one of those? Had he sunk that low?

Miles felt a stab of anxiety in the pit of his stomach and he closed the newspaper. He still felt a loathing for the man whose father had been responsible for the deaths of his parents and sister. As far as Miles was concerned, Julius had been a party to the crime. He had lured Miles away from his bed that night, and he could not forgive Julius for depriving him of the chance to try to save his family.

Miles had been devastated when his uncle, Charlie, had raped Bliss, but that did not lessen his bitterness towards Julius. Miles was afraid that he might be free of the hatred he felt for his "blood brother". They had walked the same path in their childhood years, but he did not want their paths to cross again as men.

Moses did not spend much time with the villagers at Tshotsholo. He sat alone by the dry riverbed. Sometimes, he would carve animals from bits of wood. Mostly, he would simply stare into the distance.

Bliss had not been surprised when her husband had arrived at the kraal. Many men had returned to their homes and families, but she had been shocked by his appearance. His was thin to the point of emaciation and his once handsome face was gaunt. His swollen belly and yellowing hair was testament to the fact that he was suffering from Kwashiorkor, the malnutrition that was sweeping through Matabeleland.

Many Matabele had died from the disease caused by one of the worst droughts in living memory, and the fact that the government was blocking world food aid to the south. Their misery was compounded by the dreaded Fifth Brigade whose task was to hunt down dissidents and supporters of Joshua Nkomo, who had now fled to Botswana in fear of his life.

Following the recent armed outbreak in the resettlement camps, most ex-combatants had been forced to disband. But, in the Eastern Highlands, a full Brigade of ZANU soldiers had remained at arms. Instructors had been flown in from North Korea to train them in special combat skills. They would remain outside the main command structure and be directly responsible to the ZANU Central Committee. They were called the Fifth Brigade and they knew no mercy.

Bliss was frightened when Moses arrived at her kraal. She knew that he had not come back for her. She knew that her husband had other reasons for seeking refuge at Tshotsholo. He had not just brought Kwashiorkor to

Tshotsholo. He had brought a supply of guns and ammunition, too. And they were buried under the grain store at the edge of the village.

Moses stared into the distance. His eyes were dulled from sleepless nights, but his senses were still finely tuned. He heard a baboon's bark in the distance and his skin prickled. A second baboon replied. Moses stood up and peered into the darkness. Suddenly, a flock of birds took flight from the trees.

Sensing danger, Moses turned and ran towards the bush. He did not make it.

Six men stepped out from the bushes and intercepted his path. He recognised them at once from their camouflage uniforms and distinctive red berets. They were members of the elite Fifth Brigade,

'This is a peaceful village. You are not needed here.' Moses drew himself up to his full height and glowered at the men standing before him.

'We will decide whether we are needed here, zimundebere, old man.'

The man poked Moses in the chest with the barrel of his rifle and ordered him to walk back to the centre of the kraal. Bliss was sitting on the step outside her rondavel. She jumped up in horror when she saw the armed strangers. Moses gestured to her with his eyes to stay silent, but she did not understand and she ran to him in fear.

'I see that this is your woman,' the soldier grinned. 'Perhaps she will be able to help us. We are hunting for weapons, old woman. We have heard that there are guns hidden in this village. Do you know about this?'

Bliss screamed and fell to her knees, clutching at Moses for support. The other villagers had been turned out of their huts and they stood by the fire, frightened and uncertain.

'We know this man.' The Fifth Brigade leader bellowed at them. 'His name is Moses Khumalo. We know that he is loyal to Joshua Nkomo, Father of the Dissidents, and we know that he is involved in a plot to overthrow Robert Mugabe's freely-elected government. If you tell us where his weapons are hidden, we will spare your lives. If you do not... you will die.'

No-one spoke.

The man turned to Moses and chopped at his legs from behind. Moses fell into a kneeling position and the man pressed his gun against the back of his head. 'You have one chance, zimundebere. One chance to save your miserable life and that of your woman. Where are your weapons?'

Moses looked at the young black man and his eyes glinted in the firelight. He smiled and, for a moment, he was transformed into the handsome, young revolutionary he had once been. 'I will tell you this much, comrade. I fought beside the Shona to free us from white oppression. I expected to die at the hands of the whites. I did not fear death then. I do not fear it now. I fear only for the future if black brothers are ready to kill each other for wealth and power.'

The man smashed his rifle against the side of Moses' head and pointed towards Bliss. 'Lock her inside and set fire to the hut. We will find the weapons, zimundebere.' He knelt down until his face was on the same level as Moses. 'But Tshotsholo will be no more. Your wife will be no more. And you, Moses Khumalo, will be no more. Your struggle will be over.'

Screaming with terror, Bliss was bundled into the rondavel. One of the soldiers hurled a flaming log from the fire into the tinder-dry thatch. Within seconds, the rondavel was in flames and the villagers cringed at the sound of her agonised cries.

Bliss took a long time to die, but eventually her terrible howls subsided and only the crackling fire could be heard. Moses hung his head and his tears splashed into the dirt. One of the men had tied his hands behind his back and shoved his face into the ground with the heel of his boot. The villagers, unarmed and in fear for their lives, watched helplessly.

'Will anyone tell me where the weapons are hidden, or do more people have to die?'

'They are here!' one of the soldiers ran back into the village holding a couple of guns aloft. 'They have a whole armoury over there. Comrade Khumalo must have been planning another chimurenga.'

The officer dragged Moses to his feet and punched him square on the mouth. Moses' front teeth splintered under the impact and his chin lolled against his chest. The officer grabbed the back of his head and pulled his face up to look directly into his eyes.

'Are you ready to die, Moses Khumalo?'

Moses blinked away the blood from the deep cut on his forehead and nodded. 'I am ready to die, comrade.'

The other man swore under his breath and lashed out again. Another punched Moses in the stomach so that the air was expelled from his lungs in a hot gasp. But still Moses Khumalo did not cry out in pain. His eyes shone like polished coal and his flesh was bathed in a soft glow. The barrel of a gun was pointing at his temple and he knew there was no more time. He thought fleetingly of his son and his wife who had to die. And he thought of Africa.

'Your struggle is over, Moses Khumalo,' The man placed his finger on the trigger and aimed.

'My struggle is over, comrade, but yours is only just beginning. My struggle was with the white imperialists. I think now that my struggle may have been in vain. I will never know. But your struggle is with black Africa and you can never win that war. For you, and for all the Shona, the struggle will never be over.'

A solitary black bird was perched on the top branches of a msasa tree. Its beaded eyes surveyed the scene below. The kraal was on fire and the wailing villagers huddled together in the midst of the carnage. One man knelt on the ground, apart from the others. He embraced them lovingly with his eyes as he prepared to meet death with courage in his heart.

Suddenly, a rifle shot sounded and a woman screamed. The man fell to the floor.

Startled, the bird opened its wings and flew up into the night sky. It circled silently, its inky wings tipped with silver from the moon, but then it soared into the dark, cloudless sky and disappeared.

15

Lucie Lyndon lifted her arms above her head and wriggled her hour-glass figure into an impossibly tight red dress. She tugged the shoe-string shoulder straps into position and leaned forward to jiggle her voluptuous breasts into a more comfortable position. Then, smoothing the creases over her hips, she stood back and surveyed herself in the full-length mirror.

Not bad, she decided, peering closer to dab at her lipstick. She turned sideways so that her breasts stood proud and her enviably flat stomach was shown at its best. She would certainly command centre stage at the party tonight.

And Lucie liked to be centre stage.

She pulled a hairbrush through her long blonde hair and, in a rare moment of self-doubt, thrust out her chin petulantly. She had every right to want to be the centre of attention tonight, she reassured herself. This was her party after all, held to celebrate her thirtieth birthday, and it would be packed with Harare's most successful and interesting people. A perfect way for Lucie Lyndon to be introduced to Zimbabwe's elite. Yes, there was no doubt about it, Lucie was planning to take Harare by storm. And heaven help anyone who tried to get in her way!

The event was being held at the home of Matthew and Rebecca Cloete in the pretty suburb of Sentosa. The Cloetes had been travellers in their teenage years, hitchhiking round the world with nothing more than a couple of backpacks and bedrolls. They had practised meditation in India, had joined the student demonstrations against Vietnam in London and had lived a simple life on a Kibbutz in Israel. But their most memorable year was spent travelling by Greyhound Bus across America. And it was there that they had met Lucie Lyndon, the daughter of a wealthy banker from Boston.

Lucie Lyndon, like many of her contemporaries in the late sixties and early seventies, had left the parental home under a cloud of disapproval to follow the trail to San Francisco. Her father, Bud Lyndon, was a giant in the banking world, where no man dared to question his authority, but he was powerless to prevent his wayward child from clambering into the back of a camper-van and heading for the West Coast.

Far away from parental scrutiny, Lucie immersed herself in the San Francisco scene. She embraced the drugs, the music, the lazy pace of life, and the culture of free love wholeheartedly. And San Francisco was perfectly happy to welcome this gorgeous girl, with the wide blue eyes and sexy giggle into their world.

Matthew and Rebecca Cloete were hitchhiking along the Big Sur in 1975 when they first chanced upon Lucie and her friends. The Cloetes, who had fascinating tales to tell of life in war-torn Rhodesia, were given a warm welcome. Long evenings were spent in smoke-filled rooms in Haight Ashbury, or under the stars on San Francisco Bay, when the young Rhodesians would paint vivid pictures of their homeland for their American hosts.

One member of the group, Lucie Lyndon, had been particularly captivated by their stories of Africa. With her emotions heightened by hallucinogenic drugs, Lucie had wept to hear how the blacks were ready to die to fight injustice, and she had been enthralled by the notion of a handful of white liberals who were willing to risk their lives to create a free and fair Rhodesia. It all seemed so impossibly romantic - a land of handsome white Rhodesians standing side-by-side with young black men in a glorious quest for freedom. Sitting cross-legged in front of the beach fire, Lucie fell in love with Africa and swore to her new-found Rhodesian friends that she would visit it one day.

It was a promise she would keep.

Rebecca Cloete tapped on the door of the guest cottage and called out softly: 'Lucie? Are you ready? We're all waiting for you?'

Lucie stepped out of the bedroom and paused for effect before carrying out a playful twirl in front of her friend. She stopped and then waited for signs of approval.

'You look stunning. Quite stunning!' Rebecca shook her head in disbelief and went over to hug her guest. 'You look as beautiful today as you did in San Francisco all those years ago. Happy birthday, Lucie.'

Lucie smiled and her thoughts drifted back to those early years. She had come through it all, the cocaine and LSD, and the shock when she discovered that she was pregnant with Larry Pitt's baby. She had no choice other than to have the abortion. Larry would never have coped with the responsibilities of fatherhood. He was hooked on cocaine and she would have been left to bring up the child on her own. In spite of this, after the abortion, she took up with Larry Pitt again.

Lucie paused at the top of the grassy path that led to Rebecca's vast bungalow and turned to her friend. 'That stuff with Larry Pitt – it was crazy, wasn't it?'

Rebecca reached up to brush Lucie's cheek. 'It was, but you paid the price, darling. Larry Pitt returned your love with drugs. In return, you got a cocaine habit and three years in jail for possession! Not a fair exchange in my opinion. Well, you've served your time, Lucie. You managed to study for a degree in Sociology while you were inside and, more importantly, you managed to kick the drugs. Those are pretty impressive achievements, you know.'

The sound of laughter filtered out on the night breeze and the heady scent of expensive perfume mingled with the flowers. Lucie breathed deeply and smiled at her friend. 'It was good to be able to write to you while I was in jail. You really helped me get through it all.' Then, with a mercurial change of subject so typical of Lucie, she added flippantly: 'Is my hair okay?'

She flicked her silver-blonde curls behind her shoulder and tugged the neckline of her dress down a notch. Occasionally, she would be prone to self-doubt, would have moments when she felt guilty for all the worry and hurt she had caused, but those moments never lasted long. Everyone had forgiven her for being so beastly in her teenage years. She was too young to know what she was doing, her father had said. It was all Larry Pitt's fault, her mother had declared. Lucie had nothing to worry about. She had come through it all unscathed. The wild sex, the drugs, the abortion and even a spell in jail. Nobody blamed her. Everybody loved her. There was no need to trouble herself further.

And now she was in Africa with a new job and a new circle of friends. She was only thirty years old and she looked a million dollars. It was her birthday and she was to be the belle of the ball at a party held in her honour. Suddenly, she felt a tingle of excitement travel down her spine and she squirmed deliciously. This was going to be a very special year in her life.

The party guests applauded loudly when Lucie entered with Rebecca. Matthew Cloete spotted her first and he threaded his way through the throng to plant a hearty kiss on both cheeks.

'What a girl!' he laughed with undisguised pleasure and, turning to his wife, added: 'Two beautiful women under the same roof. I am a very lucky man!'

'Matthew, could you get Lucie a glass of wine...'

'Make that a Vodka and Black,' Lucie interjected, scanning the room to size up the company.

'A large Vodka and Black it will be,' Matthew headed off towards the bar where a black waiter in a crisp, white jacket was waiting to serve drinks.

'We've got some fascinating guests here tonight,' Rebecca whispered. 'I want to introduce you to Mr and Mrs Daly-Smythe. They're huge in tobacco. Own a sprawling 50,000 acre farm up near Mana Pools. Pots of money. You'll love them. They're such fun. And there's Paul Mhlangu. He comes from a wealthy black African family. Studied at Oxford, but he's back now because he wants to be a part of the new Zimbabwe. He's a Minister in the Government. Transport, I think.'

'Who's that,' Lucie gestured discreetly with her eyes to the far corner of the room.

Rebecca giggled as Matthew handed Lucie her vodka. 'We wondered how long it would take you to spot him on your man-radar! Isn't he divine? He's got every girl in Harare swooning over him.'

Intrigued, Lucie peered at the young black man from under her lashes. She took a sip of her drink and noted the proud stance, the wide shoulders and chiselled jaw. She glanced away lest those smouldering eyes look in her direction, but could not help prevent her gaze returning to the handsome stranger who stood a full head above the other men in the room. He stood alone. He was not smiling, and his furrowed brow betrayed an intensity that burned from somewhere deep within his soul. He was no ordinary man, Lucie realised, but he was a man that she was determined to have eating out of her hand before the night was out.

'Who is he?' she hissed, frantic to know more about him.

'He's a lawyer, some say the best there is. Honest, too. Lives right here in Harare. He has his own private practice, but he also acts as a Government adviser. If you want my opinion, I reckon that young man is destined for the top. They say even Mugabe listens to what he has to say.'

'He's beautiful,' Lucie murmured, running the tip of her tongue over her lips.

'And guess who's sitting next to him at dinner tonight?' Rebecca teased. 'That's right. Our very own birthday girl. After that, though, you're on your own, lady!'

Lucie grinned and the deep azure of her eyes twinkled mischievously. 'Poor lamb,' she sighed. 'He doesn't stand a chance!'

'I wouldn't be too sure of that if I were you. He's not like other men. You wouldn't be the first to cast a net in that direction only to find it empty when you reel it in. He's not easily caught. Ask half the single women in the room, and one or two of the married ones if the truth be known, and they'll all tell you to prepare yourself for failure. I don't think he's looking for love right now.'

Lucie cast a glance at the stranger's noble bearing and she could see immediately what Rebecca meant. He did not look like a man who was willing to be ensnared by any passing female. This was a man who was used to calling the shots, a man who could dictate his own terms, and Lucie liked him all the more for that.

'Introduce me,' she pleaded. 'I'm dying to get to know him.'

Rebecca took her hand and led her through the crowd. As always, Lucie turned people's heads wherever she went and the men of Harare were no exception. More than a few turned to linger on that ample cleavage as she approached, or gawk at that shapely backside as she passed. The single women simply turned away with envy, but the married women, many of whom had read their husband's minds, watched warily as the ravishing beauty squeezed past them in a haze of perfume.

But tonight, Lucie was oblivious to the stir she was causing. Her eyes were fixed on the tall, dark stranger who seemed to grow even more handsome as she approached and whose eyes, the colour of liquid mocha, looked as though they could melt a woman's heart when he smiled.

'Lucie Lyndon,' said Rebecca, standing aside to present the blonde beauty beside her. 'I'd like you to meet Julius Khumalo.'

Dinner was served under the stars on rows of trestle tables hung with ivory silk and decorated with white roses. The Cloetes' family silver had been polished earlier that day and the goblets shone in the candlelight. The top table stood under an arch of flowers that had been shaped into the words: "Welcome Lucie". In the corner, a musical quartet of sixth form pupils from St. George's School played Happy Birthday as Lucie took her seat.

Dressed in crimson, Lucie looked stunning against the silver backdrop. The Cloetes had gone to great lengths to contrast the party's colour theme with that of their guest of honour. The results were perfect and they grinned at each other, confident that their efforts to introduce their American friend to the cream of Harare's society were going to be successful. In fact, the only outcome they could not predict would be Lucie's introduction to Harare's most eligible bachelor.

But, so far, things did not seem to be going according to plan.

Julius was a private, taciturn individual who always stayed on the edge of a crowd and did little to ingratiate himself with other guests. However, his manners were impeccable, and those who did manage to break through his outer reserve talked of an unconscious charm and ready wit. But few did manage to break through, and even an experienced socialite like Lucie was at a loss to know how to penetrate the invisible barrier that surrounded him.

'Were you born in Harare?' she asked in an effort to ease the silence that hung between them.

'No. I am a Matabele. I was born near Bulawayo.' Julius replied, turning to her with a smile. 'Have you visited Matabeleland yet?'

His voice was low and husky and his eyes seemed to glow with a gentle light when he spoke. Lucie found herself wanting to talk to him simply so that she could hear the seductive timbre of his voice and feel his eyes upon her. But Julius Khumalo was not going to be easy quarry.

'No, but I'd like to. It sounds so beautiful and I'd love to go shopping in Bulawayo. Such a pretty town by all accounts. Very colonial.'

'It is a town with a great history,' Julius replied. 'The name Bulawayo means the Place of the Killing. It has a place in the hearts of all the Matabele people.'

'It seems to have a place in your heart,' Lucie purred, looking up through her long lashes. 'Perhaps you could tell me some of its history. I'd love to learn more about this beautiful country.'

Lucie was an accomplished sexual predator who could spin her silken web around a man's heart before he knew what was happening. Confident of her allure, she leaned closer to Julius and her left bosom brushed against his arm.

Julius glanced down at the tantalising valley between her breasts and his breath caught in his throat. 'Do you intend to stay in Zimbabwe for some time?' he asked, distancing himself from physical contact, and hurriedly gesturing to a waiter for more wine.

Lucie recognised his brief moment of inner turmoil. She smiled sweetly and switched seamlessly from a hot-blooded sexual predator to an innocent girl. It was a fascinating paradox that left most men confused … and head over heels in love with her! Lucie Lyndon was quite a woman and the trail of broken hearts in America was testament to this fact.

'I have a job here,' Lucie broke off a piece of bread and nibbled at the corner. She wanted to show Julius that she was not some spoiled little rich kid from the States. There was more to her than that. She was here to work.

Julius raised his eyebrows and peered under the cascade of silky blonde curls that framed her face. 'You have a job?' He was genuinely surprised.

'I didn't get it all by myself,' she confessed. 'Daddy helped me. He didn't want me to come to Africa at all, but when I insisted, he pulled a few strings to help me get a place in the new Ministry of Community Development and Women's Affairs. Have you heard of it?'

Julius put down his wine glass and leaned back in his chair, turning to look at his companion as if for the very first time. He draped one arm along the back of his chair and frowned in an attitude of deep concentration. Lucie was delighted. She had his full attention at last.

'Of course I have heard of it. It was set up last year to enable women to play a full part in the development of the new Zimbabwe. The Government recognises that women have an important contribution to make and Robert Mugabe is doing everything he can to assist them. Do you believe that you will be able to help with this important task, Lucie?'

Lucie thrilled to the sound of her name uttered in those deeply masculine tones. She was also conscious of the intensity of Julius' gaze as he waited for her response. Her feminine intuition had already warned her that Julius would not be swayed solely by soft, creamy flesh or luscious lips. Julius was different from other men. Of course, there was no doubting his manhood - Lucie had already witnessed his discomfiture when his gaze inadvertently wandered over her curves. He was a man with fire in his loins, she was certain of that, but she would have to earn his respect first. He would be a challenge, but she had not failed to win a man's heart before. She did not believe that she could fail now.

'I don't really know whether I can make a difference,' she replied, affecting an air of modesty. 'But I'm certainly going to try. I have a degree in Sociology and I'm a woman,' she paused as though waiting for confirmation of this inarguable fact. 'I understand a woman's needs.'

Julius took another sip of wine. 'I have always said that the new Ministry should be run by women for women. Men can never hope to appreciate a woman's real needs, but I am pleased to discover that we are attracting women of such high calibre from other parts of the world to help with the cause.'

'There are lots of foreign women here,' Lucie enthused. 'Everyone wants to be a part of your new nation.'

'And you? Do you want to be a part of this new nation, too?'

Lucie lifted her head and brushed a stray hair from her forehead. 'I fell in love with Africa years ago, when I first met the Cloetes in San Francisco, but I decided I had to come here when I read a newspaper article about the treatment of women in Africa. I couldn't believe that in this day and age women are still treated as minors under the guardianship of their husbands. The article said that the Zimbabwean Government was taking steps to address these wrongs and I knew that I wanted to help. Daddy wasn't too pleased, of course. He worries about me. I'm just a little girl in his eyes...'

'I can understand his wanting to protect you,' Julius smiled at her. 'Any man would want to protect a lovely woman like you.'

Lucie blushed and looked away. Suddenly, she felt uncertain of her ground. Without even trying, Julius had managed to shift the position of power and she was helpless to prevent his gaining the upper hand. Things were not going according to plan and, for the first time in her life, Lucie Lyndon felt weak and vulnerable.

But, unlike Lucie, Julius Khumalo was not vying for supremacy. His mind did not work that way. It would never occur to him to play games or to work to a strategy that might depart from his own, true self. As always, Julius had meant what he said in all sincerity. It was not part of any complicated plan to subdue the beautiful creature at his side.

'You must be a strong supporter of the new Legal Age of Majority Act,' he said, unaware that his companion's heart was thumping in her chest. 'It will give women the rights to property and the power to make their own decisions. I have been a supporter of this law from its inception. It is a very progressive piece of legislation, don't you agree?'

'I do agree and I'm so proud that I am a part of all this,' Lucie gathered her breath and clutched at the chance to move back to neutral territory. 'American women take freedom and equality, all those things, for granted. It's not until you come to a place like this that you realise how lucky you are.'

'Western women are lucky. You are right about that. Here, when a woman's husband dies, his relatives are entitled to reclaim all his possessions and leave his poor widow destitute. Her status is based solely on the quantity of cattle in her dowry and the number of children she manages to produce. Yes, the women of Africa have suffered greatly, but it is good that their American sisters, women like you Lucie, have heard of their plight and are ready to do something to help.'

Once again Lucie shivered at the sound of her name on his lips. She found herself warming to his natural charm and honesty. She had never met a man like Julius Khumalo before and she was keen to get to know him better. But she knew that she would have to tread carefully. One wrong move and he would be lost to her forever. He was a man of principle. A man of integrity and openness. He would not take kindly to being the object of female machinations. He was no fool. She dared not treat him like one and she remained on her guard for the rest of the meal.

'Shame on you, Julius Khumalo!' Rebecca Cloete leaned forward in her chair and called down the length of the table. 'Dinner is over. Is it not time you asked our honoured guest to dance?'

'You are quite right, of course,' Julius turned to Lucie and winked at her. 'Rebecca can be a very demanding hostess! We would be well advised to do as she says!'

Lucie giggled and allowed him to take her hand and lead her into the centre of the garden. The dancing area had been roped off with paper lanterns that dangled against the ink-black sky and cast pretty shadows on the ground. People clapped as she and Julius passed to make their way on to the dance floor, and Lucie laughed happily as she waved to her new friends.

'I do not dance well,' Julius confessed. 'You will have to guide my steps I'm afraid.'

Lucie laughed. 'Trust me! No-one will know. As long as we can get through the first couple of minutes without falling over, the others will join us and we won't be the centre of attention any more.'

Julius threaded his muscled forearm round her waist and Lucie wriggled closer. His chest was damp with sweat from the heat of the night. Lucie breathed deeply, luxuriating in his hard masculinity.

'It seems to me that you are more than capable of holding the centre of attention,' Julius breathed against her neck, causing goosebumps down her arms. 'I think you were born to be the centre of attention.'

Lucie leaned back to look at him and her eyes widened. 'Whatever do you mean?' she drawled, pretending to hide her blushes. 'I am far too ordinary to stand out in a crowd. I'm just a home-loving girl from Boston.'

Julius took a deep breath and pulled her closer. 'I doubt that very much,' he murmured.

Confident that he was succumbing to her charms, Lucie threaded her arms around his neck and allowed herself the liberty of resting her head against his shoulder. He may be able to hold out when they were seated at a dinner table, she told herself, but it was quite a different matter when she was in his arms. She knew that every inch of her body, from the tip of her nose to the tip of her toes, could drive a man crazy with desire. And with a shapely bottom writhing just below his fingers, and soft, fleshy mounds pressed against his chest, even a man like Julius Khumalo might find himself ensnared.

'You are a very beautiful woman,' Julius pulled back to look at her. 'I am surprised that no man has claimed you as his wife.'

Lucie cast her eyes to the floor. 'I was married...once. His name was Kurt Klein. He was the son of my parents' oldest friends.'

Julius lifted her left hand from his arm and glanced at her ring finger. 'You are no longer married?' he asked.

'We divorced. I... I was not ready for that sort of commitment. I had only just returned from San Francisco where I had made a bit of a hash of things. My parents were desperate to see me settled and ... well, I kind of wanted to be settled... but it all happened so quickly. I just wasn't ready for it.'

'And Kurt Klein? What happened to this poor husband of yours?'

Lucie was not sure, but she thought Julius might be teasing her. 'He still lives in Boston. He works for my father. I guess he's doing just fine now that I'm out of the way and he can get on with his life.'

Julius drew her closer and his fingers rested on the upper swell of her buttocks. 'I would find it hard to get on with my life if I had once been the husband of a woman such as you.'

Lucie felt the heat in the pit of her stomach and she allowed her hips to gyrate a little against his groin. Her voice was muffled against his chest as she whispered: 'Kurt was never going to be the right man for me. I only married him to please my father. He was too weak for a girl like me. He just let me walk all over him. I really hurt him at the end, you know. I felt bad about that.'

'And what kind of husband are you looking for now, Lucie?'

Lucie slowed her movements so that she could look directly into Julius' eyes. She tilted her head to one side in an attitude of concentration and Julius smiled.

'He would have to be handsome, of course, and strong. I don't mean just physically, I mean mentally too. He would have to be strong enough to cope with someone like me. I need a man I can look up to, someone who will look after me and put me in my place once in a while. And he must be successful and kind and amusing and honest … and…'

Julius chuckled and led her off the dance floor as the music ended. 'He sounds too good to be true,' he declared solemnly. 'Do you think such a man exists, Lucie?'

'Oh he exists, all right,' Lucie fixed him with her cerulean eyes. 'In fact, for all I know, I may already have met him.'

'Then he is a very fortunate man,' Julius pulled a chair out for her to sit on, but he remained standing as he thanked her for the dance.

'Won't you sit beside me for a while?' Lucie patted the chair beside her.

'I'm afraid not,' Julius sighed, regretfully. 'I have to leave now.'

'Surely not!' Lucie was astonished. 'It's far too early to leave!'

'I am truly sorry, believe me, but I have to go. I have work to do. Forgive me. It has been a pleasure to meet you. I wish I could have stayed a little longer.'

Lucie watched, mouth agape, as Julius turned and made his way through the crowd. She saw him stop and chat briefly to Matthew and Rebecca before disappearing out of view. He did not turn to look at her. He simply said goodbye to his hosts and left. Lucie was peeved. She was not used to such indifference and she did not know what to do in the face of it. She was still staring after him when Matthew approached and dragged up the chair beside her.

'He's a strange man,' Lucie declared, her brow creased by a frown.

'He's a very busy man,' Matthew added. 'We were lucky to get him here at all. He doesn't have much time for socialising.'

'Does he have many friends? He seems so … alone.'

'There are many people who want to be his friend, but no … I can't say I know anyone who is his friend in any special way. He's had a tough life. Both his parents were killed by the Fifth Brigade in Matabeleland. It was really ghastly at the time, but it convinced Julius that the tribal conflict between the Matabele and the Shona is a real obstacle to racial integration.

In fact, he is one of the few people I know who truly believes that there should be harmony between the two nations.'

'And what about white people? Is he comfortable with white people?'

'Some, I guess. I'd like to think he numbers us among those he can trust, but he doesn't trust many white people. His mother was raped by a white man years ago. He has never forgotten that. Rumour has it that Julius' father murdered three members of that family in their beds, but one son escaped alive. It's a dreadful story.'

Lucie smiled as Rebecca approached their table. 'Ah... You're talking about Julius and the farmer's son, Miles Cameron.' Rebecca sat beside Lucie. 'It's complicated. No-one really knows for sure what went on. We only know that Miles Cameron and Julius witnessed some terrible things in their youth and each has good reason to seek revenge upon the other. We'll probably never know the truth, of course, but we always say that if Julius Khumalo were to bear a grudge, nothing... and no-one ...could prevent him from getting his revenge.'

'He sounds terrifying!' Lucie squirmed in her chair.

'He probably is terrifying if you meet him as an enemy,' Rebecca agreed. 'He's also one of the most genuine, kind and generous people I know.'

'And honest too,' Matthew interjected. 'It's amazing that, although Julius trusts absolutely no-one, absolutely everyone trusts Julius! Even Government Ministers turn to Julius for advice. He may be young, but he's one of the few trustworthy people in this country.'

'It's a pity he had to leave so abruptly,' Lucie moaned. 'I would have liked to get to know him better.'

'We knew he wouldn't stay long,' Rebecca replied. 'He's up at dawn every day and he works late into the night. We were lucky to get as much of his precious time as we did.'

'But I didn't really get a chance to say goodbye properly!' Lucie pouted, irked by his indifference.

'He asked me to apologise to you. He said something about enjoying your trip to Bulawayo. Are you planning a trip to Bulawayo?'

'No... I mean yes...' Lucie was dismayed. 'I was hoping he would tell me more about Matabeleland.'

Rebecca stood up to grab the arm of an elderly white woman who was passing their table. 'Jean darling, do come and meet Lucie. She wants to know all about Matabeleland. Jean is the descendant of one of Rhodesia's early pioneers, and the current Secretary of the Pioneers' Society. She's lived in Bulawayo all her life, and her father and grandfather before her. If anyone can tell you about Matabeleland, Jean can.'

Lucie shook the woman's hand and smiled weakly.

'My goodness!' said Jean. 'There's such a lot to tell. Where on earth shall I begin?'

That night, alone in his bed, Julius Khumalo found himself dreaming about the beautiful American woman he had met at the party. It was a deeply erotic fantasy in which she had danced, naked, before him. He had awoken with a throbbing erection and sweat pouring down his back. In a half-hearted attempt to subdue his passion, he reminded himself of the gentle soul, Esther, who had been betrothed to him since his childhood. Esther had died in the bush war, but even her sacred memory could not dampen the fire in his loins, and his treacherous mind soon returned to the American woman's fat breasts, slender waist and juicy lips.

It was folly, he told himself sternly in the cold light of day. She was an American divorcee and Julius had little time for flirtatious white women. He knew that his destiny lay with a good African wife, a woman born and raised in the kraals. But the American had bewitched him. She was quite the most exciting, beautiful and desirable creature he had ever met, and, try as he might, he could not banish her from his thoughts.

In spite of her frivolous nature and pampered life, Lucie did care about the plight of women in Africa and she genuinely enjoyed her job. Of course, she was still young, she reminded herself on more than one occasion, she could not be expected to spend all her time worrying about the poor people of Zimbabwe. But when she was at work she was more than happy to do what she could to help, and she was certainly willing to receive the effusive praise and gratitude that invariably accompanied her efforts. After work, there were parties and barbecues, tennis and trips to the theatre. Harare was fast becoming a thriving, cosmopolitan city and Lucie loved being a part of it.

Surprisingly, she had not seen Julius Khumalo since her birthday party. She had hoped to see him at other social events, but he never came. She had met many interesting people, and one or two handsome ex-Rhodesians had made it clear that they would like to get her know her better, but she could not get Julius Khumalo out of her mind. The more she longed for him to come, the more bitter her disappointment when he failed to turn up. Eventually, she became obsessed with the need to see him again. He was the one that got away and, without a doubt, the one she had most wanted to catch.

Her thoughts, as always, were with Julius as she sucked the top of her biro and gazed out of her office window. She was so engrossed in her reverie that she did not hear the woman enter the reception and approach her desk, and she was startled when bony fingers reached out and touched her arm.

'I have come to you for help,' the woman said. 'They tell me that you can help me. My name is Patience.'

'Hello Patience,' Lucie snapped back to the present and promptly took the top off her pen in a bid to look efficient. 'What can I do for you?

The woman was probably the same age as Lucie, but she looked tired and bowed. She had a sleeping infant strapped to her back and a grubby toddler with a snotty nose standing next to her. She wore a tatty black cardigan and a long black skirt. On her feet were a pair of bright pink flip-flops known as pata-patas. The little girl standing beside her wore no shoes and her feet were crusted with dirt.

'I would like to divorce my husband because he beats me. He starves me and my children. And he will not try to find work.'

'Sit down Patience and tell me everything. I promise I will do anything I can to help you.'

The woman perched on the edge of the plastic chair and leaned forward to avoid squashing the tiny baby on her back. She hunted in her skirt pocket and pulled out a crumpled piece of paper. 'I have been told I must speak to this man. I have been told that he is a good man. He will help me.'

Patience could not read, so she waited quietly while the white woman read the markings that were scrawled on the piece of paper. She watched the woman's eyes and she was puzzled when they suddenly brightened as a huge smile lit up her face. She must be a truly kind woman, Patience thought, to be so happy to help. It was a good sign.

'How do you know this person?' Lucie asked, pointing to the name that was written on the paper.

'Everybody knows him,' Patience replied. 'He is the only honest lawyer in Harare. He is a true son of the soil.'

Lucie chewed her bottom lip thoughtfully. This was the opportunity she had been hoping for and she seized it eagerly. 'I will go to see this lawyer and I will speak to him about your problem. I know this man. His name is Julius Khumalo and you are right, he is a good man. Trust me, Patience. I will see him as soon as possible.'

Julius had been surprised when his assistant, Eli, handed him the note from Lucie. It was on headed paper from the Ministry of Community Development and Women's Affairs and it sounded urgent. In it, Lucie had said that she wanted to meet him as soon as possible - that it could mean life or death for a poor African woman from one of the townships on the edge of the city. She had asked him to come to the guest cottage where she was staying with the Cloetes the following day. It seemed an odd place to discuss urgent business, Julius mused, but then Lucie was no ordinary woman.

But she was a dangerous woman, he reminded himself as he adjusted his tie in the mirror on his office wall. A white woman, and it was madness to lust after a white woman. Julius was not ready for that. Even so, he could not help a second glance in the mirror before he grabbed his pen and notebook, slung his jacket over his shoulder and made his way downstairs into the street.

'I'll only be an hour,' he called to Eli as he passed. 'No more than that. I've got a lot to do this afternoon.'

He found Lucie sitting on a bench on the stoep outside the secluded little cottage. The sun was high in the sky, but she was shaded by a canopy of vivid bougainvillaea. She was wearing a white cotton blouse and tight black skirt that had ridden up almost to thigh level when she crossed her legs. As Julius drew near, he could see that the top two buttons of her blouse were open. He took a deep breath, sat beside her on the bench and steeled himself against the temptation that he knew was to come.

He was pleasantly surprised, and secretly relieved, to discover that Lucie did have a genuine reason for wanting to talk to him. She was anxious that the woman who had been to visit her might be killed or injured by her drunken husband, and she clearly wanted to do everything she could to help.

'She seemed old,' Lucie fiddled with her watch strap. 'And yet she isn't much older than me. She was so… careworn. She had a little girl with her and she was terribly thin. Do you know, Julius, that little girl didn't even have a pair of shoes to her name? Isn't that awful?'

Julius nodded. 'It is good to know that you care so much for our people, Lucie. Africa needs women like you. Leave it to me. I can help this woman. She will be fine.'

Lucie turned to look at him. 'Oh Julius… thank you so much. I've done so many bad things in my life. It's so nice to think I might actually be useful for a change.'

Julius chuckled. 'We have all done bad things. I am sure you malign yourself unfairly.'

Lucie let her hand rest lightly on his arm. 'You don't really know anything about me. I've done some terrible things in the past. I've hurt a lot of people, including my parents. I'm not a very nice person.'

Julius lifted her chin with the tip of his thumb and turned her face back towards his. 'We all have to hurt people at some point in our lives,' he whispered in an effort to reassure her. 'You are probably no better, or worse, than most people. Besides, it is what you are now that counts. Are you a good person now, Lucie?'

'I want to be,' she murmured. Her skin tingled under his touch and her lips parted slightly. He was so handsome, so utterly irresistible… and she wanted him so much. 'Will you help me to be a good girl, Julius?'

She was so close that Julius could feel her sweet breath fanning his cheek. He turned away, but only for a moment. He wanted more of this woman. He needed more, and he could feel himself hardening at the thought of it. He groaned and pulled her closer, hoping, half-heartedly, that she would be strong enough to help him avoid such madness.

But Lucie had no intention of resisting a man like Julius Khumalo and there was no protest in the warm, wet mouth that came to meet his. It was a long, intimate kiss. A desperate kiss. Neither one had managed to forget the other, and both had been tormented by the powerful chemistry between them. Now, with this one kiss, Julius and Lucie abandoned themselves to the sexual urges that had assaulted them for too long.

'Let us go inside,' Julius pulled away and gripped her shoulders, staring at her with a savage lust in his eyes. 'God help me, but I must have you, woman. I must have you. Now!'

Julius and Lucie could not have known that their union on that day would unleash a desperate hunger that would never be satisfied. From that day forth, every spare minute was spent making love, often well into the night. Their coupling was savage, cruel almost, but it was never enough to satisfy either one of them. They were like animals who had chanced upon each other out in the wild, open bush. And their desire was insatiable.

Before long, the affair was the talk of the town and Matthew and Rebecca Cloete began to worry about their friend. Tentatively, they voiced their concerns on their verandah at sundown.

'You look stunning in that dress, Lucie. Are you seeing Julius tonight?' Rebecca's voice betrayed just a hint of nervousness. She did not want to pry, but Lucie was causing quite a stir.

'We're meeting for a drink when he finishes work and then we're going back to his house. Have you seen it, Matthew? It's amazing. It sits at the top of this incredibly steep, winding hill...'

'Lucie.... Rebecca and I are worried about you. People are beginning to talk. We don't want you to get hurt.'

'I won't get hurt,' Lucie seemed genuinely puzzled, and her hosts were once again struck by her complex mix of innocence and sophistication. 'You know that Julius would never hurt me.'

'We don't think for one minute that Julius would hurt you deliberately, darling,' Rebecca held Lucie's hand. 'It's just that... well he must know as well as we do that this relationship can't go anywhere. He couldn't possibly marry you, for example. Mixed marriages are simply not the done thing, even in the new Zimbabwe. Julius knows that, and you can't keep on ... seeing him like this. This is Africa, darling, not San Francisco, not even Boston! People here frown upon such behaviour. It may be 1982, but this is still an old-fashioned country with old-fashioned values. You must be more careful.'

Lucie's eyes brimmed with tears. 'I can't believe I'm hearing this. Julius is your friend and he's a wonderful man. I've never met anyone quite like him. I love him.... And he loves me!'

'Oh Lucie,' Rebecca glanced at Matthew. 'Are you sure? Julius is a very handsome man. Most women are a little infatuated with him.'

'I'm not infatuated with him,' Lucie replied stubbornly. 'He is the most wonderful man I have ever known. I need him. I have to be with him.'

'Then you must be prepared to be strong, Lucie, for you will be ostracised by both black and white communities.'

'I am prepared for that,' Lucie declared.

'I'm sure you are darling,' Rebecca was genuinely concerned. 'But is Julius prepared to meet such hostility? Speak to him. Ask him. For you will have to depend on his strength if you do decide to go ahead with this relationship.'

Julius knew at once that Lucie was not herself. He could tell by her strange cries as he thrust deeper and deeper into her body and by the way her fingernails drew blood as they clawed at his back. Her demands, and the pain she inflicted upon his naked flesh, drove him mad with lust, and he bore down upon her.

Later, still drenched in their own sweat, and bloodied from the ferocity of their passion, they lay entwined each others' arms, bewildered and breathless, and completely overwhelmed by their needs. Lucie lay cradled against Julius' rock-hard biceps with her arm flung across his chest. She was gazing out of his bedroom window at the moon, but her thoughts were in turmoil. Julius stared up at the ceiling, listening to the rhythmic call of the crickets. He did not speak. He knew that Lucie was troubled. He would wait until she was ready to talk. After all, he was a Matabele. Patience was in his blood.

Eventually, as the bedside clock ticked away the hours, Lucie whispered: 'Julius? Are you still awake?'

'I am awake.'

'Julius... Matthew and Rebecca are worried about our relationship. They say that I might get hurt. They say that there is no place in Zimbabwe for a relationship like ours. Are they right, Julius?'

Julius lifted himself up on to his elbow and gazed down at the exquisite creature who lay unashamedly naked on his crumpled sheets. 'They are right,' he replied. 'Zimbabwean society would not look favourably on a relationship between a black man and a white woman.'

'But why, Julius?' Lucie clutched at his arm. 'It's happening all over the world. Why should it be any different here. I thought this was supposed to be a liberated country.'

Julius smiled at her naivety. 'We may well be liberated from white imperialism, but we have a long way to go before we can cast aside the shackles of our own personal intolerance. The Cloetes are right, Lucie. We must try to stop this madness before it is completely beyond our control.'

'It's not madness!' Lucie pulled herself up to sit cross-legged in front of him. 'I love you, Julius! I have never met a man like you before. Please.... Please don't cast me away!'

Julius moaned and pulled her head against his chest. 'I am not casting you away, little bird. I am simply trying to be strong... to do what is best for both of us. I have an important job to do here. I have a part to play in the evolution of my beloved country. I dare not allow my passion for you to threaten my purpose in life. You can understand that, can't you?'

'No!' Lucie snuffled petulantly and buried her head deeper into his chest. 'I don't understand at all. I love you …. And I thought you loved me…'

'I do love you, woman. God help me. I love you so much that I fear I may go insane. Indeed, it is so all-consuming that I fear it will destroy us both.'

'Then let's go to America,' Lucie lifted her head to plead with her big, blue eyes. 'My father is very wealthy. He would look after us. He could find you a job, maybe set you up in your own law firm in Boston. And he would buy us a beautiful house and ….'

Julius laughed mirthlessly. 'Just like he did with you and Kurt Klein. No. It is nothing but a dream, little bird. I could never leave Africa. I belong here. My people need me. I have a job to do.'

'Then I'll stay with you,' Lucie wiped the tears from her eyes with the corner of the sheet. 'We can get married. Then no-one can would dare to criticise us. And they'll soon learn to live with it. It won't be long before mixed marriages are accepted and then everything will be fine.'

'We cannot marry,' Julius gripped her shoulders. 'I cannot allow my desire for you to disrupt my work.'

Lucie let the sheet slip down her body. It hung briefly on one of her taut, cherry-red nipples and then it slid into crumpled folds in her lap. She leaned forward, her breasts hanging heavily like ripe melons, and she sighed, closing her eyes as her lips parted.

Julius cupped both fat, round bosoms in his hands and pulled her closer. She squealed delightfully in mock pain, and arched her back towards him. With her head thrown back and her long silky mane tumbling over her shoulders she was utterly irresistible. Her body movements said that she was his, to do with as he pleased. She felt him shudder involuntarily. He was trying to break away from her, to avoid the heartache that he knew was to come, but he had no weapons left in his feeble armoury. He could feel her writhing and squirming in his arms, curvaceous, sweetly-perfumed and willing ... oh so willing.... and he was lost.

'You do love me, don't you Julius?' Lucie purred as she climbed astride his wide thighs.

'Yes, I love you!' Julius grabbed her buttocks and shifted her closer to his throbbing member.

'And you wouldn't want to leave me, would you?' Lucie ran her fingers over the tip of his erection.

'I cannot leave you, woman. Your web is woven too tightly. I know now that I cannot escape. I am ensnared.'

Lucie allowed the shadow of a smile to play across her lips as she bent down to kiss him fully on the mouth. 'Don't worry, darling. I am a very sexy spider. You will enjoy being trapped in my web.'

And then, with a little wiggle that left Julius gasping with pleasure, she raised her buttocks and drew his aching member into the welcome wetness between her legs.

Julius grabbed at her fleshy cheeks and closed his eyes. He had lost the battle. He knew that now. He needed this woman more than he had ever needed anyone, or anything, in his whole life. And he would have her. As God was his witness, he would have her. And nothing, not even the might of all Africa, would stop him.

Miles leaned over the balcony of the café at Harare's international airport. A bottle of beer dangled from his fingers. He took a swig and placed it on the table beside him before resuming his vigil. He peered up at the cloudless blue sky and his heart missed a beat when he spotted the gleam of the British Airways plane on the horizon. It looked like a huge silver bird as it approached the airport, and Miles was determined not to miss one second of its descent. As the plane nosed closer to the runway, the roar of its engines increased as the pilot applied its awesome brake power. Within minutes, the aircraft was safely down and coasting towards the terminal building.

Miles waited patiently while the steps were jammed up against the exit doors for the passengers to disembark. There were dozens of people on board, and Miles watched as they clambered down the steps with their hand baggage and duty-free carrier bags.

Suddenly, his heart skipped a beat as he caught a glimpse of red hair in the doorway. And then she stepped out into the bright African sun, shielding her eyes to scan the crowds on the balcony. Miles was afraid she would not see him, so he called out her name.

'Lydia!'

He did not know whether she had heard him at first, but then she looked directly at him and waved back frantically as she hurried across the shimmering tarmac.

'I'll see you on the other side!' Miles yelled, ducking through the crowd to rush downstairs.

A huge crowd of people had gathered to meet Zimbabwe's new arrivals. Miles settled down for a long wait, African passport control officers were not renowned for their speed and efficiency, but he was amazed when, after only half an hour, Lydia came through the glass doors. Miles vaulted the rope barrier to sweep her into his arms.

'Oh Miles…' Lydia felt hot tears of joy splashing down her cheeks as she was deposited back on the ground after a heady twirl. 'Oh Miles…'

Miles held her at arms' length and marvelled at her beauty, her adorable smile and her hair that glittered like sparkling rubies. He breathed deeply, intoxicated by the familiar scent of fresh peaches that threatened to overwhelm his senses.

'Do I meet with your approval?' Lydia stared at the floor, embarrassed by his lingering scrutiny.

'You're so ….perfect!' Miles pulled her towards him so that her face was pressed against his and he could whisper in her ear. 'I had forgotten just how lovely you are.'

'And I had forgotten just how much I needed to hear you say that.'

Miles led her to his car, one arm pushing her baggage trolley and the other arm wrapped tightly round her shoulder. When they reached the vehicle, he turned to face her, his eyes searching hers as though looking for answers.

'Lydia?' There was an anxious tone in his voice. 'Before we go any further …there is one thing I must ask you…one thing I need to know.'

'What is it, my love?'

'Have you come home, Lydia?'

Lydia brushed his cheek with her lips and a huge smile lit up her face: 'Yes, my darling. I have come home.'

16

Lydia tied the belt of her jeans tightly round her waist and slipped on her outside shoes. She gathered her hair into a ponytail and stuffed it under her baseball cap. Then, gulping the last of her coffee, she ran back to the barn where one of the cows was calving.

Miles had stayed up all night to help. He was worried that the dam was weak and her calf might not make it. Lydia spent most of her time ferrying hot coffee and warm blankets to and from the farmhouse, or simply sitting beside her husband hoping that nature would take its course without mishap. At four o'clock in the morning, aided by Miles' strong arms, a healthy little calf tumbled out on to the floor.

Miles wiped his sweaty brow with hands stained by blood and foetal dung. 'It's a bull calf!' he exclaimed with delight, turning to hug his wife, with hands kept well away from her face! 'What a star!' he patted the cow's rump and beamed at the complicated tangle of legs on the floor beside him.

Swiftly, he scooped up a fistful of hay and began to massage the calf to keep it warm. He wiped the area around the navel and then dressed it with tincture of iodine to prevent bacterial infection.

'He's so pretty.' Lydia was enchanted. 'He's all gangly and cute, and his coat is just like soot.' 'Can I call him Sooty?'

'You can call him anything you like, sweetheart,' Miles lifted the new-born animal to its feet. 'But first we must introduce this little fellow to his mother's teat. He'll need her natural colostrum immediately if he's going to have any resistance to infection. Right now, he's just about as vulnerable as a chap can get.'

Lydia watched in silence as her handsome young husband wiped the black, faecal jelly from the animal's backside while it suckled its mother's teat for the very first time. 'The milk acts as a laxative,' Miles explained proudly, seemingly oblivious to the stench. 'So all this gunk here is proof that the new-born is suckling properly. Amazing, don't you think?'

After almost twelve months of marriage, Lydia was still surprised by her husband's enthusiasm for the wonders of nature, although she herself was still in awe of the glorious sights and sounds and smells that accompanied everyday life at Scarfell Farm. She could hardly believe that Scarfell Farm was now her home.

Afterwards, Miles washed his arms and face under the outside tap before coming to sit next to Lydia on the bench in front of the barn. In the far distance, the magnificent Blue Hills were tinged with gold as the sun rose to greet the dawn. All around them, the tinkling of birdsong grew louder as the light and warmth of a new day spread across the land. Lydia leaned her head against Miles' shoulder and sighed happily.

'A hard day's work and it's not even sun up,' Miles chuckled, threading his arm round the back of her shoulder to act as a cushion. 'A farmer's life is not an easy one.'

'I wouldn't have it any other way,' Lydia murmured, her baseball cap all askew as she nestled deeper into Miles' shoulder and tried to prevent her sleepy eyes from closing. 'I never want to leave this wonderful place.'

'Let's hope we won't have to,' Miles stared into the distance and a frown creased his brow.

Lydia sensed the change in his tone and she sat up, instantly alert. 'What do you mean?'

'Robert Mugabe's got hundreds of thousands of homeless people clamouring at his door demanding land. They say they're entitled to it, and who can blame them? Let's face it, that's what the war was all about. Land. And the problem isn't going to go away.'

'But Scarfell Farm is protected by the Lancaster House Agreement, surely?' Lydia reasoned. 'We don't have to sell if we don't want to, do we? That's what was agreed.'

'No we don't have to sell if we don't want to, sweetheart. Lancaster House insists on a willing seller, willing buyer. Mugabe agreed that with the British Government, and he wouldn't dare to renege on it, not if he wants to keep foreign money coming in to shore up his planned resettlement programme. He'd be in big trouble without that!'

'But what about all the homeless people? What will he do with them and the families of all those people who died for this land? How can he possibly hope to find homes for them all?'

Miles shrugged and leaned his head back against the wall of the barn. 'I guess that's Mugabe's problem now that he's in power. Of course, he's got the right to seize any land that isn't fully utilised, as well as some of the vast farms owned by absentee landlords and big businesses, so that should keep him going for a while. Besides, Scarfell is only twelve thousand acres. That's pretty small in comparison with most of the white-owned farms in Africa. I don't think anyone is going to come knocking on our door. Scarfell is just a minnow by African standards. Now let's go and get cleaned up for breakfast. I'm starving!'

Lydia trailed Miles as he wandered up to the house and she luxuriated in the manly smells he emanated. His shirt was dark with sweat and clung to the muscles on his back as he moved. His shoulders were broad and his hips lean. His hair, still damp from hard labour, had gathered into a tiny curl that lay flat in the nape of his neck. Lydia reached out and touched the wisp with her fingertip and she squealed when Miles spun round to enfold her in a big bear hug.

'Stop! You'll crush me to death! You don't know your own strength!'

Immediately, Miles eased his grip. 'I keep forgetting you're just a skinny little slip of a girl,' he teased. 'We'll need to fatten you up a bit if you're going to make the grade as a proper African wife!'

'You'll never fatten me up if you keep working me right through the night!' Lydia punched his chest playfully.

'You don't normally complain when I work you through the night!' Miles laughed, pleased with his own innuendo.

'Apart from when you drop off to sleep from sheer exhaustion!' Lydia retorted, turning on her heels to race him up the path. Miles gave chase as his wife sped back to the house where she fell in a fit of giggles on the sofa. Panting slightly, Miles dropped down beside her.

'So, you dare to question my stamina, do you woman? We'll have to see about that!' Miles dragged her closer, but they sprung apart again when Sixpence tapped lightly on the door before entering the sitting room.

'Should I serve breakfast now, Nkosikazi?'

'Just give us ten minutes to freshen up please, Sixpence.'

Lydia took the Bulawayo Chronicle from the bureau and handed it to Miles who flicked it open. It was yesterday's edition, but he had not yet found time to read it. Relaxation was a luxury he could rarely afford.

Lydia leaned over his shoulder as he glanced at the front page, so she did not see his eyes narrow suddenly, but she did feel his shoulders stiffen suddenly beneath her touch and she dropped to his side.

'What is it, darling?'

Miles prodded the picture on the front page. 'Julius Khumalo. He's been elected to the new Parliament. It seems he's Mugabe's favourite son nowadays, thanks to his help in bringing about the Unity Accord between ZAPU and ZANU.'

Lydia glanced at the photograph. 'He's very handsome,' she joked, seeking to dispel the tension in the air.

'He's the son of a murderer!' Miles crushed the newspaper into a ball and hurled it across the room. 'His father butchered my family in their beds! I might have been able to help them if ... if this bastard hadn't stopped me!'

Lydia reached out towards him, but he shrugged her away.

'My family paid for his education,' He growled. 'It's thanks to the Camerons that he's now got himself a profitable law practice and, so it seems, a seat in the Government. Julius Khumalo. MP and Murderer! Ironic, isn't it?'

'Miles, please don't upset yourself like this. So what if he gets himself elected to Parliament? What do we care? It's not going to affect us here in Matabeleland, is it? Let him have his wealth and power. We have Scarfell Farm. He can't take that from us. We're safe here.'

Subdued by the anxiety in her voice, Miles turned to Lydia and kissed her upturned face. 'I'm sorry, sweetheart. It just maddened me to see him in his fancy suit, sucking up to Mugabe like that. I just saw red!'

'Oh Miles. I didn't know what to say to you. I've never seen you that angry before.'

'And you won't see me like that again, baby girl. The mean old bear who just slipped into my shoes has just had his arse well and truly kicked. He won't be back again.'

'Perhaps I should go and have my shower, now,' Lydia whispered. 'Then you can start to fatten me up like a good African wife with one of Sixpence's bumper breakfasts. I think we've both earned it, don't you?'

Miles patted Lydia's bottom and watched her leave the room. He was unsettled by his uncharacteristic outburst. Confused, he picked up the crumpled newspaper and dropped it into the bin before thrusting his hands into his pockets and wandering out on to the verandah. Outside, a trio of guinea fowl were strutting sedately across the lawn. Miles smiled wanly. Life went on at Scarfell Farm. It always had.

Julius slung his briefcase on the chair and went out on to the balcony of his hilltop home. Far below, through the tops of the trees, he could see the city of Harare spread out before him. Immediately beneath him, he could see the interwoven pathways that had been etched into the steep incline of the gardens at the front of the house. To his right, lower down on a second tier patio, the cool waters of the swimming pool beckoned. He shrugged out of his suit jacket, slung it over the balcony rail and opened his shirt collar. He was just about to make his way downstairs to the pool when a movement caught his eye as his wife, Lucie, wandered into view.

She was wearing a tight black swimsuit that was cut high and rode up into the crease of her buttocks. At the front, the neckline plunged down to her navel and its wide v-shaped opening was held together by laces that were threaded through eyelets on either side. Julius watched silently as she rubbed sunscreen oil over her skin. He was mesmerised by the seemingly innocent ritual and by the way his wife's oily body glistened as she spread out a towel on the sun-bed.

Thomas, one of the house servants, brought her a glass of wine and she gestured for him to leave it on the table beside her. Thomas bowed, but he did not turn and leave straight away. Julius was convinced that Thomas lingered longer than was necessary in order to feast his eyes upon the tantalising display of creamy-white flesh spread out in front of him. Worse, Julius could have sworn that the sole reason his wife chose to lift her arms above her head at that precise moment was to allow the lusty, young buck a better view of her bosom.

Suddenly, Julius was consumed in a grip of jealousy that was so powerful it took his breath away. The spectacular personal and political achievements that he had celebrated only hours earlier with the signing of the Unity Accord, and that he had rushed home to share with his wife, had crumbled into ashes. Furiously, he clenched his fists and stormed down to the poolside.

'I have told you before about this sort of exhibitionism!' Julius bellowed, towering over Lucie so that his huge frame blocked out the light. 'I do not want the servants to see you ….naked.'

'Oh darling! Don't be such a prude.' Lucie stretched out her hand like a cat and beckoned for Julius to sit beside her. 'I'm not "naked" as you put it. In case you haven't noticed, I'm wearing a swimsuit! Besides, it's only Thomas. He's just a servant. I'm sure he wouldn't notice if I slipped out of this swimsuit and danced the seven veils in front of him!'

'Of course he would notice,' Julius threw the towel over her body. 'He's a young African male. Any man would notice when a woman parades herself in front of him. I have told you before. I do not want other men ogling my wife. Not even the servants.'

'So I mustn't let other men see this, must I?' Lucie wriggled seductively and the straps of her swimsuit slipped off her shoulders. 'And I am forbidden to let them see…. this… am I?' She loosened the laces that held the fragile décolletage together and one of her huge, ruby nipples poked out of the flimsy material. 'Would it be okay for other big, black bucks to see me like this, Julius…?' she murmured, gazing up at him with wide innocent eyes.

Julius dropped to his knees beside the sun-bed. He buried his face in the hot valley between her breasts and groaned with the intensity of his lust. Lucie arched her back and smiled. Her husband's jealousy, although irksome at times, never failed to turn her on.

'This is a crowning moment for Zimbabwe,' Julius said later, gesturing towards the news on television. 'The signing of the Unity Accord will bring peace between ZAPU and ZANU at last. Now we can move forward and, united, we will make this nation great.'

'Amen to that!' Lucie toasted the television with her glass of wine and giggled. 'And I shall have one more teensy-weensy glass of wine to celebrate.'

Julius replenished his wife's empty glass and returned his attention to the news. 'I did not think I would live to see this moment,' he mused, still dazed by the significance of it.

'It wouldn't have happened without you. You do know that, don't you, Julius?' Lucie drained her glass and plonked it noisily on the table. 'And I for one will make sure that anyone and everyone knows exactly how much they owe you for this.'

'I have already received recognition for my efforts. I do not need any more praise. It is enough to see the Matabele and the Shona sharing power at last.'

'That may be enough for you,' Lucie reached over for the bottle of the wine. 'But I think you could have made more of it than you did. You worked your butt off to bring those two sides together. You mustn't let your efforts go unnoticed.'

Julius took his wife's hand and pulled her on to his lap. 'We have plenty of money, little bird,' he whispered. 'And rest assured that my efforts to bring about the Unity Accord have been noticed in high places. Robert Mugabe, the President, has thanked me personally and so did Joshua Nkomo when he returned to Zimbabwe. They are both glad that, at last, we are an African nation governed by all Africans.'

'I feel sorry for poor, old Ian Smith,' Lucie murmured, running her fingernails down the flesh on his forearms. 'It was a bit mean to boot him out of Parliament like that. He must be devastated.'

'Ian Smith was plotting with dissidents in South Africa.' Julius replied. 'They were planning to unsettle the nation. Mugabe had no choice other than to sack him from the Government. The Unity Accord heralds the beginning of true democracy here in Zimbabwe. In the future, blacks and whites must fight for election on the same footing. There are no privileges for whites any more, no guaranteed twenty white seats in Parliament. Ian Smith, and all true Africans, must learn to accept the changes that will follow the Unity Accord. As the President said in his speech, whites must now choose whether they are African or European. If they are African, they must support the Unity Accord.'

'There is another good thing on the horizon following your meteoric rise,' Lucie nuzzled Julius' neck. 'I've heard that MPs get preferential treatment from the big motor manufacturers. Now that you're officially an MP, we won't have to wait in line for a new car like everyone else.'

'I am not sure I approve of that practice,' Julius deposited his wife on the sofa beside him and threw open the doors on to the balcony. 'It is open to abuse. There is a serious shortage of cars for sale in Zimbabwe. If companies like Willowvale Motor Industry are encouraged to let members of the Government jump the queue, then ordinary Zimbabweans will have every right to feel cheated. I would prefer to wait my turn, along with the rest of the people of Zimbabwe.'

'But that might take years!' Lucie tucked her legs underneath her and pouted prettily. 'You've done so much for this country with the Unity Accord and everything. Surely that's enough to get one lousy car? I don't see why we should have to wait.'

Julius turned back into the room. He had unbuttoned his shirt and it now hung open against his chest. Lucie let her gaze travel over the well-toned definition of his stomach muscles and his hard, black chest. His eyes were as dark the night sky when they met hers and she felt herself melting under his brooding intensity. However, her quest for a new car took precedence on this occasion, and she was not going to allow herself to be distracted from her cause.

'You never see things from my point of view,' she complained, resorting to emotional blackmail. 'It's always "the people this" or "the people that". Never me. Never your poor, dutiful wife.'

Julius threw back his head and roared with laughter. 'If only that were true, little bird! What wouldn't I give for a "dutiful" wife! Such unimaginable luxury!'

Lucie chucked a cushion at him and swung her long legs off the sofa. 'I am a dutiful wife! You just don't know it, that's all. Anyway, just like the dutiful wife and society hostess that I am, I have arranged a little dinner party for one of the top guys from Willowvale this weekend. I thought you might like to get to know him. He's loaded and I'm sure you'll like him.'

Julius frowned at his wife. 'How do you know this man? You have no connections at Willowvale.'

'He's American,' Lucie busied herself with puffing up the cushions on the sofa. 'He knows Daddy. Oh Julius. I know you'll like him and he can do so much for the poor people of Zimbabwe.'

'What is his name, this great American philanthropist?'

'Oliver,' Lucie murmured, not meeting his eyes. 'Oliver Jordace.'

Miles shaded the sun from his eyes with the palm of his hand and squinted at the old tree house. 'I really should repair this,' he declared. 'Some of that wood is rotten.'

Lydia came to stand beside him. She had been cutting down the tall grasses that grew on either side of the paths and she was still clutching the pink feathery bundles in her arms when she stopped at the foot of the ancient ficus glumosa. She laid her bundle on the ground and plucked a ripe fig from the clusters that grew at the end of the branches.

'Yummy!' she sucked the fruit from her fingers and stared up at the rickety structure 'Yes, I see what you mean. It is looking a bit neglected.'

Miles ran his hand over the pale, creamy-grey bark. The young December leaves and petioles were sporting long, silky hairs that gave the tree a shaggy appearance. 'I can remember this tree house being built,' he mused. 'It was Joseph's idea. My Dad wasn't too keen at first, but Joseph managed to convince him that he knew what he was doing.'

'Well he did a fine job. All it needs are a few extra nails and a couple of new planks of wood and it will be looking as good as ever. I reckon you could fix it up in no time. It would be so nice to see it restored. It's such an important part of Scarfell Farm. It's a part of your childhood.'

Briefly, the light dimmed in Miles' eyes. Lydia spotted the change and knowing exactly where his thoughts were heading, she quickly sought to steer him back to happier times.

'Do you know what I think the tree house really needs?' she whispered, threading both arms around his waist and reaching up to plant a peck on his cheek.

Miles pulled her closer and returned her peck with a hearty smacker on the lips. He was as eager as his wife to dispel the gloomy thoughts. 'So what harebrained scheme would you have in mind now, Mrs Cameron?'

'Children,' came the barely audible reply.

'Children!' Miles lifted her chin to force her to meet his eyes. 'Did I hear you say children?'

Lydia nodded and blushed furiously.

'And where do you suppose these children will come from?'

'If you don't know… perhaps I could show you…'

'Hang on a minute!' Miles gasped and held her at arms' length. 'Am I hearing what I think I'm hearing? I mean…. are we talking about….our children!'

Lydia laughed and nodded joyfully. 'Yes, my darling husband. We are talking about our children. Lots and lots of adorable little baby Camerons running about, making a mess and playing in the old tree house at Scarfell Farm. Do you understand now?'

Miles whooped with delight and swung his wife round and round in a heady twirl until she pleaded for respite.

'Our children! Camerons! Are you sure, sweetheart? I thought you wanted to wait for a while.' Miles was breathless. 'Is this what you really want?'

'Oh Miles, apart from loving you and wanting to live here at Scarfell Farm, I have never been more sure of anything in my life.'

'But… what shall we do now….? When shall we start?'

Lydia giggled and took his work-callused hand in her own soft palm. 'Well, my beloved husband, there's no time like the present, as they say. And, if you're not sure what to do, don't worry, I'll show you!'

Lucie Khumalo was on top form. Her silver-blonde curls were gathered up in various bunches and held in place by tiny diamond clasps. The overall effect was stunning as each golden strand hung freely from a single diamond that sparkled in the candlelight whenever she moved her head. The hair decorations were a gift from Oliver Jordace, the wealthy American businessman who was their guest. Lucie also wore a pair of expensive diamond earrings and a matching necklace that glittered at her throat. These were a gift from her father.

Julius sat at the dinner table watching his wife. He could not deny that the diamonds complemented her black silk evening dress. He was painfully aware that his wife was looking more lovely than ever, and the presence of her fellow countryman served only to enhance her charms. Julius knew all this, but he did not like it. He did not like it at all. Try as he might, he could not hide his resentment at the closeness between the two Americans, and he could not join in with their anecdotes about a country that was, culturally, a million miles from Africa. A country that he, Julius, had never even seen.

Oliver Jordace was a well-built individual with a square jaw and an uncompromising set to his shoulders. He was tough, an ex-marine, and it showed in the bulges under his shirt sleeves and the hard lines on his face. He was not a handsome man, but he exuded a power and ruthlessness that women found attractive. He did not smile much - Oliver Jordace had little time for humour - but he could captivate a woman with the harsh intensity of his deep-set eyes. He had been married twice and divorced twice, and he paid his exorbitant alimony with undisguised reluctance. He liked women, but he was not a man to carry surplus baggage from his past. "When it's over, it's over" he would growl when challenged about his attitude. "I like to keep moving."

Oliver's rough and ready approach had certainly stood him in good stead when he first met Bud Lyndon, the wealthy banker from Boston. The two men had formed an instant bond, one based on a shared philosophy that there was no place for emotion in the world of business. Business was for making money. And money counts!

Bud was keen to exploit the business opportunities opening up in Africa. It helped that his daughter, Lucie, was now living in Zimbabwe as the wife of a prominent politician. Oliver had sat in the drawing room of Bud's elegant red-brick house on Boston's exclusive Beacon Hill and listened with growing interest as the older man outlined his plans.

'There's a chronic shortage of cars out there,' Bud had explained, chewing on the butt end of an expensive Havana cigar. 'A classic case of demand outstripping supply.'

Oliver swirled the brandy in his glass. 'Why is that?'

'Why? I'll tell you why – because the damned fool of a president, Comrade Robert Mugabe, has signed some law or other to prevent people bringing in cheap cars from South Africa, or using their funds to bring in cars from abroad. Economic suicide if you ask me!'

'So how can I be of help to you, sir?' Oliver Jordace examined the gold signet ring on his little finger and finished his brandy. The expensive liquid warmed his belly and he felt good. Bud Lyndon was a man he respected. A man he could do business with.

Bud squatted on the footstool directly opposite Oliver, planted his feet widely apart and leaned towards the young man whom he had come to like and trust. 'Okay. This is the deal. There are three major car manufacturers out there. Leyland in Mutare is one, but I'm more interested in the Willowvale Motor Industry in Harare. I have a couple of guys out there… if you know what I mean?' he nudged the side of his nose. 'They look after American interests in Africa. They're the guys who first alerted me to the growing shortage of new cars. Lucie, my daughter, that's her in the picture over there…'

Oliver let his glance stray to the voluptuous blonde in the framed photograph on the mantelpiece. He took a sharp intake of breath. 'She's a good looking woman,' he declared.

'She's her Daddy's girl. Make no mistake about that!' Bud beamed with pride. 'Now what was I saying? Oh yes, Lucie wrote to me complaining about the fact that she has to drive some beat-up old car. Damned ridiculous! My little girl without a decent set of wheels to her name! Why, it doesn't bear thinking about, especially when she tells me that her husband, who's a Member of Parliament for chrissake, could use his influence to get her a goddam fleet of new cars, if he wanted to!'

'So why doesn't he?' Oliver queried.

'Now that's the problem! My son-in-law, Julius Khumalo MP, has got what you and I might call integrity!' Bud spat out the word and a fine mist of spittle rained over his guest. 'I know! I know! A damned nuisance it is, too! "Integrity" always gets in the way of good business, but unfortunately for us, the man has got more than his fair share of it and we're just gonna have to work round that obstacle if we want to succeed.'

Oliver had a dozen questions to ask, but he kept them to himself and waited for Bud to enlighten him.

Bud shuffled the footstool closer and leaned forward conspiratorially. 'What I want you to do, my boy, is get yourself out there and help Lucie persuade Julius to use his privileges as a Member of Parliament to buy new cars at rock bottom prices. Then, you can sell them on at a profit to private buyers. Get my drift? We split the surplus, and Julius is none the wiser. A piece of cake!'

'But surely he can only get one car at a time? Not half a dozen or more?'

'Wrong! MPs are allowed to buy cars for their family and their constituency workers, and anyone else they feel should have one. He just needs to sign to say he has approval from the Ministry of Industry and Technology and Willowvale Motor Industries will let him as many vehicles as he wants.'

'And then?'

'And then you sell them on to private buyers who are willing to pay big prices for new cars. Believe me, there are plenty of folks with ready cash out there. I wouldn't be surprised if Government Ministers are already milking the motor cow. That's why you have to get out there and start working fast. Lucie will help you, and my importer in Harare, but just you make sure my little girl gets the pick of the bunch when they start coming through from America.'

'Just one question, Bud.' Oliver was interested

'Spit it out, boy?'

'How will we get Julius to sign for the delivery of large numbers of new cars.'

Bud grinned and slapped his knees gleefully. 'That's something you and I don't need to worry ourselves about, Oliver boy. That's something we can leave entirely in my Lucie's hands. I don't know how she'll do it, but I do know my little girl. She won't let us down.'

Julius peered into the bathroom mirror and rubbed his face dry with a towel. He then looked past his own reflection to that of his wife who was standing behind him pulling the diamond clasps out of her hair. He turned to her and frowned.

'I did not like the man,' he declared, moodily. 'He is interested only in money. He does not care about the people of Zimbabwe. I am sure he would import cars to sell to anyone with enough cash to buy them. He has no scruples.'

Lucie pulled a face. 'You don't like him because he is a man! It doesn't matter that he's trying to help us both, and your precious ZANU party members, by securing reliable transport for us all. You just didn't like the way he looked at me.'

Julius threw the damp towel into the basket while he reflected on his wife's words. It was true. Oliver Jordace had a way of looking at Lucie that had made his blood boil. No doubt he looked at every woman that way, rather like a wealthy investor assessing a thoroughbred racehorse, but Julius did not care about other women. He cared about his wife. And he did not like the way Oliver Jordace had raised his eyebrow in that smug, self-satisfied way when she had giggled at one of his jokes, and he had visibly scowled at the sight of Oliver Jordace leaning back in his chair, legs apart, as Lucie bent over to light his cigar. But, most of all, Julius disliked the intimacy between them. Lucie had dismissed his concerns as irrational jealousy, and perhaps she was right. But Julius did not like Oliver Jordace, and he could not subdue the jealous demons that tormented him.

'And as for being interested in money,' Lucie paused at the bathroom door. 'He's a businessman. Why shouldn't he make a few bucks for his efforts? He stands to earn his money by helping other people. I can't see anything wrong with that!'

Julius sighed heavily and followed Lucie into the bedroom where she dropped the hair clasps into a jewellery box and picked up her hairbrush. She had already removed all traces of make-up and she looked fresh and childlike.

Chastened, Julius kissed the back of her neck. 'I am sorry, little bird. I just cannot bear to see you talking and laughing with another man. I know I must learn to live with it, I cannot expect other men to ignore such a beautiful woman, but it is hard for me. Sometimes, I think I would like to kill every man who dares to look at you. I want you all for myself. I do not want to share you with others.'

Lucie reached behind her and pulled him towards her so that their heads were on the same level in the mirror. 'Silly boy,' she purred, pressing her cheek against his. 'I'm not interested in Oliver and I'm quite sure he's not interested in me. I just want a lovely new car so that I can go shopping without fear of breaking down in the middle of the bush. You can understand that, can't you darling?'

'I can understand that. And you are right, perhaps I do care too much for the ordinary people and not enough of my precious wife. Why should you have to drive a car that might break down at any time? You deserve better than that and it is my duty to make sure that you have it.'

'So you will sign the form from the Ministry of Industry and Technology?'

310

'I will sign the form,' Julius stepped back as Lucie jumped up and spun round to hug him. 'Especially if it merits such a generous reward!'

Lucie showered his neck with kisses. 'Oh thank you, Julius. Once you have signed the request form you won't have to think about it again. Oliver will do the rest. As soon as we get the okay, he will arrange for his contacts at Willowvale to let me have a car. It's so simple!'

Julius laughed and circled his wife's tiny waist with his huge paws, but she wriggled free from his embrace and skipped over to her writing desk where she scooped up the official request form and held it aloft with a grin.

'There is another reason I need a new car,' she lowered her eyes and assumed a timid pose. 'I mean, you couldn't expect the son of the great Julius Khumalo to be ferried around in scruffy old banger, could you?'

Julius stood rigid and held his breath.

'That's right, you big dope!' Lucie waved the paper in front of her. 'This piece of paper will allow your son to travel in style!'

Julius cried aloud and shook his head in disbelief. 'You are carrying my child? My son?' he asked.

'Well, it could be a daughter,' Lucie teased.

'Are you carrying a child of the House of Khumalo, Lucie? Tell me now!'

'Lucie snuggled into his embrace. 'Yes, Julius. That's precisely what I am doing. Now, will you kindly sign this wretched form so that we can begin celebrating?'

Julius whooped with joy and snatched the paper from her fingers, scribbling his name at the bottom. He then tossed the pen on to the writing desk and swung his wife up into his arms. She was carrying his child. A child of the House of Khumalo. And all she wanted was one decent car to travel in. It was not much to ask and, suddenly, Julius felt ashamed. He had every right to buy his wife a car using a minor Parliamentary privilege. He owed it to Lucie to exercise that right.

Lucie screamed playfully as Julius swept her off her feet and carried her across the room to lay her carefully on the bed. As she slid over to accommodate his bulk beside her, she glanced at the request form on the table. She would get it to Oliver first thing in the morning and he would see just how resourceful she was. Oliver was adamant that Julius could only be persuaded to ask for one car. He did not believe that Lucie could dupe her husband into requesting six new cars, but Lucie had been determined to impress the beefy American with the sexy, southern drawl.

She had been excited by his ruthlessness and personal dynamism, and she wanted to show him that she could match his ambition. All she had to do was trick Julius into signing a request for six vehicles instead of one. The others could then be sold on at a vast profit.

Of course, Lucie had not expected to discover that she was pregnant in the middle of her plans, but she saw at once how she might use it to her advantage. She knew that Julius would be so thrilled by the news that he would not give a moment's thought to the wording on the request form and he would not notice how many cars were being ordered.

Nor would he give one moment's thought to the devastating impact that pregnancy might have on his wife's perfect hour-glass figure, Lucie thought with a frown. But she was not unduly worried. She had already survived one abortion unscathed. There was nothing to stop her taking a trip back to Boston for another. She still had a few weeks left to decide what to do about the baby. Even if she did choose to go through with it, she would have a full-time nanny to look after it. Lucie would not let something as insignificant as motherhood interrupt her carefree lifestyle.

Meanwhile, she had secured Julius' signature, and the promise of enormous profits from this first batch alone. Her beloved father would be delighted with her efforts and so, too, would Oliver Jordace. But, for now, she had a huge, handsome man lying naked beside her. She had done enough work for one day. Now it was time to play.

Miles shielded his eyes from the sun with the back of his hand and watched as his wife's Datsun sped up the drive. He never ceased to marvel at Lydia's driving skills, nor her nerves of steel! Many times, he had been forced to avert his eyes as she slammed her foot on the accelerator to overtake some particular irksome truck or bus. He had complained that she might kill them both with her passion for speed, but she had retorted, proudly, that she was far too good a driver ever to crash a car. With a helpless shrug of his shoulders, Miles had to agree. She did seem to lead a charmed existence behind the wheel. Now, he just shrugged his shoulders and grinned as the vehicle raced towards him before screeching to a halt in front of the house.

'I need a new car!' Lydia threw open the passenger door. 'This old wreck is falling apart at the seams. It's a disgrace!'

Miles laughed. 'Are you sure the car is a wreck, or is it simply knackered after a trip into town with you?'

'It's a wreck!' Lydia pulled off her straw hat and flung it, frisbee-style, on to the verandah. She then bounded up the steps and flopped into the rocking chair.

She was dressed in a black cotton tee-shirt and jeans. Her lustrous ruby-red mane lay curled on her shoulders and her emerald eyes glistened in the noon-day sun. She kicked off her shoes and tucked her bare feet underneath her, pouring herself a glass of iced lemonade from the jug on the table.

Miles was delighted to see the rosy glow on her cheeks and the sparkle in her eyes. He had been worried about her. Despite their determined efforts to start a family, Lydia had not conceived, and this had left her feeling inadequate and anxious. She had always been skinny, but Miles had been concerned to see her losing weight in the last few weeks, and he did not like her unhealthy pallor. But when she started feeling nauseous, Miles had insisted on her seeing a doctor in Bulawayo.

'You shouldn't fuss,' Lydia had said at the time. 'I've always been scrawny. You know that.'

'Not as scrawny as you are now,' Miles had argued. 'You're not eating enough. How do you expect to bear my child if you don't eat, huh? The Camerons always make big babies. You're going to have to toughen up, girl, if you want to carry my offspring.'

Suddenly Lydia eyes filled with tears and her fingers plucked nervously at Miles' shirt sleeve. 'I'm not sure I will ever bear your child, Miles,' she whispered. 'It's been a whole year since we started trying.'

'One year! Big deal! Some couples try for two or three years. One miserable year hardly signals failure.'

Lydia dabbed at the corners of her eyes. 'I'm not like other women, I'm not as strong as other women. Maybe you should have married one of the Shaw sisters. I hear they are both pregnant at the moment.'

Miles threw back his head and laughed, masking his anxiety, but he knew that she was right. She was not as strong as other women. In fact, he had often marvelled at her body, which was as smooth and slim as teenager's. Miles had always loved the way she looked, but he did not like it when her weight began to drop. It had taken a lot to persuade her to see a doctor, but he was glad now that he had forced her to go.

'Judging by the smile on your face, I gather Doctor Bennett has given you a clean bill of health?' Miles took the chair next to her. 'So what did he have to say?'

'Lydia sipped her lemonade through a straw and glanced at Miles from under a veil of thick lashes. 'He said I've got to eat more.'

'Sounds sensible!'

'He says that I am not to be troubled in any way.'

'Did he say that?' Miles was puzzled. He leaned forward and lifted her coppery fringe from her eyes. 'Does he reckon we're trying too hard… for a baby, I mean? Is that what the problem is? Maybe he's right. We are a bit obsessed about it all. Maybe we should just relax and enjoy making love for a while, instead of fretting about whether it's the right time of the month. They do say that worry can prevent a woman conceiving.'

Lydia smiled and reached out for his hand, holding it tightly in her own. 'I'm not going to worry about getting pregnant any more, Miles, because I am pregnant. That's why I've been feeling so sick recently. I can't imagine why it never occurred to us, but I'm pregnant. Can you believe it?'

'Pregnant! You're pregnant! How long? I mean, when's it due? Christ! How did we manage that?' Miles grinned widely and pulled her face towards his. Cupping her cheeks in both hands, he kissed her fully on the mouth and declared proudly: 'I love you Lydia Cameron. By God, I love you so much!'

'And I love you, Miles Cameron,' Lydia whispered through her tears then, patting her stomach, she added: 'We both love you.'

Miles laid his hand on the perfectly flat plain of his wife's belly. Lydia curled her fingers over his and leaned against him. She was suddenly subdued and Miles pulled her closer.

'What's wrong, baby girl?' his words were muffled by her hair.

'I'm just a bit frightened, I guess.'

'You don't have to be frightened, silly girl!' Miles gripped her shoulders. 'I'll be with you every step of the way.'

'I hope I'm going to be strong enough to carry this baby, Miles. Doctor Bennett said I must take care. He said I might have a difficult pregnancy. He wants to talk to you and says he will have to keep an eye on me.'

Miles turned his gaze to the far distance, to the quiet hilltop where his parents and sister were buried. Silently, he promised himself that one day soon he would take his own child to stand beside those graves. He would tell the child that it was a great honour to bear the name Cameron and to live in this beautiful part of Africa. He wanted his child to love Scarfell Farm as much as he did, and to see the Camerons live on in Matabeleland.

Softly, Miles brushed Lydia's cheek with his fingertips. 'You will be strong enough to carry our baby, Lydia. There's nothing to fear, my darling, because I'll always be there for you.'

Two days later, a hearty bellow rang out in the private ward of Harare's top maternity hospital. Outside the delivery room, Julius heard the cry and his heart raced. Anxiously, he paced up and down the corridor, and then he stopped dead in his tracks when the midwife came out and beamed at him.

'Congratulations, Mr Khumalo. You have a beautiful daughter.'

Julius swallowed the lump in his throat and stared uncomprehendingly at the stout, middle-aged woman standing before him.

'You can go in now,' she said, gesturing towards the double doors behind her. 'Your wife is ready to see you.'

Julius hurried to Lucie's bedside in the private maternity ward. The tiny infant lay sleeping in a cot next to her. Tenderly, Julius kissed his wife's brow before peering anxiously at his new-born daughter. He towered over the cot and gazed down at the little puckered face.

'She is beautiful,' he said. 'Like her mother.'

Lucie grimaced. 'Please do not compare me to that! A scrunched-up, red-faced baby is not what I call beautiful, thank you very much!'

'She is beautiful, and she will grow to be even more beautiful.'

Gently, Julius lifted the infant and enfolded her into his arms. Hot tears pricked the back of his eyes as he held his daughter for the very first time. She was so small, so fragile and so lovely that he thought his heart would burst with love. Never, in all his born days, had he felt such an intense emotion. This child was his, a true descendant of the House of Khumalo and the blood line of the Great King Mzilikazi. He reached out and touched her delicate fingers. Instantly, they curled around his and he marvelled at how pale they were.

This child carried the blood of Africa and America in her veins. She would belong to both worlds. His child would be one of the new generation of Africans who were born without the shackles of racial hatred and cultural divide. She would be able to make her own choices and she would be free.

'She will be the first of many children for us, little bird.'

Lucie took up the ivory hand mirror from her bedside table and peered at her reflection. She hated her puffy cheeks and the way her normally taut flesh seemed to sag. She would have to get back in shape and fast. She was heartily sick of being fat and uncomfortable and unattractive. She had hated being pregnant and, having experienced the agony of giving birth, she had sworn that she would never put herself through that again. She had provided Julius with one baby. To her mind, she had fulfilled her duty as a wife, but there would be no more pregnancies for Lucie Khumalo. She would make sure of that.

'What shall we call this daughter of ours?' Julius held the precious bundle in his arms and grinned at his wife.

'I'd like to call her Devon,' Lucie replied.

'Then Devon it shall be,' Julius brushed the tiny face with his lips. 'Welcome to Africa, Devon Khumalo. Welcome to life.'

17

Lydia reached across her drawing board and accidentally knocked her pencil on to the floor. It rolled under the chair and came to rest against her cat, Bala. Roused from her slumbers, Bala stretched out and tried to hook the pencil with her claws. Her half-hearted efforts were doomed to failure and, instead, she lifted her redundant paw to her mouth and proceeded to wash it leisurely.

'Lazy old puss!' Lydia remonstrated as she tried in vain to bend over and pick up the pencil. 'Too sleepy even to play!'

Bala yawned and inclined her ear towards Lydia's finger in the hope of a tickle.

'I'll get that!' Miles strode up to the stoep and picked up the pencil. He then stood behind his wife to inspect her drawing. 'It's brilliant!' he enthused.

Lydia looked at her work and tipped her head to one side. 'It's okay,' she mused. 'It just needs a touch more contrast in this corner.'

Miles knelt down beside her chair. 'How are you feeling, sweetheart? Better now?'

Lydia nodded. 'I've been feeling sick all morning, but I think it's finally settled. I must be the only expectant woman on the planet who's actually losing weight during pregnancy.'

'Will you be okay here on your own for the next few days? I can always drop out of the conference if you need me here.'

'I'll be fine....as long as I don't have to bend over! The bump is really getting in the way now. No, it's important that you attend this conference. This will be the first opportunity for the Commercial Farmers' Union to air their concerns about land reclamation. White farmers from all over Zimbabwe will be there. I think you should be with them.'

Miles squatted on the edge of the step at his wife's feet. Bala, sensing the opportunity for more attention, sidled up to him and pressed herself against his outstretched hand. Dutifully, he stroked her head until she flopped over on her side and exposed a soft, furry stomach for further pampering. Absently, Miles ran his hand over the silky fur while Bala gnawed at his fingers playfully.

'I'm banking on Scarfell being too small to be of any use to the Government, but Mugabe's getting desperate. He's threatening to abandon the terms of the Lancaster House Agreement when it expires in two years time. White farmers are going to have to act swiftly if they want to prevent major land seizures in 1990.'

'I can understand his dilemma,' Lydia said. 'When the Lancaster House Agreement was signed, everyone wanted to leave the country. The whites were quite happy to sell their land and start a new life abroad. Now, eight years later, they all want to stay. Life under a black Government isn't as bad as they had feared, and they want to keep their land.'

'Exactly.' Miles agreed. 'But if the whites won't sell their farms, how can Mugabe get his hands on enough land to give to the blacks who fought for it? It's a Catch 22.'

Lydia stood up and arched her back, rubbing her swollen belly. Miles looked up and felt the familiar stab of alarm at the sight of her skinny legs supporting such an enormous burden. It was proving a difficult pregnancy and, once again, Miles felt a flicker of doubt at his proposed trip to Harare.

'Oh Miles, please don't worry. In comparison with those poor African women giving birth out in the bush, I've got no problems. Now stop fretting about me and get ready for the trip tomorrow. You'll need to be off at the crack of dawn if you want to get to KweKwe for lunch. It's a long drive north.'

'I'm just glad I'm not taking the our car,' Miles followed his wife into the cool shade of the kitchen. Bala padded along behind them. 'I reckon the wheel bearings are on their way out. Little wonder given the state of the local roads these days. There are potholes everywhere. I don't think the Government rates road repairs very highly right now.'

'We need a new car. It's as simple as that.'

'Easier said than done. New cars are like gold dust,' Miles opened the fridge and pulled out a square sachet of orange juice. He cut open a corner at the top and gulped it quickly before the juice spurted out over the floor.

'You should pour it into a jug, greedy!' Lydia moaned. 'It'll tip over if you put it back like that.'

'I won't put it back,' Miles wiped his mouth with the back of his hand and grinned at her. 'I'll finish it in one gulp!'

Lydia rolled her eyes. 'Heaven help you if you behave like that at Harare's International Conference Centre. They'll think you're a real bush-boy farmer.'

'I am a real bush-boy farmer! That's why I'm going in the first place. I've lived on this farm all my life. If I don't want to sell it, I don't see why I should have to. And I certainly don't think that people should be allowed to simply take it away from me. This land has been in my family for generations.'

Lydia leaned over to plant a kiss on his cheek. It would have been a long, tender kiss, but the "bump" as it was affectionately known, got in the way. 'Save your speeches for the conference. Right now, you should get yourself cleaned up and packed for the trip. What time is Mike picking you up?'

'At the crack of dawn, knowing Mike. Andrew's hitching a ride with us as well, along with Doug Macintosh.'

'The reporter from the Bulawayo Chronicle? Why is he going?'

'He's covering the story for the newspaper. It's a major event and it's likely to be news for some time to come.'

'Well thank your lucky stars that you're not going in the Datsun. It couldn't possibly cope with the weight of four grown men. It can barely get me to Bulawayo and back.'

Miles screwed the empty juice sachet into a ball and dropped it into the bin before turning to Lydia and pulling her into his arms. 'Will you miss me while I'm away, Mrs Cameron.'

'Every minute of every day, Mr Cameron,' Lydia nuzzled his unshaven chin. 'Just make sure that you get yourself there and back in one piece. You have a wife and unborn baby waiting here for you.'

'And a dumb cat,' Miles added, noticing the furry bundle that had just spread itself over his left foot.'

Lydia laughed. ' And a very dumb cat,' she echoed.

The journey from Bulawayo to Harare, took around six hours with a stop for lunch at a pretty hotel just outside KweKwe. The main roads through the towns were in good condition, but some of the smaller ones were deteriorating. However, even the occasional pothole and cracks in the tarmac could not detract from the awesome grandeur of the open savannahs that flanked the route.

Miles sat in the back of car with Doug Macintosh enjoying his companion's good humour and lively conversation. Miles had always respected Doug for his honest reporting and for his refusal to follow any one party line. Doug was a kindly, honest individual whose recent application to join the Bulawayo Club had been met with wholehearted support by all the members. And, of course, Miles was a great fan and loyal reader of Doug's newspaper, the Bulawayo Chronicle.

Doug turned to Miles with a broad grin on his face. 'It seems that Graham Hick is doing very well for himself over in England. It came through on the wires that he's currently 405 not-out against Somerset.'

Miles whooped with joy. 'Did you hear that, lads? Another batting record for Hick! I'll bet Worcestershire are celebrating the day that they signed that guy.'

'Ja, but he still isn't allowed to play cricket for England,' Andrew Saville swivelled round in his seat. 'It seems he can't find a bone fide parent or grandparent to justify his claims to British citizenship.'

'No, but he'll be playing for the national side before long. You mark my words.' Doug interrupted. 'He'll just have to sit out a longer qualifying period, that's all. But be in no doubt, Graham Hick will become the first white Zimbabwean to play for England - and the Bulawayo Chronicle will be sure to cover the story when it happens.

'And it will be a great day for Zimbabwean sport when he does,' Mike added. 'Now then guys, we're about fifteen minutes away from KweKwe. Everyone ready for lunch?'

With its pretty whitewashed walls and roof of golden thatch, the Golden Mile Hotel just outside KweKwe was a popular stopping-off point for people travelling between Zimbabwe's two main cities. With clean toilet facilities, excellent food, and gardens crammed with beautiful blooms and shrubs, it was an oasis of cool on the long, dusty road north.

Mike's suggestion was greeted with a chorus of approval. Travelling in Africa could be arduous at times, but with good friends, stunning scenery and welcome breaks along the route, it was also one of life's more pleasurable experiences.

The International Conference Centre in Harare was filled to capacity. White farmers and their families strained to hear the words of the President of the Commercial Farmers' Union, Bob Rutherford, as he outlined CFU plans to help the Government tackle the escalating problems regarding the land issue. The Minister for Lands, Agriculture and Rural Resettlement, Comrade David Karimanzira, sat stony-faced and implacable.

Both sides agreed that the fundamental problem was a shortage of land. The Government had a duty to house hundreds of thousands of homeless Africans, but white landowners were no longer willing to sell their homes for resettlement. They had grown accustomed to black majority rule in the new Zimbabwe, and the anarchy that they had first anticipated had not materialised. Now, few were willing to abandon the only life they had ever known to start again elsewhere. As a compromise, Bob Rutherford put forward the suggestion that white farmers would be willing to help retrain homeless settlers in basic agricultural skills given that the Government had finally recognised the devastating effects of putting urban poor on to a patch of land and simply leaving them to get on with it. He pointed out that the economy was suffering from the destruction of productive farmland that had already been procured by the Government. It would be commercial suicide to strip yet more white Zimbabweans of their land simply to fulfil a moral obligation. In the end, all would suffer and the country would no longer be able to sustain itself.

Unmoved by this argument, Comrade Karimanzira reiterated his party's obligations to the war veterans. Black Zimbaweans had fought and died for the right to own land in their own country. The Government could not be seen to renege on its promises now. To justify their standing on the world stage, and to try to win the support of the white farmers, the Minister pointed out that eight million black Africans were forced to eke out a living on the same amount of land as that owned by a mere four thousand whites. It was unfair, and ZANU (PF) were honour bound to redress the imbalance and ensure that black people were given a fair proportion of the country's richest natural resource.

The conference had reached a stalemate. The Government had to find land to resettle the homeless, but the whites were not prepared to give up their land for resettlement. By the end of the day, the tensions inside the Conference Centre were at boiling point, and when the meeting finally drew to a close, delegates poured out of the doors with heavy hearts.

'I can't see a way out of this mess,' Miles supped a long, cool glass of Lion lager in the bar of the Sheraton Hotel.

'I wouldn't be too worried if I were you,' Mike reassured him. 'Scarfell is only twelve thousand acres. They need to get hold of the big farms if they want to make a dent in the numbers claiming resettlement. Take my place, for example, that would be a prime target. I'm surprised they haven't shown any interest in it before now.'

'And we've got the farm that my wife inherited from her parents,' Andrew added. 'They're not going to let us get away with having two farms for much longer.'

The three men sat on their bar stools in the magnificent surroundings of the Sheraton Hotel and pondered their fate. All three were anxious as to what the future might bring. The Lancaster House Agreement was due to expire in April 1990, at which time the Government would be free to make its own decisions about the land issue. Many white farmers dreaded the day, fearing that their homes would be forcibly taken from them. Others had convinced themselves that the British Government would find a way to resolve the issue that would satisfy the demands of both sides. Lancaster House still had two years left to run. There was plenty of time to sort things out.

Miles stayed behind to finish his drink when Mike and Andrew retired for the night. He sat at the bar, staring into his drink, thinking of Lydia. He had called her earlier to let her know how the day had gone and to check on her health. She had spent the day in bed, she said miserably. She had been hoping to visit a friend on the other side of town, but was too sickly to go. She was hoping to go tomorrow, but Miles begged her not to. The Datsun was unreliable and she was too frail. Reluctantly, she agreed to stay at home and rest. Miles was worried about his wife all alone at Scarfell, and he looked forward to an early start back to Bulawayo in the morning.

'Mind if I join you?' a deep American drawl penetrated Miles' thoughts and he looked up to find a stranger standing before him.

'No... please... take a seat.'

The stocky American sat on the vacant bar stool and thrust out a hard, hairy hand. 'The name's Jordace. Oliver Jordace. I hope you don't mind. I'm not one for solitary drinking.'

Miles took the outstretched hand and returned the iron grip. 'Miles Cameron. Good to meet you Mr Jordace. Are you a tourist, or on business over here?'

'Business!' Oliver grunted with mirth. 'Definitely business. And you?'

'I'm from Bulawayo. I'm here for the farmers' conference.'

'Ah yes,' Oliver pulled out a fat cigar. 'Nasty business. Can't see how they're going to sort that problem out. Are you a farmer?'

Miles nodded. 'We have twelve thousand acres of dairy farm in Bulawayo.'

'Probably too small to be of any consequence,' Oliver lit the end of his cigar and blew a strand of grey smoke into the air.

'That's what we're banking on,' Miles agreed.

'You got family down there?'

'My wife, Lydia. She's pregnant.'

'Is that why you're sitting all alone in a bar at midnight?' Oliver joked.

Miles laughed. 'Partly that, and partly because I couldn't trust my car to get me to Harare and back. I had to hitch a lift with some buddies.'

Oliver leaned back in his chair and signalled to the waiter. 'Can I get you a drink, Mr Cameron? Another lager? I'll have a scotch on the rocks.' Oliver thrust the dollar notes at the waiter and turned back to Miles. 'What kind of car do you have?'

'A Datsun, but it's on its last legs.'

Oliver shook his head. 'New cars are hard to come by out here.'

'I'll probably shop around for a second-hand vehicle. I'd prefer to have a new car, but I know I don't have a cat in hell's chance of getting one.'

'So you would like a new car, would you, Mr Cameron?'

'Sure I would!' Miles laughed aloud. 'But I've lived in Africa too long to expect the impossible. A new car would be great, especially when the baby's born, but I can't see that happening.'

'I may be able to help… if you'd like me to?'

Miles' brow furrowed. 'How? Are you in the car business?'

'Call me a dealer of sorts,' Oliver drew heavily on his cigar and the red tip glowed. 'I might be able to lay my hands on a new car if you want one. A Toyota Cressida perhaps?'

'Is it legal?' Miles took a slug of his drink and took a closer look at the man sitting opposite. He was a tough-looking individual with deep lines at the corners of his eyes and a chin that was rough and blue from frequent shaving. His back was straight and his shoulders square. In fact, his bearing was that of a military man and Miles was intrigued.

'Let's put it this way,' Oliver Jordace waved away his change irritably. 'It's not actually illegal …. It's more a case of having the right connections… do you get my drift?'

'And you have "connections" here, do you?'

Oliver nodded and leaned closer. He had been drinking heavily and his breath was stale with whiskey. 'A good friend of mine from the States is married to a prominent MP right here in Harare. Between us, we've got the whole car scene sewn up. Are you interested? It will cost you, though. There are risks.'

Miles' thoughts were racing and his heart began to beat heavily in his chest. Oliver Jordace had mentioned that his Government contact was married to an American woman. That could only mean one thing – Julius Khumalo! Was Julius implicated in some sort of racket? Miles fought to keep his expression neutral.

'What kind of money are we talking about?'

'Depends on the vehicle,' Oliver replied. 'But I need to cover my costs.'

'So there is a mark-up?' Miles asked.

'Just enough to make it worthwhile. We're talking about a Government Minister and his wife here. If this story got out, they could lose a helluva lot. So, are you interested or not?'

'Oh I'm definitely interested. You can count on that.'

'So, do you want to work out a deal, Mr Cameron?' Oliver peered with alcohol-blurred eyes at Miles.

'I do, Mr Jordace. I certainly do.'

The sun room ran along the left-hand side of the house. It was Lydia's favourite place. She loved the huge picture windows with their magnificent views across the garden and the sight of the birds flocking to gather the nuts that she had hung in baskets from the tree branches. She had even installed a bird bath within view of her favourite armchair where she could watch the manikins playing in the sparkling water.

Inside the sun room, the wide window sills supported huge Zulu baskets woven in a variety of bright colours and geometrical shapes. One wall had wooden shelves that housed Lydia's stunning collection of African beadwork. The amber paintwork and polished wooden floors gave the room a warm, golden glow in the sunshine.

Lydia's collection of pens, paper and inks were stored in various boxes in the corner, and her latest artwork was leaning upright against one of the boxes. She had been influenced by Art Nouveau and the ornate lines of Aubrey Beardsley, and she was delighted with her recent efforts. So much so, that she was thinking of producing a series of greetings cards in various designs to sell at one of the arts and crafts shops in town. Lydia's creative flair had already proved popular in Bulawayo and Mutare, and friends had said there was a market for her designs in Harare, too. As soon as the baby was born, and she was feeling fit again, she was determined to expand the thriving cottage industry she had already started.

But, right now, her back was aching and she felt tired. She looked up at Miles who was pacing the room with a determined set to his jaw and deep frown lines etched into his brow. He was agitated and had been so since his return from the capital. Impatiently, he checked his watch and glanced out of the window waiting for their guests to arrive. He agreed to sit down when Lydia pleaded for respite, but he perched on the edge of the chair ready to pounce the minute the car came into view.

'Darling, please try to relax. You'll give yourself a heart attack at this rate.'

Miles shrugged helplessly. 'I'm sorry, sweetheart. It's just that this is important. If I'm right, and Julius Khumalo is up to his neck in corruption and double-dealing, I want to have a hand in exposing him.'

Lydia shuffled uncomfortably in the armchair and rested her cup of tea on top of her bump. Miles jumped up to rearrange the cushions behind her back, but she took his hand and begged him to sit still for a minute.

'They said they'd be here by noon,' Miles glanced at his watch. 'It's gone that now.'

Lydia laughed. 'It's ten past twelve. They're hardly late. They're busy people. Doug Macintosh never stops working, according to his wife, and Geoff Nyarota is a newspaper editor. He must find it impossible to get away from his office on time.'

'But this is important,' Miles persisted. 'We're talking about a major scandal involving top politicians. Doug reckons that there are a number of Ministers involved in the scam. He said that he and Geoff have been investigating the rumours for months now. This might be just the lead they're looking for.'

'And it might just lead to nothing,' Lydia cautioned. 'So be prepared for a disappointment.'

'I won't be disappointed. I know that for a fact. That American guy I met in the hotel said he could get me a car if I had the money to pay for it. He said that he had contacts in the Government.' Miles was cut short by the sound of tyres crunching over the gravel in the drive. He jumped to his feet and ran outside where two men were climbing out of a dusty vehicle.

'Welcome to Scarfell Farm!' Miles extended his hand to the editor of the Bulawayo Chronicle.

Geoff Nyarota took the outstretched hand in a firm grip and his kindly African features broke into a huge grin that lit up his face. 'Good to meet you, Miles.'

Doug Macintosh followed them into the sun room where Lydia was waiting. In spite of her pregnancy, she looked thin and gaunt and her huge green eyes seemed almost luminous against her alabaster skin. She had cut her hair short in a fashionable spiky crop and she looked far too young to be a pregnant mother.

'Hello Doug,' Lydia offered her cheek for a kiss. 'Mr Nyarota. What a pleasure to meet you. I'm one of your most avid readers.'

'It's true,' Miles gestured for them all to sit down. 'She reads the Chronicle from cover to cover. I don't know how she finds the time.'

'Well I do have rather a lot of time on my hands at the moment,' Lydia pointed towards the bump and they all laughed. 'Most of my normal activities have been curtailed. Now, can I get you all a drink?'

The three men waited politely until Lydia had left the room then they drew up their chairs and leaned forward. The house was quiet and all that could be heard was the merry chirping of a blue warbill outside.

'Geoff reckons that your conversation with the American could be dynamite.' Doug said. 'He thinks it could open up many more lines of investigation.'

'So you're already investigating the allegations?' asked Miles.

Geoff Nyarota nodded and his deep sonorous voice dropped to a whisper. 'We've had a tip-off from one of the Willowvale Directors claiming that Government Ministers are using their powers to buy cars at cheap prices and then sell on at a profit. We've been looking into it for months now. We're calling the investigation "Willowgate" after the Watergate scandal that two newspaper reporters uncovered in America. We already have a number of names, but we've not been able to pursue an actual transaction. If what you say is correct, the American, Oliver Jordace, might lead us straight to Julius Khumalo himself.'

That's right,' Miles confirmed. 'Jordace said his contact was an American woman who was married to an MP. There's only one man in the Government with an American wife. It has to be Khumalo.'

'I agree,' Geoff's forehead glistened with sweat and he patted his domed pate with a clean white handkerchief folded into a square. Gratefully, he took the cold drink from Lydia and downed it in one go. 'There is one thing that puzzles me,' he continued, belching quietly behind the handkerchief. 'Why is this fellow, Jordace, so indiscreet?'

'He was drunk.' Miles declared. 'He'd been swigging scotch on his own all evening. I think the liquor had loosened his tongue.'

'That's very likely,' Doug chipped in. 'Besides, I reckon they're starting to get a bit too cocky for their own good. They've been getting away with it for so long that they're not bothering to be cautious any more.'

'We're also puzzled as to why Julius Khumalo would want to risk his reputation for a simple money-making exercise,' Geoff mused. 'He's renowned for his honesty and integrity. It seems strange that he should be prepared to throw all that away.'

'Nothing surprises me where that guy is concerned,' Miles growled. 'And as for his honesty and integrity…. what are they in comparison with an easy buck? The Julius Khumalo I know has no integrity. He has no honesty. It's all a sham. So what do you want me to do?' Miles chewed his bottom lip - a sure sign that he was anxious.

'Go through with the deal,' Geoff replied. 'Let Jordace think that you're in the market for one of his cars and we'll follow you every step of the way.'

Lydia felt the unborn baby kick against her stomach and she gasped. Immediately, Miles rushed to her side, but she pushed him away with an apologetic wave of her hand. 'Sorry folks. I think I must have a rugby player in here. When he kicks, he can take my breath away. It's nothing, please ignore it. I'm fine now.'

'I want you to take it right through to purchase,' Geoff waited until Miles was seated again. 'Are you okay with that?'

'Oh Miles, are you sure this is the right thing to do?' Lydia interjected. 'It could be dangerous. Why not let the Chronicle continue with its own investigation. It seems that they already have a plethora of evidence concerning Willowgate.'

'They don't have anything against Julius Khumalo,' Miles' eyes narrowed and his jaw muscles clenched. 'He was involved in the murder of my entire family. He got away with that, but he won't get away with this.'

'Well there's no doubt that if this little lot breaks, and Julius is involved, his career will come crashing down around him like a house of cards,' said Doug. 'He'll be finished.'

Miles stared into the distance. 'And I'll be the one who pulled his house down. I'll be there to watch as Julius Khumalo falls, just like he watched while I buried my entire family. It will be a just revenge, I can tell you that.'

The Bulawayo Chronicle's relentless pursuit of Government corruption gathered momentum after Miles led them directly to Oliver Jordace and his top level connections. With concrete evidence that corruption was rife, President Robert Mugabe was forced to set up an official committee to investigate the so-called Willowgate scandal.

The Commission was chaired by Justice Wilson Sandura. Its brief was to look into the irregular sales of new cars by the Government-owned Willowvale Motor Industries. Their findings would be published the following year. The Government reassured the people that, if politicians were abusing their Parliamentary privileges, heads would roll. It was a pledge made by President Robert Mugabe himself. And the people could trust their President.

Julius was shocked by the allegations. He knew that such a scandal could break the fragile Unity Accord and destroy the Government's credibility, but he was too much of a realist to believe that the allegations were unfounded. He knew that many of his African brothers were motivated by money, and that their lust for wealth and power far exceeded their desire to serve their country, but he did not believe that the malpractice was as widespread as these early reports were suggesting. He knew from his own experience that it was impossible for MPs to obtain cars without their request being sanctioned by the Ministry of Industry and Technology. It was unlikely that the corruption would reach that far.

Even so, Julius was troubled as he pulled into the driveway of his home. His spirits sank even deeper when he spotted Oliver Jordace's car parked there. The man was a pest, Julius thought with a sigh. He had lost count of the times when he had been compelled to share his evenings with the blunt American. But Lucie seemed to enjoy the man's company. On one occasion, Julius had complained that Lucie's affections might be misconstrued, but she had resented his accusations and had flounced out of the room. Exhausted after a long day at work, and too angry to trust his temper, Julius had left her alone until they had both calmed down and could pretend that nothing had happened.

Wearily, Julius climbed the steep steps that led up to his front door. He vowed not to make a scene tonight. His head was aching and he did not want to start a fight in his own home.

'Julius! You're back early.' Lucie jumped up from the sofa where she had been sitting with Oliver Jordace. Her cheeks were flushed and her eyes were bright. Julius noticed that she accidentally spilled a drop of wine on the carpet, but she did not seem to care and he said nothing. But he did search his wife's eyes as she leaned forward to kiss him, puzzled by the way she avoided his gaze. He was dismayed to find that her breath was tinged with alcohol and he wondered just how much she had drunk so far.

Tenderly, he took her chin between his thumb and forefinger and raised her face to meet his. 'Are you all right, little bird?'

Lucie shook herself free. 'Of course I'm all right. Oliver has only just arrived. We were just talking about you.'

Julius threw his briefcase on the chair and accepted a drink from the maid. 'I hope I was a sufficiently engaging topic of conversation!'

'We were talking about Willowgate,' Oliver felt physically disadvantaged by being seated in the presence of this towering giant and he got to his feet. Standing upright, the two men were on a par and Oliver felt more confident. 'It could spell trouble for some people.'

'It will certainly spell trouble for those who have courted trouble,' Julius agreed. 'I have every faith in the Sandura Commission to root out any corrupt and evil influences.'

Oliver stood with his legs slightly apart. 'That's a bit strong buddy. We're talking about a few guys trying to make a quick buck, that's all. We're not talking genocide!

Julius glared at the man standing in front of him. 'We are talking about corruption by the people's elected representatives,' he spat out the words. 'We are talking about people abusing their positions of trust and undermining the entire credibility of the Zimbabwe nation.'

'Don't you think you're overreacting just a little? I mean, do you really think that politicians here are any different from those the world over? Of course not. Everyone's out to make a fast buck! Money makes the world go around, remember?' Oliver slugged the last of his whiskey and dropped the glass on the table. 'And if you can't accept that, old buddy, you're living in cloud-cuckoo-land!'

'I will never accept that, buddy.' Julius gritted his teeth and hot Matabele blood pumped through his veins. 'Nor will I accept being spoken to in that fashion in my own home. I must ask you to leave. I do not want you here.'

'Julius!' Lucie thrust herself between the two men. 'Don't be so ridiculous. Oliver is my guest... my friend! It's not for you to say whether he's wanted here. I want him here!'

Julius grabbed Lucie's arm and pulled her to one side. 'You, woman, would do well to keep your mouth shut. This is my home and I will say who is welcome.'

'I'm not one of your servile African wives, you arrogant bastard!' Lucie turned on Julius with fists flying. 'How dare you talk to me like that!'

'Take it easy, baby,' Oliver gripped her hand and dragged her away from Julius. 'The guy's all screwed up by his own integrity. He's never gonna understand.'

'Baby?' Julius echoed in disbelief. 'You call my wife "baby"?'

'Yes he does,' Lucie snuffled through her tears. 'Because he cares about me. He cares more about me than you ever will.'

'He cares about you! Julius cried out in disbelief. 'I am your husband! I love you more than my own life.'

'No you don't! You love "the people" far more than you could ever love me. I'm sick of it. I'm going out. I need some air. Will you take me for a drive, Oliver?'

Julius grabbed her wrist and she screamed in pain. 'You will stay here, woman.'

'No I will not!' Lucie wrenched herself free and ran to the door. 'I will do what I like when I like. I'm a free woman and I'm not going to play second fiddle to some crummy African country any more. And as for this stupid Willowgate scandal, I don't care if it all blows up in your face! I don't care if you and your entire Government come crashing down. I'm an American. I don't give a shit about Africa!'

Lydia was hot. She had kicked the bedcovers on to the floor, but still her sleep was fitful. Beneath her, the white cotton sheet was damp with sweat and crumpled. Her short hair was pressed against her head like a boy's and her pale skin glowed eerily in the moonlight. She glanced at the bedside clock. It was only half past two. It was going to be a long night. She wanted to lie on her side but her belly was too big and heavy, so she lay on her back instead. Outside the window, bathed in silver, the African night was still.

Miles lay beside her, sleeping. His breath was deep and even and she turned her head towards him and watched him quietly. He was so handsome. His long lashes lay curled against his cheeks and his hair was tousled against the pillow. He looked so tanned and strong that she almost felt ashamed of her own scrawny body with its bulbous belly and pallid hue. Silently, she vowed to get back in shape as soon as the baby was born and, with the warm African sun on her face, it would not be long before she had some colour in her cheeks and flesh on her bones. By then, of course, she would be a wife and a mother and the mistress of Scarfell Farm. Who could possibly ask for more?

She tried to turn over, but the baby moved and she felt a sudden searing pain in the pit of her stomach. She screamed and shot out a hand for support. Miles was awake in an instant.

'What is it, sweetheart?' he sat up and tried to take her into his arms.

Lydia wanted to be comforted, but a second crucifying pain cut her in half and she let out a howl of anguish. She turned to him, her eyes wide with fright, as another spasm tore into her.

'Hang on! I'll ring the doctor. Don't try to move!'

'No time!' Lydia gasped. 'Just get me to the hospital…. Hurry!'

Miles tugged on his jeans and yanked an old tee-shirt out of the dirty linen basket. He rummaged around for one of Lydia's dresses, but panicked when he saw her drag herself out of bed and lurch towards him.

'It doesn't matter,' she cried, clutching her belly with both hands. 'Just get me to the car. We don't have much time. The pain…. I can't bear it!'

After a nightmare journey in which every pothole, every corner and every gear change seemed like agony, they finally pulled up at the entrance to the Lady Halliwell Hospital in Bulawayo. Staff swung into action as soon as they saw the dishevelled young farmer stumble into the maternity unit with his pregnant wife in his arms. Relieved of his precious burden, Miles could only stand by and watch helplessly as Lydia was laid on a stretcher and urgently wheeled out of sight into the labyrinth of corridors beyond the swing doors.

And then she was gone and Miles was left alone and forlorn, gazing stupidly at the doors that had seemed to open up and swallow his beloved wife whole in those last few crazy seconds. He did not know what to do. He was still standing there when one of the doors swung open again and a young nurse emerged. Unconsciously, Miles backed away from her, afraid to hear what she might have to say.

'Mr Cameron?'

'That's me. How is she, nurse?'

'She's in a bad way, I'm afraid.' Gently, the young woman led him to one of the plastic chairs that were lined up against the magnolia walls. 'She's gone into premature labour. Your wife is very weak.'

'She was in such pain! You have to help her!'

'There is another problem, I'm afraid. The baby is in the wrong position. We cannot guarantee that the baby will survive….'

'Oh my God!' Miles held his head in his hands. 'What about my wife? She'll be okay, won't she?'

'It's too early to say. She may have to have an emergency caesarean. Please try not to worry, Mr Cameron. Your wife is in good hands. We're doing everything we can. Would you like a cup of tea before I go?'

Miles shook his head. 'For God's sake, please take care of them,' he begged as the nurse stood up to leave. 'They're all I have.'

The night was hot in Harare, too, but Julius did not even try to sleep. He knew it was impossible. After last week, when the Willowgate scandal had first hit the headlines, he doubted he would ever sleep easily again. Instead, he paced the bedroom floor. He picked up the framed photograph of his wife and stared at it. Lucie's lovely blue eyes gazed back at him. They had hardly spoken since that terrible night when she had stormed out with Oliver Jordace, but Julius knew that events today eclipsed even those ugly memories. Angrily, he tossed the photograph on to the bed, but it missed and the glass splintered as it fell on to the floor.

Julius slammed out of the bedroom and went into the study. His desk was strewn with papers, but there was one piece of paper that stood out amid the other debris. Julius picked it up and began to read it, but the words swam before his eyes. It was his resignation. All it needed was his signature. Sadly, he leaned his elbows on the desk and pressed his knuckles into his brow. He knew that this piece of paper represented the end of his good name. Henceforth, his reputation would be in tatters. But he had no choice.

He had not known why he had been called into the urgent top-level meeting earlier that day. He could tell by the sombre expressions of those present that the matter was serious and he was puzzled, but not alarmed.

It did not take long for him to realise the enormity of their accusations, delivered in grim, solemn tones. At first he had been shocked and confused. He did not deny that he had requested new cars from Willowvale Motor Industries on more than one occasion, but these were for his wife and a small number of party officials, he explained. It was a minor parliamentary privilege, and he had merely exercised that right. The cars could not have been sold on for profits because he had seen the recipients driving their vehicles recently. They were clearly still in the hands of their rightful owners.

But Julius had not been prepared for the incontrovertible evidence of his culpability that was spread on the table in front of him. He had not been expecting to see his signature at the bottom of requests for three, four and even six new cars at a time! And no, he had not been able to explain how such a thing could have happened. Nor did he know what had happened to the surplus cars that had been purchased at rock bottom prices in his name. Julius had read the list of private buyers that was handed to him, and he groaned inwardly when he saw the vast amounts of money that had exchanged hands and the profits that had been made.

He realised immediately what had happened. He saw with cruel clarity how he had been duped by his wife's skilful machinations and his shoulders sagged with shame. He knew he was innocent, and the three men sitting across the table knew he was innocent, but all accepted that he would never be able to prove it without dragging his wife's good name, and his marriage, into the mire.

'How did you find out about this?' Julius' voice croaked with emotion.

'It appears that your wife was in league with an American businessman, Oliver Jordace. You know him, I believe? It appears that Mr Jordace had been boasting to a young Bulawayo farmer that he could get cars on the black market with the help of your wife. The farmer was suspicious and contacted the editor of the Bulawayo Chronicle. Mr Jordace sailed blindly into a trap, which, as you can see, led directly to you. You may well have avoided being named in the scandal if it hadn't been for the efforts of that young farmer from Bulawayo.'

'This farmer,' Julius frowned darkly. 'What was his name?'

'Cameron,' came the reply. 'Mr Miles Cameron.'

Miles Cameron. The words were still echoing in Julius' head as he clutched his resignation letter in his hands later that night. Miles Cameron had been instrumental in his downfall. It was a bitter pill to swallow, but Julius knew that he had no choice other than to resign. His political career was finished. Wearily, Julius flattened out the paper creases and picked up a pen. He took a deep breath and signed his name in his customary bold hand. He then folded the letter into an envelope and sealed it. The deed was done. His parliamentary career was over.

But Julius had yet to confront his wife.

He did not know where she was, but he knew that she would be with Oliver Jordace. There was nothing he could do about that for, not only had he lost his reputation and his good name tonight, he had lost his wife, too.

Julius waited at the window of the darkened room for Lucie's return. Before long, a car's headlights swept into view and he moved back out of sight. Oliver Jordace was driving with Lucie in the passenger seat. Sick to the stomach, Julius watched them chatting together, clearly at ease in each other's company. And then their heads moved closer until they were joined in a long, intimate kiss.

Julius tried to tear his gaze away, to avoid the torture of betrayal, but he could not escape his demons. He witnessed every minute of their passionate embrace and his heart was truly broken. Silently, like a dangerous predator, he waited in the shadowed hallway as his wife made her way up the steps and fumbled in her bag for her key.

'Welcome home!' Julius flung open the door and Lucie took a step back in horror.

'Are you spying on me, you bastard?'

'You whore!' Julius seized her arm as she tried to push past him. 'You lying, scheming whore!'

'Let me go!' Lucie screamed and swung out at him with her fists clenched. 'I hate you! Let me go!'

'I will let you go,' Julius twisted both her arms behind her back and pinned her against the wall. 'But first you must tell me why you did it. I know why you and Jordace wanted my signature for the cars. That is easy. That is just greed. But why.... why did you have to betray your marriage vows? Why, Lucie?'

'Because it was fun!' Lucie tried in vain to wriggle free. 'And because he cares more about me than you ever will. He isn't obsessed with Africa or its people, and neither am I. I'm sick of Africa. I want to go home to Boston. I want to be free!'

'I will set you free, whore. But you will never see your daughter again. Devon stays here. You can go back to America with your lover. I do not care about that. But Devon stays here. She will grow up with her feet firmly rooted in African soil.'

'Screw you! And screw Africa!' Lucie yelled. 'I don't need you and I don't need to be saddled with your kid, either! I'd rather be with Oliver! I don't love you any more. Get it? I just don't love you!'

Julius heard the words, but they seemed come from a great distance. His head was spinning and a red mist floated in front of his eyes. Suddenly, he felt calm and suffused with strange powers. He heard the crunch as the knuckles of his clenched fist met Lucie's high cheekbone. He felt the soft, creamy flesh tear under the impact, but he did not know how it had happened. Impassively, he watched her fall like a rag doll at his feet, and only then was he able to tear himself from his trance.

Lucie lay slumped against the front door. There was blood on her face and she was sobbing. Terrified of what he had done, Julius knelt down beside her, stammering his apologies, but she pushed him away and struggled to her feet.

'Don't you ever come near me again, Julius Khumalo,' she leaned against the door and spat at him. 'I'm leaving you! Do you hear me? I hate you!'

Julius did not try to stop her as she staggered out into the night. He simply waited until the tail lights of her car had disappeared from view and then he closed the door and sat at the foot of the stairs with his head in his hands. His career was in ruins and now his marriage was over. And his pain was so intense that he felt sure it would kill him.

'Daddy!' He heard Devon's voice crying in the darkness - a tiny child's voice trying to make itself heard above the chaos.

'Daddy's coming, little one,' Julius took the stairs two at a time and burst into his daughter's bedroom where he plucked her out of bed and crushed her against his chest. She was warm and soft and small. So small. He buried his head in her pink fluffy pyjamas and forced back his tears. 'It's okay, little one. Daddy's here. Everything is going to be fine. There's nothing to worry about. Nothing at all.'

Dawn broke and the day shift arrived at the Lady Halliwell Hospital in Bulawayo. People began milling about and the sights and sounds of everyday life resumed. Few people noticed the young man sitting there with his head leaning awkwardly against the wall. They did not know his pain, nor his fear.

Miles jumped to his feet when the nurse arrived and tapped him on the shoulder. The doctor was with her. 'How is she?' he asked nervously.

The doctor smiled kindly. 'She is going to be fine. So, too, is your son, Mr Cameron. We may have to keep them both here for a while, just to make sure, but mother and son are doing just fine.'

'I have a son?' Miles did not know how or why, but he suddenly burst into tears. 'I'm sorry. I'm so sorry,' he spluttered. 'It's just....'

'I understand,' the doctor nodded. He had witnessed too many tears of grief to be embarrassed by tears of relief. 'Perhaps you would like to see them for a couple of minutes.'

Miles followed the doctor into the side ward where Lydia was lying in bed attached to a drip. She looked frail. Anxiously, Miles bent down and brushed her lips with his own. 'Hello, sweetheart,' he whispered.

'Miles....' Lydia tried to talk, but her voice was barely audible. 'Miles, they say that I will never have any more children. I'm so sorry, Miles. I didn't mean to let you down. Can you forgive me?'

'There's nothing to forgive, my darling. You've given me a son, and you're alive. What more could I possibly want?'

'But you always said you wanted lots of children at Scarfell Farm.'

'Our son will carry the name of Cameron. Through him, Scarfell Farm will live on. I'm happy, sweetheart.'

'Are you Miles? Are you really happy?'

Miles paused and stared into the distance. 'I am happy, Lydia! I am really, really happy because I have a son! And now, Mrs Cameron, I would like to go and meet this boy of mine.'

'He's in an incubator. He's very weak.'

'He may be weak now,' Miles declared proudly. 'But he will grow strong soon enough. He is Ewan Cameron of Scarfell Farm. And he will never be weak again.'

18

It was autumn and the recent rains had transformed the lowveld into a sea of lush green crops and golden wheat fields. The Masvingo province was a fertile land and the abundance of natural water from the Runde River and Lake Mutirikwe had encouraged early settlers to build vast citrus estates and a thriving sugar industry there. With a huge dam spanning the Mutirikwe River, and extensive irrigation, the land was now a rich source of revenue for Zimbabwe.

Masvingo was steeped in history. It was there that Cecil Rhodes had established the first permanent white settlement in the nineteenth century. It was also the site of one of Africa's most ancient and holy places – the vast granite ruins of Great Zimbabwe. It had taken successive kings and high priests more than four hundred years to build this mighty citadel. Great Zimbabwe had once housed a thriving community of thirty thousand people, but as time passed the ancients were driven from their homes by drought, locusts and attacks from marauding tribes. Over the centuries, the gigantic hill complex became a silent, brooding place standing against a backdrop of looming cliffs and rocky hills. Creepers grew over the outer walls of the Great Enclosure and long grasses swayed at the foot of the proud Conical Tower. The ruins had been discovered in 1867 by a white hunter who stripped away the remnants of neglect and helped restore the magnificent structure to a semblance of its former glory. Now, Great Zimbabwe was one of the country's premier tourist attractions.

And one particular tourist, a young Master Ewan Cameron on holiday with his parents, was about to receive his very first history lesson of the wonders of his ancient homeland!

'Just look at this great, big wall.' Miles pointed at the eleven metre high wall that snaked like a python around the crest of the rocky hill. 'It's five metres thick in some places.'

'Big wall!' Ewan jabbed a chubby forefinger at the massive structure and grinned delightedly.

'That's right,' Miles beamed with pride and deposited the wriggling child onto the ground where he promptly squatted on his haunches to examine a blade of grass.

'He may be a tad too young for a detailed history lesson, darling,' Lydia suggested tactfully.

'He's never too young to learn about his heritage,' Miles replied. 'This is the largest ancient stone structure in sub-Saharan Africa. I've been reading up on it. They reckon over a million granite blocks were used to build it, and every one was cut to size and fitted without mortar. Incredible!'

Lydia stood behind her husband and wound her arms around his waist. She then reached up and planted a damp kiss on the back of his neck. 'Not as amazing as you are, my darling. Your enthusiasm never fails to amaze me…. Ewan! No!'

Lydia disengaged herself from her husband and swooped down on her two-year-old who was about to stuff a clump of dried grass into his mouth. She lifted him up in her arms and swung him round until he was squealing with joy. Miles stood by with his hands thrust into the pockets of his jeans and watched them happily.

Lydia had recovered well from the trauma of childbirth and she had filled out with a diet of good food, warm sun and the sweet, clean air of Africa. She was still as slim as a reed, but her body was soft and supple and her gentle curves suited the line of her fitted tee-shirt and black cycle shorts perfectly. Her legs were tanned and a pair of white socks and chunky white trainers complemented her shapely legs and trim ankles. She had grown her hair into a soft bob with a wispy fringe that ruffled like silk in the breeze and shone like fire in the midday sun. She held her excited toddler at arms' length as she spun round on the spot. Ewan was transported with glee.

'Phew!' Eventually Lydia had to draw the dizzying game to a halt.

'More!' Ewan yelled, raising two little arms to reinforce his demand.

'No more. Mummy's exhausted. You're a big boy now. You're much too heavy to spin round for long.'

With the easy good nature that he had inherited from his father, Ewan toddled off to explore the intricacies of Great Zimbabwe and, before long, was rewarded with the discovery of a tiny pile of rocks at floor level that had crumbled away from the main wall. With a child's unerring instinct for exploiting the most minor structural defect, he promptly added to the monument's architectural decline by prodding the loose earth around one of the stones until it fell in a puff of dust into his lap. Delighted by his achievement, he jumped to his feet and ran back to his parents who were chatting nearby. After being suitably impressed by the pile of dust in his palm, they then took a hand each and swung him back and forth as they ambled around the Great Enclosure.

The weather was warm and the sky was a clear duck-egg blue as the family wandered around the ruins. They ate a picnic lunch of biltong and cold chicken sandwiches followed by pawpaws and sweet bananas in the shade of the Conical Tower. After that, they wound their way through the labyrinth of stairways and passages that led to the top of the hill complex.

They were exhausted when they finally reached the top and even Ewan's boundless energy was sapped. His sun hat had fallen down his back and was now hanging on by two cotton threads sewn on by Sixpence's wife, Grace. His chubby cheeks were flushed with exertion.

'Me ride, Daddy!' He stood in front of his father and craned his neck upwards. Miles settled the lad on his shoulders and held on to his ankles with both hands as he and Lydia continued to cross the red carpet of earth that formed the plateau on the roof of the complex.

Great Zimbabwe was built into the cliff walls, eighty metres above the valley floor. It was a magical place, and Miles and Lydia gazed around with awe. The spirits of the ancient Kings and the tribes who had once lived and worked here filled the senses and there was an aura of calm that even young Ewan seemed to feel. Unsurprisingly, however, his characteristically brief reverie was easily interrupted by the sight of two strange birds striding across the open veld in the distance.

'Bird!' Ewan cried, stabbing the horizon with his busy little forefinger.

'They're Secretary Birds,' Miles turned to Lydia. 'Members of the eagle family. See their black leggings and wing feathers and their sober grey fronts? People thought they looked like nineteenth century office clerks.'

'Yes! I see what you mean,' Lydia peered into her binoculars. 'They're very staid... apart from those funky orange circles round their eyes! They look like they're wearing stage make-up. What an odd looking pair they are.'

Conscious that he was no longer the centre of attention, Ewan bobbed up and down on his father's shoulders, begging to be let down. Miles dutifully obeyed, but the boy's natural propensity for danger was curtailed by the restraining grip of his father's hand when he ventured too close to the edge.

'And there's Lake Mutirikwe in the distance,' Lydia raised her sunglasses on top of her head and let her binoculars dangle on their cord. 'It looks so beautiful from up here.'

'It sure does,' Miles agreed. 'And I reckon we had better be getting back there pretty soon. This little chap is starting to get tired.'

With that, the Camerons trudged back to their car and set off for their rented holiday chalet on the shores of Lake Mutirikwe. The luxury lodges were popular with local and foreign tourists. They had been built in the early years of independence, when Zimbabwe was emerging as a popular destination for travellers, and they had flourished. Lake Mutirikwe was a perfect holiday spot where visitors could enjoy scenic drives around the shoreline and water sports enthusiasts could indulge their passions for water-skiing and sailing. Barbel, bottlenose, red-bellied bream and black bass swam in abundance in the deep waters of Zimbabwe's second largest lake, and proved an irresistible magnet for fisherman of all ages. For those who simply wished to sit and stare, the glorious sight of the gently rippling waters, and the dusky-blue backdrop of the distant Beza and Nguni mountains, guaranteed peace and tranquillity.

And Miles was not the first tourist to bask in the warmth of sundown, sipping cool white wine as the sun slid below the horizon. Their lodge had been built in the style of a traditional rondavel with polished local stone and a heavy thatched roof that hung over the balcony. Inside, the solid wooden furniture was carved from mukwa. A brass fan hung from the centre of the wooden poles that supported the open thatched roof and lacy mosquito nets were gathered at the corners of the bed. The room smelled fresh and earthy and the small windows, although keeping out the light, also kept it cool. The lodges, erected in the midst of the acacia trees and the wild wisteria that dominated the local bushveld, felt private and cosy.

'He's spark out,' Lydia opened the door that led on to the balcony and sat in the chair beside Miles. She placed her glass of Coke and a bar of milk chocolate on the patio table and then took a deep breath and sighed contentedly. 'He wouldn't settle without his teddy, though. I'm so glad we remembered to bring it.'

Miles reached across the table and took her hand in his. 'I used to have a panda called Pandaloo,' he recalled. 'And my sister used to suck a tea towel before she went to sleep. It was known as Beth's GoiGoi. She would suck them until they wore out and had to be replaced with new ones when she wasn't looking.'

'I remember that ridiculous orange ball of yours.'

'Chuff!' Miles laughed.

'That's it. Chuff! What a daft name.'

'I'll have you know that ball had magical properties. Chuff meant a lot to me.'

They both giggled and Lydia let go of his hand to take a sip of her drink and break off a piece of chocolate. 'It's so nice to be here. This place is heaven.'

'They've done wonders with the bush. It wasn't like this when I was a kid. They've obviously tapped into Zim's growing tourism market. There's a lot of money to be made from tourism these days.'

'We ought to be doing something like this,' Lydia said. 'Scarfell Farm would make an ideal base for tourists to visit places like Chipinga, the Matopos and Matabeleland in general. We could turn some of our less productive land over to holiday chalets and make a small fortune!'

'Ever the entrepreneur!' Miles teased.

'Well you've got to look to the future, darling. Nothing stands still, you know.'

Miles watched a pretty impala doe grazing on the plains below the lodges. The rest of the herd were allogrooming - mutual grooming to keep those hard-to-reach places clean and parasite free. 'I used to think that time stood still here in Africa,' he mused. 'But I guess old Harold Macmillan was right when he said the winds of change were sweeping across Africa. They're still blowing today.'

'The winds of change will always blow across this continent,' said Lydia. 'But they're warm and welcome winds now. They brought me back to you, and gave us little Ewan.'

They fell silent as the sun shot mauve and crimson rays across the coral pink sky. All was quiet, apart from the aloes rustling in the breeze. Swiftly, as was the way in Africa, the night cloaked them in its coal-black mantle and they gathered up their drinks and went indoors.

Ewan was sleeping soundly. His dark brown hair, tinged with copper highlights, was ruffled against the pillow and he was sucking his thumb in a contented sleep. Teddy was squashed face down against his chest and secured in a vice-like grip. Gently, Lydia leaned over the sleeping infant and tried to remove the furry toy, but Ewan tightened his hold on his precious sleeping companion and Lydia gave up with a smile. He was such a beautiful boy, she thought with pride. He had his father's handsome eyes and devilish smile. And he was a precious, much-loved son.

Miles threaded his arms around his wife's waist as they stood beside the bed and then, quietly but firmly, he led her to their own king-sized bed where he lay her down on the soft quilt and cupped her face in his hands.

'I love you,' he whispered, running his finger over the sensuous lines of her breasts.

'I love you, too,' Lydia responded, instinctively arching her body towards his.

Devon Khumalo was only three years old, but she was quite convinced that she looked very grown up indeed in her denim dungarees with the shiny pink buttons. Most of all, she liked her pink Barbie Doll ankle socks with the sparkling flowers embroidered up the side. As she sat on her chair directly opposite her father, her little legs stuck out so that her glittering socks could be seen and admired by fellow diners in the fashionable Harare restaurant.

Her black hair was soft and curly and hung in bunches held together with Barbie Doll hair clasps. Her skin was the colour of fresh honey and her big dark eyes glistened under a curtain of long lashes. But when she looked across the table at her father this seemingly sophisticated young lady betrayed her tender years, for her rosy cheeks were smeared by a liberal spoonful of ice cream that had somehow missed her mouth.

Now, reluctantly squirming in her chair, she was subjected to the ruthless flannel of her nanny, and the outwardly stern, but privately amused, expression of her doting father. Only when her nanny had inspected her cheeks and chin was she allowed to resume the task of demolishing the huge ice cream sundae in front of her.

Her father, Julius, sat opposite, reading a letter that had arrived in the post that day. Devon was pleased about the letter because it had made her father laugh out loud and hug her tightly. Devon had grown used to the sight of her beloved father standing quietly at the window. Sometimes, she had seen him hold his head in his hands and swallow hard as though he was trying not to cry. She did not know why he seemed so sad and distant sometimes. All she knew was that when she called out his name, his face would light up with a smile and she would run into his arms for the comforting hugs she loved so much. Today, her father was playful and light-hearted with her. And he had brought her to their favourite place where the ice cream sundaes came in big glasses with an umbrella on the top.

Julius folded the letter and placed it on the table beside his coffee. Even so, he could not help but stare at it and recall every word that was printed on it. His father, Comrade Moses Khumalo of Matabeleland, had been officially classified as a National War Hero by the ZANU-PF Government and, as such, would be afforded a full military funeral at Zimbabwe's prestigious resting place, Heroes' Acre. His body would be brought up from Tshotshololo and laid to rest with the other great war veterans. As a National Hero, rather than a District or Provincial Hero, Moses Khumalo would receive the highest commendation given to those who had sacrificed their lives for freedom. President Robert Mugabe himself had attended every funeral of the thirty three National Heroes who lay at Heroes' Acre, and he would be present at the burial of Moses Khumalo, too. Thenceforth, the soul of this great freedom fighter, who had lived and died for Africa, would be celebrated on the nation's official Heroes' Day in August. And his spirit would live on in the hearts of the people.

'This is a great day for the Khumalo family,' Julius delcared. 'Your grandfather will be laid to rest at Heroes' Acre and President Mugabe himself will be present at the burial.'

Devon peeped out from behind the towering sundae and grinned at her father with a creamy white moustache. 'Bear..reyall...' she mouthed the unfamiliar word.

'Burial,' Julius corrected, but tenderly. 'It is a great honour for us. It means that my shame, and the disgrace heaped upon the House of Khumalo by the woman who was your mother, has not corrupted the honour of the family name and ancestry. It means that one of this country's finest warriors, your grandfather, will not bear the same dishonour as his son. You are too young to understand this, my daughter, but you will understand it one day. And you will be proud.'

Devon nodded happily before tucking into the rest of the ice cream with a hearty gusto. 'Bear reyall,' she repeated the strange word as she licked the delicious strawberry flavour from her spoon.

'And, as a true descendant of the Great King Mzilikazi and the grandchild of Comrade Moses Khumalo, you will stand by my side at Heroes Acre, little one. You are untainted by my shame, my child. Your blood is still pure.'

The sun beat down on the gun carriage that transported the latest National Hero, Moses Khumalo, up the hill that led to the graves at the top of Heroes' Acre. The drive was flanked by msasa trees and kirkia, and by tall lights, painted grey with a white globe on the top. The pinnacle was a magnificent bronze statue of two men and one woman that symbolised those who had fought side-by-side in the liberation war.

The gun carriage was draped with the flag of Zimbabwe, upon which the coffin of the fallen comrade was bedecked with vibrant flowers. Julius walked behind the coffin with his head bowed and his eyes downcast. Next to him, clutching his hand tightly, Devon skipped along, trying not to pick the pretty flowers that lined the route.

Heroes Acre had been built in 1981, shortly after independence, and was constructed with help from the Koreans. The majestic sculptures were carved in bronze with black granite from Mutoko. The walls at Heroes Acre were made from the same stone as the walls of Great Zimbabwe. A central sculpture commemorated the tomb of the unknown soldier and an imposing tower housed the symbolic flame which burned each night. Julius was keenly aware that only great men were buried here. The lawyer, Herbert Chitepo, was here, as was Leopold Takawira, Robert Mugabe's friend and mentor, and his neighbour during the years of imprisonment at Sikombela. Now, Comrade Moses Khumalo, Julius' own father, would join them.

At the top of the hill, Julius and his daughter took their places at the right hand side of the grave. Opposite, the stalls were crowded to bursting with onlookers, well-wishers and those who had come to hear the words of their President.

Julius stood under the massive memorial to the freedom fighters and his dark eyes scanned the eager faces of the crowds. These people were his brothers and sisters. His father had lived and died for them. As he watched them standing there, happy and smiling under the fierce African sun, Julius knew that his father had contributed to their freedom. He knew that his father had been called upon to make some difficult decisions. Moses Khumalo had been asked to set aside love and former loyalties and give his life to the cause. He had accepted this calling, and had remained true to his beliefs to the bitter end. And the end had been cruel and painful, as it would have to be for a man like Moses Khumalo. But it had not been in vain. Julius knew that now.

Beside him, dancing quietly to some unknown tune in her head, his own child had been born in a free land. Devon Khumalo was the beneficiary of the selfless dedication of men like her grandfather, Moses. She, and all the young children born in the new Zimbabwe, should never know the misery of subjugation and oppression. She was free. And she would always be free, for that was the reason why so many had to die. For she was the future for Africa.

When President Robert Mugabe completed his speech, a full gun salute commenced. The heavy guns bellowed out their reports and crashed into the silence of the day. Terrified by the thunderous noise, Devon clutched her father's thigh and tried to hide behind his massive bulk. Gently, he disengaged her and she knew then that he wanted her to be strong and stand alone. Tremulously, she stood small, but proud, and tried hard not to jump when the guns blasted.

Finally, to the sombre strains of a military band, the coffin that bore the remains of Comrade Moses Khumalo was gently lowered into the grave. His body would lie there forever, but his soul would soar to magical places with those of his fallen comrades. Julius watched the coffin sinking into the dark pit. Silently, he asked for forgiveness for the shame he had brought upon the great name of Khumalo. He hoped that his father would understand how easily he had been blinded by love ... and lust ... and he prayed that this moment of national recognition for his father's greatness would somehow atone for his own sins. He swore that he would devote the rest of his life to Africa, and to honouring the Khumalo family name. And his eyes shone with tears.

In March 1990, ten years after the Lancaster House Agreement was first signed, the people of Zimbabwe were once again called upon to elect the party that would govern them for the next ten years.

President Robert Mugabe spoke eloquently and forcefully of the injustice suffered by the indigenous people at the hands of the white minority. He promised them that, if re-elected, he would review the laws governing the acquisition of white farmland that had been agreed at Lancaster House ten years earlier. His assertion that the previous agreement was not working was met with resounding applause at each of his many campaign rallies. White farmers had refused to give up their land voluntarily, he roared, and there were still hundreds of thousands of black Africans without homes. Yet the right to own their own land was one of the reasons they had fought the war in the first place. Without land, the descendants of those brave warriors could never hold up their heads and be proud in their own country, he warned. But if the people of Zimbabwe voted for ZANU-PF in this, their first election that was free from British intervention, things would change. And he, Comrade Robert Mugabe, would be the architect of this change. This was his pledge to the people of Zimbabwe.

And Robert Mugabe won the election on the promise of more land, for land was what the people craved above all else. Now, Mugabe had no choice other than to implement the reforms that had formed the key part of his manifesto. The people of Zimbabwe had spoken and they had made their views clear. They wanted to reclaim the land that was theirs by right. They had given ZANU-PF and President Robert Mugabe a mandate to seize white lands and return them to their rightful owners. They had been promised land under the Lancaster House Agreement ten years ago and it had not been forthcoming. They were not prepared to sit back and wait a further ten years for what was rightfully theirs. The Lancaster House Agreement was due to expire in April 1990. After that, Africa would be rid of its colonial ties with Great Britain and ZANU-PF would be free to govern according to the needs of black majority.

President Robert Mugabe was an intelligent man and he understood full well that he had no choice other than to fulfil his pledge to redistribute white land. He had to move quickly while the people were still buoyed by the optimism of his political rhetoric. Within weeks of winning the 1990 election and taking up office, his Government had established a team of top political and legal advisers. Their brief was to draw up a new Land Acquisition Act. The new law had to be in force within two years and should tighten up on existing loopholes that had enabled white farmers to hang on to their land in the past. The Land Acquisition Act would need to be tough, but it had to be seen to be just in the eyes of the western world. After all Zimbabwe was a democracy, and as such was subject to the codes of conduct for all Commonwealth Nations.

Mugabe knew that the Land Acquisition Act could be a time-bomb if handled badly, and it had the potential to destroy Zimbabwe's social and economic structure if it was implemented without due care and attention.

And everyone knew that only one man could be trusted to act as a legal consultant on such a complex and dangerous piece of legislation. Everyone accepted that Julius Khumalo had been forced to resign from the Government following the Willowgate scandal, but he was still one of Harare's top legal men and they needed his sound judgement.

Miles and Lydia heard the news of the ZANU-PF victory on the radio at their holiday cottage. Although they were both concerned about the result, knowing full well that Mugabe had won the election on the promise of land reform, neither one wanted to spoil the magic of their last day at Lake Mutirikwe. They had enjoyed a carefree two-week break. They were relaxed and happy and determined to stay that way as long as possible.

'Are you still up for a safari drive?' Miles leaned back in the armchair with his feet on the coffee table and watched his wife drying her hair in the mirror.

'I wouldn't miss it for the world,' Lydia shook her tousled locks into shape and turned to look at him. 'A leisurely drive through the Gonorezhou Game Reserve with my family. Now what could be better than that?'

Miles smiled and opened his arms to invite Ewan on to his lap. Chuckling merrily, the youngster clambered up his father's legs and, grabbing at a clump of shirt for support, managed to pull himself into a upright position. Miles held on to his son's outstretched hands and began to move his knees up and down to create a deliciously bumpy ride. Ewan squealed and screamed for more.

'Don't let him get too excited,' Lydia called over her shoulder as she disappeared into the en-suite bathroom. 'He's going to be stuck in a safari truck for quite a while. We need him to stay calm!'

'Calm! You! Not a chance, eh buster?' Miles increased the rough ride and Ewan flopped on to his knees, clinging on to his father's hands with tight little fingers. 'Too much for you, huh? You'll need to toughen up, my boy if you want to ride the rodeo when you grow up.'

Lydia re-emerged from the bathroom in a tight-fitting black vest, white cropped pants and a big, black leather belt. Miles slowed down the bucking bronco and let out a long, slow wolf whistle.

'That's my woman!' he nodded appreciatively. 'And hell, what a woman! Hang on though… have I missed something here? I mean, is the driver some gorgeous Rhodie hunk, or is this all sexy dressing up just for me.'

'It's all for you,' Lydia blushed self-consciously. 'Not that you deserve it. Now get your son ready or we'll miss the start of the drive…. And I wouldn't want to upset the gorgeous truck driver!'

Gonarezhou, "The Place of the Elephants" was a sprawling wilderness in the south-eastern Masvingo Province. There, under a fierce African sun, the mighty Runde River meandered through the plains, its banks ablaze with apple-ring acacia, monkey orange trees and exquisite sabi star blooms of white and crimson.

Sitting in the back of the open safari truck, Miles and Lydia were enchanted by the spectacular Chilojho Cliffs that towered above the open veld and dwarfed the breeding herd of elephants that had ambled down to one of the Runde River pools to drink.

'We'll pause here for a while, if that's okay with you guys,' the driver whispered over his shoulder to avoid disturbing the animals. 'These jumbos will be here for a while. If you look further down the river bank, you'll see that hippo bull is looking pretty irritated right now.'

'Why is that?' Lydia was astonished by the sight of a huge gaping maw with yellowing teeth only a stone's throw away.'

'Oh he's just complaining about the presence of humans in his territory. Don't worry. It's all for show. They're a pretty laid-back bunch out here. We've got hippos sharing their territory with crocodiles in some places.'

'And do they leave each other alone?' asked Miles.

'Mostly, but a big croc' might snatch a young hippo if he was hungry enough. They're still predators, and all predators are opportunists.'

'Sounds pretty much like the human race,' Lydia added, disengaging her camera strap from Ewan's sticky fingers. 'Look darling! Look at those baby elephants playing.'

Ewan followed the direction of her gaze and bounced up and down on the seat beside her. 'Lelephants!' he cried delightedly. 'Lelephants, Mama!'

Enchanted, Miles and Lydia sat in the back of the truck, watching the wonders of nature unfold before their eyes. Elephants were a matriarchal society, with females dominating the herd, and aunts and sisters helping to rear the young. Bulls left the herd at puberty, returning only to mate. Although clearly protective of their young, the adults were content to let the babies push and play at the waterhole, pausing only to deliver a stern reprimand in the form of a shove with a trunk, when the gambolling became too exuberant.

'See,' said Lydia. 'Baby elephants are naughty just like you.'

'And they never stay still, just like you!' Miles added with a frown as he squeezed himself into the far corner to allow Ewan even more space to clamber and climb. 'How come the smallest guy gets the most room, that's what I want to know?' he queried with a grin.

'Because the smallest guy wriggles the most,' Lydia answered on behalf of her frisky child. 'Now don't take your hat off, darling, or you'll burn. Here, let Mummy tie it on again.'

The drive back was slow and easy and, well before they reached their lodge, Ewan had snuggled into his father's arms and was sound asleep. Holding on to his precious bundle with one hand, and with his other arm wrapped around his wife's shoulders, Miles felt that he was happier at that precise moment than he had ever been in his entire life. He kissed the head of his sleeping infant and longed for the day when Ewan would be old enough to recognise and understand the majestic beauty of his African homeland.

And yes, ZANU-PF had won an election today. And yes, they had won that election on the promise of land redistribution, but Ewan Cameron was a son of the African soil. And nothing, and nobody, could take that from him. It was his birthright.

It took Julius Khumalo and the crack team of lawyers and Government ministers two years to bring the Land Acquisition Act on to the Statute Books. Two long years spent in hot, airless rooms, with men in suits sweating under their shirt collars, and tempers flaring when a particularly thorny issue could not be resolved. Two years to ensure that the Government's brief was met in full and that, henceforth:

"The President may compulsorily acquire any land where the acquisition is reasonably necessary in the interests of defence, public safety, public order, public morality, public health, town and country planning or the utilisation of that property for a purpose beneficial to the public."

And it was during those two long years, that Julius Khumalo, for the first time in his life, was forced to question his own integrity and acknowledge the real reason as to why he was prepared to devote so much of his time and energy on the new legislation. For at some point in those long, hot days and nights, Julius realised that he was motivated by something stronger than the desire to right the wrongs of Zimbabwe's colonial past. Something far less honourable.

He knew that the political survival of ZANU-PF depended on a workable solution to the land issue, and he accepted that fact, especially as homeless war veterans would be the main beneficiaries of land redistribution. He also recognised that many of the whites who now owned the farms were second or third generation African born. But, in his opinion, that fact should not be allowed to influence the land reforms. The whites would have to pay for the sins of their forefathers. They were the victims of war and it could not be helped. Julius knew all this, and was able to justify it in his mind and continue to support the black man's case.

But it was not as easy for Julius to justify his own motives for ruthlessly sealing up loopholes that may have protected innocent white farmers from unscrupulous land grabs, nor did he fully understand the uncharacteristic passion with which he had fought to get the new law passed by the House. All he knew was that one man's name had haunted him as he argued his case to his fellow lawyers, or sat pouring over some legal obstacle late at night. That name was Miles Cameron. And when Julius pictured the faces of jubilant blacks as they claimed white-owned lands as their own, it was always the rich red earth of Scarfell Farm upon which they stood.

Julius had yet to come to terms with his political downfall and the heartbreaking collapse of his marriage. He had not wanted to learn about his wife's duplicity. He would have preferred to live in blissful ignorance, he told himself, if only so that his precious daughter could be nurtured by a mother's love. But Miles Cameron had come crashing into Julius' world, shattering all that he held dear, and Julius could not forgive him for that.

Now, with land reforms looming, Julius had the power to exact revenge upon the Camerons of Scarfell Farm. One stroke of his pen could strip away their rights of ownership to Scarfell Farm and return the land to the Matabele people. His father had died for the Matabele and for their right to own the land that the early white settlers had stolen from them. Now, Julius, the son of Moses Khumalo, could turn his father's dreams into reality.

Julius did not feel comfortable with this element of his character. He did not like the fact that some of his decisions were governed by self-interest and lacked the honesty and professional integrity which he had always valued. But the thirst for revenge had to be quenched, and Julius would not dishonour his father's name by shirking the task ahead. It was his duty and he was ready to meet it.

The winds of change had reached storm levels when they finally blew through Parliament on Thursday 12th December 1991, and the Land Bill was passed by the House on its third reading. Immediately, there were whoops of joy and Parliamentarians erupted into spontaneous song. Three people had voted against the Bill, hoping against hope that it would never become law. Now they sat stony-faced and silent for more than two minutes while the euphoria continued. Outside, Julius Khumalo raised his fist to the heavens and saluted his father.

'We have won baba. I now have the weapons to avenge my beloved mother who was raped by the Camerons and I have finished the deed that you began on that Night of the Slaying. The Camerons will be defeated very soon, and Scarfell Farm will be returned to the people of Matabeleland. Rest easy, baba, and be proud of your son.'

The summer temperatures were soaring when Lydia spotted the parking space outside Haddon and Sly in Bulawayo. Relieved, she swung her vehicle into the vacant spot and let out a long, deep sigh. She grabbed her bag from the passenger seat and shoved open the driver's door to be met by the usual gaggle of beggars and street sellers.

'Not today, thanks,' she said politely, ignoring the outstretched hand laden with cheap watches and the fat woman who tapped her arm and thrust a bunch of over-ripe bananas in her face. 'No thanks,' she repeated, slightly irritated now.

'You want me to look after your car, Madam?' the teenage boy was tall and thin, clad in a shabby tee-shirt and torn denims with no shoes on his feet. 'I will keep these people away from your car, Madam.' To demonstrate his efficacy as her protector, the teenager shoved the older woman away and glowered at the watch salesman who removed himself from arm's length, but still loitered on the pavement in the vain hope of a sale.

'My car will be just fine, thanks.' Lydia hurriedly locked the door and clutched her bag to her chest. 'Now if you will let me through...?'

The teenager adopted a surly expression, but he stood aside to let her pass before strolling over to another potential customer. Lydia made her way along the busy streets, ignoring the beggars who sat huddled on the pavement and the scruffy children who skipped along beside her with eager smiles and outstretched palms. Normally, she would be moved by their plight, for these people were the true victims of the so-called liberation war. These helpless beggars and starving children had been given freedom, but they did not know what to do with it. Now, hopelessly, they filled the streets of Bulawayo. They had no jobs, no homes, no money and no pride. All they had was their freedom - the freedom to stand by and watch their black leaders grow rich and fat under the banner of independence. But for them, independence brought only hardship, hunger and death.

Now, with the heat reaching unbearable temperatures, and her head pounding, Lydia did not have the strength, nor the will, to help these poor creatures. She had only one thing on her mind. She had to get to the post office before it closed for lunch. There was a letter waiting for collection. It was an urgent letter and Lydia's throat was tight with fear as she made her way along the tree-lined streets to collect it.

She had left Miles back at the farm with Ewan. She had seen the look of dread that clouded his vision when he first heard about the letter. Her own heart had missed a beat and she felt a strange urge to run out of the room, to pretend that nothing was happening and thus avoid her fate. But she could not avoid the hand that destiny may have dealt her. She was a Cameron, and she would have to play the cards she had been dealt.

Quietly, she had reached across the breakfast table and pressed a comforting hand on her husband's shoulder. She would be strong for him and for Ewan. It was the least she could do. 'It may not be what we think,' she volunteered feebly.

Miles snorted and shook his head. 'It is. I just know it. I can feel it. Oh Christ, Lydia, what the hell is happening to this country?'

Lydia squeezed his shoulder. 'I'll drive into Bulawayo to collect it. You wait here with Ewan.'

Miles stood up and gripped the sides of her head in his powerful hands. 'I love you,' he ground out the words. 'But I can't let you go on your own.'

'Miles! Listen to me! If this government is going to seize my home and my family's livelihood, I want to be standing on my own land when they tell me. We're stronger here, darling. We don't want to be learn about our fate in some crowded street in town. We want to be right here at home, surrounded by our own things and the people who care about us. Now let me go, darling. It doesn't matter what ZANU-PF has in store for us, we will be ready for it. And, if necessary, we will fight it.'

Miles followed her outside. 'You're right as always. And, as you say, it might be a letter from your mother, or even something boring about dip tanks and milk yields. Christ, will we feel stupid if that's the case!'

'Stupid, but very relieved I reckon. And very happy!'

'Mummy!' Ewan had wriggled free from his nanny, Martha's embrace and was now hurtling across the lawn towards her.

Laughing, she bent down to hug him. 'I'm just going into town for a little while, my angel. Will you be a good boy and help Daddy with the farm. You know how much he needs you.'

Ewan regarded his mother steadily before glancing up at his father. 'Okay,' he said having weighed up the two alternatives. 'But you can take this with you if you like.'

'A present!' Lydia chuckled and held out her hand. 'Why thank you, darling.'

Delighted with the unexpectedly rapturous response, Ewan opened his little fist and dropped his newly-discovered pet worm into his mother's hand. 'It's still mine of course, but you can borrow it.'

Lydia screwed up her face in horror and then burst into spontaneous laughter. 'He's beautiful,' she giggled. 'Thank you so much. But will you do me one little favour, sweetheart. Will you keep him right here with you until I get back. It may be a bit too hot for him in the car, and he might be hungry. Perhaps lie him over there, under the roses.'

Now, as she pushed through the crowds outside the post office in Main Street, Lydia could barely raise a smile at the fond memory. Doggedly, she kept repeating her silent plea that the letter be nothing more an innocent missive from her parents. Something pleasant. Something that would make Miles laugh when she showed it to him. But the letter that was waiting for her at the post office did not bear the familiar airmail stripes. It was from Harare. And it had a government stamp on it.

The letter lay unopened on the passenger seat as Lydia wound her way out of town and along the Gwanda Road that passed Scarfell Farm on its way to Beitbridge. She glanced at it from time to time, but her heart was beating so fast, and her courage was so sorely depleted, that it was all she could do to keep her car on the road. Did that letter contain the seeds of their destruction? Would this shatter her husband's dreams and leave them homeless and destitute? And did this letter herald the end of the great legacy that the early Cameron pioneers had entrusted them with? She did not know the answer, but as she pulled into the drive and made her way up the steep track that led to the house, she was afraid. For she would know the answer very soon.

Grace Dube had taken all the pictures down from the walls in the sitting room and was busily polishing the frames when Lydia burst in to the house. She looked up from her cross-legged position on the floor and beamed at the Madam.

'Where is the Nkosi?' Lydia asked, gesturing towards the unopened letter in her hand. 'It is important that I get this to him.'

'The Nkosi is at the top of the hill at the cemetery,' Grace replied. 'Shall I fetch him, Madam?'

'No, it's okay. I'll go up there myself. Thank you Grace.'

That year had seen the worst drought in living memory and many of the fields were parched and tinder dry. Even Lydia, who had been raised under the intensity of the African sun, felt herself wilting from exhaustion as she climbed the hill to the burial site of the Cameron family. The boreholes were dry and the animals were starting to suffer. This was Africa at its most cruel. And it could be a formidable foe.

Lydia spotted Miles at the top of the ridge, standing under the old marula tree that shaded the graves of his parents and his sister. He had his hands thrust deep into his pockets and his shirt collar was open at the neck. Beside him, Ewan was blissfully happy attending to his self-appointed task of gathering an eclectic assortment of leaves, twigs and weeds to place on England's grave. The little boy loved to hear stories about the big Labrador called England. They made him laugh. He liked to think of England lying up there in Dog Heaven and he regularly supplied the earthy mound with toys and flowers and just about anything else he could lay his hands on for decoration. Indeed, the grave of the faithful hound called England was an exceptionally well-tended spot.

Lydia had almost reached the ridge before Miles turned and spotted her. A smile flickered briefly on his lips, but it disappeared in an instant when he saw the ominous brown envelope in her hand. He waited while she skirted the grave of his uncle, Charlie Cameron, and then beseeched her with his eyes when she drew close.

'It doesn't look good,' Lydia whispered, handing the letter over to her husband. 'It's got a Government stamp on it.'

Miles wiped the sweat from his brow with the corner of his shirt and then tore open the gummed seal. 'It's from the Acquiring Authority. Shit! Is it really going to happen to us?'

Lydia looked at him with eyes brimming with tears. 'I brought a copy of the Gazette back with me.'

'Is there a Notice in there? They have to publish a Notice if they're going to take your land.'

Anxiously, Lydia flicked through the newspaper until she reached the page that normally carried public notices. It was there. A big, bold Garamond typeface officially proclaimed the Government's intention to compulsorily acquire part of the land known as Scarfell Farm.

Lydia dropped the newspaper on to the floor and held out her hands. 'What shall we do, Miles? They want to take our home away from us. Oh my dear God…. What shall we do?'

With that, her shoulders sagged as she sobbed helplessly against her husband's chest. Miles screwed up the letter and lobbed it down the hill where Ewan instantly scampered after it. He then enfolded her in his arms and let his own tears fall into her hair. They stood like that for some time, neither one able to speak, to comprehend the enormity of what had just happened to them. The Government had selected Scarfell Farm as one of the areas that should be taken from its legal owners. They had given themselves the right to take it from the people who had loved it, and nurtured it, and spent their entire lives transforming the once arid bushland into the irrigated fields and farms that had become the lifeblood of Zimbabwe. These farms had turned Zimbabwe into the "bread basket of Africa" and now the people who had struggled and toiled to build them would be dispossessed, and their land parcelled up and handed out to uneducated, untrained Africans who could not possibly know what to do with them.

Miles and Lydia stood among the graves of the dead Camerons and wept for themselves, for their future and for the legacy that these brave and dedicated souls had left in their care. They wept also for Zimbabwe, for the future of their beloved country looked bleak.

'I'm sorry!' Miles stared at the silent graves. 'Mum, Dad... Beth... I'm so sorry. I've let you down. I've let us all down.'

With that he fell to his knees and thrust his fingers into the dry red earth, wracked by helpless, defeated tears. He looked up at Lydia, silently pleading for an answer, for a reason. But there was none. Instead, his wife fell to her knees beside him and sobbed with him.

'Daddy?' a little voice penetrated their despair and they both sat up and hurriedly disguised their grief. 'Look...I fetched it back for you. It rolled down the hill, but I fetched it for you.' Delighted with his own initiative, Ewan held out the crumpled letter from the Government's Acquiring Agency and grinned when his father took it from him. 'Am I a good boy, Daddy?'

Miles swallowed his pain and smiled, taking the tiny boy into his arms and pressing his head into the warm, sweet softness of his child's neck. 'Yes,' he mumbled against the beloved young flesh. 'You are a very good boy, Ewan. Thanks for bringing the letter back to me. I have a lot of work to do because of it, so it's good that you brought it back to me so soon. I haven't got time to waste.'

'Why did you throw it away then?' Ewan persevered with the simplicity of youth.

Miles laughed and got to his feet. 'I threw it away because I didn't like what was in it,' he replied. 'But when you brought it straight back to me, I knew I had to accept it. Now, thanks to you little fellow, I intend to stand up for my rights and fight. This is Cameron land. This land was given to me by your grandparents who are lying right here and should be allowed to rest here in peace. I owe it to them to protect Scarfell Farm, and I owe it to you and your mother. And I will not give it up without a fight.'

'You will not fight alone,' Lydia said, rising to her feet and wiping away the tears with dusty hands. 'I will be with you every step of the way.'

'And me!' Ewan bellowed. 'I want to be with you and Daddy, too.'

'You will be, my boy. We will deal with this together. I promise you.' Miles took his son in one hand and his wife in the other and made his way down the hill to the beautiful old house that was the very heart of Scarfell

Farm. Behind them, a gentle breeze rippled across the marula tree on top of the hill so that one or two leaves floated gently on to the earthy mounds that marked the final resting place of Ralph and Rachel Cameron and their daughter, Beth. Further down, Charlie Cameron had found peace at last on the land that he had loved as a boy all those years ago. A short distance away, decorated with various childish items, the faithful dog, England, still lay beside the family he had served so well.

Miles let go of Ewan's hand and watched as the youngster hurtled down the hillside and off to his favourite play area. He was already halfway up the rope-ladder of the tree-house by the kopje when Miles and Lydia reached it. Excitedly, Ewan shinnied up the ladder and peered over the walls of the recently refurbished structure.

'Look at me, Daddy! Look at me!' he cried with glee. 'I'm the King of the Castle!'

19

Julius turned the airmail envelope over and tore along the gummed seal. It was from America. From Boston. He pulled up one of the plastic patio chairs at the side of the swimming pool and sat down. It was a short letter, no more than one side of a sheet of paper, but Julius' hands were trembling as he began to read it.

It was from Bud Lyndon, Lucie's father. In it, he explained that Lucie's drinking had escalated since her return to Boston, and when Oliver Jordace had thrown her over for an attractive divorcee from New Orleans, Lucie had spiralled into a despair fuelled by alcohol and cocaine. In the end, Bud had little choice other than to commit his daughter to a sanatorium. It was a very expensive sanatorium, he added hastily in a desperate attempt to appease his own guilt, and Lucie was getting the best medical care and attention that money could buy. At the end of the letter, Bud had written the name and address of the sanatorium, suggesting that Julius might want to contact his ex-wife at some time. Bud thought it might help to cheer her up.

Julius stared at the letter for a long time, but then his reverie was distracted by the tinkling laughter of his own daughter who was playing with two friends in the swimming pool. He watched the happy trio tossing the beach ball between them, diving into the crystal waters to retrieve it and delivering squeals of protests when it flew over someone's head.

'Not so high next time,' Devon remonstrated with her friend, Georgia. 'That's cheating!'

'No it's not!' Georgia retorted, her pale pink cheeks flushed with indignation.

'It is too!' Ruth Ndweni added her considered opinion to the debate.

'You only say that because you can't catch properly!' Georgia argued, scooping up handfuls of water to douse her friend who promptly screamed and swam off to the deep end to escape the spray.

Devon, spotting a new game, discarded the beach ball and, sleek as an otter, struck off for the deep end, too. Georgia slipped into an easy crawl and followed them, yelling in between gulps of air: 'Hang on for me. We can have a race back to the shallow end. If I win, I get to wear Devon's new hair-band!'

Julius smiled to himself and watched the three girls skimming through the warm, sparkling water. Georgia was a fast swimmer, but she was trailing behind Ruth whose slim young body, glistening like polished ebony, cut through the water. Devon was neck-and-neck with Ruth and Julius found himself calling out encouragement from the poolside table. When his daughter touched the wall first, he whooped with joy and his heart lurched when she turned to deliver a broad smile in his direction.

The letter from Boston was still in his hands. He glanced at it briefly and then looked at his daughter who was enthusiastically defending her right to the title of "Champion" with her sceptical chums. Julius laughed at their good-natured squabbles and then he stood up to leave. As he did so, he tore the letter up into small pieces and dropped them into the garbage container.

That letter was from his past. From a distant, different place. That honey-coloured child, who was giggling and squabbling merrily, with her hair hanging damply around her cheeks, and her face wet and shiny, that child was his whole life now.

'I saw the Public Notice in the Gazette, both weeks, and the one in the Bulawayo Chronicle. It's all being done by the book, I'm afraid, Miles.' Bob Potter peered at the site plan of Scarfell Farm that was spread out across his desk and then pushed his spectacles on top of his sweaty brow. 'Not much hope, lad, but we can give it our best shot. Just don't get your hopes up.'

Miles sank into the creased and tattered leather chair on the opposite side of the desk. Bob Potter had been the Camerons' family lawyer for as long as he could remember and he trusted his judgement completely. Unfortunately, if Bob Potter said there was not much hope, then there was not much hope, and Miles was devastated.

'So what can I do, Bob? I can't just sit back and let them rob me of my livelihood and my home. I've got to do something.'

'Well, we can appeal. That's for certain. You'll have to lodge a written complaint within thirty days. I'll draft that for you. I think the best argument we've got is, paradoxically, that they're not taking the whole estate. By my calculations, they're acquiring just over half of Scarfell Farm. Am I right?'

'Yes,' Miles replied, standing up to lean over the map and trace the perimeter of the land acquisition. 'Oddly enough, it's the land on the other side of the Gwanda Road. They seem to have ignored the house and the hilltop pastures.'

'Well that's one small mercy,' the lawyer declared.

'Yes, but it's not enough to run a dairy farm. There's no way I could support my family on the land I have left. I'll be finished.'

'And the land they intend to take? Will that be sufficient for commercial dairy farming?'

'Not a hope,' Miles shook his head. 'There are only a few boreholes active up there and the land isn't good enough for large-scale grazing for any length of time. By splitting Scarfell into two halves, they're effectively going to destroy it as a productive dairy farm.'

'That's it then! That's our case. The Land Acquisition Act states that, if an owner can prove that the land reclamation will render the land unfit for its original purpose, he has a case to fight the seizure.'

'But can we win?'

Bob Potter sighed and replaced his old-fashioned spectacles back on his nose. He then peered at the young man sitting before him. He had watched Miles Cameron growing up on that farm. He had known his father well, a decent chap and a first-rate farmer who loved the land and loved Africa. Bob Potter was not a man to indulge in emotional displays, but he could not help pitying the lad. He had endured some pretty harsh knocks that would have floored a weaker man, but with a gritty determination, he had pulled himself up and carried on. Now, this last blow had all but devastated him, and Bob Potter was not sure how it would all end. One thing he did know for sure was that the Acquiring Authority did not consider appeals with the due care and consideration that their Constitution allowed. Most white lawyers, and farmers, agreed that the Authority was simply paying lip-service to justice and that, once a Notice had been served, very little would budge them from their original plans.

'It'll be touch and go, Miles. I can't promise anything, you know that. I agree that you have to put up a fight, you can't just let them walk in and take over your land, but I would spend some time looking at alternatives if I were you. Your wife is from the UK, isn't she? Maybe you could start a new life over there. Our farmers are packing up and taking their skills away in droves. America, Australia, Great Britain, Canada - you name it. It's a sorry loss for this country, but they're thinking about their families and their children's future. Many have no choice. Many have lost all their land and are left with nothing. The Government's so-called land reform is crippling the agricultural stability of Zimbabwe. It's madness. Sheer madness, and God knows where it will all end.'

'I'm not leaving my home,' Miles said stubbornly. 'Don't ask me how, but I'll find a way to stay in Zimbabwe. I'm not going to let the bastards grind me down.'

'That's the spirit, lad.' Bob Potter poured two glasses of brandy from a decanter on his desk. 'But don't go breaking any laws or you will be in trouble. The lawyer, Julius Khumalo, has put his mark on some of this legislation and has effectively sealed up many of the loopholes that might have helped you in the past.'

'Such as?'

'Well, one of Khumalo's bright ideas was to prohibit farmers from building on any land, or disposing of any land that has been identified for reclamation. If you damage the land they want to acquire, then you could face a hefty fine or two years in gaol. So be careful what you do.'

Miles gulped the brandy and banged the glass on the desk angrily. 'That Khumalo bastard has plagued me all my life. How the hell he managed to survive the Willowgate Scandal and still come up smelling of roses, I'll never know.'

'Well, as a fellow lawyer, I have to say that he has a brilliant legal mind. The Government were never going to keep him out in the cold for long. Okay, he may have lost his seat in Parliament, and some say his good name, but his legal skills will always be in demand. He's always been on a winner there, and his position on the Board of the Acquiring Authority is proof of that.'

Wearily, Miles held his head in his hands and breathed deeply. 'Looks like he's already won,' he mumbled through his fingers. 'In one way or another, he and his father will have managed to destroy three generations of the Cameron family.'

'You haven't lost your home, Miles. Hang on to that fact. They may have taken the larger chunk of land, but they've left you with your beautiful house and a roof over your heads. Some farmers haven't even been granted that. The land seized for personal use by corrupt Government ministers is virtually left abandoned. They just want to live in the big houses that the whites used to own. Julius Khumalo, on the other hand, seems to be more interested in giving the land back to the Matabele. He doesn't seem to be motivated by personal gains of that nature. Now go home, lad, and talk to that lovely wife of yours. She's a spirited lass. Together, you'll come through all this. You mark my words.'

Miles did mark the words of his old family friend and lawyer. In fact, he clung on to them all the way from Bulawayo to Scarfell Farm. They were wise words and, by the time he swung his vehicle on to the drive that led to the house, his courage and optimism had returned. Bob Potter had called Lydia a "spirited lass" and he was right. She was spunky and tough and, together, they would come through all this. All he had to do was keep his family together and it would all work itself out in the end. It had to.

Miles drew to a halt outside the main house and sat in the car with the windows down, marvelling at the vibrant bougainvillaea that clambered over the wooden windows and the heady perfume of jasmine that filled the air. The sky was a perfect blue and the freshly painted roof sparkled in the sunlight. Birds twittered all around and filled the air with their merry birdsong. The cattle were lowing in the distance and the vast open savannahs rippled with golden grasses. This was his home. And he loved it so.

At that moment, the doors opened and Lydia came out into the sunshine. Her hair was speckled with paint where, as she had tugged her artist's smock over her head, she had left a tiny smudge of yellow ochre on her nose.

'How did it go?' she whispered, unable to interpret the look in her husband's eyes.

'We're going to appeal, but don't hold your breath. We don't stand much chance.'

Lydia's shoulders sagged, but Miles took her chin between his thumb and forefinger and tilted her head back to look directly into her eyes. Hurriedly, she blinked away the tears.

'There's no need for tears, sweetheart,' he cooed gently. 'I reckon we can make it even if we do lose the south pastures.'

'You do?' Lydia's perfectly pink lips formed into a surprised "O".

'I do, and it's all thanks to you and your brilliant idea.'

Lydia stepped back and regarded him at arm's length. 'Which brilliant idea might that be?'

'We're going to turn the top land over to tourism, build some of those holiday lodges you've been talking about, and make our living in the tourist industry. What do you say?'

Lydia giggled and flung her arms around her husband's neck, almost knocking him off his feet. 'Did I come up with that idea? Then you're right! I truly am brilliant! Wow! What a genius!'

'Save a bit of praise for me, madam. I'm going to have to build the bloody things if this idea is going to get off the ground.'

'Sure... but that's just boring manual stuff. Anybody can do that. The brilliance lies with the idea and I can safely say that's down to little old me!'

It was not long before the noisy taunts and laughter caught the attention of young Master Cameron who had been helping Sixpence to prepare lunch. He had been given a clump of pastry to make jam tarts and he was thoroughly absorbed in his task. The pastry had been kneaded and rolled and generally mauled until it was a rather unappetising shade of grey, and the soggy circles could barely contain the huge dollop of strawberry jam that was dunked on top of them. But the sounds of commotion outside quickly distracted the boy and, tugging at Sixpence's apron, he pleaded: 'Daddy's back! Come on Sixpence. I want him to see my jam tarts. He might even want one now!'

I think it might be better if we waited until they have been cooked, Nkosizana.'

Ignoring Sixpence's culinary wisdom, Ewan grabbed the old servant's hand and dragged him outside to where his parents were still making an exhibition of themselves. They blushed when they saw Sixpence and drew apart.

'Look what I've made,' Ewan gestured for Sixpence to hold up the tray of motley jam tarts. 'You can have one now if you like,'

With that, Ewan tried to prise one of the tarts off the tray with his fingers, but the jam oozed over the edge and the pastry hung in a shapeless heap.

'They look delicious,' Miles enthused. 'But I think we ought to let Sixpence put them in the oven first. We can have them later. Now give me your hand... not that one, it's sticky with jam... this one. That's it. Now lick your fingers clean and grab Mummy's hand.'

Ewan was excited. 'Where are we going?' he asked, transferring the jam from his fingers to his cheeks.

'We're going for a walk around Scarfell Farm.'

'Can Bala come, too?' Ewan glanced at the cat who was sitting at their feet using one of her front paws to wash behind her ear.

'She can come, but she'll probably fall asleep on the path within five minutes. You know what a lazy puss she is.'

'I'm not lazy though, am I daddy?' Ewan skipped along between his parents.

'No son. You're not lazy, which is a jolly good thing because you and me and Mummy have got a lot of work to do from now on. A helluva lot of work to do!'

Three months later, a remarkable achievement by African standards, the Acquiring Authority formally responded to their appeal. It was quashed. They had the right to pursue their case if they wished, but Bob Potter counselled against it, warning that they would not be able to claim any compensation while the dispute continued. And that could take years. Miles knew it would be foolish to put his new plans on hold in the vain hope of beating a Government intent on appeasing the thousands of homeless blacks who were waiting for the land they had been promised.

'Let the case drop and you'll get half the compensation immediately,' said the lawyer. 'A further twenty per cent will follow in two years' time and the rest will be paid within five years.'

'How much will it be?' Miles asked.

'Can't say exactly, but they take into account soil types, crop yields and any buildings on the land.'

'There are several good outbuildings and plenty of housing for farmhands. The paddocks are well-fenced and the grazing land can accommodate small domestic herds. If you ask me, they're getting a bloody good bargain.'

'Right now, all that matters is that you get as much compensation as you can and it sounds as though the land is highly productive at the moment.'

'At the moment, yes, but I can't imagine what will happen to it when hundreds of individual peasants settle on it. They'll have no idea about farming on such scale. All they'll do is plant a few mealies and leave the rest to go to pot.'

'The Commercial Farmers' Union have offered to provide training and support in resettlement areas. Maybe you could do the same. Who knows, you may have labour on your doorstep to help service the new safari lodges. Never say never, Miles, especially in Africa!'

Miles laughed. 'Thanks Bob. Wise advice as always. I may look to find ways of working with the new settlers. They're on the south side of the Gwanda Road, so they won't impinge on any plans I have for the rest of Scarfell Farm. And you're right, maybe they can help. God knows we're all of us going to need help in the months ahead. It's far better that we work as a team.'

'Good lad! That's the spirit. Now I'll respond to the Acquiring Authority accepting their decision as final. After that, we can sit back and wait for the compensation which will be more than enough to finance the first phase of the building programme. And, for the record, tell that young wife of yours that old Bob Potter thinks it's a brilliant idea. She's worth her weight in gold that lass of yours. Worth her weight in gold.'

'Baba! Guess what? Guess what? Guess what?'

Julius knelt down on a level with his daughter and frowned in concentration. 'Now then,' he mused. 'Does that mean there are three things I have to guess, or do I have three attempts to guess one thing?'

'Oh baba... please! This is serious.' Devon adjusted her straw boater that had been knocked awry when she ran to hug her father at the school gates. 'You'll never guess what happened today...'

'Well then, if I'll never guess, maybe you should just tell me. It is obviously something major to warrant such excitement.'

'It is!' Devon scrambled on to the passenger seat in her father's Mercedes and bobbed up and down in the chair while she waited for Julius to take his place behind the wheel. It was always exciting when her father met her from school instead of her nanny, but today was even more special because she had something to tell him that he would never guess in a million, billion years.

Julius did not start up the engine, but turned to face his daughter instead. 'Well? What is this earth-shattering news?'

'Baba, I've been chosen to sing in the choir at the Zimbabwean Schools' Festival.'

Julius beamed. 'That is truly splendid, child. I am very proud of you. You have the voice of an angel. I have always said that.'

'Will you come to see me?'

'Of course! Nothing would keep me away from such an important event. Where will it be held?'

'Rufaro Stadium.'

'Rufaro Stadium! My, it must be an important event to be held at such a prestigious venue.'

'It is,' Devon agreed, delighted with her father's response.

'And now then, little one, I have something to tell you, too.'

'Is it a surprise?' Devon swivelled round in her seat to face her father full on.

'Well it is a surprise at the moment, but it will not be a surprise once I tell you what it is.'

'What is it, baba? Don't tease me so!'

'We are going away for a few days.'

'Just you and me?'

'And Nanny, of course.'

'Where are we going?'

Julius looked deep into the little girl's eyes and whispered: 'It is time you learned about your Matabele heritage, my child, so I am taking you to Matabeleland. We are also going to Tshotshololo where your grandmother is buried and to the Matopos where the great King Lobengula still lies. I will show you the beautiful town of Bulawayo, and I will take you to see the place where I grew up.'

'Scarfell Farm!' Devon gasped. 'We are going to see Scarfell Farm where you used to be a little boy and play just like me. Oh baba... I can't wait. That's even better than my secret.... Well, almost!'

Julius smiled and started the engine.

'When are we going?'

'Now that school has broken up for the holidays, and I can get some time away from my desk, I thought you might like to go this weekend.'

'So soon! Oh baba. That would be wonderful!'

Julius had not imagined, even for a moment, just how much his daughter would need to pack for such a trip. If he had, he might have been tempted to abandon the project. Bella, her favourite dolly, and Lulu, Bella's best-friend-dolly, would have to travel in the car with her, and then there were the various soft toys that always sat at the foot of her bed. The unopened box of crayons might be needed and her colouring book, of course. And then there were the various reading books and comics "in case she got bored". Satisfied that she had all the toys she might need, Devon then turned her attention to the kind of clothes she might want to take. And this, make no mistake about it, was no easy task!

'No! Absolutely not!' Julius cried despairingly. 'You will not need to take a party frock. We are not going to any parties. We are going to visit your grandmother's grave and to see the town where I grew up. You will need little more than the clothes you are currently wearing.'

'But I want to look nice when I visit Grandmother's grave,' Devon argued reasonably. 'You would want me to look smart, wouldn't you baba?'

'Yes child. I would want you to look smart.' Julius sighed and looked away. For one brief moment, those wily charms had reminded him of her mother who could always wind him around her little finger. Sometimes, when Devon smiled, or laughed, or pouted prettily, Julius would catch a glimpse of the beautiful, sensual woman who was her mother. Devon was so like Lucie in so many ways that Julius knew he would never be truly free of the woman he had loved, and still loved if the truth were known, with such destructive passion. Now, Lucie's daughter was growing into the great beauty her mother had been. She was nearly eight years old and quite a manipulative little lady when she needed to be.

'Do you think we might meet someone you used to know in Bulawayo, baba?' Devon was rummaging through the boxes in the bottom of her wardrobe.

Julius did not reply. He had not actually thought about the consequences of his visit. He knew only that he would stand, once more, on the land that was Scarfell Farm. His boyhood home. It was a place of ghosts and memories. Would they be kind to him? He did not know.

'There!' Devon re-emerged from the depths of her wardrobe clutching an old photograph in a broken frame. She handed it to her father with a triumphant smile and stood back to await the praise that would invariably accompany such a thoughtful gesture. 'I found it in those boxes out in the garage. I'm going to put it on Grandmother's grave.'

Julius gasped at the sight of the photograph and he frowned deeply in a bid to prevent unexpected and unmanly tears from falling. His daughter had just presented him with a glimpse of his past. He remembered the very moment the picture had been taken. The farmer, Ralph Cameron, had been experimenting with his new camera and had grouped Julius and his parents together for the shot. Moses had been working in the fields and his face was dusty. He had hastily wiped his cheeks with the back of his hand and left a zigzag smear that gave him a handsome, devilish look. Ralph Cameron had asked them to smile and Moses had dutifully obeyed, but his eyes were not smiling. They were dark and fathomless, as though looking into another world.

His mother, Bliss, was wearing the neatly-pressed uniform of the family's nanny. She was a big woman, beautiful and kind and honest. The sort of mother a little boy could feel safe with, could love and trust for ever. Bliss was holding on to Julius' shoulders in an effort to keep him still for the photograph. She had not succeeded, for Julius had been determined to keep his childhood friend, Miles, out of the family group and he had been too busy shooing his troublesome chum away to notice that the camera had clicked.

'We're blood brothers!' Miles had protested loudly. 'I'm allowed to be in it.' Miles had managed to get half his body into the frame, but his head was a blur, while Julius had been snapped staring moodily at the unwelcome intruder.

After the photograph had been taken, Miles and Julius had rolled about in the dirt in an indignant scrap, both equally convinced that they were right to take such a stand. They had fought until Julius had scraped his knuckle on a stone and started to cry, and then they had sparred verbally with Miles taunting Julius for being such a baby. The squabbles continued as both boys headed out into the bush, but as soon as they had passed the kopje, they were suddenly distracted by the impressive amount of blood that Julius' superficial wound was generating, and they had huddled together to examine the phenomenon. Within minutes, their earlier falling out had been forgotten and replaced with the more congenial challenge of a race to get to the msasa tree first. They ran as fast as they could, barefoot across the open fields. They were giggling and yelling and hollering with excitement and delight, for they were young and they were happy and they were blood brothers.

Now, many years later, Julius the man stood at the gates of Scarfell Farm with his young daughter, Devon. His silver Mercedes was parked on the roadside opposite the rows of craftsmen who were anxious to show him their exquisite wood carvings, soapstone animals and Zulu baskets. Julius had been happy to indulge Devon's wish to browse among the brightly coloured stalls and had allowed her to use her pocket money to buy a bead necklace from one of the women. But Julius' gaze had been fixed on the far side of the road, and he was relieved when Devon, thrilled with her purchase, had finally taken his hand and followed him across to the wrought-iron gates that led to Scarfell Farm.

Julius was speechless. So much had changed since he had lived here as a boy and yet it was all so familiar. The long drive had been recently resurfaced with gravel, but the old acacia and soft-wood marula trees still stood proud on either side. The distant Blue Hills still looked the same, a hazy, romantic backdrop to the beautiful hills and savannahs that surrounded the house. And the house was still there, nesting like a precious jewel amid the luscious velvet swathes of land that undulated around it.

Julius looked up at the house, fearful that the ghosts of the long-dead Camerons might see him standing there and come to claim justice for their deaths at the hands of the Khumalo family. But he had nothing to fear, for there were no ghosts, only the gentle rippling of the leaves in the breeze and the sweet smells of freshly cut grass and wild flowers.

Julius had tried to imagine the impact that the land seizure would have had upon Miles Cameron and his family, but rather than desolation and despair, as was the case with many of the former white-owned farms, Julius was surprised to see a freshly painted sign at the gate that said in neat capital letters: SCARFELL FARM SAFARI LODGES. And there, dotted among the hills behind the house, were a dozen or so pretty little rondavels, brightly painted and newly thatched.

Opposite the gates to Scarfell Farm, on the south side of the Gwanda Road, a thriving community of black Africans had made their homes on the small parcels of land they had acquired. Most were existing on their own mealie crops. Some were supplementing their income by selling their arts and crafts to the many tourists who flocked to stay at the Safari Lodges. A number were employed to serve in the main house, or in the tourist lodges across the road.

Julius had spoken to a few of them and they had all praised the kindness and generosity of their employer and neighbour, Miles Cameron. He had helped them build their villages, they had said with gratitude shining in their eyes. He had offered advice and guidance on irrigation, and had suggested that they might want to reap the benefits of the large numbers of tourists who now flocked to the area by selling native crafts or working for him as paid safari guides.

Julius had found a blossoming partnership between the white farmer and the Matabele who now occupied the southern bush. Black and white citizens were helping each other to survive in the beautiful, but harsh world of Africa. They had found a way to live in harmony and peace, without enmity and without pain.

Was this what it had all been about, Julius mused with tears welling in his eyes? Was this the end product of a long and bloody liberation war?

Not the destruction of innocent white Zimbabweans, but a true and genuine racial integration based on mutual needs, hopes and dreams. Was the bitterness that Julius had nurtured over the years all for nothing? Was it time to move on, to leave the past behind and to embrace a new kind of future borne of tolerance and partnership? He would need time to think about that.

'Who are those little boys, baba?' Devon tugged at her father's elbow and pointed to two tiny figures who were playing outside the main house.

The little white boy looked about six years old, the black boy was a few inches taller, so could be slightly older. It was difficult to tell from such a distance. Julius did not reply to Devon's question immediately. He was transfixed by the sight of the two youngsters, one black and one white, playfully teasing a golden Labrador puppy who was barking hysterically in delighted anticipation. Julius swallowed hard. His mouth was dry and he ran his tongue over his lips. It was a familiar scene, one that he had enacted many, many times during his own childhood years. The two boys were laughing, fighting, teasing the silly puppy in exactly the same way that Julius and Miles had done with the dog called England.

Was this a vision of the future? Or a glimpse of the past?

The scene being played out before his eyes had not changed. Nothing had changed. The children of Zimbabwe would always play together. Julius understood that now. But Julius also knew that those two little boys were the beneficiaries of a long and bloody war that had given them the liberty to play together without fear for their future. The war was over, and these two children would not have to witness tragic events that would tear them apart and fill their young lives with harsh memories. They were the children of the new Zimbabwe and this was their inheritance

'Do they live here, baba?' Devon was insistent.

'I do not know for sure, little one, but I believe so.'

'They look very happy. Do you think they are friends like Georgia and me?'

'I am sure they are friends, little one. They may even be blood brothers. And yes, they do look very happy.'

'Martha,' Lydia paused in her flower arrangement and turned to Ewan's nanny with a look of helpless resignation. 'See if you can haul my son inside for a wash and brush up before lunch. And do tell him to stop goading poor Chaucer. He's only a puppy, it's not fair to get the wretched creature so excited.'

369

Martha inclined her head politely. 'Yes Madam, but I fear my own son must take the blame. He loves to play with that dog.'

'Well, all three are as bad as each other, if you ask me. A terrible trio and that's for sure! Now if you could just forewarn Master Ewan that he must calm down and get ready for lunch …. or there will be no ice-cream for him. That should do the trick.'

Martha giggled softly and padded outside to where the boys were fighting a mock duel with sticks. Chaucer was barking at every movement and skidding round on the spot in a frenzy of joy when one of the boys playfully thrust in his direction.

'Master Ewan! It is time for lunch.' Martha ignored the protests. 'And Jacob, you must tidy away these toys before you go.'

Both boys dropped into a sulk, while Chaucer abandoned his former loyalties and bounded up to Martha to lick her hand. Martha ruffled the dog's head and repeated her instructions before going back into the house.

'I'll help you clear away,' Ewan offered, more to delay the inevitable wash and brush up than to help his friend complete the task.

Jacob shrugged nonchalantly and set to work. 'I'm going to sing at the Zimbabwean Schools' Festival,' he declared with a vaguely superior tone as he dismantled the fort made out of stones at the top of the drive.

'So am I, so there!' Miles retorted, gathering up the twigs that had served as soldiers.

'You cannot sing!' Jacob taunted.

'Can too! Better than you can, so there.'

Having reached a stalemate in this particular dispute, the two boys continued to clear away the remains of their various playtime activities in companionable silence. Suddenly, Jacob stood up and pointed to the entrance gates at the bottom of the hill.

'Who is that at the gate?'

'Don't know,' Ewan replied. 'Tourists probably.'

Standing side-by-side, Ewan and Jacob stared at the man and the little girl who stood at the farm entrance staring back at them. And then the little girl lifted her hand and waved.

'She's waving at us!' Ewan observed excitedly. 'Wave back. Look, she's waving at us!'

And, for one brief moment, the three children had become friends.

'There was a little girl by the gate and she was waving at us,' Ewan proceeded to overload his spoon with a dollop of ice-cream at the lunch table.

'That's nice. And did you wave back?' Miles watched the heavily-laden spoon making its way into his son's open mouth, knowing that it would be touch and go as to whether it would reach its destination intact.

Ewan nodded and presented the spoon with a wide, gaping maw.

'Don't be greedy, Ewan,' his mother remonstrated. 'Now wipe your mouth. Here, use this napkin.'

'Jacob says he's going to sing at the Zimbabwean Schools' Festival. Is he, Daddy?'

'If he says he is, then I'm sure he is.'

'You and Mummy are going to come and watch me, aren't you?' Ewan washed the ice-cream down with a huge gulp of lemonade. 'You won't have to watch Jacob. Martha can watch Jacob. You can watch me.'

Miles and Lydia laughed out loud. 'Don't worry, son. Mummy and I will have eyes only for you. We won't even notice the other children on the stage. Now then, I'd better get back to work. I've got to look at the plans for the new lodges.'

'Can I come, too?'

Miles glanced at Lydia who nodded. 'Come on then, but don't plague me with questions all afternoon, okay? I've got lots of work to do.'

'Okay. I'll just play with Chaucer.' Chaucer, who had been lying on the floor under Ewan's chair, instantly pricked up his ears at the sound of his name. 'Come on dopey dog!'

Miles stood up to leave the table, but he was almost knocked off balance by his young son and his faithful hound as they bounded out of the house in a frenzy of joyful hollering and excitable barking.

'What do the new lodges look like?' Lydia remained at the table with the newspaper.

'They look great. At our current rate of bookings, we'll have the second phase of the build programme completed long before the rest of the compensation comes in. I can't believe how well they've taken off. And it's not just foreign tourists. We seem to have captured a fair chunk of the home market, too.'

'The South Africans seem to love it here.' Lydia added.

'You're right, and we've got a family of six from Botswana arriving next week. They've taken the last of the lodges, so I'll be glad when we get the next phase finished.'

Lydia stood up and held out her arms for a hug. Miles pulled her into his embrace and kissed the top of her head. Happily, she snuggled against him and squeezed him as tight as she could. 'Oh Miles, I can't believe it's all turning out so well. It's like a dream come true.'

'It's no dream, sweetheart. This is real life. It's our life and we've fought long and hard to get here. I reckon we deserve a bit of happiness, don't you?'

Lydia smiled and nodded. It had been a hard road for both of them, but Miles was right. This was not a dream. This was real. This was their life. And she would not change a thing.

Rufaro Stadium was freshly painted and decked out with garlands of flowers and the brightly-coloured flags of Zimbabwe. At the northern end of the stadium, a vast stage supported the children who had been selected to sing at this prestigious national event. Parents, friends and representatives from all over the country filled the stands and the grounds and cheered when Ministers and other dignitaries took their seats to hear their children sing. The Zimbabwean Schools' Festival was a chance to celebrate the true brotherhood of Africa, and Rufaro Stadium was buzzing with the collective pride and joy of thousands of people.

The event had been scheduled to take place at sundown when the fierce heat had abated. Already the golden orb was slipping from its zenith, and lilac and magenta hues were beginning to stain the great canopy. The intense heat of the summer's day was cooling, but it was still a balmy evening and the people were content.

Miles had stopped to buy coffee before making his way into the auditorium, and he was delighted to see that Lydia had secured seats in the centre section. Careful not to spill his drink, he made his way down the aisle that separated the centre block from the seats on the left, and he scanned the rows to pinpoint where his wife was sitting.

In the right-hand aisle, another proud parent was happy to discover that he had been allocated a seat in the centre section close to the stage. The man glanced at his ticket to check the number of his row and then proceeded to make his way down to the front.

Miles caught sight of the other man on the far side, but he did not recognise him at first. He was just another father who had come to see his son or daughter sing at Zimbabwe's premier children's event. But there was something in the way the proud parent carried himself that seemed familiar and, when Miles pushed his hat back on his head, he realised that the man was Julius Khumalo.

Miles' heart skipped a beat and his hand shook slightly. He wanted to avert his eyes, but invisible threads held him there. Julius, sensing the other man's gaze, lifted his hooded eyes to stare straight into the face of Miles Cameron. Julius' skin prickled, but he too was transfixed by the man who had once been his childhood friend.

Time seemed to stand still as the two men started at each other across a sea of heads and strangers' faces, and a peculiar hush descended upon Rufaro Stadium. And then, in one magical moment, both Miles and Julius were transported back in time to a far distant place. A place of laughter and joy and trust. A place where innocence was treasured and where happiness was taken for granted. A place where two young boys had sealed their friendship with a pact of blood brotherhood.

And now, separated by a few rows of plastic seating, Miles and Julius had come together again as men. They had both suffered on their long journey into manhood, but each had found his own way out of the darkness of the past and into the light. Neither could have known that the precious bonds of blood brotherhood that had joined them together all those years ago would still bind them in their adult lives. They had fought their own battles in a war where each man had won and each man had lost. But now their war was over. It was time to embrace the future.

Still locked in the other man's gaze, Miles gently tipped his hat in Julius' direction in a tacit, but heartfelt acknowledgement of those early blood ties. Slowly, politely, Julius inclined his head in silent recognition, but he did not smile. Neither man smiled as they took their seats to watch their children sing. But each man felt his spirit soar as though a great burden had been lifted from his shoulders.

And then, in perfect unison, the black and white children of Zimbabwe rose up from their benches on the stage. There was a thunderous applause for the youngsters, who were smartly turned out in white cotton shirts with the national flag emblazoned across their chests. Their faces were scrubbed clean and they gleamed in the golden rays of the dying sun.

Standing on the stage, small and nervous, Ewan Cameron was suddenly over-awed by the magnitude of the event. His fingers plucked at the hem of his shorts and there were tears welling at the corners of his eyes. He had been placed next to a little girl with honey-coloured skin and liquid chocolate eyes who turned to him with a puzzled smile.

'Why are you crying?' she asked.

'Because I'm frightened.' Ewan said.

'You don't have to be frightened,' the little girl replied. 'I'll look after you.'

Ewan smiled gratefully and blinked away his tears.

'My name's Devon Khumalo. What's yours?'

'Ewan Cameron.'

'Would you like to hold my hand, Ewan?'

Ewan nodded and grasped the outstretched hand. It was a small and childish gesture of friendship, but it spoke a universal language that had transcended the confines of race, colour and creed since the beginning of time.

And then, illuminated by the awesome majesty of Zimbabwe's setting sun, Ewan Cameron and Devon Khumalo raised their hands high above their heads and opened their hearts and voices to sing a song of Hope for Africa.

Shirley Carnegie was born in the West Midlands but lived most of her life in London.

Her passion Africa was inspired by her husband's experiences of a childhood spent in colonial Africa, in war torn Rhodesia, and their travels across the country she grew to love as her own.

The Africa Series demonstrates Shirley's unique ability to transcend the limits of an individual literary genre and explore the world of storytelling in the widest possible sense.

A Shadow Passing is an historical novel. It chronicles the war of independence that led to the formation of Zimbabwe. *Sons of Africa* is a high action thriller set against the backdrop of the Zimbabwean Government's genocide of the 1980s. *A Wedding in Africa* will satisfy those readers who enjoy the twists and turns of a typical romantic novel.

Shirley and her husband, Andrew, now live in rural Shropshire with their two dogs and two cats.

Made in the USA
San Bernardino, CA
16 November 2012